WEBDANCERS

WEBDANCERS

BOOK 3 OF THE TIMEWEB CHRONICLES

BRIAN HERBERT

FIVE STAR
A part of Gale, Cengage Learning

GALE
CENGAGE Learning

Detroit • New York • San Francisco • New Haven, Conn • Waterville, Maine • London

GALE
CENGAGE Learning

Set in 11 pt. Plantin.
Printed on permanent paper.

LIBRARY OF CONGRESS CATALOGING-IN-PUBLICATION DATA

Herbert, Brian.
  Webdancers / Brian Herbert. — 1st ed.
    p. cm. — (The timeweb chronicles ; bk. 3)
    ISBN-13: 978-1-59414-218-5 (hardcover : alk. paper)
    ISBN-10: 1-59414-218-1 (hardcover : alk. paper) 1. Space warfare—Fiction. I. Title.
PS3558.E617W44 2008
813'.54—dc22   2008037091

December 2008.
Published in 2008 in conjunction with Tekno Books and Ed Gorman.

Printed in the United States of America
2 3 4 5 6 7 12 11 10 09 08

DEDICATION

This book is for Jan. When I met you on that summer day in California, all of the stars in the heavens were in alignment for us—and my darling, they have been ever since. Thank you for being my loyal, loving companion and for teaching me everything that is meaningful about life.

CHAPTER ONE

Eddies and currents of time flow through the galaxy . . .
and immense whirlpools beckon everything into chaos.
—Eshaz, timeseeing report to the Council of Elders

A tiny figure, the Parvii woman clung to the forward wall of the glowing green sectoid chamber. Using her touch and a telepathic linkage to the Aopoddae podship, she guided the creature past uncounted star systems, which she saw through multiple eyes on the craft's hull. At the vanguard of the Liberator fleet, she led the other Aopoddae vessels toward the galactic fold of the Parviis. Their destination drew near.

Tesh Kori's dominion over the sentient spacecraft was an evolving relationship, a symbiosis between two ancient and very different galactic races in which she merged into the psyche of the creature in the ancient way. Now she felt an increasing closeness to this flagship that she had named *Webdancer*. The connection gave her a glimmer of hope for the future, that perhaps her people would finally see the error of their ways and agree to cooperate with other races.

But she didn't hold out much hope for that outcome. More likely, there would be a terrible battle in the sacred fold. And she would be responsible for leading a powerful military force to that secret location, for an attack on her own people.

She tried to set aside the feelings of guilt, if only for a few moments. Her thoughts drifted to something infinitely more pleasant, her feelings for an alien Human named Noah Watanabe. . . .

In the passenger compartment behind Tesh's sectoid chamber, Noah stood beside a blond young man, both of them staring out a wide aft porthole at the formation of nine hundred podships behind them. Unlike the flagship, the trailing vessels were all piloted by Tulyans that had merged into the flesh of the spacefaring vessels, causing reptilian Tulyan faces to protrude from the prows. He recognized several of them, including that of his close friend, Eshaz.

The journey had taken longer than anticipated—more than two days so far—due to the extreme distance involved and poor conditions of the podways that had required the fleet to take alternate routes. They'd been forced to go around entire galactic sectors that had collapsed from the entropic decay of the Timeweb infrastructure.

The young man nudged him. It was Noah's nephew, Doge Anton del Velli. "While we've been looking outside, our ship morphed again. I think it's bigger now."

Noah looked around the grayness of the large cabin, which was illuminated by hidden sources that flickered faintly green at times. Many of the uniformed officers and other personnel stood at forward viewing windows that jutted out on the port and starboard sides. He heard the murmur of their voices.

Everyone had noticed the changes. Since embarking on this critical mission, the passenger areas and cargo holds on the lower levels had become at least half again as large as they had originally been. None of the Human, Tulyan, or robotic passengers had left the vessel, and all of the fighter craft were parked in the holds, yet everyone agreed there was considerably more space for everything now.

"You're right," Noah said. "There's another row of benches,

and the ceiling seems a little higher."

Anton rubbed his thick blond mustache. "*Webdancer,* she calls this one, and from the reports I'm getting, it's bigger than all the rest of them."

With a grin on his freckled face, Noah said, "Well, it is the flagship, and seems to sense its relative importance." He paused. "Perhaps our ship is just puffing up its chest in pride."

"Odd, the way podships can configure themselves at will," Anton said, "expanding, changing layouts, and even adding gun ports on the sides of the hulls that are perfect for our space artillery pieces. I find it most peculiar."

"Indeed."

"With your connections, Noah, you should know why."

"But I don't." Noah's incredible psychic powers came and went, enabling him to take paranormal journeys far across the heavens, and sometimes to pilot podships, these mysterious creatures that had their own communication methods and secret motivations. It had all started after he'd been mortally wounded in an attack by Doge Lorenzo del Velli's forces, and Eshaz healed him by connecting him to a strand of Timeweb. It had been much more than a physical healing process.

Timeweb.

He shuddered slightly as he thought of the name that Parviis and Tulyans had given to the cosmic green filigree connecting everything in the galaxy, the vast network on which these Aopoddae craft were traveling now. Most of the races could not see it, but after Noah's miraculous survival he'd been granted unprecedented private access to the web, although without explanation or guidance. Still, through it all, Noah had come to suspect that a higher power was guiding him, and had been doing so for some time. He sensed this force with him now, and with the entire fleet.

We're doing the right thing, he assured himself, *the only thing we can do.*

As he looked at the young leader beside him, Noah thought his nephew carried his responsibilities well, and comported himself as if he had been groomed to become the Doge . . . the prince of all merchant princes. That was hardly the case, though Anton did have royal blood on his father Lorenzo's side, albeit from an extramarital relationship he'd had with Noah's sister. Only serving as the Doge for a short time after his father was deposed, Anton had managed to coordinate much of the galaxy-spanning military effort, working with the various allied races and factions so that none felt slighted, and all believed they were indispensable to the success of the mission. It helped that this actually was true. Each of the groups in the assault force—the Red Berets, the MPA troopers, the Guardians, the Tulyans, and even the sentient robots—had important roles to play.

Just then, a clamor of excited voices arose at the front of the compartment. Noah and Anton hurried over there, making their way around the extruded benches, tables and other furnishings the podship had provided. Noticing the approach of the two leaders, the other passengers moved aside, allowing them to reach one of the forward viewing windows.

Looking through it, Noah sucked in a deep breath, and suppressed a gasp. Ahead he saw what looked like a large, luminous hole in the black fabric of the galaxy, casting subdued illumination like a dull cosmic searchlight.

"The Asteroid Funnel," Anton murmured. "The Parvii Fold is on the other side, but Tesh will need all of her piloting skills to get us there."

"She can do it," Noah said. Both of them had heard of the terrible dangers of the galactic funnel, the hurtling asteroids, the extremely perilous flying conditions.

For several moments time seemed to stand still around Noah

Watanabe, and all went silent. So much rested on this military venture, the fate of all the galactic races and their worlds, the fate of all they had ever known and all they had ever imagined. Countless dreams hung in the balance, made precarious by the dark clouds that had seeped into the galaxy.

Closing his eyes, Noah attempted to mind-range and peer into the cosmic web, trying to see into the Parvii Fold beyond the funnel. But the paranormal network had only been accessible to him intermittently, and almost never of his own volition. Now he beheld a pocket of blackness in his mind, and felt cold fear washing through him.

Just as Noah opened his eyes again, *Webdancer* plunged into the hole, with the fleet right behind.

CHAPTER TWO

The most ancient patterns of the heavens are falling victim to new laws of science. Since time immemorial, comets, asteroids, and planetary systems have traveled through space at regular, predictable orbits, speeds, and inclinations. Previously it was possible to calculate exactly when a particular comet would transit Venus, to the hour and minute. It was like clockwork then, but no more. Cosmic bodies, even entire galactic sectors, have vanished into timeholes.

—Professor Daviz Joél, report
to the Merchant Prince Alliance

Two mottled gray-and-black podships sped along the galactic web, one right after the other. Though they traveled so rapidly that a Human eye would not be able to see them, their speeds were nonetheless diminished from the norm, in large part due to the decline of the infrastructure.

Bred in a laboratory, these large sentient vessels were not piloted like their natural cousins. Instead of Parviis inside the sectoid chambers, or Tulyans merged into the flesh of the creatures, each was under the control of a Mutati operating a Hibbil navigation unit. Behind the pilot in the lead craft stood the Emir Hari'Adab, leader of the shapeshifter race . . . a position he had attained after assassinating his own father, the Zultan Abal Meshdi.

Hari had Hibbil and Adurian prisoners in the cargo hold, all of them soldiers. For a reason they refused to divulge, they had landed a small military force on his own planet of Dij. The Emir's fighters had overcome them, killing most and taking the rest into custody, along with their two unusual ships. His own demented father had authorized the breeding of what were known as "lab-pods," but these two spacecraft were of a higher order. They actually had Hibbil nav-systems that worked quite well, in sharp contrast with those of the Zultan.

The prisoners were members of the "HibAdu Coalition." One of them had carried a document fragment bearing the name of that military force, inscribed on a remnant of papers the soldiers had tried to destroy, along with all electronic records. But the salvaged document and other articles found with the soldiers had only succeeded in generating more questions, which none of the captives would answer.

Historically, Hibbils were allies of Humans, while Adurians had a similar relationship with Mutatis. And, since Humans and Mutatis had been the archenemies of one another since ancient times, everyone had assumed that Hibbils and Adurians should be the same. Perhaps it was only a splinter group that had landed on Hari's planet, but he sensed it might be something much more significant, and dangerous. The well-armed soldiers had carried the sophisticated weaponry and communications equipment of a much larger, well-financed force. They appeared to have been on a reconnaissance mission.

They call themselves HibAdus, Hari thought as he watched the Mutati pilot seated ahead of him, operating the touch-panel controls of the ship. *Very strange.*

Perhaps the Tulyans—with their ability to determine truth or falsehood through physical contact—could determine who his prisoners really were. And Hari had an additional motive for approaching the reptilian people in their legendary starcloud.

13

They were rumored to be close to Noah Watanabe and other Human leaders of the Merchant Prince Alliance. Perhaps the Tulyan Council of Elders could broker a peace agreement between the warring MPA and the Mutati Kingdom, ending the insane, ages-old hostilities between the two races. No one could even recall why they had been battling for so long, and Hari had always believed that there should be some way of bringing it all to a peaceful end. This had put him in direct conflict with his stubborn father, but now—after the unthinkable act Hari had been forced to commit—perhaps the Humans would believe him. If necessary, he would even submit himself to the truthing touch of the Tulyans.

At the sound of the cockpit door sliding open behind him, Hari turned to exchange smiles with his girlfriend, Parais d'Olor. While Hari and the pilot (like most other shapeshifters) were terramutatis who walked, she was an aeromutati, able to spread her wings and soar into the air, should she ever desire to do so. Just before departing on the trip with him, she had metamorphosed into the guise of a colorful Alty peacock, a very large bird with a red-and-gold body and black, silver-tipped wings that were now tucked tightly against her body. In the confinement of the lab-pod, she got around by walking, and from her own morphology she had developed a way of walking smoothly on her two bird legs, instead of hopping around in the customary avian fashion.

Behind her stood Yerto Bhaleen, a career military officer who held the rank of kajor in the Mutati High Command. A small, muscular terramutati with the standard complement of three slender arms and six stout legs, he was a four-star kajor, just beneath the highest of ranks. Like Hari, he had refused any higher designation, in Bhaleen's case because his own commanders had died in the tragic loss of the planet Paradij, the horrific collateral damage involved in the assassination of the Zultan.

"We should be there soon, My Emir," Bhaleen said. "All is in readiness."

"Very good," Hari said.

The officer moved back a couple of paces and stood rigidly, awaiting any further commands.

Glancing at Parais, the Mutati leader said, "You can't wait to fly on your own, can you? Perhaps after we arrive the Tulyans will permit you to soar around their starcloud."

"Only if we gain their trust," she suggested.

Rubbing up against his side, she smiled gently at him. Her lovely facial features were fleshy, with a small beak and oversized blue eyes that were totally without guile. "But I don't need to fly," she said. "Wherever you are is where I want to be."

Hari adored her. Without Parais' guidance and inspiration, he would not be able to go on with his life, and with the new, very ambitious purpose he had undertaken. If anyone deserved to lead the Mutati people, it was her, and not him. But the shapeshifter race was very traditional, and Hari had the right of ascendancy by birthright, no matter the terrible thing he had done to accelerate the process.

It had been an act of violence that went dreadfully wrong, in the trajectory calculation of a planet-busting Demolio torpedo. Aimed at a moon his father was visiting, the missile went off course and destroyed the Mutati homeworld of Paradij instead, wiping out billions of Hari's own people. The orbiting moon and the mad Zultan Abal Meshdi had been annihilated in the cataclysms as well, but that had been little solace. Hari could hardly bear to think of the scale of the tragedy.

Not yet having admitted to the Mutati people what he did, or the reason, Hari carried a terrible burden of guilt on his shoulders. At Parais' encouragement, he continued to lead the shapeshifter race, but he insisted on doing it as Emir, a princely governor's designation, rather than the customary Zultan title his father and most predecessors had held. It was Hari's way of saying privately that he did not yet deserve the higher title, that he had not earned it, and perhaps he never would.

CHAPTER THREE

After we defeated the Parviis, the Eye of the Swarm withdrew his survivors, taking more than 100,000 podships they control to the remote Parvii Fold. Earlier, he had already cut off regularly scheduled podship travel to Human and Mutati worlds, and now he's done the same for the rest of the galaxy. A few Parvii pilots who are out of contact with their leader are continuing routes in non-Human or Mutati sectors, but that won't last long. In addition, there are disturbing reports of laboratory-bred pods out in the galaxy.

—Excerpts from confidential report
to the Tulyan Council of Elders

From the window of a small office suspended inside the immense building, Jacopo Nehr looked down on his manufacturing and assembly lines as they produced new machine components and robots for export. He heard the steady drone of machinery, and felt the vibrations of manufacturing beneath his feet. This plant, located on the largest of the Hibbil Cluster Worlds, was one of many industrial facilities that Nehr owned around the galaxy.

But to his dismay, he was not there voluntarily. He cursed and smashed the side of his fist against the plax window. It flexed, but did not break.

Down on the factory floor he saw a scruffy little silver robot engaged in oddly animated conversations with subordinate workbots of varying sizes and designs. The little one's name was Ipsy, an odd mechanical runt who had an officious, irritating personality. He certainly grated on Jacopo, and other sentient robots took offense to him at times as well, as they seemed to be doing at the moment. Jacopo had tried to teach him personal interaction and management skills, but Ipsy had been resistant to learning them.

Now, Ipsy pushed another robot in the chest, knocking him backward against others. Three more of them tumbled over like dominoes. Jacopo had seen this mechanical emotionalism and physicality before, and always Ipsy won out. Someone had programmed him to be quite aggressive.

Despite his gruff methods, the little guy had taken charge of the facility, causing it to hum at high efficiency, producing more robots and machine parts than ever before. Jacopo knew where some of the products were being shipped around the galaxy, but not all of them. He only knew for certain that business was booming. Ipsy didn't seem to know all of the end-user details either, or he was keeping the information to himself. As a large part of this factory's business, it produced electronic instruments and control panels—components that could be used for a variety of purposes.

Unfortunately, the facility was making money Jacopo could not spend. The Hibbils allowed him access to heavily edited financial reports, but he couldn't get his hands on his share of the funds themselves, and he was not allowed access to any form of transportation. The factory complex was ringed with an electronic containment field that penned him in. The furry little bastards even forced him to live in a rudimentary apartment on the grounds, a stunted, boxlike abode that had been designed for one of *them,* not for a Human being.

Each day Nehr woke up in a foul mood, then spent much of

his time dithering around the factory, hoping something would change, that the Hibbils who had essentially imprisoned him there more than a week ago would set him free and allow him to return to Canopa. But he saw no sign of that happening.

He hadn't seen any fellow Humans at all since being forced to fly across the galaxy on a strange podship, one that was unlike any other he'd ever seen. From Ipsy he'd learned it was a craft that had been bred in a laboratory, and guided by a Hibbil navigation system. The thought of an artificial podship boggled his mind, not easily done to an inventor and businessman of his stature. One of the leading merchant princes in the Alliance, Jacopo Nehr had discovered the nehrcom cross-space communication system, and had built an impressive multi-planet business empire around that connective tissue. Before falling out of favor with the princes, he had even been appointed Supreme General of the Merchant Prince Armed Forces—the primary Human military force.

Down on the floor, Ipsy was getting increasingly aggressive, and he pushed other workbots out of his way as they pressed in around him.

Jacopo hardly cared. Ipsy would get his way, as always. The merchant prince was more concerned about being held prisoner in his own factory complex, with no one to talk to except the robots that ran the facility. Why was he being treated this way? It seemed like a cruel joke, but he wasn't laughing.

To make it even more perplexing, a Hibbil had done this to him, and not just any furball, either. It had been Pimyt, the Royal Attaché to Lorenzo del Velli, former Doge of the Alliance. Pimyt was so trusted that for a time he had even been appointed regent of the entire multi-planet empire, until the princes could agree on the selection of a new doge. Nehr had suspected for some time that Pimyt was involved in war profiteering, but he'd found no evidence of it, and had been unable to determine exactly what the attaché wanted with him.

He'd been able to come up with a pretty good guess, though, one that made sense the more he thought about it. *Leverage.* Holding him hostage on the Hibbil Cluster Worlds in order to force his powerful daughter, Nirella, to cooperate. She was not only married to Doge Anton del Velli; she was Supreme General of the Merchant Prince Armed Forces, having succeeded her own father in that position.

Nehr wondered if he would ever see her again, or his wife, Lady Amila. His mood sank even more, as he realized that the Hibbils could just keep him there for the rest of his life, and maintain the leverage they wanted. But Hibbils were supposed to be allies of Humans. Why would they do this? It went beyond war profiteering. Nehr didn't want to imagine how far beyond.

Noticing that the altercation down on the production floor had escalated, he sighed. Robots were streaming toward Ipsy, leaving their work posts, slowing down the operation. It looked like Jacopo would have to intervene this time.

Taking a lift down to the main floor, he found hundreds of robotic workers surrounding Ipsy, glaring at him with orange visual sensors that were much brighter than usual and shouting at him in a din of mechanical voices. Jacopo pushed forward through their midst. Noticing him, the robots grew quieter, but he heard them whispering around him, a peculiar and disturbing mechanical hum.

"I want all of you to calm down and return to work!" Jacopo shouted, raising his arms in the air.

The robots grew completely quiet, each one just staring at him. But in the multicolored, blinking lights around their faceplates and their bright orange, ember-like visual sensors, he saw that Ipsy's supervision methods had triggered their anger programs to a much higher level than Jacopo had ever seen.

They were operating in concert, too. Like a mob or a pack.

A wave of fear passed through him, as he saw the blinking-light patterns intensify, and the ember eyes burn even brighter. Under a strict code of honor programmed into all robots created by Humans (or stemming from those creations), robots were intensely loyal to Humans. But since his incarceration, Jacopo had grown increasingly concerned about the factory bots, because many of them were of unfamiliar designs and didn't always behave according to known industrial parameters. Some of their personalities seemed oddly unpredictable, and he had decided that this must be due to the fact that they'd been manufactured by the Hibbils, under standards that were not known to Humans. The Hibbils had long manufactured their own robots, but until recently Jacopo thought he knew all of the basic designs, since he had often worked in concert with them on the development and manufacture of sentient machines. Now, something had changed.

"We demand that you get rid of Ipsy," one of the robots howled in a tinny voice.

"Yes!" said another. "He goes, or we stop work!"

"Don't be silly," Jacopo said. "Robots can't go on strike. Now stop this foolishness and get back to work immediately."

The robots advanced on Jacopo, their faceplate lights blinking furiously, their eyes afire. He felt their hard bodies pressing around them, and it hurt. Then he heard Ipsy shout in his officious mechanical voice, telling them to clear away. The little mechanical man managed to reach Jacopo's side, but now the other robots pressed hard around both of them.

Jacopo panicked as he felt them crushing him, and he couldn't breathe. He cried out in pain and rage as they crushed his bones. Broken and smashed, the inventor slumped in the midst of the hard metalloy bodies around him.

When it was done, the robots packaged Jacopo's body into an

export box. And they tossed Ipsy . . . what was left of him . . . onto a scrap heap.

Chapter Four

"There is a certain glamour and allure to very old ways, and in particular to those that are the most ancient of all. It is almost as if the Supreme Being got it right in the very beginning with the various races and star systems he spawned, but only then. Thereafter, under pressure from countless directions, things declined, and continued that way until the entire cosmic engine started to run out of steam. Scientists describe it as entropy on a huge scale, with energy systems winding down and life forms eventually returning to the soil and cosmic dust. But I have a different, less scientific, way of putting it: Sentient life forms have a way of making selfish decisions and mucking things up."

—Master Noah Watanabe, speech to
the seventh Guardian graduating class

Horrendous. Ghastly.

Onboard the flagship, Noah and Anton conferred. Tesh stood with them, having temporarily left the sectoid chamber and used her magnification system to enlarge her image. They all faced one of the viewing windows in the large passenger compartment, staring in shock at the impediment to the fleet's forward progress.

A short while ago, when they first entered the narrowing funnel, there had been the expected hurtling, luminous white stones that Tesh and the other pilots had been forced to negotiate. Then the rolling, oncoming stones had ceased altogether, and an unexpected obstacle had presented itself to the fleet. As a result, all the way back up the funnel the entire Liberator podship force came to an abrupt halt, and floated freely in the frozen vacuum, unable to proceed any further.

Noah grimaced at the sight ahead of *Webdancer*. Like an immense cork, the way forward was blocked by immense clusters of tiny, horribly mutilated and frozen Parvii bodies, all clumped together to form a grisly barrier.

Tears streamed down Tesh's cheeks. "I saw bodies floating the last time I was here, but got past them." She paused. "When we entered the funnel this time, I wondered at first why there were no bodies. Now I know."

"We must reach the Parvii Fold," Anton said, staring out the window. "Everything depends on us capturing the rest of the podships."

"It's obvious what we have to do," Noah said. He put a reassuring hand on Tesh's shoulder. "I'm sorry, but we need to open fire and blast our way through."

Her eyes looked tortured and red.

"But will we find anything on the other side?" Anton asked.

"I think so," she said, wiping her eyes. "Woldn must have created this barrier in order to protect himself, and the others who remain with him." She scowled at the mention of the Parvii leader, the Eye of the Swarm.

Moments later, six Liberator podships opened the gun ports on their sides and commenced fire on the horrific barricade. In the fiery onslaught of white-hot projectiles, dead Parvii flesh melted away, revealing a dark tunnel beyond. . . .

Doge Anton sent two podships ahead into the darkness to scout for further hazards or traps. One of the vessels was piloted by

Eshaz. His passenger compartment thronged with Human fighters and Tulyan pilots, along with Acey Zelk and Dux Hannah, a pair of young Humans who were friends of Eshaz.

Anton's wife, General Nirella, had considered off-loading the pilots onto other vessels, but the Tulyans resisted, saying their telekinetic mindlink powers could be of added value against any Parviis they encountered. Even though the combined telepathic power was much weaker away from the Tulyan Starcloud, it was at least another dimension that might be useful in battle, and the Parviis had shown themselves to be susceptible to it.

"If we get through this, we can call ourselves men," Dux said. He and his cousin—still teenagers—sat on one of the extruded organic benches. The reptilian Tulyans towered around them on the hard seats.

"Don't get all terrified," Acey said, with a smirk on his wide face. "If you go hysterical when I'm needed for a crisis, I'm going to have to let you go."

Dux gave him a less-than-good-natured shove. Acey always considered himself the braver of the pair, but Dux thought he was rather foolhardy instead. Now they were committed, with no turning back.

"I'd rather be at the controls of one of these space blimps," Acey said.

Dux nodded, remembering a time that they had gone on a wild podship hunt, along with Eshaz and Tesh. An excited Acey had been allowed to pilot one of the wild pods shortly after it was captured. Afterward he said it was the highlight of his life, and he couldn't wait to do it again. Eshaz had told him, however, that Humans were limited in their ability to pilot the sentient creatures, and were not skilled enough for battle. All logic said this was true, but Acey showed stubborn determination. He felt he could do more than Eshaz had seen, so he kept pressing.

Now the boys and all other Human military personnel had backup life-support suits aboard, and Acey hoped to use his for going outside and mounting a podship to guide it. The insistent Acey had also obtained permission to bring along a gilded harness and Tarbu thorn-vines for basic piloting, just in case he was given the opportunity to stand atop a podship and pilot it, even if it was only on a backup basis.

Dux hoped it wasn't necessary for Acey to do that. Not in this distant region, filled with unknown dangers.

As the scout ships made their way through the narrowing funnel, luminous white stones reappeared and hurtled toward them. One glanced off the companion scout craft, causing it to veer off course, before the pilot regained control. Dux watched in horror as a much larger rock tumbled toward his own podship at a high rate of speed. Eshaz, immersed into the Aopoddae flesh and, piloting the podship as if he had been born in this form, veered hard to starboard, narrowly averting destruction.

Both scout ships made it to an adjoining gray-green passageway that was clear of stones, and then passed completely through, into the immense, pocketlike Parvii Fold. There, Dux saw thousands of the sentient spacecraft tethered in a moorage basin, and many more floated loosely in the airless vacuum, as far as the eye could see.

From the hidden, faintly green realm, Dux sent a comline message back that no Parvii swarms were massing in battle formation, not even a defensive arrangement.

"Just a swarm around the Palace of Woldn," he reported. "They look lethargic, like hibernating insects."

"And their podship fleet?" General Nirella asked, over the connection.

"Lots of ships are here, ma'am. Too many to count."

After hearing the report, Doge Anton ordered the Liberator task force to advance. In minutes, the fleet streamed through the rest of the funnel, and out into the pocketlike galactic fold.

By this time, Parvii sentries were sending alarms, and the swarm was beginning to awaken.

The Palace of Woldn—constructed of interlocked members of the Parvii race—floated in the vacuum of the Parvii Fold. High-pitched sirens went off throughout the structure. Having been ill, the Eye of the Swarm was in a deep sleep when the intruders arrived. In his diminished state, he had not anticipated an attack, nor that a Parvii would lead enemies into their midst.

Slowly struggling back to consciousness, Woldn probed telepathically, and learned from his sentinels that a fleet of Tulyan-controlled podships had arrived, behind a podship that did not have a Tulyan face on its prow. Based on this, he wondered if a Parvii could be piloting the lead craft. If so, it would be a betrayal of epic proportions. Via relay, he saw that this particular podship did look familiar, albeit larger than the last time he'd seen it. And he recalled the name of its rebellious pilot, a woman he had banished from the swarm.

Tesh Kori. But could she have brought the enemy here, at the head of an armed fleet? He didn't want to believe it.

The Eye of the Swarm sent high-pitched telepathic signals to his followers, alerting them even more than the sentries already had, and sending specific instructions to the remaining swarms. . . .

During the doomed Parvii attack on the Tulyan Starcloud, the Tulyans had surprised Woldn with a defensive strike that sent comets, meteors, and radioactive asteroids into the swarms, scattering them into space and resulting in the death of more than eighty percent of the Parvii population. It had been the biggest disaster in Parvii history, going back millions of years.

In the days of Parvii lore, long, long ago, there had been tens

of thousands of war priests and breeding specialists—two powerful factions that had worked together to enlarge the influence
and domain of the galactic race. In modern times, prior to the
devastating "Tulyan Incident" that killed so many of Woldn's
people, a small number of war priests and breeding specialists
had continued to practice the old ways, keeping their skills
sharp in case they were ever needed. During Woldn's rule there
had never been more than a hundred members of each group,
far diminished from the old days. With the Tulyan disruption of
the energy fields that connected Parviis paranormally with their
brethren, however, most of the modern war priests and breeding specialists had been killed, so that Woldn was left with only
two female breeding specialists, Ting and Volom, and one male
war priest, Ryall.

Following the disaster, in the perceived security of the Parvii
Fold, Woldn had set in motion old forces, resurrecting ancient
programs that his race had once employed successfully against
their enemies. In short order, the breeding specialists had
established an intense propagation program from old cellular
stock, and their population had begun to increase, with
hundreds of thousands of young Parviis reaching adulthood in a
matter of weeks. It had been a comparatively small amount, but
a promising beginning nonetheless.

Then something had gone terribly wrong. Shortly after reaching adulthood, the newly generated Parviis had developed a
mysterious metabolic ailment that killed almost all of them, and
even infected some of the general populace, including Woldn
himself. Ting and Volom had been forced to set up quarantine
procedures and start over. In the process, they discovered that
some of the cellular material retained from ancient times was
contaminated, and any Parvii created from it was genetically
defective, doomed to suffer a slow, lingering death. Some, but
not all, of the infected general populace fared better.

For more than a week Woldn had been ill, feeling lethargic

and hardly able to move. In the last couple of days, he had felt a little better, but he still slept most of the time, in an attempt to regain his strength. He would awaken for brief periods to do telepathic checks, then would go back to sleep. During Woldn's recovery process, Ting and Volom worked long hours, trying to figure out the problem and get things going again with uncontaminated cellular material. It was going very slowly, and both were hindered by moderate forms of the illness themselves.

Hidden in the genetic structure of Woldn's race, there were others like Ting, Volom, and Ryall, waiting to come back from long inactivity. The knowledge of breeding specialists and war priests still existed in the cellular structures of Woldn's people, having gone into dormancy. And the Eye of the Swarm had been hoping that the strongest of the ancients would reemerge.

So it was that inside one of the wings of the palace, Parviis had been working in a laboratory to resurrect the old ways. Tapping into old cellular material and into the brains of their living people, the breeding specialists had discovered the ancient memories of a few additional war priests and breeding specialists—memories in the minds of Parviis who became known as "latents," those persons with fertile memories that had been lying dormant in the collective unconsciousness of the entire race. It was like growing plants in the most receptive cellular material, weeding out intrusive thoughts, nurturing the old knowledge, bringing it back. But it wasn't going rapidly enough, and now the enemy was attacking at exactly the wrong moment. If only there had been more time to prepare, if only the war priests had been able to re-create the powerful weapons of yore. But it was not meant to be. . . .

White-hot bursts of light hit the palace and structures around it, and Woldn heard the screams of his dying people through the morphic field that connected him to them telepathically. The outer walls of the palace, constructed of densely and intricately interlocked Parviis, held up against several blasts, allowing Woldn, his personal guards, and other key personnel to escape into the airless vacuum. Leading them toward the podship basin, Woldn narrowly avoided the blasts of enemy weapons. Some of his guards were hit, and he heard their telepathic shrieks of agony.

Behind him, the Palace of Woldn disintegrated, its living components killed or scattered.

Gathering his survivors, Woldn commanded them to take control of the floating podships in his own fleet. But most of the Parviis, like their leader, were weak and phlegmatic. They attempted to swarm the podships and gain control over them with neurotoxin stingers as they had done in the past, but the stingers had little or no effect. The Parviis also tried to attack a handful of the Tulyan-piloted podships that were away from the rest of their fleet, but the Tulyans used mindlink energy to keep the attackers at bay, while MPA and Red Beret fighters opened fire with hull cannons.

Through his paranormal linkage, Woldn heard the terrible screams of his people as they died by the millions.

With Parvii numbers diminishing and unable to fight back, the Eye of the Swarm led only a couple of hundred thousand followers in a desperate retreat through an opening in the gray-green membrane of the galactic fold, passing through a small hole, so tiny that none of the attackers could follow.

In darkness on the other side, he reassessed. No active breeding specialists or war priests survived, only a handful of the budding "latents," Parviis who did not yet have use of their skills or powers. Two potential war priests and five potential breeding specialists.

To Woldn's further dismay, he had left more than one

hundred thousand podships behind, floating in the vacuum of the galactic fold, waiting to be taken by his enemies.

CHAPTER FIVE

All of us are prisoners of something, and ultimately of our
own mortality.

—Ancient Saying

Visibly upset, three Hibbils marched through the factory, looking at all of the assembly lines that had been shut down by the
disturbance. In an unprecedented event, the entire sentient
machine work crew had rebelled against their robotic supervi-
sor, smashing him into useless metal and killing the Human
factory owner.

"This shouldn't have happened," said one of the Hibbils, his
red eyes glowing angrily. He had flecks of gray fur and a thick,
salt-and-pepper beard. On either side of Pimyt a furry little
companion grunted, and their eyes glowed nearly as brightly as
his.

Pimyt watched as the two others inspected several robots,
inserting interface probes into their control boxes and reading
the results.

"Doesn't look good," one of them said. Squat and overweight,
Rennov took his job seriously.

"I don't see how this happened," the other said. This one was
younger, a Hibbil with glistening, golden-brown fur.

The two of them kept using probes to check the sentient
machines.

Overseeing the procedures, Pimyt was unhappy on multiple

levels. He and the division managers with him didn't like to see the factory operation interrupted, since the new robots and other machine components produced there—especially the control panels—were needed for the war effort of the HibAdu Coalition, the union of Hibbils and Adurians. In addition, the last thing he had wanted was for Jacopo Nehr to die, since that eliminated any potential leverage with the Human's powerful daughter, Nirella del Velli. So far, it had been a stand-off with her. She'd accused Pimyt of blackmailing her father and had even threatened to torture him into talking. Not backing down, Pimyt had threatened to release technical information about the workings of the nehrcom instantaneous cross-space communication system—revealing how simple its operation really was. It would be a scandal that would ruin her father's reputation as a famous inventor, and destroy the Nehr company. Hearing this, she had stormed off.

Shortly after that, Nirella's husband, Doge Anton, had ordered Pimyt and the former Doge Lorenzo taken into "protective custody." Enfuriated, Pimyt was ready to make good on his threat, but he and Lorenzo had been placed into solitary confinement at a prison on Canopa, with no one to talk to except for uncooperative guards. And Pimyt had not yet set up a mechanism to release the information if certain things happened to him.

While the two of them were so rudely confined, Doge Anton, General Nirella, and Noah Watanabe had departed on their foolish military venture to the Parvii Fold, an operation Pimyt had learned about just before being taken into custody. Then, from his cell, Pimyt had hoped the Parviis would succeed in wiping out all of them with the powerful telepathic weapons they were said to have.

Three days had passed. Finally, one morning the glowing electronic confinement bars on the cells went dark, and the guards said the pair was free to leave. No explanation. Lorenzo had returned to The Pleasure Palace, his opulent gambling facility orbiting Canopa. Pimyt had considered getting even with Nirella—assuming she had a part in his incarceration—but had decided to think it over first. Nirella (or whomever she left in charge) had the power to confine him at any time, for any reason. Perhaps the jail time had been her way of telling him exactly that.

Considering his options (which Pimyt often did), he had slipped away to rejoin his HibAdu conspirators, and resumed his involvement in facilitating the downfall of both the Merchant Prince Alliance and the Mutati Kingdom. This had brought him, on a secret lab-pod flight made easier by the diminishment of MPA military forces, to the Hibbil Cluster Worlds. . . .

Even now, through all of his intelligence sources, Pimyt didn't know what was happening at the Parvii Fold. It did amuse him that the Humans—reportedly with Tulyan allies—were spending so much time and effort going after Parviis. The HibAdus, learning of the military operation from Pimyt, had seen it as an opportunity to strike merchant prince planets that were left inadequately defended, because of the diversion of ships and armaments to an ill-advised distant operation. In addition, HibAdu leadership—while Pimyt had never met any of them personally—had sent a message agreeing with his assessment. The Parviis, even if they failed to completely destroy the attacking force, were sure to damage it seriously.

Now the scheming, highly organized HibAdus were almost ready to launch their simultaneous surprise attacks on key planets. Just a few essential details remained to be completed, with this additional complication. The robot uprising would have been just an annoying nuisance, if not for Jacopo's death.

The division managers completed their inspection, spot-checking robots throughout the factory. Finally, Rennov announced, "Every workbot in the factory will have to be reprogrammed."

"Get started, then," Pimyt ordered.

Ipsy, with the weight of industrial scrap on top of him, burrowed his smashed and broken body into a cavity in the pile and began to rebuild himself, converting the junked parts he found around him. He took on an even smaller body form this time, using microcircuit boards and fiber optics that he salvaged from the scrap heap, after testing each of them. His arms and legs were essentially the same, but he was considerably thinner now, and even shorter than before.

Then, as he connected a small, silver-and-green panel to his brain, he fell backward, his limbs freezing into immobility. The panel had a defect that he had not noticed.

While he lay there, looking upward and trying to repair the problem internally, Hibbil workers started dismantling the scrap pile with a mechanical, remote-controlled arm and claw, intending to melt the metals down and recycle them. Ipsy saw patches of daylight as pieces above him were removed. He noticed a zoomeye on the mechanical arm, and the claw hesitated over him for an instant—bathing him in orange light—before going on to other, larger pieces. But Ipsy knew it would be back.

The little robot was like a paralyzed man, unable to move.

CHAPTER SIX

Once, the number of Parviis in the galaxy was far beyond our capability to measure. Now the Eye of the Swarm is in a desperate situation, fleeing with what little he has left. This is not a time for us to gloat. It is a time to be wary. Like a cornered animal, he may be at his most dangerous.

—Tulyan report to the Council of Elders

After all the eons of Parvii glory, the successes that went back farther than anyone could remember, Woldn couldn't understand how things had gone so terribly wrong. Certainly, it was not due to any errors of leadership he had committed. He was far too careful for that, always using the resources of his people—and the podships under their control—prudently.

At the moment, he and his drastically diminished swarm huddled in the darkness of an unknown place. The hole through which they had escaped had not been there previously, or it would have been noticed by his people, who had been constantly checking every square centimeter of the Parvii Fold, making certain it was absolutely safe. They had all been taught from an early age that this was their sacred nest in a dangerous galaxy, one they had to protect at all costs. Never before had holes appeared in the fabric of the fold. It seemed an impossibility, because the immense protective pocket was at the farthest end of the known galaxy. They'd always thought that nothing lay beyond the gray-green membrane, that it marked the edge of existence.

And yet, he and his remaining followers had gone through. Less than two hundred thousand individuals.

Now Woldn reached telepathically into his morphic field, and opened up some of his own thoughts for his followers to read. In the process he felt the Parviis flowing to him mentally and probing him, reading the particular thoughts he had opened up to them. In turn, all of the Parviis made the totality of their own thoughts more easily accessible to the Eye of the Swarm, so that he could read them at will himself. He did so selectively, a few at a time.

Where are we? Woldn wondered. No one seemed to know.

He and his swarm remained close to the tiny hole through which they had come, as if gaining some reassurance from its proximity. At least it gave them their bearings. They were very close to their beloved Parvii Fold, and yet so far from it. The galactic membrane separating them from the fold had not proven to be very thick, but it may as well have been the entire width of the universe. Woldn had stationed alternating sentries at the hole, peering through one at a time to the other side, and they continued to report extensive military activity in the fold.

Will we ever return? Woldn thought, *or are we doomed to remain here forever?*

One of his followers transmitted weakly: *I think we're in the undergalaxy.*

Then another, equally diminished Parvii thought reached him: *I agree.*

But throughout the rest of the swarm, no others ventured opinions. They shivered and huddled, and flew nearby, ever alert to dangers.

A shudder passed through Woldn as he remembered the Tulyan legend of an "undergalaxy." Parviis had always dismissed such a concept as just one of the harebrained ideas that their rivals, the Tulyans, had. Since their fall from glory long ago, when Parviis had taken control of podships away from them, the Tulyans had descended into superstition and stories of how things used to be. They were an odd race. Oh, they had their uses. On occasion Woldn and other Parvii leaders had used them for their timeseeing abilities, for that peculiar way they had of looking through what Tulyans called the "lens of time." Bordering on the supernatural, the ability seemed to work. But not consistently.

Woldn wondered now if their stories of the undergalaxy could possibly contain a grain of truth. Or more than that.

Is that where we are? The undergalaxy?

Gazing past an opening in the huddled swarm, some of the darkness seemed to melt away, enabling him to barely make out faint and unknown star systems that seemed oddly configured. In happier times, he had led his swarms to every corner of the known galaxy, and this was not anyplace he'd ever seen before. Had he overlooked a portion of the galaxy, or could this actually be an entirely different place?

He strongly suspected the latter.

Woldn was terrified, but concealed it from his followers, and steeled himself. Two hundred thousand survivors didn't amount to much, but they would have to form the nucleus of Parvii recovery. He was determined to not only survive as a galactic race, but to rise once more in power so that Parviis regained their former glory.

According to Tulyan legend, a dark terror resided in this nether galaxy, but details were murky. Woldn did not reveal it to anyone, but he began to wonder if this legend of his enemy could possibly be true, and if Parviis had ever been to such a stygian realm. Perhaps the horrors of the undergalaxy were buried in the collective unconscious of the Parvii race, and could only be brought out in a laboratory.

Telepathically, he probed the minds of the seven latents, and absorbed their thoughts. At the most protected center of the tiny swarm, with their brethren clustered around them to preserve their body heat, these latents—two potential war priests and five potential breeding specialists—represented the future or doom of all Parviis. Seeds of the past grew in their physical bodies, which were of varying ages. Woldn probed deeply into the minds of the seven, into their memories and racial past. Through the long tunnels of their minds he went, probing, searching for facts. The paths joined, and continued back in time. From the embryonic war priests he found circumstantial evidence that an undergalaxy might actually exist.

But there were barriers to more information, to meaningful details. He found no personal accounts of the other dimension, suggesting that the two young men did not have those particulars yet, if there were any. As moments passed, Woldn was beginning to suspect that his people had been to this place at one time, but the memories were too horrible and had been collectively repressed by his race.

Leading the paltry swarm, Woldn skirted the edge of the alternate realm and circled back to the tiny bolt hole, hoping that the awful danger on this side—what could it possibly be?— did not sense their presence. When things quieted down on the other side, he intended to lead the way back through, to the Parvii Fold. Then he would take precautions to seal the area off so that no intruders could ever get back in.

But his medical personnel and his own telepathic probes were revealing disturbing information about the condition of the swarm of survivors around him. Only a small percentage of them (including Woldn) had effective neurotoxin stingers in their bodies, which explained why most of them had little effect on the podships of the military attack force.

We are far, far from home, with no way to retake it.
It was a private, very lonely thought.

CHAPTER SEVEN

"I don't see what's still holding this galaxy together."
—First Elder Kre'n, comment to her Council

While the fleet was being consolidated and organized at the Parvii Fold, Noah inspected the area. He and Eshaz rode in the flagship while Tesh piloted it around the immense galactic pocket, alternately speeding up and slowing down as Noah required. By touching the skin of the sentient vessel, Eshaz was able to link with its consciousness, a variation on the truthing touch of his people. In turn, this connected the Tulyan with Tesh, who clung in her tiny humanoid form to a wall of the sectoid chamber, guiding the craft. Thus, Tesh and Eshaz could communicate directly—transmitting to each other through the podship's flesh.

"She is describing details of the fold," Eshaz said to Noah. The reptilian man held one hand against the rough, gray podship skin on the interior of the passenger compartment. "Every crease and basin in the fold has a name, a purpose, and a history behind it." He pointed out the window. "The Parviis say that the long scar on that membrane is where the Universal Creator put the finishing touches on the galaxy and stitched everything together."

"Interesting," Noah said. "How does the Parvii concept of a Universal Creator compare with your Sublime Creator, and with our Supreme Being?"

"Some of my people would be surprised to hear you ask such

a question," Eshaz said with a toothy smile. "They believe you are the messiah."

"So, you think I should know all the answers?"

"I wasn't necessarily speaking for myself. Tell me, my friend. Are you saying, then, that you are not our messiah?"

"If I am, I have a lot to learn." Noah paused. "I don't know what I am, or why special things have happened to me. My life changed dramatically after you healed me the way you did, touching my skin to the web, causing its nutrients to flow into my wound."

"Do you regret any of it?"

Noah hesitated. "No. I don't think I do." He stared at the place on the wall where Eshaz continued to touch the podship.

"Try connecting with Tesh yourself," Eshaz said. "You've had a special relationship with podships, and with her. Touch the skin and communicate with her, as I am doing."

"I don't know. My . . . I hesitate to call them powers . . . come and go. I never know when I'm going to be able to journey through the web, and when it will keep me at bay."

"Give it a try now."

Instead, Noah looked out the window. The podship had come to a stop very close to the gray-green membrane of the fold, near the long scar that Tesh had spoken of. The sentient craft nudged against the membrane, like a ship bumping up against a dock.

Over the last four days, Noah, Anton, and the Tulyans had been consolidating the immense podship fleet at the Parvii Fold. Instead of nine hundred ships in the Liberator fleet, they now had a vastly larger number of vessels—and all of them had morphed to produce a gun port feature on their hulls, controllable by the various pilots in the battle group.

With their increased assets, the Liberators had a new mission: Use the podships to transport Tulyan teams all over the galaxy, enabling them to perform the infrastructure repairs on an emergency basis, staving off the damage that was occurring to the fabric of the universe. . . .

But before leaving, Tulyan hunting crews needed to round up all of the podships that had drifted around inside the Parvii Fold, away from the moorage basin. Acey Zelk, always anxious to pilot the arcane vessels, had been permitted to join one of the crews. Already they had found more ships than the one hundred thousand Tulyan pilots they had brought with them, so the Liberators would need to send some of their original fleet back to their starcloud to pick up thousands more pilots. The exact number was unclear, because they kept finding more podships, in hidden places.

"A nice problem to have," Doge Anton had said that morning, when he and the others began to realize the enormity of the prize they had captured from the Parviis.

Through the web, Eshaz had sent a message back to the Tulyan Starcloud, notifying the Council of the logistical challenge. They made arrangements to send four hundred podships from the original Liberator fleet back to the starcloud, to get more Tulyans. They needed enough pilots to transport the rest of the huge fleet of recovered vessels, and none of the new ships could be moved yet.

This was because the Tulyan pilots and web maintenance crews needed time to familiarize themselves with the new podships, and to practice operations with them. Since the beginning of recorded time, there had always been a methodical breaking-in process in which the various personalities and talents—Tulyan and Aopoddae—were sorted out and meshed properly. If this was not done correctly, the ancient legends held that there could be extremely adverse results, even disasters in which podships rebelled and caused destructive havoc. Thus, it was worth taking the extra time to ensure safety, and—to the extent possible—to enhance predictability.

In addition, the Liberators were setting up defenses, securing the galactic fold militarily to prevent Parviis from returning and regaining multiswarm strength there. General Nirella had set up a guard post near the tiny bolt hole where the Parviis had disappeared, and had made plans to leave a guard force of one hundred podships and military personnel in other key areas of the fold, including the entranceway to the Asteroid Funnel. . . .

Continuing the inspection tour on a prearranged route, Tesh caused *Webdancer* to hover over the bolt hole. Using a magna-viewer aboard the flagship, Noah saw the barely perceptible opening through which the Parviis had escaped. Inside the hole, he saw something move, and identified it as a solitary Parvii. A sentry, Noah surmised.

Noah set the viewer aside, and said, "We must guard this area well."

"Where there's one hole, there may be others," Eshaz said.

Both of them knew Tulyan teams were looking, but so far nothing had turned up.

Once more the podship nudged up against the membrane, this time near the bolt hole. Inside the passenger compartment, Noah touched the skin of the vessel, but unlike the experience of Eshaz, Noah did not link with Tesh. The skin trembled, as if in fear of Noah. Then it calmed, and abruptly his vision shifted, flooding his consciousness with a wash of gray-green. Presently it focused, and one star seemed to twinkle in the broad field of view, but for only a moment before turning the blackest black.

With his mind, Noah Watanabe—this most unusual of all men—peered into Timeweb and absorbed the entire vast enclosure of his own galaxy, including the decaying infrastructure and this remote, intricately folded section of membrane that had once protected the Parviis.

The opening through which they had fled was a tiny point of blackness in the midst of the gray-green membrane. With his inner eye, Noah peered through the hole into another galaxy, and saw distant, twinkling star systems, nebulas, and belts of undefined, streaking color.

He then experienced an even more peculiar sensation, and felt his consciousness shifting, spinning, making him dizzy. Presently he regained his internal balance, and found that his mind was now *inside* the alternate galaxy, experiencing it paranormally. From this new vantage point, he saw the small Parvii swarm near the other side of the bolt hole.

They're in the undergalaxy, he thought, feeling both a rush of excitement and deep trepidation.

Oddly, Noah could not see very far in this realm, and he wondered if his own anxiety had something to do with that. In his own galaxy, he had learned to overcome physical fear, for he was as close to immortal in that realm as any person could be. But in the undergalaxy, he sensed the rules of physics and laws of nature were entirely different. Nothing was as it seemed there, and he curbed his own curiosity, didn't really want to venture further. Everything he had been through in his own galaxy was more than enough for him, and he couldn't afford to lose focus, couldn't afford to leave his duties and spin off into the unknown.

But Noah also sensed very strongly that something in the undergalaxy was causing the decline of Timeweb, or at least contributing to it. He could not avoid considering the ramifications of this second galaxy. His entire concept of galactic ecology had potentially been broadened by a great deal, and beyond that the implications were exponential. A universe of them.

Seeing the vastly diminished Parvii swarm hovering by the bolt hole, Noah had mixed feelings—an urge to destroy them and feelings of pity. Tesh was one of that devilish breed, and he thought he might even love her, and that he might do virtually anything for her if he ever managed to fulfill the galactic duties that seemed to have been thrust upon him by fate.

I am not a god or a messiah.

He did not want to even consider such possibilities. It could only cause harm to his focus, to his intentions. He felt an innate sense of rightness about the course he had followed with his life thus far, about the choices he had made. But he hesitated to believe that he might be anything more than an enhanced form of a human being. Eshaz, in his zeal to heal Noah, had pressed his wounded flesh against the infrastructure of Timeweb, but the strange and powerful nutrients of the infrastructure could never alter certain basic truths.

I was born of a Human mother and father. There is nothing miraculous or particularly heroic about that.

Despite all he told himself, and his sense that he was highly ethical, part of Noah wanted to eliminate this Parvii swarm violently, leaving Tesh Kori as the only survivor of her demented race. In the undergalaxy, the troubled Noah stirred his mind, and felt a cosmic storm forming. Was he causing it? He felt uncertainty about this. But then, as if caught in a great wind, he saw the Parvii swarm buffeted, so that its members flitted about in confusion and fear. Some scattered into the distance, and did not return.

The swarm grew even smaller, and Noah felt compassion for the terrified creatures.

Wondering what had just occurred, he struggled to extract himself from the peculiar visions. Finally he succeeded in withdrawing, and returned to his physical self, in the passenger compartment of *Webdancer*.

Conflicting emotions raged in his mind, giving him an intense headache.

Eshaz looked at him with concern in his slitted, pale grey eyes. "You saw something, didn't you?" the Tulyan asked.

Noah nodded, but for several moments found himself unable to organize his thoughts or form them into words.

CHAPTER EIGHT

Noah worries incessantly about his genetic linkage to Francella Watanabe, and her severe mental health issues. But
there is an ancillary problem, something he has not
discussed with me, and which I have not had the courage
to bring up: Is not Doge Anton genetically linked to Francella as well, and might there be psychological repercussions because of that?
                                        —Tesh Kori, private notes

Thousands of additional Tulyan pilots had arrived from the
starcloud, and were being meshed with the podships like alien
marital partners, using the ancient techniques to ensure the
maximum efficiency of the Tulyan-Aopoddae linkages. Now,
counting the original nine hundred podships that the Liberator
fleet had brought to the galactic fold, Doge Anton had a force
of more than one hundred twenty-two thousand vessels. As had
earlier occurred with the original fleet, when the new pilot-ship
matchings were completed, the sentient podships took on the
reptilian faces of their pilots, and opened up gun ports on the
sides of their hulls.

The process was going well. Only two hundred and fourteen
podships remained to be synchronized by the Tulyans, plus a
few more out in the reaches of the fold that needed to be
brought in.

Noah, Anton, and Eshaz stood at a viewing window inside a

48

modular headquarters structure that General Nirella's military technicians had constructed. Held in place by space anchors, it was positioned exactly where the Palace of Woldn used to be, which was considered the most central—and most command-ing—position in the entire fold.

The three leaders stood with a number of dignitaries who had been brought in after the victory here over the Parviis, including two members of the Council of Elders and a number of merchant princes. They watched while teams of Tulyan podship handlers worked in the airless vacuum with the remain-ing, unsynchronized Aopoddae.

The entire Liberator fleet had been delayed while Tulyan experts synchronized and stabilized the vast fleet, necessary to ensure that there would be no rebellion in the Aopoddae ranks, and that every one of the sentient ships was working in concert with the pilots. This involved subtle methods of synchronicity and mutual respect, ways that had been known to the Tulyans since time immemorial, and by which they ensured the integrity of the immense fleet.

"It has been very difficult to integrate so many ships," Eshaz said, "but we're almost there. Long ago, the Parviis did something similar, using their own methods. We're replacing their bonds with our own, then checking and rechecking."

"And those are the most difficult of the bunch," Anton said, pointing out at the podships that were still being worked.

"Precisely. We've separated them from the others, and are performing final tests on the others as we speak. Keep in mind, too, that this is not a process of breaking or taming the podships. Rather, we must harmonize with them."

"Just as Humans and other races need to do in nature," Noah said.

"Well put, my good friend," Eshaz said. He touched Noah's left arm affectionately before pulling away. Then, looking at

Doge Anton, the Tulyan added, "If final tests go as anticipated, the rest of the fleet should be able to depart for the starcloud in two days."

"And the recalcitrants?" Anton asked, gesturing again at the podships outside.

"They can be left behind for more work. Eventually, they will be integrated with the others. These just have more difficult Parvii bonds to overcome."

Anton tapped on the window plax. "Can they be merged with the guard force of one hundred armed vessels that we're leaving?"

"Some, perhaps. We'll see."

Outside, Noah saw three additional podships being brought into the mooring basin, including one piloted by Acey Zelk. In the only way that a Human could do this, the teenager was secured to the top of the vessel with an ornate harness and wore a life-support suit. Using thorn-vines to guide the creature, he could travel at high speeds, as fast as the podship could go. The young man was grinning as he came in atop the hull, and he waved toward the viewing window.

Noah and Eshaz waved back.

But Noah withdrew his hand quickly. He wore a long-sleeve shirt, and the extension of his left arm had revealed something that had been troubling him for several days . . . a rough area of gray-and-black skin that ran from the forearm to the shoulder and down across his torso, like a mineral vein.

He had not wanted to see a doctor about the condition, suspecting that it was far beyond anything a medical practitioner could understand. Much of his own paranormal abilities undoubtedly stemmed from the time that Eshaz had healed him of a serious head injury by connecting him to a torn fragment of Timeweb. Afterward Noah's twin sister, Francella, had attempted to kill him by the most brutal of methods, by hacking him to pieces. Through some miracle, he had survived the dismemberment attempt, growing back all of his severed body parts like an exotic lizard.

The doctors had been dumbfounded.

Even after all that, Noah's demented, dying sister had injected him with a dermex of her own tainted, contaminated blood. Since then, Noah had been increasingly concerned, but had not wanted to consult with anyone about it, not even Eshaz. Whatever was happening to his body would happen, and Noah sensed—very strongly—that neither he nor anyone else could do anything about it.

The night before, while sleeping in accommodations that had been provided for him in the headquarters building, he'd experienced an odd dream about Francella in which she had chased him across the Parvii Fold. It had seemed so real, but had been utterly impossible, since Francella had died after injecting herself with an immortality elixir—a substance that turned against her and made her age rapidly. It was with that tainted blood that she had injected Noah, just before dying herself prematurely. His relationship with her had been a real nightmare. No matter how many good things Noah had tried to do for her during his lifetime, nothing had worked and she had never appreciated any of it. To the end she had remained bitter toward him, irrationally blaming him for her troubles and trying to kill him.

Now Noah saw Eshaz watching him closely, as the Tulyan sometimes did.

Then Noah remembered Eshaz touching his affected arm a few minutes ago. With their truthing touch ability, Tulyans could read thoughts if they desired to do so. But Noah had been wearing the long-sleeve shirt, and Eshaz hadn't felt the skin directly. Noah had always assumed that direct skin contact was necessary, but what if that wasn't the case? What if Tulyan mental probes could penetrate the fabric?

With Noah staring back at him, Eshaz lowered his gaze.

In privacy that evening, Noah examined his arm closely, and an unavoidable thought occurred to him. The affected area that he'd been trying to hide reminded him of podship skin.

CHAPTER NINE

Great historical events can be illusory to their participants, and to the historians who write about them afterward. Even with the passage of time and the seasoning of history, the truth can still be elusive.

—Sister Janiko, one of the
"veiled historians" of Lost Earth

After reading a holo-report that floated above his desktop, Pimyt paused and looked up. "This looks good," he said to the dignitary sitting across from him, an insectoid man in a white-and-gold suit.

Ambassador VV Uncel did not respond. He stared at a small handheld screen.

"VV?"

"Eh?" The Adurian's voice squeaked. "Oh, sorry, my room-mate gave me a list of things he wants me to do. Household tasks."

"Ah yes, what Humans call the 'honey-do' list."

"Yes. He's quite demanding."

Even though Uncel and his male roommate were in what the Adurians called an "affectionate relationship," Pimyt knew it was not sexually intimate. The androgynous Adurians, renowned for their laboratory breeding methods, even relied upon them entirely for the propagation of their own race, and had taken genetic steps to make sexual acts impossible.

"Now what were you saying?" the Ambassador asked.

"Just that the report looks good. The results are exactly as I expected."

"As *we* expected," Ambassador VV Uncel said. Like all of his race, he was entirely hairless, a mixture of mammalian and insectoid features with a small head and large bulbous eyes. His skin was a bright patchwork of multicolored caste markings, symbolizing high social status.

"Don't take that tone with me. The minute I learned about Human military operations on Canopa, I found out their purpose, and I knew instantly they would fail against Parvii telepathic weapons. That was all in *my* initial report to the Coalition, predating anything you wrote."

The Ambassador raised his chin haughtily. "Your report would not have gone anywhere if I hadn't concurred with your *guess.*"

"What do you mean, *guess?*" Pimyt felt his face flush hot, and considered hurling something at the irritating diplomat. For a moment, he scanned the objects on his desk, a glax paperweight that could kill him, a paper spike that could do the same, or put out an eye. . . .

The Hibbil's gaze settled on a book that was heavy enough to cause pain if hurled accurately, but wouldn't do lasting physical harm. He'd never taken such action before, though, and knew he shouldn't even consider it. Too much was at stake.

Taking a deep breath, Pimyt continued. "In my position as Royal Attaché to the former Doge, I gained extensive military experience. I was personally responsible for moving MPA troops and equipment around, taking steps to weaken merchant prince military capabilities while maximizing our own. I was also on the team that came up with the idea of inserting sabotaged computer chips into the firing mechanisms of merchant prince space cannons, ion guns, and energy detonators. The weapons will seem to operate perfectly, until our warships come into range and are identified—which automatically shuts the weapons down. What a delightful image: totally defenseless Humans, ready to be slaughtered."

The elegant insectoid smiled. "You are so like your Human friends, aren't you? Always exaggerating your contributions, trying to take personal credit for everything. We Adurians are not that way, and understand the need to share credit, to work as a team. You know quite well that I had similar devices installed surreptitiously on the biggest Mutati warships, but I'm not bragging about it."

Pimyt grabbed the book. Perhaps if he threw it just right it would strike the Ambassador hard enough in the head to knock him out for a few minutes. Yes, he could do it quickly, without warning. Then he could. . . . The Hibbil salivated, but he set the violent thought aside, and the book.

"Let's stop bickering," Pimyt said. "We agree the Humans have gone on a fool's mission against the Parviis, and soon we'll learn the scale of it." He pointed to the holo-screen, which displayed a report sent back by HibAdu observers who had positioned lab-pods out on the podways to watch for enemy activity. "The Humans have big problems tying them down at the Parvii Fold, so much that they even had to send hundreds of ships back to the Tulyan Starcloud for reinforcements."

"Our Coalition forces are in perfect position, my furry friend. With the merchant princes tied up in a distant battle, their planets will be easy pickings for our massive fleet of four hundred and seventy-six thousand lab-pods, filled with military armaments and fighters." Uncel gestured with his wiry hands as he spoke. "The only question being worked out now is how to distribute our forces for the simultaneous attacks on Merchant Prince Alliance and Mutati Kingdom targets. The Humans have spread themselves too thin, so we're assigning more of our forces to the attacks on Mutati worlds."

Nodding, Pimyt said, "Our enemies have weakened themselves by warring against each other, and now the shapeshifters have been further weakened by the destruction of their homeworld, Paradij."

"Close call for me," Uncel mused, tapping a long finger on the desk top. "I got away just in time."

A pity, Pimyt thought. His eyes felt hot as he glared at the Ambassador.

Uncel paused, seemed nervous as he continued to speak. "Only two days before the destruction, I was with the Zultan Abal Meshdi, spent a night in his palace. He was completely insane, you know, with that Demolio program to blow up merchant prince planets—wiping out our potential prizes of war."

Pimyt nodded again. "It is a double-edged sword, isn't it? Fewer planets left for us to share as spoils of war, but the Mutatis are weaker because of the loss of Paradij."

"Lucky for me, I had to get back here for an appointment." Uncel scratched his wiry neck. "Hard to believe Meshdi's own son did it, a murder conspiracy with a huge miscalculation that blew up the most important Mutati planet. Even though rumors are rampant that Hari'Adab was responsible, most Mutatis seem willing to forgive him."

"No figuring shapeshifters," Pimyt said.

"That's for sure. Even so, both target empires still have many valuables for us. We'll hit them hard, out of the blue."

"I'd like to meet our own leaders one day," Pimyt mused, "especially High Ruler Coreq."

"Many things are far more important," the Ambassador said, his tone sharp.

Pimyt fumed. "Don't you see? We have a lot in common, you and I, including important assignments from HibAdu commanders we've never met."

"No matter. Our careers are assured. Reports from each of us have proven invaluable to the HibAdu effort."

Pimyt grinned. "To make up for my *perceived* selfishness, I must give credit to your own resourcefulness in the not-too-distant past."

Uncel's already-large eyes widened, and he smiled. "But I have so many accomplishments, my friend. As a *team* member, of course. Of what do you speak?"

"I'm thinking of the time you obtained raw information from the Mutatis on the nehrcom cross-space communication system, a system that the Mutatis could not perfect. But our scientists certainly had no problems figuring it out, did they?"

"No. Truly, our forces are poised, and are fortunate. With Hibbil manufacturing skills and Adurian biotech knowledge, it is a combination of the best. No longer will our people be under the boot heels of the Humans and Mutatis."

"We live in legendary times," Pimyt said. "After the great HibAdu victory, perhaps historians will write of our own contributions, VV. To the *team,* of course. Incidentally, I was just teasing you when I exaggerated my own contribution. Sometimes it is quite simple to agitate you."

"Yes, *friend,* but rile me at your own peril. You think I'm a pushover, don't you?"

"I think a lot of things about you that are not productive to mention. A pushover? Perhaps, but I have never required a weak opponent to prevail." The Hibbil leaned forward over the desk. "But let us turn our talents elsewhere, shall we?"

"Ah yes, an excellent suggestion. Combined, we are much stronger, aren't we? And that's what the Coalition is all about."

CHAPTER TEN

I ought to exercise more caution, but it is not in my nature.
My father was a risk-taker of the highest order, and it is
my weakness that I have inherited this tendency from him.
Hopefully, I have not also acquired the Zultan's madness.
—Emir Hari'Adab

The Mutati delegation should have been able to reach the Tulyan Starcloud in a few minutes, but it was taking them much
longer to cross the galaxy. Hari's two lab-pods had been in the
far reaches of space for more than a day so far, but they had not
yet reached their destination. At the moment the vessels were
dead in space, having been stopped by their crews to assess the
unexpected situation. In the lead craft, Hari'Adab and his followers were in comlink contact with the other crew, trying to
figure out the problem. And inside the holds of each vessel,
HibAdu prisoners were being interrogated intensely.

One thing seemed clear. The Hibbil navigation units on each
ship, which the Mutati crews originally thought they understood,
had sent them off-course by millions and millions of light years.
But that could be made up quickly, if they could only determine
where they were. At the speed of podships, even traveling along
a damaged infrastructure, such distances could be covered in a
relatively short time—and these lab-pods, like their natural
cousins, were biological entities with seemingly unlimited travel
capabilities. But the lab-pods were acting like blind birds flying

headlong through space, not knowing where they were going.

According to one of the prisoners, in all manufacturing tests the Hibbils had performed, covering multiple star systems, the nav-units had functioned perfectly. Apparently, he claimed, they did not function well in all sectors—and in the deepest reaches of space, far from the Hibbil Cluster Worlds, they were undoubtedly giving erroneous readings.

Dismayed and frustrated, Hari conferred with Kajor Yerto Bhaleen. They sat at a small table in the spacious passenger compartment, examining an electronic clip pad that displayed an astromap of this galactic sector. Tapping a button on the pad, Bhaleen called up a holo image of the sector, showing planets, suns, an asteroid belt, and a stunning, butterfly-shaped nebula in the distance that glinted with golden light.

"It's incredibly beautiful in this region," the Kajor said, "but that doesn't help us figure out where we are. My officers are running and rerunning programs now, searching for answers. The prisoners may have thrown us off intentionally, providing false information."

"You think they're fanatics?"

"Maybe. Hard to tell."

"Give me your best guess," Hari said. "How much longer do you think this will take?"

"To figure out where we are, or to get to the starcloud?"

"Both."

"Hard to judge, because even if—I mean, *when*—we figure out our location, we are still having problems with the nav-units. Even so, my officers are confident that we can compensate for the errors. They're taking astronomical readings, and the ships' computers should be able to figure out what we did, and how to correct it."

"But the computers allowed us to go off course?"

"They did, but there have been problems with the podways

on which these ships travel, with entire galactic sectors damaged so badly that we couldn't travel through them, requiring
that we go around."

"And now?"

"With all the navigation mistakes and corrections we've
made, we're way off course. But don't worry. My nav officers
will come up with new settings."

"At least that's what they're telling you."

"True enough, My Emir." The Kajor smiled cautiously. "But
you've always liked my optimism in the past."

With a broad grin, Hari patted him on the back.

Just then, Bhaleen took a comlink call from the other ship.
Under intense interrogation, the captured Hibbil and Adurian
soldiers were offering no real assistance whatsoever. The Kajor
went on to discuss a mechanical question with someone on the
other end of the line. Bhaleen was the most loyal of all military
officers Hari had ever known, and could always be relied upon
to perform his work well.

That took some of the load off the young leader's shoulders.
But it had not been an easy journey for Hari to arrive at this
point. In sharp contrast to the radical, demented militarism of
his own father, he had always considered himself something of a
moderate—a person who was willing to talk to the enemies of
the kingdom and negotiate with them for the mutual benefit of
two very different galactic races. And, just as he loved Parais
d'Olor, he was certain that all of humankind was filled with
relationships such as the one he enjoyed with her, involving
people who didn't care about ancient enmities and just wanted
the fighting to stop.

Normally, Hari was not an appeaser; while he was willing to
negotiate, he also believed in negotiating from strength. In the
present circumstances, however, that tactic was no longer possible. With the total destruction of the beloved Mutati home-

world of Paradij (an event that would always weigh heavily on his conscience), the shapeshifters had sustained a grievous setback. His people were still in possession of considerable military strength in other Mutati star systems, but the command center and the most powerful forces had been lost with Paradij. The brightest of the brightest had been wiped out, along with the greatest of all military minds and much, much more.

He tried not to dwell on the troubling details, but they kept surfacing to torment him, almost beyond the limit of his endurance. His heart sank at the thought of the great libraries that had been destroyed on the beautiful world, with all of the priceless ancient documents. All of the historical and cultural treasures. And most of all, the lives that had been taken, especially the young ones. Their imagined faces spun through his thoughts, and he fought off tears.

Suddenly, Parais d'Olor burst into the passenger compartment. Excitedly, she almost lifted her wings, though she had no room to fly in there. "One of the Adurians is talking," she said. "He's a navigation technician who refused to say anything before. Now he's telling our officers what we did wrong, and how we were misled by other prisoners."

"But can we trust him?" Bhaleen asked. He hurried past her, heading for the hold where the prisoners were.

"Wish we had a Tulyan to use the truthing touch on him," Hari said.

When Hari and the others entered the spacious hold, he saw his officers and soldiers standing around one of the hairless, bulbous-eyed Adurians. The alien was spewing words like automatic projectile fire, technical information about astronomical coordinates and settings on the nav-units. One of Hari's men was recording him, and another was entering notes on a clip pad.

Finally, the HibAdu soldier fell silent.

Pushing his way past the others, Kajor Bhaleen unfolded a knife and held the sharp blade against the throat of the prisoner. The Adurian technician had dark eyes that were comparatively small for his race. His gaze darted around nervously.

"Why should we believe you?" Bhaleen asked. He drew a trickle of yellow blood from the alien's neck.

"Please don't kill me! I'm telling the truth because I don't want to die out here, marooned. I have told your men what they need to do."

"If he's lying, we will know soon enough," Hari said, placing a hand on Bhaleen's shoulder.

The Kajor hesitated, then withdrew the weapon. He wiped off the blade and folded it back into his pocket.

The Adurian pleaded to be sent back to join his companions, and received assurance from his captors that his actions would be kept secret. Afterward, Mutatis checked and rechecked the new information. All calculations and projections showed that it was correct, and finally the ships got underway again.

Three hours later, the Adurian was found dead in his sleeping quarters, having been strangled by a fellow prisoner.

CHAPTER ELEVEN

Sometimes it is possible to think about a thing too much.
                                        —Master Noah Watanabe

For weeks, the Liberator fleet had been in the Parvii Fold, occupied with essential tasks. The complete vanquishing of the Parviis and their flight from the galactic pocket had only been the beginning. Now at last, virtually all of the podships had Tulyan pilots and the region had been secured against the return of enemy swarms, to prevent them from ever using it as a home base, or an area of racial recuperation.

In addition to their concerns about Parvii survivors, the Tulyans in the Liberator force had devoted themselves to preparing the vast Aopoddae fleet for deep-space galactic recovery operations, matching them up with pilots and taking steps to remove and replace the ancient bonds that Parviis had placed on the sentient spacecraft in order to control them.

Inside the main corridor of the flagship *Webdancer,* Noah had just spoken with Tesh Kori. Then she had returned to her isolated position in the sectoid chamber, from which she would pilot the vessel in the Parvii manner. She was about to get underway, but this time fleet command had decided that the big flagship would be among the last of the vessels to depart for the Tulyan Starcloud. For hours now, the rest of the fleet had been streaming out through the Asteroid Funnel, into deep space.

As Noah hurried through the gray-green corridors of the vessel, he had mixed feelings. Some of his companions, including Anton del Velli and Subi Danvar, had said they hoped the entire Parvii race went extinct, for the greater good of the galaxy. To Noah that sounded horrific, but privately he'd admitted that it did make some sense. Still, he wanted to believe it was overkill, so he had been telling the others that there were worthwhile Parviis in the race. Tesh Kori had proven that, and her intentions had been verified by the Tulyan truthing touch.

If only the remaining Parviis could be separated from the Eye of the Swarm and his influences, many of the race might be rehabilitated. For that matter, while Noah had seen the survivors through a Timeweb vision, and they had been hovering near the bolt hole on the other side, he wasn't at all certain if Woldn remained with them. For security purposes, he had to assume they still had the same leader, and that he remained a danger.

Noah stopped as something small scurried past his feet and disappeared around a corner. He'd gotten a good look at it, and his eyebrows lifted in surprise. A dark brown roachrat.

"On a podship?" he murmured. Then, considering it more, he felt confident that the podship could selectively kill the rodent if desired. The sentient spacecraft must be aware of its presence (and perhaps others), just as it was aware of the pilot and passengers aboard.

Continuing down the corridor, Noah entered the passenger compartment, which was filled with MPA and Red Beret soldiers and the noise of conversations among them. He nodded to Doge Anton, who was speaking with one of his officers.

Finding a chair by a porthole, Noah sat down and gazed outside, at large and small stones tumbling by in the Asteroid Funnel, obstacles that Tesh eluded skillfully. Previously the stones had only tumbled in one direction. Now Noah noticed them coming from both ends of the funnel, at varying speeds. Some of them bounced off the hull, transmitting dull thuds to the interior, but Tesh kept the ship going. Finally, the huge fleet was getting underway.

When Noah's ship reached open space, he felt a slight vibration in the chair and in the deck, which meant they were on a rough section of podway, where the strands of the paranormal infrastructure were frayed. Ahead, he saw other Aopoddae ships veering onto a side podway, and presently Tesh followed.

Sitting by the porthole, Noah ran a finger up his left forearm, beneath the long sleeve of the tunic. Feeling the rough skin on the arm, he still didn't want anyone to know about it yet, and perhaps never. The gray-and-black streak ran from his wrist all the way up his arm to the shoulder, and down the front of his torso. Grayness now covered the spot beside his belly button where his sister had stabbed the dermex into him, but the vein had not started there. In his questing mind, this did not necessarily mean that she was not the cause of his strange physical changes. In fact, he strongly suspected that she had something to do with the phenomenon, perhaps as a catalyst.

But beyond anything Francella might have had to do with his metamorphosis, it was as if . . .

He took a deep breath before continuing the thought.

Noah feared thinking about it, and couldn't imagine it really being true, but his skin definitely looked like the surface of a podship hull. On a much smaller scale, of course, but the colors and texture were remarkably alike.

Now, as he had done previously, he touched the actual podship skin, the interior of the wall. This time the creature did not tremble in fear.

A note of progress? Noah thought.

He made an attempt to connect with Timeweb again, but after several moments he realized it was to no avail, perhaps because the vessel was not nudging up against a galactic membrane like the last time. Apparently, the linkage to podway strands was not enough, perhaps due to breakages in the infrastructure. But as Noah withdrew his hand and stood straight, he realized that he was developing a headache, and it was quickly growing intense.

He heard the voices of fellow passengers around him. Motioning to a tall Red Beret soldier, Noah asked if he had anything to help his headache.

"I have just the thing, sir," he said. "Acupuncture robotics."

Noah nodded. He'd tried the technique once, and it had worked.

The soldier activated a small acu-robot—the size of a freckle—that scampered over Noah's skull and through his hair, along the scalp. He barely felt the needle prick, just a little tickle. Gradually Noah's thoughts calmed and his head began to feel better. But he still had an ache in the back of his head. In an attempt to relax more, Noah raised the back of his chair and leaned his head against a pad.

While he was able to tune out the conversations around him, his mind continued to churn, dredging up a panoply of thoughts—from the most minuscule to the most significant.

Abruptly, Noah felt a surge in his mind. Through sharp lances of eye pain he saw an internal vision of the planet Canopa, and a huge timehole near it, just beyond the atmosphere. The hole spun like a pale gray whirlpool, encircled by a luminous band of green light.

The headquarters of the Merchant Prince Alliance was on Canopa now, along with Noah's genetic roots . . . the birthplace of virtually everyone in his family, going back for many generations. But his mother, father, and even his vile sister were all gone, and Noah had created new roots for himself around the galaxy, with successful business operations involving ecological recovery operations. Until a series of crises—one on top of another—interrupted.

The timehole grew larger, and the planet drew closer to it. He wondered if this was reality. He thought it was, but there were so many unanswered questions about the paranormal realm.

Canopa was Noah's homeworld, and he felt a deep sadness at the prospect of its loss. If the entire planet disappeared into the hole and presumably into the adjacent galaxy, he assumed that all life on the world would perish. For him it was more than personal feelings; it was a galactic ecology issue and a military matter. It was the loss of his personal and Human underpinnings, and extremely unsettling to him. But from this remote distance, what could he do to rescue Canopa?

Squinting, he saw an orbital station move into view and drift near the timehole. With a start, he realized it was EcoStation, which the former Doge Lorenzo had renamed The Pleasure Palace, and which he used as a gambling casino. Noah missed the facility that had long been close to his heart, and a source of immense pride for him.

Then, just as quickly as it had appeared, the images of Canopa, the space station, and the timehole faded away. Noah felt an immense emptiness at the potential cataclysm, and bemoaned his inability to do anything to prevent it.

He would send a message to Canopa as soon as possible to warn them, and would alert the Tulyan Council of Elders to send a repair team—in case the images proved to be true. Inexplicably and against all of his logic and moral base, he worried more about EcoStation than anything. He wasn't proud of the thought and didn't understand it, but it lingered with him nonetheless.

CHAPTER TWELVE

We wear our mortal skins like cloaks, protecting us until
the fabric rots away. Then at last we are left naked, exposed
to the entropy of the universe.
                                        —A Saying of Lost Earth

Princess Meghina of Siriki had led an interesting life.

One of the most beautiful women in the galaxy, she had married the Doge Lorenzo del Velli twenty-two years ago, when she
was only fourteen. As her loveliness became renowned throughout the realm, she had—with her husband's concurrence—
become a courtesan to other powerful noblemen in the
Merchant Prince Alliance. An independent woman, she had
lived separately in a marvelous palace on the planet Siriki, and
ostensibly bore seven daughters for Lorenzo. Afterward, having
escaped the destruction of her homeworld by Mutati military
forces, she had moved to the orbital gambling facility over
Canopa, to live with her husband.

There, her darkest secrets had been revealed. Through
intrigues by Francella Watanabe, she had been exposed as a
Mutati, but one who had always wanted to be Human, and
whose shapeshifting cellular structure had locked into a form
that looked Human. Her daughters, it turned out, had all been
fake pregnancies, with the baby girls obtained from clandestine
sources. She had never given birth to any of them. The MPA
public, and Lorenzo himself, had ultimately been sympathetic

to her, despite the deceit.

Living with her husband on the orbital gambling facility for some time now, she had become a mysterious, glamorous figure, occasionally seen out on the gaming floor, but more often frequenting the back corridors and glittering chambers of the facility, where she spent time with a most unusual group of friends. . . .

One evening, Lorenzo invited Meghina and these friends to dinner in his elegant dining hall. Months earlier, he had been forced to abdicate as doge, in part because of the revelations about Meghina, which his political enemies used to their advantage. Now the nobleman was essentially an outcast on the orbiter, living in a velvet-lined cocoon.

At the appointed hour, Princess Meghina sat on one end of the gleaming wooden banquet table, opposite Lorenzo on the other. With her golden hair secured by a jeweled headband, she wore a long black velveen dress, trimmed in precious gemstones. She smiled down the long table at her husband, and sipped from a large silver goblet of red wine, a fine Canopan vintage.

Along the sides sat her five extraordinary companions—three men on one side and two women on the other. They formed an exclusive little club, often getting together socially in Meghina's royal apartments on The Pleasure Palace orbiter. All the while, the six of them were under continuing medical supervision.

This was because they had apparently become immortal.

Under a research program established by the medical division of CorpOne, a remarkable elixir had been developed from the DNA of the purportedly indestructible Noah Watanabe. The new solution (dubbed the Elixir of Life) had been injected into two hundred thousand persons from all of the galactic races, and had resulted in immortality for a scant six of them, including Meghina. It had been like winning a lottery, and initially they had all considered themselves lucky.

Then they had heard that Noah's insane sister had injected herself with the elixir, and had suffered a rapid cellular decline—an artificial form of progeria that caused the accelerated aging of her cells, and her premature death. There had even been rumors that Francella, shortly before dying, had injected her own tainted blood back into her brother, trying to harm him. The attempt had apparently been unsuccessful, because he didn't seem to have experienced any associated medical problems.

So far, neither had Princess Meghina or the other Elixir of Life "winners."

In a chair on Meghina's immediate left sat a large black pet that she had recently taken a liking to, a rare Bernjack dagg from her private animal collection. Once it had been owned by a very old woman, but she had gone into a rest home and had been unable to care for the dagg any longer. The shaggy animal was very special to Meghina now, and she called it Orga, because the old lady had been Mrs. Orga. Using the solitary bulbous eye above its snout, it peered around the long fur overhanging its face.

At the other end of the table, on Lorenzo's right, sat what looked like another pet but really wasn't. Rather, it was her husband's furry little attaché, the feisty Hibbil, Pimyt. Meghina had never liked the graying, black-and-white alien, but had gracefully concealed her feelings from him.

Raising his own goblet, Lorenzo said, "A toast to the good life."

He and his guests quaffed their drinks, then set the goblets down with thumps that were almost in synchronization.

Just then, the dagg leaned its long snout over the table, and gripped its water bowl in its mouth. Lifting the bowl high, the animal leaned back and slurped from it, before losing its grip. The bowl crashed to the floor, shattering and spilling the water.

Several guests tittered, but Lorenzo scowled at the animal, as he often did. He only tolerated the dagg. A servant hurried over to clean up the mess.

"Perhaps we should put wine in Orga's bowl!" suggested one of the guests, a ruddy, aging man named Dougal Netzer. Once an impoverished portrait painter, he now earned large sums for his work. More than any of his cellular peers, he had been able to capitalize financially on his overnight fame as an immortal.

Servants brought in platters heaped with steaming game hens, cooked in a dark, aromatic sauce. At Meghina's order, they even had a plate of boned hoglet for the dagg. The moment it was placed in front of him, Orga tried to grab a piece of meat. But Meghina waggled a finger near the plate, causing the animal to let go of the food and pull his head back—awaiting permission to eat.

"As my lovely wife has probably told you," Lorenzo said, "I am in *de facto* exile on this orbital facility, with little opportunity to get away from it." He paused. "Tell me about events on the surface of Canopa—news, gossip, bits of information. Pimyt doesn't have the connections he enjoyed while working for me on-planet, and I've been feeling isolated."

Pimyt shot him a hard stare, but for only a moment. Two of the female guests and one of the men provided the former merchant prince leader with details, how Doge Anton, Noah Watanabe, and others had formed a military expedition and departed in a big hurry.

When Lorenzo had heard enough, he permitted the table to fall into witty, light-hearted conversation, much of it about the immortality of Meghina and her friends.

At first, Pimyt said very little. Finally, he asked the woman seated next to him, "What do you intend to do with your own extended life?"

"I have so much time now to consider such matters," she

said. A robust, big-chested woman in a blue tunic, she smiled. Since gaining immortality she had abandoned her original name, and for unexplained reasons now called herself Paltrow.

"And the answer is, after all the time you've taken to consider it?" the Hibbil asked.

"I have put off such matters, such *worries*, really. I've hardly thought about them at all."

"A nice luxury to have." The little Hibbil tugged at the salt-and-pepper fur on his chin. It was a nervous mannerism that Meghina had noticed previously.

"I'm sorry," Paltrow said. "I don't mean to be rude, but I honestly haven't given it much thought."

Most of those at the table had paused to listen to the exchange.

"Perhaps our additional time is not so important as you might think," Meghina suggested. "What, exactly, does living forever mean? Living forever in relation to what?"

"Intriguing observation," Dougal Netzer said.

The guests began to pitch in. Finally Paltrow asked, "Is a million years in our galaxy only a moment, or a mere fraction of a moment?"

Theories and more questions went around the table in rapid succession, and it developed into a game in which several people tried to ask the most clever question, some of them rhetorical.

The repartee intensified, and Lorenzo seemed to enjoy it. Meghina couldn't help noticing, however, that Pimyt appeared to be somewhere else in his mind, perhaps far across the galaxy on his alien homeworld.

CHAPTER THIRTEEN

Each moment is slightly different from the one preceding it.

—Parvii Inspiration

In the alternate realm, the cosmic storm subsided, and the huddled swarm of Parviis stopped being buffeted around. But to the Eye of the Swarm, this provided little comfort.

Drifting in the airless darkness with the remnants of his once-mighty race, Woldn felt dismal. He had always been a leader who visualized things and made them happen. For him, that was a key aspect of command, envisioning what others could not, and making them come to pass. But in his wildest imaginings, from his first recollections of life more than two thousand years ago, he'd never thought it possible that he could fall to this level, soundly defeated and relegated to hiding in an unknown galactic region, perhaps even in another galaxy altogether.

More than anything, Woldn wanted to fight back, to stream back through the bolt hole into the Parvii Fold and dispatch his enemies with raw telepathic violence, killing and scattering them, chasing them to the ends of the universe and wiping out all remnants of them. But he didn't have the power to do that. Not even close.

Even worse, troublesome thoughts had been creeping into his consciousness like vermin infesting his mind, and he could not avoid asking himself, *Have I done anything to cause this?*

The Eye of the Swarm wondered if he might . . . or *should* . . . have done anything differently. Somehow the realities of the galaxy had slipped his notice, and passed him by. A sense of deep gloom and foreboding came over him as he realized that his leadership methods had been inherited from previous Parvii rulers . . . and hardly modified at all. Methods that did not contemplate the modern challenges confronting him. Never before had a leader faced such immense trials and tribulations: the decline of the galactic infrastructure on which podships traveled, and the enemies of the Parvii race who wanted to destroy them. But he realized this was no excuse. Millions of years of relative sameness in the galaxy had lulled him and his predecessors into a false sense of security.

We didn't adapt to changing conditions. I *didn't adapt. My people followed me to destruction.*

He shivered in the dim void. Though his people hardly ever felt the frigid extremes of temperature in deep space, for some reason it seemed much colder to him here. But how could that be? It probably wasn't the case, not according to the laws of physics and the galactic principles that had been around since the beginning of time. Perhaps extreme stress was affecting him, compromising his Parvii bodily functions.

And . . . this might be another galaxy, one that really is colder.

He drifted toward the tiny bolt hole, and telepathically commanded the sentry at the opening to make way for him. That one hurried out of his way, back into the alternate realm.

Woldn entered. The hole was actually a tunnel—only a few hundred meters in length—through the membrane that defined and protected a large portion of the sacred Parvii Fold. In a matter of seconds, he reached the other end, but stopped just before emerging.

Then, ever so cautiously, he pushed his head out of the opening on the other side and peered into the fold. Not far away, he saw a few dozen podships that looked as if they had been stationed to guard the hole. Extending his range of vision (as only the Eye of the Swarm could do), he made out additional sentient vessels in the distance, engaged in what appeared to be practice maneuvers, and other podships that he thought were on patrol.

Scanning around the fold, he didn't see that many vessels. Then, at the entrance to the Asteroid Funnel, he saw podships going through, departing. Looking farther, he saw to his vexation that they were making their way expertly past the tumbling, luminous white stones and out into deep space.

They're stealing my fleet, damn them!

Right there, as never before, Woldn vowed revenge. Even if it required every ounce of his remaining strength, to the very last conscious thought he had, he would make the effort. And so would every one of his followers. If any of them didn't show enough commitment, he would kill them. For a matter involving stakes this high, he could do no less, could expect no less.

CHAPTER FOURTEEN

Many people want to predict the future, so that they can be ready and position themselves most advantageously—protecting themselves and those close to them. Every organism has an innate need to survive, but I have no curiosity about the moment and method of my own death. Rather, I choose to observe larger issues that affect all living organisms, so that I might contribute to the whole. If we do not take the long view as a species, the short view that happens to each of us no longer matters.

> —Master Noah Watanabe, classroom instruction

On board the flagship, while the pilot searched for safe podway routes along a decaying infrastructure, Noah had additional concerns. Layers of trouble seeped through his thoughts as he paced back and forth across an anteroom. It was one of several that the sentient vessel had formed around the perimeter of the main passenger compartment, using its mysterious manner of extrusion and changing shape, and of changing size. Now she was easily the largest vessel in the fleet, with the most complex arrangement of interior rooms.

She, Noah thought. *Yes, assuming* Webdancer *has a gender, it seems female to me.*

Through an open doorway, he heard the voices of Doge Anton, General Nirella, and Subi Danvar coming from a room across the corridor. He'd been in there with them earlier, telling them about the paranormal image of a timehole he'd seen near Canopa and EcoStation, and how real it had seemed to him. Now he tuned out the voices in the other room, didn't try to listen in on the words.

His main concern was much closer to him. Noah's body had been changing for some time now, though it remained to be seen if it was a bizarre evolutionary process, an uncharted disease, or something he had not yet considered.

I may be immortal, but what am I becoming?

He felt vibration in the floor as they passed over a rough section of podway. It grew worse for perhaps a minute, then gradually smoothed out.

During the past year, Noah had taken a number of fantastic mental excursions through Timeweb, and he had peered into what seemed to be an entirely different galaxy, where a small swarm of Parvii survivors had fled. While held prisoner by his own sister, Noah had survived her vicious butchery, and had even regrown severed limbs and other body parts like a lizard. Now, in recent weeks, the skin on his torso and arms was becoming different, morphing into something unfamiliar. He'd been able to conceal the changes beneath his clothing so far, but he didn't know how much longer he could do that.

Am I turning into an alien . . . no longer Human?

His mental incongruities seemed to have come first, followed by the physical. But he had no way of studying the history of his own cellular structure to confirm that, so the physical changes might have actually started the process. Most perplexing. Perhaps it all had been occurring simultaneously. Certainly both the cerebral and the corporal were apparent now, and they had not locked into any semblance of stability. He was in a constant state of flux, leaving him with infinite questions and no good answers.

Terror washed through him, but abated in a few moments

when he realized that part of him actually *wanted* the changes to continue. On many occasions he had tried to enter the Timeweb realm of his own volition, but for the most part he had been unable to do so. And even when he had been able to go into the web at all, it seemed to be through a back or side door, one that the gods of the realm had only left ajar accidentally. Perhaps it was a symptom of the declining infrastructure, the strange and baffling ecological malaise that was spreading through the galaxy. Without warning, as if sensing his presence where he was not supposed to be, the rulers of the realm kept locating him and throwing him out summarily.

The podship vibrated again, and slowed. Through a porthole Noah saw a flickering blue sun and a system of ringed planets. Then the podway improved once more, and they sped past the system, through the heart of a purple nebula.

In the end Noah realized that it didn't matter what he wanted himself. All of the bizarre things that were happening to him were far beyond his personal control. His tormented sister Francella had complicated any hope he ever had of figuring the transformation out, stabbing that dermex of her own poisoned blood deep into him.

Now he lifted his tunic and stared at his muscular abdomen, the place where she had struck. The vein of his morphing, gray-and-black skin had started on his chest, not at that spot beside his belly button. Even so, there might be a time correlation. The physical changes had begun a short while *after* her attack, and now included the place she had stabbed him, a small oblong area that was darker than the rest of the altered skin.

He paused and fixed his gaze on the open doorway, the gray-green natural light out in the corridor, and the mottled gray skin of the podship. Just focusing on various sections of the sentient vessel seemed to have a strange fascination for him, reminding him of how he'd felt as a small boy when he stared transfixed into pools of water, hypnotized by the changes in light and ripples of liquid in motion. The interior of each Aopoddae vessel was like that in a sense, as he detected tiny shiftings in the illumination and skin surfaces all the time, subtle differences in hue and texture that he didn't think the other passengers noticed.

Perhaps Tesh, as the Parvii pilot, could see such things. It might be possible. *Beautiful Tesh.* His thoughts drifted toward her, and then away again.

Abruptly, he found himself plunging outward, beyond the confines of the podship and into space. As he hurtled into the frozen void he saw *Webdancer* and the rest of the huge fleet behind him, with porthole lights visible along their hulls. Quickly, the fleet vanished from view, and a new awareness came over him.

Noah's motion stabilized, and he found himself standing motionless inside the sectoid chamber of yet another podship, piloting it in the Tulyan manner along the decaying infrastructure at much higher speeds than *Webdancer* had ever been able to attain. He changed course repeatedly, finding optimum strands for the ship to utilize. In a state of hyperawareness, Noah realized that it was not his Human body in the sectoid chamber. Rather, he had become a metallic green mist within an amorphous, unidentifiable shape, perhaps the form he had been evolving into before this happened.

But, as if in contradiction of that, on the prow of the vessel he saw—somehow—his own Human face in an enlarged form, suggesting that he had discovered a modified Tulyan method of piloting the craft. Did the form of the pilot lose its separate features inside the sectoid chamber when its energy merged into the podship flesh?

Another question without an answer.

Far off in the distance, he recognized some of the major

planetary systems of the Merchant Prince Alliance, and as he flew on he made out the galactic sectors of other races. He made his way toward some of the regions that he recognized. But soon he found, strangely, that he was flying right through them as if they were no more than holo images. On previous excursions into Timeweb he had been able to see activity in the galaxy, particularly other ships as they negotiated the podways. Now it was different. He could not make out details such as that, only increasingly blurry views as he neared and passed through the systems.

And he sensed—but could not see—a great but undefined danger out in the galaxy, beyond the crumbling infrastructure that everyone knew about. As he turned around and went back in the direction he had come, he wondered what the feeling meant.

On the way Noah recalled an earlier venture into the paranormal realm in which he saw Hibbil and Adurian soldiers inside strange podships that were piloted by Hibbils using computerized navigation units. It had been peculiar and unexplained, and he had reported it to Tesh Kori and Doge Anton.

Alas, with no way of reentering the web at will, and no way of verifying what he had seen, Noah never could tell if that startling vision had been real or not. It had not made any sense at all, since Hibbils were aligned with Humans, and Adurians were the long-time allies of Mutatis. Since then, there had been no other sightings of the odd soldiers or the highly unusual ships, so nothing could be done about it.

Might that be the additional menace he sensed now? He let the question sink in. No, he decided. The threat came from something else.

Just ahead he saw the rear of the podship fleet. The larger and more impressive *Webdancer* was out in front, leading the others. At the immense rate of speed that Noah had attained, the fleet seemed to be traveling slowly through space, and he caught up with it easily. None of the vessels noticed him, and as he neared he found himself hurtling out of the sectoid chamber toward *Webdancer,* and back into the anteroom he'd been in before embarking on this strange journey.

Moments later he was standing in that room, staring through the doorway into a gray-green wash of light.

And abruptly, as if emerging from a trance, Noah jerked to awareness and hurried across the corridor, to the room occupied by Anton, Nirella, and Subi. The three of them sat at a table, engaged in intense conversation. At first they didn't notice him enter. Then Subi called attention to him, and they all looked at Noah in a similarly odd manner, leaning close and squinting their eyes. Under their intense scrutiny Noah felt warm. Drops of perspiration formed on his brow.

"I sense a terrible danger out there," Noah said, at last. He could hardly get the words out.

"Are you feeling all right?" Nirella asked. She wore a red uniform with gold braids and insignia, designating her rank as Supreme General of the MPA armed forces. But now she conducted herself more like a caring woman than a military commander, looking at him with concern and urging him to sit down.

He resisted her efforts and pulled his arm away from her grasp. "I'm fine. Listen to me. I sense an additional threat, more powerful than anything else we've ever seen or discussed."

"But what?"

"I can't say, but it's out there, and seems like even more than the disintegration of the galactic infrastructure."

"It can't be military," Nirella said. "We've defeated the Parviis, and the Mutatis don't have anywhere near the power we have now. We control all the podships, so we can go and attack their planets at anytime."

"It's not Parviis or Mutatis," Noah said. "Or any other galactic race. It's something else entirely. I think . . . I *fear* . . . that it's beyond anything we're able to comprehend."

"For hours we've been in range of deep-space nehrcom relay stations," Anton said, "and the reports from our planets are all good. Nothing significant is happening in our sector, or anywhere near it."

"Maybe it's only the infrastructure after all," Noah said. He slumped into a comfortable chair that the podship had created, off to one side. He smiled grimly. "*Only* the infrastructure. As if that isn't enough."

"The repair and restoration of the galactic network needs to be our top priority," the young Doge insisted.

"I don't dispute that," Noah said. "I just wish we'd get to the starcloud faster so we can get on with it."

But no one in the room had any idea what was really occurring. Or the fact that HibAdu conspirators were using their own technology to relay false nehrcom messages. In actuality, a terrible thing *had* happened, which Noah and his companions would soon discover. . . .

CHAPTER FIFTEEN

We are a galactic race that no one has ever noticed. Doesn't the intelligence of our members—at least the best of us—compare favorably with that of any recognized galactic race? Admittedly, we look different from any of them, and we don't have their cellular structures, but who's to say that a galactic race has to be biological? Why can't it be mechanical instead, with metal and plax parts, and computer circuitry?

—From one of Thinker's private data banks

Unable to move, Ipsy watched as a mechanical claw reached for the remains of a large, dented unit that had once been the central processing unit for an entire factory assembly line. As the claw lifted its load, the pile shifted, and the broken little robot was jostled to one side.

He'd been there for weeks outside the factory, bumped around and constantly ignored. No one seemed to need his parts for anything. He was small and easily overlooked, but the claw had a zoomeye on it, projecting a beam of orange light that enabled it to see the tiniest part anywhere in the heap, even at the bottom, underneath everything else.

At the moment, with the heavy CPU no longer on him, Ipsy found himself on the very top of the scrap heap, warming under a bright sun. He didn't really want to be taken, because then he might lose what little independence he had left, if only what remained of it in his own mind. All he had now was his ability to observe what went on around him, and to remember better days.

The claw moved its load and released it, then returned and hovered over another part, a couple of meters away from Ipsy.

Just then, without being touched, the pile shifted, settled. And, for the first time since being thrown on the scrap heap, Ipsy moved one of his mechanical arms, and a leg. His circuits had reconnected, but only partially. He tried to move his other arm and leg, but without success. It would be difficult to escape this place with only two of his four major appendages, but he decided to give it a try anyway.

Like a cripple, he dragged himself over the top of the heap, away from the claw. His improvised body was even shorter than before, and much thinner. With one of his rear visual sensors, he saw the claw's orange beam of light move toward him, and almost catch up with him. Abruptly, more key components of his circuitry came to life. He scurried like a rodent down the slope of junk, and entered the factory through a side door.

Reaching the main aisle and then crawling up on a ledge for a better view, the little robot saw that the factory was not operating at all. Hibbils and workbots busied themselves at assembly-line stations, adjusting the machinery, connecting raw material feeder units to it. On the far end of the aisle, robots stood motionlessly, awaiting the signal to return to their stations.

Hearing voices behind him, Ipsy dropped down behind a bench.

He saw the furry lower legs of two Hibbils, standing near him. The diminutive men spoke rapidly, excitedly. From their conversation, he figured out they were military officers for something called the HibAdu Coalition, checking on the production of war materials. Listening attentively, Ipsy heard more.

"We're getting close to zero hour," one of them said. "It'll be unprecedented. Simultaneous sneak attacks on Human and Mutati planets. Imagine the scope of it, all the destruction and death."

"From what I hear, it could already be underway."

"I wish I was on the front lines, instead of on this assignment," the other said. "I hate Humans, the way they've always lorded over us, treating us like children."

"We each must do our part. Most of the instrument systems and parts coming out of this factory are for the HibAdu fleet." This Hibbil laughed, and added, "If you want to go on the front lines, why don't you hide inside one of the weapon-control boxes?"

The two officers walked away, and their conversation faded.

Ipsy's artificial brain whirred. He wondered if he might commit an act of sabotage . . . perhaps even blow up the factory. But this was one of many factories, and they would just resume operations elsewhere. Besides, it sounded like most of the Hib-Adu attack force was already in place and ready to attack.

Then Ipsy had an even more intriguing idea. If he could do something *during* a military engagement, he might be able to wreak much more havoc.

Considerably smaller than a Hibbil, he crawled inside one of the weapon-control boxes just before it was sealed up, and awaited its delivery to the war.

CHAPTER SIXTEEN

Trust is like quicksand. It can lull you to your death.

—A Saying of Lost Earth

At opposite sides of a dual-console machine, two aliens of differing races stood inside a glax tower building in the Hibbil capital city, surrounded by a sea of industrial structures that stretched to the horizons of the planet. The shorter alien, a Hibbil with graying black-and-white fur, glanced up at his companion, concealing his own enmity.

This Adurian diplomat was a major irritation.

Whenever VV Uncel wasn't looking, Pimyt glared at him with red-ember eyes. Then, the moment Uncel looked his way with those oversized insectoid orbs, the little Hibbil was all smiles on his own furry, bearded face, and his eyes had reverted to red dullness. Pimyt knew how disarmingly cute he could look whenever he wanted, like a cuddly Earthian panda bear. He also knew that Adurians didn't trust Hibbils, and vice versa. The two races were only working together for their own interests, with each constantly trying to get a leg up on the other. On some occasions the methods were subtle, but most of the time they were not. Even so, racial preservation and advancement had a way of causing Hibbils and Adurians to overlook the perceived slights committed by the other. The leaders of the two races understood this, and knew they could go farther together than apart.

In other circumstances, and perhaps sometime in the not-too-distant future, Pimyt might eradicate Uncel with shocking suddenness, moving in for the kill in a surprising blur of speed. But for now, they would play this little game together.

It was an Adurian form of entertainment, actually, in which the two of them stood at linked holovid consoles, operating touchpad controls that immersed each of them into a holo-drama, shown on a large central screen. The Adurians loved their games of chance and competition, and this one had a couple of twists that rigged it in the Adurian player's favor. And, though Uncel had taken pains to keep it secret, Pimyt knew that the decisions the Hibbil player made were being sent by hidden telebeam transmitters to an office full of Adurian bureaucrats, where they were further studied, to analyze sincerity and trustworthiness.

Pimyt smiled to himself. As a race, the Adurians were notoriously paranoid. On their homeworld and throughout their foreign operations, everything was under surveillance, and they were quite adept at tech gadgets. But Hibbils were considerably better at devising clever machines and mechanical systems than Adurians, and for every tech system the Adurians had, the Hibbils had one that was superior. It was only in diverse biological and biotech products that the Adurians held the upper hand, particularly in the improvement of lab-pods, which had originally been discovered by Mutati scientists—but not developed very well by them.

This machine could be set to play a variety of games. At the moment, the participants were in a simulated competition of space baseball, with their holo images dressed in uniforms, standing in batters' boxes on an asteroid. Each of them faced the same tall Vandurian pitcher who threw two balls simultaneously, one with each arm. The first player to hit the tricky pitches, or to get the best hit if both of them connected simultaneously, won the game.

Uncel swung, and missed. "Damn!" he exclaimed.

Smiling to himself, Pimyt hit a line drive that carried into the asteroid belt. His virtual ball kept going and going, and soon it was out of sight. Gleefully, the holo image of the little Hibbil ran and leaped from asteroid to asteroid around the simulated deep-space base path, and finally he came back around to home plate on the original asteroid.

"Going, going, gone!" he shouted, as if he was an announcer describing a long home run. "You lose!"

Uncel had an expression on his face like a man who knew he had been hoodwinked, but couldn't figure out how. In fact, the Adurian machine had been rigged to give Uncel the advantage, but Pimyt had transmitted an overriding signal into it to give him the edge instead.

"This is impossible," Uncel said. "You did something to the game, didn't you?"

"You sound so certain of that, my friend. Why is that, do you suppose?" Pimyt knew why, and saw a look of guilt on the Ambassador's face. The cheater knew that he had himself been cheated.

"You're wasting my valuable time," Uncel snapped. Lifting his head in disdain, he marched to an ascensore and entered it, leaving Pimyt alone in the tower room.

"Pompous ass," Pimyt muttered under his breath.

Left to himself, he fiddled with the game controls, changing the settings in rapid succession, bringing up a variety of games, some of which he'd never heard of. Many of the diversions involved cards, dice, or balls, while others were animal races, with the players riding on the backs of alien beasts.

All the while, his thoughts wandered. The little Hibbil led an uncommonly complex life, balancing his various duties, his lay-ers of subterfuge and intrigue. His biography was not linear, and would be impossible for anyone to write accurately without his candid cooperation.

Pimyt was, without doubt, a very important person. And not just in his own estimation.

Though Hibbils did mate, and the vast majority of them enjoyed the company of the opposite sex, he had been involved in very few dalliances in the past, and expected the future to be the same. He was proud of the fact that his libido had no influence on his decision-making processes. Or at least, that he had subdued it enough to make it ancillary.

There had been undeniable temptations, such as the attractive Jimlat dwarf that had caught his eye on the remote, unaligned planet of the same name. He'd never seen a face and figure to match hers. And the way she *moved!* She had almost derailed his entire career with her charms. Pimyt had made love with her in her apartment, and she'd told him of her own ambitions and dreams, of how she would like to marry him and move to the Hibbil Cluster Worlds.

He had smiled and nodded, and had popped a pill to diminish his passions. Then, when her back was turned, he had strangled her to death, moving against her with a suddenness that she could never have anticipated. It wasn't that Pimyt liked to kill anyone. He didn't go out of his way for anything like that. But she had been a distraction, one he could ill afford. He'd done her a favor, actually. Undoubtedly he would have been more brutal with her if he'd really gotten to know her. Especially if—as he thought might happen—he actually fell in love with her.

For someone in Pimyt's position, with so much riding on his shoulders, he could never allow that to happen. He was responsible for a major portion of the HibAdu plan, and it had to proceed without impediments. He was, in his own estimation, far more important to the cause than the pretentious

Adurian Ambassador.

At that moment a telebeam message came in, and he activated his ring to open the connection. A bright red banner opened in the air, a holo image with white lettering on it:

BULLETIN: OUR HIBADU FORCES HAVE MADE SURPRISE ATTACKS AGAINST ALL HUMAN AND MUTATI WORLDS. DEFENDER SHIPS PROVED USELESS, DUE TO SABOTAGED FIRING MECHANISMS ON THEIR ARTILLERY PIECES. WE ALSO USED SIGNAL-BLOCKING DEVICES TO MUZZLE THE DEFENDERS' TELEBEAM TRANSMISSIONS, SO NONE OF THEIR EMERGENCY MESSAGES GOT OUT. ALL MPA WORLDS EXCEPT FOR CANOPA AND SIRIKI HAVE FALLEN, AND ALL MUTATI WORLDS EXCEPT FOR DIJ. FIGHTING RAGES FOR THESE LAST THREE PLANETS.

Grinning from ear to furry ear, Pimyt linked the ring to a panel box on the wall, and transmitted the same banner—in much larger form—into the sky outside the tower building. Tonight, there would be dancing in the streets.

CHAPTER SEVENTEEN

"Any moment could be your last—individually and collectively."
—Eshaz, comment to Subi Danvar

At the head of the podship fleet, *Webdancer* plunged into the
ethereal mists. Thousands of ships in the first wave followed her
into the starcloud, while the balance of the fleet went into holding patterns in that galactic sector, awaiting instructions by
comlink to proceed.

Noah sat solemnly on a hard bench in the passenger compartment. Looking up, he saw a blank white screen appear, covering
the viewing window on the forward wall. Like a schoolteacher,
the big Tulyan Eshaz stood near the screen, holding a black
control device in one of his thick hands.

He activated the device and the screen went on, displaying
multiple views of the starcloud planets—all showing throngs of
Tulyans celebrating in the streets.

"Word has reached them that the fleet is returning," Eshaz
said, his voice and expression filled with pride. "After millions
of years, we can once again return to our caretaking duties."

"We've rescued the podships," another Tulyan said. "Truly,
this is a joyous occasion."

But Noah felt a deep despondency, and a sense of foreboding. He knew something terrible was wrong, but couldn't
determine what it was. He was focused so far inward, questing

and wanting answers, that events around him seemed as hazy as the mists of the starcloud. In a short while, he disembarked the podship at the moorage basin and boarded a glax, self-propelled space platform. Tesh, Eshaz, Anton, Subi and a number of soldiers from the flagship accompanied him.

From the platform, the others stared in amazement at tens of thousands of podships moored around them in the pale mists. Like a small child, Tesh pressed her face up against the clear-glax, for a closer view. Then she pulled back and looked at Noah. "As a galactic race," she said, "the Aopoddae are known to date back even farther than the Tulyans . . . to the very origins of the galaxy."

As Eshaz gazed out on the wide mooring area, he said in a reverent tone, "Some of these creatures are exactly the same pods that once transported us on our important maintenance and repair assignments, millions of years ago. The ancient podships are well-known from the oral history of my people. Each ship has a name and a historical record of accomplishments. Some of the most legendary pods are Spirok, Elo, Dahi, Thur, Riebu, Thees, Lody." He pointed. "There! That one is Riebu!"

The one he designated had deep, rippled scars on its side, as if it had suffered the space equivalent of Moby Dick, and survived.

"Podships have mysterious life cycles," Tesh said to Noah. "While many of them live almost eternally, that is not the case with all. Some die from accidents and diseases. Breeding is inconsistent. It goes in spurts, and then seems to stop entirely for centuries."

"This is true," Eshaz said. He looked at her thoughtfully. "Your people have had time to observe the creatures."

She nodded, her expression growing sad.

Outside, a number of Tulyan pilots emerged from the

podships, then stood atop the creatures and bowed their heads.

"An ancient ceremony," Eshaz said, his voice choking with emotion. "These pilots have been reunited with their original podships, from long ago."

At his side, Noah saw Tesh crying softly. He wiped the tears away from her cheeks, and kissed her tenderly.

"My feelings are complex," she said. "Tears of joy for the Tulyans and their podships, but intense sorrow for my own people."

"I understand," Noah said, putting an arm around her.

"Why did it have to come to this?" she asked. Then she added quickly, "Of course, I already have the answer to that."

In a comforting tone, Noah said, "I know it's impossible to ask you not to feel distress. But Tesh, please don't feel guilty for what you had to do. Maybe you're like Meghina. Both of you were born to other races, but you each wanted to be Human. You are Human now, my darling."

She smiled, but only a little. Her green eyes opened wide. "Well, almost Human, anyway. Cellular tests would say otherwise."

"You and Meghina both look Human and act Human. It's beyond cellular structures, beyond anything physical. It goes to your hearts."

"Listening to you, I could almost imagine that any other differences are inconsequential."

"They are." He pulled her close, embraced her. It amazed him how the Parvii magnification system could make this tiny person seem much larger, in all respects. He wondered what the fate of her decimated race was, and knew she spent much more time thinking about that than he did.

Noah heard a low hum, and felt a gentle vibration at his feet. The glax platform shuttled them from the moorage basin toward the floating, inverted dome of the Council Chamber. After a few minutes, it nudged up against a docking module and locked into position. Glax double doors slid open, revealing the interior of an entrance deck that skirted the chamber.

A pair of Tulyans marched forward stiffly, dressed in green-and-gold uniforms. They each carried a cap. "Right this way, please," the shorter of the reptilian men said to Anton and Noah, as they stepped off the platform. "We are your escorts." He bowed, then put his cap back on. "The Elders are extremely anxious to speak with you."

"It is an emergency," the other Tulyan said as he put on his own cap.

"What do you mean?" Doge Anton asked.

"I am not authorized to say."

Noah felt a sense of foreboding.

Emerging from the gathered passengers, Eshaz said, "I'll go with them. This doesn't sound good."

"As you wish." The shorter escort led the way up a wide, travertine tile stairway, while Eshaz motioned for Tesh and Subi to join the group.

On the next level they hurried through an arched doorway, then over a wide bridge that crossed a reflecting pool. Well-dressed aliens of a variety of races were gathered in a reception area, talking in hushed tones. They looked angry. Noah noticed that other alien dignitaries were being led out of the Council Chamber, just beyond. None of them looked at all happy.

The escorts led the small party into the immense Council Chamber, onto a clearglax floor that seemed to float on air, with the curvature of the inverted dome below, and beneath that the ethereal mists of the starcloud. Their footsteps echoed on the floor. The immense chamber was nearly empty, with no one in the rows of spectator seats, and a few last aliens being led out, despite their protestations.

Ahead of them sat three stern-looking Tulyans at the center of a wide, curving bench.

"Something is terribly wrong," Eshaz whispered to Noah. "Just three Elders, and no one in the visitors' gallery. I have never seen anything like this before, and I have lived for a long time."

The female Elder in the center looked down solemnly from the bench, and waited for the chamber to be sealed. Noah recognized her as First Elder Kre'n.

"We have very grave news, indeed," she said.

Noah and his companions stared upward inquisitively. His feelings of foreboding intensified.

"Terrible tragedies on Human and Mutati worlds," said a much larger Elder on her left, Dabiggio. "Our operatives got messages off to us describing the disasters."

"Web transmissions," Kre'n said. "While we have had difficulties with them, due to galactic conditions, they remain more reliable than your nehrcoms."

"Tragedies, disasters?" Anton asked. "What are you talking about?"

Kre'n scowled at him. "You don't know? While you were away, didn't you receive any nehrcom messages?"

"We've been in relay range for a while now. Several reports came in, but nothing about any big problems."

"Fake transmissions, I suspect. Every Human and Mutati planet has been attacked."

Anton and Tesh gasped. Noah glowered, waiting for more information.

"The attackers cut off authentic nehrcom transmissions from all MPA planets," Kre'n said. "It took them longer, but they also managed to cut off our web transmissions. We fear the worst for our operatives."

"What the hell happened?" Anton demanded. "Who attacked us?"

"Hibbils and Adurians," Dabiggio said. "The Human and

Mutati empires are lost. Surprise assaults, with overwhelming force. We lost communication three hours ago, but at that time only Canopa and Siriki were holding out in the MPA, and the Mutatis only had Dij left."

"My God!" Anton said.

"We have incontrovertible proof that the Hibbils and Adurians are in alliance," the third Elder said.

Is this what I sensed? Noah wondered. "Hibbils and Adurians?" he asked. "How could that possibly be?"

Nodding solemnly, Kre'n said, "They call themselves the HibAdu Coalition. They must have been plotting the attacks for some time. Coordinated military assaults against all targets."

"Traitors," Tesh said. "What a bunch of sneaky bastards."

Noah thought back, and again he remembered seeing Hibbil and Adurian soldiers in a Timeweb vision. He'd reported it to Doge Anton, but there had been no indication of the scope of the treachery, or the direction it might take. Noah also remembered now that Lorenzo had a Hibbil attaché named Pimyt. The last Noah heard, Lorenzo and Pimyt were in Noah's former EcoStation, where the deposed Doge was in exile.

The HibAdu Coalition, he thought in dismay, letting it seep in.

But his gut told him that wasn't all he'd been sensing. There was something more than this dire military news, something even worse, and he couldn't put a finger on it.

Kre'n raised a hand. "Bring the Mutatis in," she said.

"The Mutatis?" Anton exclaimed. Obviously stunned, he exchanged nervous glances with Noah.

A side door burst open, and a large Mutati strutted in, wearing a purple-and-gold robe. He was accompanied by an entourage that included several uniformed military officers and a female shapeshifter—of the aerial variety—who flew beside him.

"Meet the Emir Hari'Adab," Kre'n said, "ruler of the Mutati Kingdom."

CHAPTER EIGHTEEN

If you look hard enough, there are always surprises in this universe.

—Tulyan Wisdom

Inside the inverted, floating dome of the Council Chamber, Hari'Adab addressed the small gathering, choosing to emit synchronized, pulsing sounds from his puckish little mouth. It was not an orifice that had been part of his natural-born state, but was instead something he had improvised (and varied slightly from time to time) when he became old enough to care about his appearance. Now, dressed in a flowing robe that cascaded over his mounds of fat, the Emir paced in front of the wide Council bench.

"Since you know my name and I know some of yours, allow me to introduce two of my companions." He motioned back to the aeromutati who stood off to one side, just behind him. "This is Parais d'Olor, the gentlest of all Mutatis, a person who brings peace to my heart."

He nodded somberly in her direction, then looked back to the other side, where Kajor Yerto Bhaleen stood with military erectness. After introducing him by title and name, he said, "Yerto is the highest officer in the Military High Command. He gives me advice in matters of war. But he knows, and fully understands, that I seek peace as the highest priority of my people."

Noting skepticism on the faces of Doge Anton and Noah Watanabe, Hari gazed at them with oval, bright black eyes and said, "The Elders told me of your tremendous military victory over the Parviis. Unfortunately, while you were occupied with that, the Merchant Prince Alliance and the Mutati Kingdom fell to conquerors."

The Humans glared at him. Then Anton responded, "Between us, we may have three planets left. Whatever the case, we *will* fight back."

Beside them, a large Tulyan and a Human-looking woman watched Hari warily. The young Emir, with a racial ability to detect subtle details of physical appearance, noticed immediately that the female was not really Human, but had altered her appearance to look that way. She was not, however, a Mutati. What was she, then? Wondering if her companions knew of her secret identity, the Emir decided she would bear close watching. That one could be dangerous.

In a careful tone, he said, "We each have our own terrible burdens to bear, Doge Anton. And we must face reality. Our peoples need to put our wasteful, ancient feud to rest."

"Mutatis have never shown us anything but aggression," Anton said, glowering.

"That will change, now that I am in charge. The old ways have not been productive or kind to anyone, so I refuse to continue them. Over the centuries, billions and billions of Mutatis and Humans have died due to our ongoing wars. It makes no sense."

"War is the biggest polluter of all," Noah said, somberly.

"Ah, yes, the famous galactic ecologist. I have heard many things about you, Mr. Watanabe. My father used to speak of you derisively, but he and I never agreed on much of anything." The Emir smiled, but it didn't hold, and tears began to stream down his face.

Haltingly, as if hardly able to utter the words, Hari'Adab told of the horrendous error Zad Qato had made in the trajectory calculations on a Demolio shot, and how it had destroyed the beautiful Mutati homeworld of Paradij, killing all of its populace. Billions of lives lost due to one miscalculation. As he spoke he trembled, and tears streamed down his face. "I, I'm so sorry about that," he said, wiping his face.

The big Tulyan stepped closer to Hari. "I am Eshaz," he said. "Do not be alarmed, but I must make skin contact with you. Is the back of your neck all right?"

"The truthing touch." Hari looked up at the seated Elders. "But they have already done this to me, to Parais, and all of the other Mutatis with me. They have also done the same with Hib-Adu prisoners we turned over to them."

The Tulyan hesitated, looked to his superiors for guidance.

"Go ahead," First Elder Kre'n said to Eshaz. "You are especially gifted in this area. Perhaps you will find something we missed."

Eshaz touched the back of Hari's neck, and the Emir felt the coarseness of the reptilian hand on his skin. It remained there for only a few moments, before Eshaz withdrew and announced, "He is being honest with us. The shapeshifter leader bears us no ill will, and he intends to take the Mutati people in a new direction."

"If he can save the remains of his race, of course," the peculiar woman said.

Hari nodded, trying to be dispassionate.

"We were aware of the loss of your homeworld," Noah said.

"Oh? How?"

"I have certain . . . um, paranormal . . . abilities that permit me to peer into the universe from time to time. Where Paradij used to be, I saw only a debris field floating in space. I did not, however, know how it happened, or why."

100

"It has been said that we live in a universe of magic," Hari said. "You are, perhaps, one of the primary examples of that."

"And an entire race of shapeshifters is another," the woman said.

"And you are?" Hari asked, in his most polite tone.

"Tesh Kori. I've noticed you looking at me strangely. Is there a particular reason for that?"

"Maybe it is a defect of my personality. If I have offended you, I apologize most sincerely."

"It's not that, not at all." She exchanged glances with Eshaz, then added, "You have discerned something about me. Please, share with everyone here what it is."

"Are you certain you want me to do that?" Hari looked around at the Humans and Tulyans in the great chamber.

"I have nothing to hide from them. These are my friends. And if Eshaz's report on you is correct, you might become one of them yourself."

"We shall see about that." He smiled. "For one thing, I see that you are a woman of considerable charm. In my experience, I must tell you that charming people are to be watched more closely than others."

"Because they can be manipulative, you mean?" she said, looking past him at Parais d'Olor.

"Precisely."

She lifted her chin haughtily. "And you have come all the way from the Mutati Kingdom to warn everyone about me?"

Laughter echoed around the large chamber, from the Elders and from her own companions.

Maintaining his composure, Hari said, "Madam, I would have said nothing about anything I might have noticed, but you have pressed me to speak. Very well, you are not what you appear to be. By that, I mean, you are not Human."

"She's a Parvii, and we all know it," Eshaz said. "Do you

think we didn't achieve full openness with her, just as we have verified from you?"

"I see." Hari looked at her. "A member of the defeated race. I have heard of you. Not exactly shapeshifters, from what I hear. Some sort of magnification system, I am told."

"Your reports are accurate," Tesh said. "Science or magic? Where does one end and the other begin?"

"Where, indeed?" Hari said. "We're going to need a lot of both, if our races are to survive the present catastrophe."

"You refer to the HibAdu matter, of course," First Elder Kre'n said, from the bench. "But there are other, even more pressing matters that you might not be aware of." She looked at the two other Elders with her, at Eshaz, and then at Noah Watanabe.

"Something worse than the HibAdus?" Hari said. "But how can that be?"

"The galaxy, we're sad to inform you, is crumbling. We took a huge podship fleet away from the Parviis in order to set up a massive galactic repair program. When there is more time, we will tell you more. But suffice to say now that in ancient times the Sublime Creator of the galaxy assigned an important duty to the Tulyan race. We became the caretakers of the weblike galactic infrastructure, with jurisdiction over all podships, for the purpose of performing our important work."

Hari struggled to keep up with the new information, but decided not to ask questions. He and the others here knew there had been a feeling-out process among those present as they got to know one another, and that the apparent small talk had not been that at all. It had been important to get the relationships sorted out among themselves. It still was.

"I want to work with you in any way possible," Hari said. "The last I checked, much of my most elite military force remained intact, holding out against the attackers at Dij."

He formed a frown on his fleshy face, and his snout twitched as he turned his gaze on Doge Anton. Then the shapeshifter leader asked, "I assume you are going to assign podship assets to the defense of the Merchant Prince Alliance?"

"We're working through those details now," the youthful Doge said.

"Might I ask that some military assets be assigned to assist the Mutati Kingdom as well?"

"It is possible," First Elder Kre'n said. "Now, we must move quickly. Far beyond Human and Mutati domains, the entire galaxy is a battlefield, and we must triage it, assigning our assets on a priority basis."

The Tulyan leader looked around at the small assemblage, and announced, "You have all come to me, my Human and Mutati friends—and my one Parvii friend, of course—and all of us should consider ourselves caretakers of the galactic web. It is a shared responsibility among races, at a time of crisis like none other in the annals of history."

Doors opened around the chamber, and robed Tulyan dignitaries marched in, from several directions. They took seats at the remaining Council chairs on the curved bench. The Tulyan Elders—twenty of them now—all conferred for several minutes in a language that Hari could not understand.

Then Kre'n leaned forward and announced, "Eighty percent of our podships will be assigned to galactic recovery operations, and twenty percent to Human and Mutati military operations. Doge Anton, you shall have the authority to work out the proper allocation of those assets."

Anton and Noah nodded in deference to the Council leader. Then the young Doge said, "I concur fully. The welfare of the entire galaxy must take precedence over the military threats."

"We would prefer to allocate fewer ships to the HibAdu matter, but our technicians are studying the two laboratory-bred podships that the Emir brought with him—and they've already determined that such vessels cause damage to the podways on which they travel. Tiny green fibers of the Timeweb infrastructure have been found in the undercarriage tracks of the lab-pods." Kre'n scowled. "Those ships are burning up the podways. As you can see, Doge Anton, your duties coincide with our own ecological recovery operations."

"I understand," Anton said.

Kre'n continued in a solemn tone. "When you succeed in your military operations—and I have every confidence that you will—we shall expect to reassign your podships to galactic restoration projects. Initially, your primary responsibilities will be to remove the artificial podships from service, and to save Human and Mutati worlds."

"It will be done," Anton said. "We'll hit the HibAdus with everything we have, starting from the three planetary fronts."

With a sense of urgency in the air, the Council of Elders adjourned the meeting and called for new sessions to begin in different portions of the large chamber—to deal with the galactic ecology and HibAdu crises. Decisions had to be made quickly, so that the ships and crews could be dispatched where they were most needed.

Chapter Nineteen

Noah is a composite man, a puzzle person forged in a galactic crucible. I can't help being drawn to him.

—Tesh Kori, private notes

In only a short time, Doge Anton del Velli made the most important decision of his brief political career. After consulting with the robot leader Thinker, as well as with his other top advisers, Anton divided the twenty-four thousand podships under his control into three task forces. Anton and Nirella would take twelve thousand vessels to the merchant prince homeworld of Canopa, while Noah would lead six thousand in the Siriki mission. Another six thousand podships would be assigned to the military needs of the Mutati planet of Dij.

As the meetings and submeetings formed, military officers and Tulyan caretakers flowed into the large chamber and headed for their various sessions. To separate the groups acoustically, the Elders used shimmering energy fields as dividers.

In nine hours, all of the plans were essentially complete, and the various groups began to break up. The ecological recovery operations would essentially follow ancient patterns, with certain modifications. On the military side, the tactics for the rescue of each of the three planets had to proceed with caution, because of the lack of clear intelligence from the field.

As Anton concluded his Canopa meeting, he and Tesh talked with the largest Tulyan Elder, Dabiggio. The stern Elder looked down at Tesh and said to her, "Before you depart, I must comment on your own pod, the one you call *Webdancer*. Prior to your involvement with the vessel, it was marooned on Plevin Four for a long time."

"That is correct." She felt perplexed.

"I must tell you that the podship had a different appellation in ancient times—*Clegg*. It was one of the strongest and fastest ships, high-spirited but unproved, and only known to the Tulyans for a short while before the entire race of podships was swarmed and taken by the Parviis. You didn't know that, did you?"

"I know some things about *Webdancer*, but the vessels are enigmatic, as you know."

"So, you didn't know what I told you?"

She smiled. "I didn't say that."

"And how did it get marooned?" Anton asked.

Dabiggio hesitated, appeared to calm himself with a heave of his wide shoulders. Then: "We have learned from a variation of the truthing touch that the vessel rebelled against its Parvii masters and fled into space. For hundreds of thousands of years it roamed the cosmos, and no one could capture it. The rest of its story remains, thus far, unrevealed to us."

"My podship has a rather independent personality," Tesh said, giving the Tulyan a gentle smile. "Perhaps it will reveal its full story to me one day."

He stared at her rigidly. "Unlikely. Parviis do not have the telepathic skills of Tulyans, so you would have difficulty conversing with him."

"But we do have some of those skills, as you know."

"True enough, but beside the point. Here's what I want to tell you. By tradition, the names of podships have always remained unchanged. Once *Clegg*, always *Clegg*."

The remark hit Tesh hard, and took something personal away

from her. She looked at the clearglax floor and the starcloud mists visible beyond.

"Do you understand what I am saying to you?" Dabiggio asked in a gruff tone.

"You want me to change the name back?"

"Exactly. It is not good luck to do otherwise."

"Nonsense," First Elder Kre'n interjected as she came over to them. "Tell her what we decided as a Council, not what you believe independently."

Dabiggio wrinkled his reptilian face in displeasure. He said nothing.

"I'll tell her, then," Kre'n said. She looked at the Parvii woman and said, "Tesh Kori, you are admired by the Council of Elders, and there is widespread recognition of your contributions to the success of the Liberators. Even Dabiggio—who tries to argue with everything—cannot really dispute this. In honor of your service to the cause, we have decided that you may continue to use the appellation *Webdancer* for the pod."

"That pleases me very much," she said. "I appreciate it."

As she and Anton left the chamber together, the young Doge said, "I would have allowed you to keep the name, anyway. Those old Elders can't tell us everything to do, even though they might think they can."

"Would that really have been a battle you should have picked?" she asked, remembering for a moment how close the two of them had once been.

Darkness came over his features. "Maybe I'm a bit of a rebel myself. Now, let's move on to the battles that really matter."

Tulyan wranglers separated twenty-four thousand podships from the main fleet, and further divided the smaller portion into three even smaller fleets, earmarked for Canopa, Siriki, and Dij.

For the Sirikan rescue mission, Noah Watanabe controlled six thousand sentient warships, which he quickly calculated to be five percent of the entire Liberator fleet. After receiving the ships, he and Subi Danvar supervised the details of their military assault force, passing instructions on to their subordinates about how they wanted personnel and equipment loaded into the podships.

All the while, the wranglers and other Tulyan specialists coordinated and synchronized the various vessels in each of the military fleets. Anton's portion, the largest, would get underway first, in part because of the already proven leadership qualities of the flagship, *Webdancer*. But there were larger reasons. Canopa was inarguably the most important of the surviving planets, and Noah had reported to Anton his troubling vision in which the planet—and Noah's former EcoStation orbiting it—appeared to be drifting toward a dangerous timehole. Noah had also arranged with the Elders to have a Tulyan repair team sent there.

Discussing that in the Tulyan Council Chamber, Anton had said, "I know what you're thinking, Noah, that you would prefer to go on the Canopa mission. But I need you to head up the Sirikan operation instead. I'm weighing all the factors, and that is my decision."

Noah had nodded, but recalled chewing the inside of his own mouth to the point of rawness, as he resisted arguing with his superior . . . a wound that still hurt a little.

"A timehole," Anton had said. "If that additional element is indeed added to the already ongoing military operations on Canopa, I'm not certain what any of us can do to keep the planet and the orbiter from vanishing into the cosmic whirlpool. I only know that I have to be there firsthand, to do whatever I can."

It was the mission that Anton wanted, so he would have it.

Noah's smaller fleet, and the one of matching size assigned to the Mutati rescue mission, would have their own flagships, thus requiring more preparations and coordination—work that was not commenced until after the Tulyan Elders decided on the allocation of the vessels.

Finally, having rushed around tending to numerous important matters involving his task force, Noah sent an aide to summon Subi Danvar for a brief, final meeting. While waiting, Noah settled into a deep-cushion chair in his onboard office. Subi would arrive any moment, so Noah closed his eyes, intending to do so for only a few seconds.

As he sank into the fleshy podship cushion, Noah sighed, and a deep sense of calm came over him. Minutes passed, and he felt himself sinking into the most restful state of relaxation he could imagine.

Subi seemed to be taking a long time to arrive. Not wanting to fall asleep, Noah decided to open his eyes. As he did so, however, he experienced a sensation like opening an unusual circular door, one that irised open with shocking suddenness. Abruptly, he felt himself catapulted through an amorphous opening, and he hurtled and spun out into the starry, eternal night of space.

He was back in Timeweb, via a slightly different entry point.

A rush of excitement passed through Noah, tempered by the realization that he could not remain there long, that he needed to go back and get his podship fleet underway. But at the same time, he couldn't pass up this opportunity either. . . .

CHAPTER TWENTY

War has a way of shortening some men's lives, and lengthening others.

—Doge Anton del Velli

"Only twelve thousand ships," Doge Anton said. "Just a small portion of the fleet we brought back from the Parvii Fold."

He and the cerebral robot Thinker stood on the command bridge of the flagship *Webdancer*. Tesh was still at the controls, but the podship had metamorphosed internally to create new military-purpose rooms, and had grown even larger than before, so that it now appeared to be at least twice the size of any other vessel in the fleet. Anton didn't know how the ship changed (or the impetus for the alterations), but he rather liked the new internal arrangement, which included a spacious dome on top of the vessel where they stood now—with wide viewing areas in all directions, through filmy windows.

"I appreciate you coming with me," Anton said.

"You are the commander-in-chief. I follow your bidding. Everyone interpreted your 'request' for my assistance as considerably more than that."

Anton smiled gently as he looked back to see other vessels behind them, picking up speed to keep pace with the flagship, cutting through the milky mists of the starcloud. "Somehow," he said, "I've always thought of you as a strong and independent personality, more impressive than any other machine and more

110

than most men."

"You are too kind, My Lord. I only hope to be of service on this, the most important of the three military missions. I must say, Sire, you were wise to allocate your ships the way you did. Canopa merits the most consideration, and the most firepower."

Anton nodded. In the ongoing, mounting crisis he had made quick decisions, after receiving advice from his wife Nirella, from this robot, and from the other top minds in the new alliance, including Noah and his strategy-wise adjutant, Subi Danvar.

Webdancer accelerated onto a main podway, bound for Canopa. It would take longer than in the old days. Supreme General Nirella rode in another ship with the main navigation team of the Humans, and they had made predictions and projections of the route the ships would probably take. For all practical purposes, the fleet would select its own course, following the lead of Tesh when she—enmeshed with *Webdancer* in the Parvii way—got a good view of space and determined the best route.

With all he had been through, and the tremendous burden of responsibility on his shoulders, Anton felt like a man in his middle age. But as he reviewed the actual mileposts of his life, the chronology only added up to twenty-one years.

As stars blurred past, he realized that he seemed to have lived two entire lifetimes. In the first, comprising a bit over twenty years, he had been the rather ordinary Anton Glavine, a mere caretaker and maintenance man. For a while he had been close to the exciting Tesh Kori, and they had been lovers. But they'd never connected in a deeper sense, and their relationship had ended when Anton and Noah were taken prisoner by Lorenzo. The two had escaped, but by the time Anton saw Tesh again, she had already drifted toward Noah.

During his so-called "second lifetime," Anton was the

fledgling Doge of the Merchant Prince Alliance, and he'd been forced to learn on the job, facing the challenges of managing the various competing powers in the realm. Not the least of the problems he'd faced had been his late mother Francella Watanabe, but he had found ways to sidestep even her. As for his father, the former Doge Lorenzo, Anton had not had much to do with him at all, other than making certain he didn't interfere in merchant prince affairs.

Now, as he embarked for Canopa at the head of twelve thousand armed podships, Anton felt yet another lifetime beginning. Only a few hours ago he had met Hari'Adab, and now—at breakneck pace—the three portions of Anton's fleet were speeding toward different destinations.

But significant restrictions had been placed on the Mutati Emir and his mission to Dij. After conferring with his advisers, Anton had sent what Nirella called "military chaperones" to monitor him. Ostensibly, they were following Hari'Adab's commands, and to an extent they would do that. But—despite the Tulyan lie-detection tests Hari and all of his Mutati followers had passed—Anton's Human officers were alert for tricks and traps, and on a moment's notice they were prepared to take control of the Dij-bound fleet. Robotic troops had also been sent with that rescue force, led by the loyal robot Jimu.

In yet another precautionary measure, Anton had ordered that the Emir's lady friend, Parais d'Olor, be separated from him and placed with Noah's forces on the Siriki mission—for at least the duration of the three initial military campaigns. Both Hari and Parais had objected to this, but the young Doge had insisted upon it. The more indignant they were—and they showed considerable vehemence—the more certain he became that it was the right thing to do. Obviously Hari cared deeply for this aeromutati, so Anton had gained some leverage over him by keeping them apart. How much, though, he was not certain.

Now, as he thought back on these things, and on his own place in the critical events unfolding around him, Anton murmured, " 'Trust but verify.' "

"What did you say, sir?" Thinker asked.

Anton repeated it, louder this time. Then: "It's a saying of Lost Earth. I don't know where I picked it up."

Thinker whirred. "I have it in my data banks. It was a Russian adage, one of the major nations on the doomed planet."

"I wonder how much of the MPA we can save," Anton said.

His thoughts were very dark. Just before departure he had received a report that the HibAdus had enslaved trillions of Humans on every merchant prince planet with the exception of the two where the defenders were still holding out. He hoped, at least, that this had not worsened, and that he was not too late.

"Odds unknown," Thinker said. "Not enough data on the enemy."

"The people of Canopa and Siriki have fought bravely," the Doge said. "We can't abandon them to the HibAdus when they've shown such determined resistance."

He felt his blood pressure rising from the frustration of how long it was taking to cross space. Then a comlink transmission came from General Nirella: "On final podway approach to Canopa system, sir. With luck, we're only a few minutes away."

"Any evidence of a timehole in the vicinity?"

"The Tulyans are checking on that. No report from them yet."

"Visual confirmation that we are approaching Canopa, sir," Thinker said. Even at the extreme speed of the podship, he was rapidly accumulating data on the star systems they were passing.

Anton steeled himself, wondering what awaited them. It could

113

be a carefully laid HibAdu trap, and the same held true for Siriki and Dij.

CHAPTER TWENTY-ONE

There is no such thing as a perfect secret.
—Adurian Admonition

It required a considerable amount of bravery for the guests to have come here, to Lorenzo del Velli's opulent gambling hall on The Pleasure Palace orbital station. At any moment, HibAdu forces could reappear from space and blast the facility into oblivion.

Of course, Pimyt knew otherwise. He just smiled to himself as he stood listening to the nervous chatter around the long diceball table. On his right, Lorenzo stood at the head of the table watching the game, occasionally interjecting to regale his guests with gossip-laden conversation. This gray-haired old man might have been deposed as Doge of the Merchant Prince Alliance, but he still retained his memories of many of the interesting noblemen and ladies in the realm. And if he had trouble remembering some of the details, he made some up in convincing fashion.

Though he kept it undisclosed in such company, Pimyt had been leading a hectic, though fascinating, life himself. If anyone ever wrote about the events and compiled them, his secrets would fill numerous thick volumes.

"The enemy could strike from any direction," one of the noblemen said, looking around nervously at the wide view of space they had from the glax-walled main casino on the top level of the space station. Dozens of the Doge's defensive ships patrolled the area, but Pimyt knew how paltry they would prove against any real attack. So, it seemed, did a number of the guests.

"Just being here is rather like a game of chance, wouldn't you say?" Princess Meghina observed from her place opposite Lorenzo. As beautiful as ever, the blonde courtesan was a constantly smiling, perfect hostess. She sipped red wine from a crystal goblet, and asked, "Do we feel lucky or not?" Beside her, Meghina's pet dagg emitted a low growl. She petted the large black animal.

"But what if the luck for any one of us has run out?" a giddy noblewoman asked as she rolled the diceball and watched it bounce from obstacle to obstacle on the table. Her hair was coiffed in a high bun on her head, and adorned with glittering rubians and saphos that cast prismatic red and blue light around her head. "What if it's you, Lorenzo?" she asked, looking at him. "You've always had quite a run of good fortune."

The automated table tallied her score, and three gold chips popped into a tray in front of her.

"Until forces conspired to remove me from office," he snarled. "Don't delude yourself. I've already had my share of misfortune. No, it isn't *my* luck that would run out."

The gamblers bantered and quipped around the table, as they tried to figure out who among them might either be ready to lose their luck, or who might be a Jonah that could bring bad fortune on the entire orbiter. Then the subject of conversation changed, and they talked about dagg races many of them had attended earlier in the day, at the recently completed racetrack that encircled the bottom level of the space station.

Pimyt tuned out their voices. His HibAdu conspirators had made powerful military strikes against every Human and Mutati world, and had overrun all but three of them. Ironically, Pimyt was now in orbit over one of the unconquered planets, Canopa, aboard Lorenzo's space station. For several days, fighting had been fierce down on the surface, as well as in the air and orbital spaces over the planet . . . but had since died down. For a time, Lorenzo had suspected him of being one of the conspirators, but Pimyt had convinced him otherwise. And the Hibbil's credentials, especially as a former Regent of the Merchant Prince Alliance, gave his word considerable weight. All Hibbils and Adurians were not against Humans, just because some were. For the time being, Pimyt's story had been believed, but he would need to take extra care in the future to avoid detection.

Through good fortune or divine salvation, the space station had been spared thus far. Or so the defenders thought. In reality, Pimyt had played a behind-the-scenes role in that, having convinced his secret superiors that it was a useful facility, worth saving. To preserve it as a prize of war, he'd made certain that HibAdu forces launched only token attacks against the facility, so diminished that Lorenzo's own ships had been able to drive them away.

But even after all he had been through and all he had accomplished, Pimyt had never met any of the HibAdu leaders, nor did he know anyone who had. Prior to the emergence of the HibAdu Coalition, the Hibbils and Adurians had been ruled by their own planetary councils and committees, with largely ceremonial heads of state. That was all suspended with the onset of the HibAdu military buildup, which took precedence over prior forms of government. Now the Hibbils and Adurians were one political and military entity.

Most of Pimyt's associates, such as the Adurian VV Uncel, said they did not care if they ever met the HibAdu leaders in person. To Pimyt, though, it had always seemed peculiar that the coalition high command only distributed audio recordings of themselves delivering inspirational speeches, and had never made personal appearances to the public or to the armed forces. While their names and titles were known—High Ruler Coreq, Prime Lord Enver, and Warlord Tarix—no photos had been disseminated of any of them. Sometimes, in his wildest visions, Pimyt's thoughts would run amok and he would imagine that the leaders were not what they seemed to be . . . not Hibbils or Adurians.

Of course, he constantly assured himself, that was not possible.

Jolting Pimyt to awareness, the floor suddenly shuddered beneath his feet. Gaming pieces rattled on the table and slid off in a series of increasingly loud, crashing clatters. He heard an explosion, and the shouts and screams of his companions.

Noah experienced dual realities, the pleasant sensation of the soft podship chair around him, but the suspicion that it might have drawn him down like quicksand into Timeweb. Normally, he might have welcomed a journey into the paranormal realm. On numerous occasions he had attempted to enter it himself through varying doorways that always seemed to open of their own volition. Now, unexpectedly, he had been drawn in at a time when he could least afford it.

If he didn't wake up quickly, it meant he had essentially gone to sleep on the job. Not like him at all. Noah had always been a hard worker, but now as he considered the prospect of going back, he suddenly felt very tired—the fatigue of an entire lifetime weighing him down.

Here in Timeweb, on the other hand, he had an odd sense of exhilaration and tremendous energy, that he could journey on and on through the cosmos, like a stone skipping forever across a very, very broad pond.

His motion through space slowed dramatically, and just ahead he made out the Canopa Star System and its largest planet, the homeworld of the Merchant Prince Alliance. As if his eyes were a holocamera, Noah zoomed in on the planet. He searched for the timehole he had seen in an earlier vision, and didn't see it. But beyond Canopa, space was murky, with a peculiar fog that he found troubling.

Abruptly, time seemed to go in reverse, and once again Noah was a small boy living in the Valley of the Princes on Canopa, at his father's vast estate. A redheaded girl ran toward him, calling his name. "Noah! Noah!"

For an instant, he hesitated. Then he answered her back with her name. "Francella! Where have you been?"

"I don't know," she said. "But I'm back." Francella smiled sweetly, prettily. Her dark brown eyes glittered.

Like long-lost siblings, the two children hugged. Noah felt the warmth of her embrace.

When they withdrew and he looked at her he saw that she was pointing in wonder at the sky, her eyes open wide in astonishment.

Noah looked up at a vault of grayness that was dissipating, like a thinning fog. Through an opening in the vault he made out the faint green filigree of Timeweb against the backdrop of space and glittering stars. Reality turned inside out, and he was an adult again. His vision zoomed in, and he saw his former space station high overhead, now the orbital home-in-exile of Lorenzo del Velli. Seeing the facility again gave Noah a warm, comfortable feeling. He still thought of the orbiter by his own original name for it, EcoStation, even though it had been substantially changed after the merchant princes took it away from him and Lorenzo turned it into a gambling casino.

His gaze searched in the vicinity of the space station, and to his alarm Noah detected a crack in the fabric of the webbing, a fine line running through the green threads that stretched larger and larger and widened, until he could identify the defect as a whirling timehole, with the blackness of eternity visible beyond. The stygian hole pulsed on its luminous green edges like a living thing. It grew in size until it dwarfed the space station, which drew close to it, as if pulled by a magnet.

In a previous vision, Noah had seen a huge timehole in the vicinity, and now it seemed apparent that it had diminished in size for a time, and then had re-enlarged. Through the luminous perimeter of the opening, he saw a view of space beyond that looked like the blackest place in the entire universe.

Inside the glax-walled gambling hall, people screamed and cried out in pain as the space station rolled and tumbled, and the onboard gravitonics system failed. Meghina's dagg barked and whined. Pimyt tried to find something stable to hold onto, while avoiding being hit by the loose, heavy objects. He grabbed the edge of the big gaming table. Something slammed into his left hip, and a sharp pain lanced through his body.

Everyone tumbled over in a deafening crash of sound, as the table, guests, and chairs slid against the viewing windows.

In what seemed to Noah like a nightmare instead of reality, EcoStation vanished into the galactic maw in a bright green flash. He gasped in horror. A shift in the strands of the webbing ensued, and the timehole sealed over, so that Noah could no longer see it.

He awoke, and found himself back in the soft chair in his office. The chair, part of the podship and created by it, pulsed around his body, as if massaging him and trying to draw him back into it.

But Noah leaped to his feet. He shouted for Subi Danvar, and moments later he saw the rotund adjutant standing in the doorway.

"Everything's ready," Subi said, as if nothing unusual had happened.

Glancing at his own wristchron, Noah was surprised to see that only a few minutes had passed since he'd taken the break. It hadn't done him any good, and he didn't feel rested at all. But he had no time to consider such matters, and he couldn't worry about EcoStation. That was not his mission.

From deep inside, he drew strength, and hurried with Subi to the passenger compartment of the flagship, a room they had converted to a command center for the fleet.

Arriving there in the midst of his officers, Noah told an aide to send a message to Anton about what he had seen. Then he shouted, "On to Siriki!"

In a matter of moments, the command was transmitted to the Tulyan pilot in the sectoid chamber. The vessel—named *Okion* since ancient times—accelerated toward the podways.

CHAPTER TWENTY-TWO

All battles are not won by those who seem to prevail on the field and are left alive. Sometimes, it is better to have died the quick way.

—General Nirella del Velli

After emerging from space, *Webdancer* flew toward Canopa, bathed in bright light from the system's yellow sun. Inside the command-bridge dome atop the sentient vessel, Doge Anton stood with his wife and supreme military officer, General Nirella.

"What's that?" he asked, pointing ahead. Not far from the planet, a green flash lit up space, then vanished.

"Give us a reading," Nirella said, to a junior officer who sat at one of the consoles.

"Lorenzo del Velli's space station just disappeared," he said. "It looks like one of those timeholes the Tulyans need to fix." The officer conferred with a Tulyan woman who wore a red MPA uniform like his own, then added, "Timehole confirmed."

"Noah was right," Anton said.

"Notify the Council of Elders," General Nirella said to the Tulyan. Nodding, the reptilian woman pressed a hand against the filmy window surface, thus putting her in telepathic contact with Tesh and the podship. From Tesh, the message would be relayed to another vessel in the fleet and to a Tulyan webtalker, who would then tap into Timeweb for a transmission to the starcloud. The Elders had already assigned an eco-repair team, and were undoubtedly aware of the confirmation. But this was too important to assume anything.

"Now enter the atmosphere," Anton said.

The Tulyan transmitted the instruction to Tesh Kori, who caused the Aopoddae vessel to dip toward the atmosphere. Some of the other ships remained behind to patrol space, while the majority followed the flagship in a series of "v"-formations that looked like immense flying wings.

Comlink reports flowed as the fleet made contact with military and civilian authorities on the ground and in the air. The defenders reported that battles had subsided in this vicinity, but that the HibAdus had been using a variety of deadly weapons, including warheads filled with Adurian-developed plague viruses. Fortunately, medical personnel on the ground had the situation under control, so the fleet command made arrangements to land.

Five kilometers above the surface of the world, one-quarter of the trailing formations broke away to form patrol sections in the skies. Anton saw one of the formations chase the podships of a HibAdu squadron—small, dark gray aircraft that were much smaller than podships, with orange cartouches on their hulls. The pursuers then divided into smaller formations and fired cannon shots at the fleeing craft, sending bright orange tracer fire through the sky. Several hit their marks, and explosions erupted in the air like fiery red flower blossoms.

The main body of Anton's fleet continued downward. At the vanguard, *Webdancer* circled the cliffside metropolis of Rainbow City, then flew down into the Valley of the Princes and set down on the main landing field. Hundreds of ships followed, while others found additional landing sites at nearby commercial and industrial sites.

As Anton disembarked on a ramp, ahead of Nirella and Tesh, they were greeted by two MPA officers in red-and-gold uniforms. On either side, hundreds of soldiers stood at attention, and beyond them sprawled the towers and structures of the field.

The tallest MPA officer saluted. After introducing himself as Vice-General J. W. Hacket and a dark-skinned officer with him as Starcap Avery, he said, "Sire, thank you for coming to our aid. As I said over the comlink, there is much death here, and not all from battle wounds. The HibAdus disseminated plague and other biological scourges before we succeeded in driving them off. So far, our medical personnel have the illnesses under control, but we've had to devote tremendous resources to the problem."

"Any quarantines?" Anton asked.

"Not necessary anymore. CorpOne research personnel have identified the biologicals, and have already distributed antidotes."

"Some of the enemy are still in the vicinity," Anton said. He heard Nirella on the comlink behind him, getting reports from the air-and-space patrols.

Presently she reported: "Not much activity. Enemy is on the run."

"We didn't kill anywhere near as many HibAdu ships as we saw," Hacket said. "They've been preparing for a counterattack, but it might not come now that you're here. How many pod warships did you bring?"

"Twelve thousand."

The Vice-General smiled. "That should keep 'em at bay."

"Maybe not. Our best robots have calculated that it must have required hundreds of thousands of enemy ships to conquer so many Human and Mutati planets. We may have slowed them down a bit here, that's all."

"But even outnumbered, we're still better than they are," Hacket said. "We already proved that here, and your forces can only help." He looked back, and motioned for a square-jawed man to step forward.

"This is Doctor Bichette," the Vice-General said. "He runs the CorpOne medical research division, and has come up with capsules to immunize you from the HibAdu diseases. He will be coordinating the treatments for all of your officers and soldiers."

After shaking hands with Anton and Nirella, the doctor looked past them and said, "Hello, Tesh."

"Hurk." Her reply was icy, and Anton knew why. Bichette was yet another man from her past.

"We used to know each other well," Bichette said to the Vice-General, with a curt smile.

"He was the personal physician for Prince Saito," Tesh said. "Noah Watanabe's father."

Following an awkward silence, an aide to Dr. Bichette handed out packets of capsules to Anton and his entourage.

After taking the medications, Anton, Nirella, and Tesh boarded a survey aircraft, along with Hacket and Bichette. Thinker accompanied them, as did other top MPA and Liberator officers. Their civilian pilot flew them away from the valley and the city, out toward the coast.

Below, on a broad field bordering the sea, Anton saw tens of thousands of bodies and the burned-out hulks of warships from both sides of the battle, including the rotting remains of dead podships.

"The enemy pods aren't natural," Hacket said, pointing to several decaying wrecks on the ground. "They're growing them in Adurian bio-labs, and fitting them with Hibbil navigation machines."

"We saw a couple of them back on the starcloud," Anton said. "The Tulyans are analyzing them."

"We've done some of that ourselves," Hacket said. "We'll have to compare notes."

They toured four more death-fields where ships had fallen and soldiers on both sides had died. Many enemy robots lay on the ground beside Hibbils and Adurians, but Anton didn't care about any of them. Then a tinge of emotion went through him as he realized how many of his own loyal robots had fallen fighting at the sides of his fighters.

Presently Anton and his entourage flew over the smoldering remains of Octo, one of Canopa's largest cities. "We lost over a million people down there," Bichette said in a somber tone. "But it could have been worse."

"You're a military expert now?" Tesh said.

"Just quoting the Vice-General," he replied.

"That's right," Hacket agreed. "The HibAdus arrived in force, but we drove them back."

Starcap Avery, a slender officer with almond-shaped eyes, pursed his lips. "The enemy seemed to pull their punches, as if they didn't want to wipe everything out. We counterattacked, and they fled too easily."

"In your opinion," Vice-General Hacket said. "It's not the majority opinion."

"I have the vote that counts," Doge Anton said. He narrowed his gaze. "I think the HibAdus could have hit harder, but they wanted to save the planet as a war prize. Even with us here, they probably think they can strike a killing blow any time they feel like it."

Avery nodded, while Hacket just glared silently.

Tapping General Nirella on the shoulder, Anton said, "Send an emergency message to Noah Watanabe at Siriki. Tell him in detail what happened here, and not to let his guard down."

CHAPTER TWENTY-THREE

Most people do not know why they hate the members of another race. The reasons fall away, like leaves from a tree. But the hatred remains.

—First Elder Kre'n

Noah's fleet split space in brilliant bursts of green as it emerged over Siriki. While his warships formed into battle groups, the flagship *Okion* went into geostationary orbit over the planet. On the command bridge of the vessel, Noah stood at a wide viewing window with Subi Danvar, watching violent splashes of color in near-space and in the atmosphere below. They had arrived on the night side of the planet, and from his high vantage point Noah received reports from spotters about the ferocious battle raging below.

He heard their voices over his comlink headset, and on a display screen he saw smaller HibAdu and MPA ships engaged in fierce dogfights and larger vessels in cannon exchanges, lighting up orbital space and the skies over the planet with orange tracer fire and brilliant, multicolored explosions.

Before Noah and Subi could put a rescue plan into operation, a Tulyan woman received permission to enter, and strode heavily onto the command bridge. The reptilian Zigzia had always been what her people called a "webtalker," but Noah had not heard of the vocation until recently, from Elders at the starcloud. Prior to that, he and other Guardians had only known that Zigzia could send and receive messages across the galaxy, through an arcane method of communication.

But the name of her specialty said a great deal about how she and others like her accomplished it. In recent days Noah had asked questions, and had learned that they tapped into Timeweb in a variety of ways, and transmitted telepathically along the strands of the infrastructure.

"Urgent message from Doge Anton at Canopa," the webtalker said in a trancelike voice. "He advises you not to trust anything you see, and suspects that the HibAdus are adept at trickery, at laying deadly traps for our forces. On Canopa it is relatively calm, but there are indications of a storm brewing."

Without hesitating, Noah dictated a response to Doge Anton. "Sire, I have encountered a difficult situation on Siriki. The HibAdus are attacking in considerable force."

Completing his comments, Noah waved the Tulyan away. She hurried off to transmit. By prior arrangement, the three divisions of the Liberator fleet—at Canopa, Siriki, and Dij—were on their own, unless Doge Anton decided to change that.

Keeping his main force back, Noah ordered one of his battle groups to attack, and it dove into action. Podships disgorged thousands of fighter craft into the sky, which immediately sped to the aid of the Sirikan defenders, guns blazing. All the while, in orbital space some of Noah's larger ships hunted for the biggest, most powerful enemy targets, which were not making themselves apparent thus far.

Just then, firing their powerful cannons, two enemy podships came out of nowhere and raced toward Noah's flagship. It was a moment of vulnerability, but *Okion*—either from instinct or the Tulyan pilot operating it—darted out of the way in the battle-lit darkness as if it were a smaller, more agile craft, and fired volleys that destroyed both vessels. They blew up in bursts of color that quickly flashed out in the airless vacuum.

In the next half hour, the tide of battle swung decisively in the Liberators' favor. Soon no more enemy lab-pods appeared, and the smaller warships were being scattered or destroyed. Confident that he could go on to the next stage, Noah sent more commands by comlink, and to the flagship's sectoid chamber through a Tulyan on the command bridge. Now *Okion* led the main body of Noah's fleet downward, into the atmosphere. Fighter craft and other podships cleared the way. Hib-Adu ships were no match for the natural podships, or for the smaller vessels operated by highly trained crews. Reports came in to Noah over comlinks that the HibAdus were in full retreat.

Followed by other podships, *Okion* flew to the sunlit side of Siriki, where there were no ongoing battles. The ship circled the grounds of Princess Meghina's palace and then set down in a broad meadow of flowers. Hundreds of ships followed, while additional craft found their own landing sites in the nearby countryside.

As Noah and Subi disembarked in bright sunlight, they were greeted by three MPA officers who wore red-and-gold uniforms. Hundreds of soldiers stood at attention, and behind them rose the glittering turrets and spires of the Golden Palace. The Princess had not returned since the cessation of regularly scheduled podship travel.

"I'll go ahead and check things out," Subi said. "Let's see if her palace keep matches its reputation."

Noah nodded, and watched as Subi and a half-dozen men marched down a flower-lined path toward the elegant structure. Looking around, Noah saw no signs of war here. The grounds were immaculately maintained.

Reportedly the Princess had set up an attack-proof capsule inside the palace structure, her version of the ancient concept of a fortified castle keep, where the royal family and key associates resided. Subi—with his security expertise—wanted to see it firsthand.

At a gesture from Noah, a dark-skinned aide hurried over, and saluted. "Sir?"

"Bring the Mutati to me," Noah said.

Within minutes, two soldiers brought Parais d'Olor to him. Under close supervision, she had ridden in the passenger compartment of one of the other podships.

"Another test I need to pass?" the Mutati asked in a weary voice, when she reached Noah. She looked much the same as the last time he'd seen her, just before his fleet disembarked, but he thought her peacock feathers were of a slightly different color now. A woman's prerogative, he supposed. Her small beak moved as she spoke.

"No," he said.

Before departing from the starcloud on this mission, the Council of Elders had confirmed Parais' veracity and lack of duplicity by administering the truthing touch on her. The Tulyans had done the same with all of the other Mutatis who had arrived in the two lab-pods, including the shapeshifter leader, Hari'Adab. Now, according to a report that had been transmitted to Noah's flagship, Parais d'Olor had passed an additional series of truthing tests that had been administered by Tulyans in Noah's fleet.

In his experience as Master of the Guardians, Noah had developed a sixth sense about the people he admitted into his environmental organization. Inarguably, one of the best choices he had ever made had been Subi Danvar, a man who had risen quickly through the ranks to become his adjutant. Another had been the Tulyan Eshaz, who had performed excellent ecological recovery work for the organization. In accepting Tesh Kori as a Guardian, Noah had assessed her heart correctly, but had not realized until later that she was really a Parvii, and not Human. He had also allowed the cerebral robot, Thinker, to join his inner circle. Thus, an interesting pattern had developed around Noah, as he interacted closely with a variety of galactic races, as well as sentient robots.

Subi Danvar, always security conscious, had expressed concern over this when he saw the pattern taking shape. In response, Noah had authorized him to complete any background or other security checks he wanted, and the adjutant had done so. For non-Humans, that proved to be difficult, but in his own way, Subi had satisfied himself that the eclectic assortment of Guardians were an asset to the organization, and not a liability.

Noah had never suspected anything else. Just as he saw the entire galaxy as one ecological unit, so too did he view all galactic races—and even sentient robots (who were inspired by Humans)—as cut from the same essential cloth. Honor was honor, and betrayal was betrayal. Though he had been through his share of battles and could justify feeling otherwise, Noah invariably tried to find the good in people, instead of assuming the worst about them. He even did this with his enemies, trying to understand their rationalizations, their motivations. It helped him cope.

Now, as he looked intently into Parais' cerulean blue eyes, Noah was trying to determine the sincerity of the member of yet another race. And this time it was not just any galactic race. This was a *Mutati,* and they had been the mortal enemies of humankind since time immemorial.

"I believe I can trust you," Noah said.

She smiled, revealing upturned creases around the sides of her beak. "You remind me of my Hari," she said, "always thinking, always evolving in your thinking. You look *through* people."

"I'm sorry. I don't mean to, but these are not ordinary times."

"No, they aren't."

131

He told the soldiers with her to allow her freedom of move-
ment, then said to Parais, "I'll talk more about this with Doge
Anton, and see if we can come up with duties for you.
Something befitting your position and your unique skills."

"Thank you." She bowed slightly to him.

"Excuse me," Noah said, as he received a vibrating comlink
signal. When Parais left, he took the call over a handheld
transceiver. It was from Subi.

"The palace is everything I hoped," the adjutant said. His
visual came up from the trasceiver, a holo-image. Subi grinned,
put his hand on a pistol that was holstered on his hip. "Ten of
us convinced the caretaker to give us a tour. Meghina's central
keep is virtually impregnable, so it should be as good a place as
any to coordinate our military operations. There are some
surprises, though, as you'll see when you get here."

Followed by the MPA officers and some of his own men,
Noah marched along the dimly lit main path toward the palace.
Just before going in the main entrance, he saw Acey Zelk and
Dux Hannah, in a lighted section of the gardens. The teenagers
were with a group of men setting up temporary structures and
equipment for a security perimeter around the grounds. Dux
said something to a non-commissioned officer, who looked in
Noah's direction and then nodded to him deferentially.

The boys hurried over to join Noah, and Acey spoke first.
"Master Noah, we really sent the HibAdus packing, didn't we?"
The young man, having never really retired from the Guardians
or been dismissed from them, apparently felt comfortable using
Noah's title as the leader of that organization.

"Don't trust anything you see," Noah said, passing Anton's
advice along. "We can't let our guard down for a moment."

"Our Grandmamá Zelk lives on Siriki," Dux said. "In the
back country. We're worried about her, sir."

"Can we go and check on her?" Acey asked. He grinned

awkwardly. "We're just a couple of kids and not worth much. No one will miss us."

"You're hardly worthless," Noah said. "I've been getting good reports on both of you." He looked the boys over, noting that much of the baby fat had left their faces.

"We know how to use local transportation," Dux said in an imploring voice, "and we won't take long."

Hesitation. Then: "OK, I'm going to let you go. You've both earned the right." He patted the boys on the shoulders. "But take care of yourselves and come back safe, all right?"

"Thank you sir," Dux said, with a wide grin. "We will."

Acey, less mindful of decorum, was already hurrying off, down the dimly lit main path. Dux saluted Noah and ran after his cousin.

CHAPTER TWENTY-FOUR

> The ultimate crisis can bring out the best in a galactic race . . . or lead to its complete extinction.
>
> —Woldn, in his darkest hour

The Eye of the Swarm clustered in the midst of the surviving members of his race, in what he thought must be the blackest, coldest region of the universe. All hope seemed to be lost. He felt the collective loss of body heat in his race, sensed the slowly fading members around him.

Focus, he thought, *I must focus and find a way.*

The Parviis had their secret treasures, going back for millions and millions of years, to the very beginnings of their collective consciousness. It comprised a vault of arcane information that had worked well for them in bygone days to establish their position in the cosmos, but which had not been needed in later times. Or so it had seemed to a long succession of leaders. But Woldn was questioning the old ways.

As the Eye, I did as my predecessors did.

But Woldn didn't want to make excuses for the extreme difficulties in which he now found himself, because rulers were supposed to lead and show strength. He wondered when the changes began, the slippages in ways of doing things, the entombment of important knowledge. At various points along the course of history, Parvii leaders had gradually decided not to emphasize some of the old ways, and in the process important concepts and activities had piled up on intellectual dust heaps. He may even have contributed to the steady decline himself, in some barely perceptible manner. Admittedly, he had not made the decision to resurrect the old knowledge soon enough.

In his great despair, Woldn realized that he had lost touch with the ancient truths and principles of his race, the roots of what it meant to be a Parvii.

We have drifted.

And in drifting, the Parvii race had lost its compass. How fitting that he would make this analogy now, when he and the surviving members of the once-vast swarms were huddled in an uncharted region, probably in another galaxy entirely.

But all living Parviis are not here, he thought. *Tesh has joined our ancient enemy, has thrown in her lot with the Tulyans.*

Woldn lamented over how many key Parvii secrets she might have revealed to them. Some, obviously, like the location of the Parvii Fold. But not all of them, certainly. The traitorous female had never gone through the rituals and training required to become a Parvii Eye of the Swarm. Thus, she could not possibly know certain things.

Secrets layered into secrets.

But she did have important contacts, like Noah Watanabe. If the rumors about him were true, if he was the first Human in history who could access Timeweb and utilize its vast powers, he was a dangerous wild card. He might even be able to peer into the secret treasure vaults of the Parvii race. The reputed "galactic ecologist," combined with Tesh's betrayal, could be why Woldn found himself where he was now.

Cast off, floundering, and sinking into oblivion.

To his dismay he noticed that some of the Parviis who had been clustered around the latents had died, but remained in place even in death. Through his morphic field, he counted them telepathically. Eight hundred and thirteen. Just then, another passed on, right in front of his mind. Eight hundred and fourteen brave souls so far, and surely more would follow. He appreciated their contributions, their loyalty.

Something spiked in his consciousness. Telepathic waves coming from the center of the cluster, from one of the war priests. This one had a name now, resurrected from ancient times. Yurtii. As moments passed, Woldn sensed Yurtii drawing closer to him. The name was unfamiliar, so he must not have been one of the most famous of the ancients.

Like a chick hatching from an egg, Yurtii shoved several of the dead Parviis aside and emerged in the physical form of a boy, then pushed his way out of the swarm and flew into space. Woldn followed him. Entirely hairless and without clothing, the boy hovered near Woldn, making a buzzing noise that the Parvii leader could hear, despite the absence of atmosphere.

The Eye of the Swarm felt his spirits lift, but he could not put the sensation into words for anyone to hear, did not even know if the feeling was justified, or if it was foolish.

"What was old is new again," Yurtii said.

In the war priest's presence, confronted by the potent ancient mind that had regrown in a child's consciousness, Woldn felt grossly inadequate. Though he had known war priests before, his initial probings of Yurtii indicated that they were only faint shadows of this one. Woldn had never been in the presence of a war priest of such talent.

"I am no longer qualified to command the swarm," Woldn said, his voice weak. "Perhaps I should pass the mantle on to you."

Yurtii's bright blue eyes flashed from depths that seemed far beyond his corporal form, like twin stars in the alternate galaxy. "It is in the specialty of a war priest that I can do the most for our race." The hovering youth bowed his head. "I defer to you."

"Very well." Falling silent, Woldn closed his eyes and probed

Yurtii's reawakened mind even more. In the process, he learned interesting things about this war priest's past successes. It gave Woldn hope for the future, especially if the other latents were on the level of this one. But Yurtii had faced opposition from other war priests of his era, and the historical record had not been as kind to him as it might have been. His military successes, while numerous and important, had been downplayed by those who served after him. A cesspool of politics.

Reopening his eyes and staring at the war priest, Woldn said, "Long ago, our race had many masters of illusion. I wish to restore what is good about the old days."

Simultaneously, Woldn and Yurtii focused their gazes on the tiny timehole through which their small swarm had escaped. As seconds passed, a telepathic bubble emanated from the two linked minds, an invisible enclosure that passed through empty to the other side, unseen and undetectable by the guardian ships of the enemy. The swarm could enter it and travel undetected, concealed from view.

With new excitement, the Eye of the Swarm led the way through, into the safety of the bubble. Then, filled with Parviis, the invisible bubble floated away, to a remote corner of the Parvii Fold. Behind, the timehole appeared to seal over, so that it no longer seemed to exist.

Under Woldn's leadership the tiny creatures were coming back to awareness. They were angry and single-minded, and wanted to regain control of the podships. They saw this as their only purpose in life, their sacred and eternal destiny. But their numbers were far too small to even consider resurrecting the ancient glories, at least not yet. All of them were feeling better physically and mentally, but most of the individuals no longer had the effective neurotoxin stingers that were needed to capture and control podships.

Still, inside the Parviis' invisible bubble lay potential salvation, because it offered the means of escape, a tiny pocket within the traditional galactic fold that had always been their sacred place. It was warmer inside the bubble, much better for breeding than out in space.

But the five latent breeding specialists had not yet returned to consciousness. And without their guidance, the Parviis could not breed at all. They could only die.

CHAPTER TWENTY-FIVE

Timeweb holds this galaxy together. But there are galaxies on top of galaxies in this vast universe. Are they also linked to the cosmic web that we know, or are their structures entirely different and unimaginable to us?

—Tulyan report to the Council of Elders

In times long past, so many years ago that Eshaz could hardly remember them, he had been a skilled podship pilot for the Tulyans, transporting web caretaker teams around the galaxy. After the insidious, selfish Parviis took away control of the podship fleet, Eshaz—having lost the means of performing his specialty—had been forced to adapt. As a consequence, he had perfected other skills authorized by the Council, among them the ability to timesee. In addition, he had become a web caretaker himself, performing occasional timehole repair duties in the limited travels that became available to him.

Eventually he'd met Noah Watanabe, the first Human to ever grasp the concept of galaxy-wide ecological interdependence. Joining Noah's idealistic team of "eco-warriors," Eshaz and scores of other Tulyans engaged in ecological monitoring operations, and—in secrecy—they occasionally used ancient Tulyan methods to complete timehole repairs.

In recent years, Eshaz had seen conditions worsening, but he had been unable to do much about it until now. With more than ninety-six thousand podships dedicated to their tasks, the Tulyans were mounting the most massive ecological recovery operation in history. After assembling reports from web caretakers, the Elders were looking at the vast galaxy as if it were a battlefield, with wounded soldiers lying all over it. In their way of prioritizing, each of the timeholes became like an injured person, and the Tulyan leaders were using a triage method to determine which wounds needed attention first.

At long last, the Tulyans—who had always considered themselves a peaceful people—were going to war, in a very aggressive, organized fashion.

As the leader of one of the repair divisions, Eshaz stood with a throng of other Tulyans on a space platform while the craft floated past the immense fleet of rescued, moored podships. Presently the glax-enclosed platform came to a stop and rocked gently in the vacuum, an optimal moorage basin at the stationary center of the planets of the Tulyan Starcloud. In recent months, Eshaz had been resurrecting his old piloting skills, having gone on a hunt for wild podships and having piloted one of the sentient vessels in the Liberator fleet.

Now the Tulyan portion of the fleet was embarking on an even greater task. In a sense it was linked to the military operations of the Humans and Mutatis in their efforts to save their planets and stop HibAdu lab-pods from damaging the podways—but this was a far more delicate and wide-scale operation. Everything had to be done perfectly. The fate of the galaxy rested on their skills.

For some time the Tulyans had been retraining themselves, updating their old aptitudes and methods. Because they led exceedingly long lives, hundreds of thousands and even millions of years, many living Tulyans recalled the old days. But after so long, memories had a way of slipping in the clutter of events, and some of Eshaz's race were better at recalling details than others. There had been numerous arguments about the proper methods to use, but the proof had been in the tests they had performed. Handling a few wild pods—which Tulyans had continued to do for centuries—was not the same as organizing and coordinating the actions of thousands of them. Large numbers of Aopoddae behaved quite differently from smaller numbers, and needed specialized techniques to manage them. Determining which methods to use was like a filtering process, eliminating the ideas that didn't work and implementing those that did.

Just getting the podships here from the Parvii Fold had involved much of that, perfecting ways of piloting the vessels in large formations to selected destinations. Now the ships no longer had gun ports on their hulls, for their passengers had different requirements, and the sentient spacecraft had made adjustments. Their passenger compartments and cargo holds were filled with ecological repair teams, with all of the esoteric equipment needed for that purpose. The articles taken along weren't things that could be manufactured in a conventional factory. Rather, they were thorn-vines, pouches of green dust, and books of incantations that would be needed to ward off the evil spirits of the undergalaxy.

To an extent the Tulyans understood what they were up against: Galara, the powerful evil spirit of the undergalaxy, was punching holes in the Known Galaxy, penetrating the protective membrane at numerous points in order to undermine and conquer. For millions of years the malevolent one had been working at this, and finally, with the momentum of the decay Galara had set in motion, the adverse conditions were accelerating. Long ago, the Tulyans had an easier task, because they could respond quickly whenever timeholes appeared, and could seal them quickly. But with all the years of decline the job was much bigger now, and the prospects were uncertain at best. Certainly, all of these thousands of podships and teams of Tulyans were a formidable force to save the galaxy. But was it too late? Could they make enough of a difference to reverse an immense-scale decline?

Just as Tulyans knew that there were ancient enemies among the galactic races, so too they believed there were competing spirits and gods of the various galaxies. And just as people wanted to dominate one another, it was like that in higher orders of existence as well, where the stakes were much greater.

Eshaz bowed his bronze head in reverence to Ubuqqo, the Sublime Creator, and whispered a prayer for the salvation of the galaxy. *"Ubuqqo, anret pir huyyil."*

A benign spirit seemed to encompass the reptilian man now, and he felt supremely comforted in its presence. Closing his slitted eyes, Eshaz murmured an incantation to beckon a nearby, familiar podship in the ancient way, commanding it to come closer: *"Aopoddae, eyamo ippaq azii . . . Aopoddae, eyamo ippaq azii. . . ."*

When Eshaz opened his eyes moments later, the large gray-and-black pod was bumping up against the platform, and an access hatch was open on the hull. The ship drifted back just a little, but remained close. With a rush of excitement, Eshaz leaped off the platform into space. Like an eager lover, the podship scooped him up, and he found himself inside.

Once more it was like old times, when Eshaz had been a caretaker-team pilot. He placed his hands on a warm interior wall and felt the pulsing consciousness of the ancient creature, and repeated its name, which he knew well. In the times of lore, this had been one of the podships he had piloted across vast distances.

Agryt.

Walking down the corridor, Eshaz reached the sectoid chamber, and found the access hatch open as expected, revealing a glowing green enclosure beyond. The podship awaited his commands.

Eshaz took a deep, satisfied breath and stepped across the threshold into the core of the vessel. The access hatch closed behind him, bathing him in green luminescence, but he was not afraid. In the age-old way of his people, the Tulyan touched the glowing flesh and merged into it.

On the prow of the podship, Eshaz's face appeared, very large now in his metamorphosed state. He felt euphoric, like a reborn creature ready to leap and frolic across vast expanses of the heavens. But he knew he could not do that, could not do anything trivial or selfish with this critically important assignment that had been entrusted to him.

Instead, as the leader of a five-hundred-ship ecological repair team, Eshaz guided *Agryt* around the other vessels assigned to him, signaling to them telepathically, as they had practiced. Tulyan faces appeared on the prows of ship after ship, and the vessels fell into formation behind him, their countenances rigid and expressionless.

The Tulyan caretaker had many things on his mind, the concerns of the day. And of all those matters, one surfaced above others. Noah had been telling everyone that he sensed a "terrible danger" out in the cosmos, beyond anything they already knew. Eshaz wondered if his friend could possibly be right, and if so, what it might conceivably be. Something to do with Galara that was even worse?

A chill ran down his spine. In this galaxy, anything seemed possible.

CHAPTER TWENTY-SIX

Just as there are byways and hidden passages within any sentient mind, so too is it with larger groups of living beings. As individuals, and as groups, conscious organisms have an obsession with doing things that others do not know about. It is their way of controlling situations—or of altering their perception so that they *believe* they are in control.

—Thinker, data bank file 34ΩÆØ

Having been summoned to his homeworld of Adurian, the Ambassador waited patiently for the dignitaries to arrive. His pulse quickened. Uncel had received notification that the three leaders of the HibAdu Coalition would finally identify themselves and would make a major military announcement. At last, he would learn who they were!

VV Uncel stood with other diplomats and local Adurian leaders, all gathered in a grand reception hall that had been converted from the remains of an old spacecraft. A buzz of anticipation filled the air, and people kept looking up at the speaking balcony and at the grand staircase that descended to their level, where the triumvirate might appear.

In its original form the large spacefaring vessel had contained numerous reception halls and meeting rooms, and had been built in an opulent style for one of the early Adurian emperors, Oragem the Third. The walls and ceilings were hand-painted and framed in gold filigree along the moldings and on the railings and banisters.

A tall Churian with thick red eyebrows worked the gathering, offering drinks that he balanced precariously on two trays.

"I'll have a ku-royale, please," Uncel said, pointing.

Nodding, the Churian contorted a very flexible leg that had long, prehensile toes on the foot, which he used to grasp the drink and pass it on to Uncel.

As the servant moved away, the Ambassador took a long sip of the alcoholic beverage, and tasted its delicate, minty sweetness. Surrounded by conversations in which he was not participating, he took a few moments to reflect. Though born to wealth and privilege, Ambassador VV Uncel had always worked hard to improve himself, and took pride in his achievements. A pureblood Adurian born on the planet of the same name, his father had been a successful biochemist who earned numerous patents, while his mother had been a product designer who worked on the team that developed *Endo*, the most popular of all Adurian games.

Educated at the elite Sarban University in the capital city, Uncel had always known he would succeed. Everyone who knew him commented on his many attributes, especially his keen intelligence, his way of getting along with virtually anyone, and his burning desire to succeed. He had graduated first in his class.

For years, Uncel had been on the ascendancy in his career, culminating with his appointment as Ambassador to the Mutati Kingdom at the very young age of sixty years, quite youthful by the biologically enhanced Adurian standards. In his professional life he had known the Adurian emperor and his advisers very well, and had established a vital communication line with the Mutatis and their difficult Zultan, Abal Meshdi.

Uncel had even been in on the early planning sessions of the Hibbil and Adurian rulers, in which they resolved to form a clandestine alliance to defeat both the Mutati Kingdom and the Merchant Prince Alliance. When the HibAdu alliance got underway, however, Uncel had been frustrated to find himself increasingly out of the loop, becoming one of the people who only received information on a "need to know" basis. In answer to his queries about various issues, the Adurian Emperor and his advisers began to defer to what they called the Royal Parliament, which they said was making the key decisions about Hib-Adu military plans. Three names and titles had surfaced as members of that governing body, but not their faces: High Ruler Coreq, Premier Enver, and Warlord Tarix.

Prior to that, Uncel had never heard of the trio or their governing body, and he'd never been able to determine where they convened. Rumor held that the Royal Parliament had been established on one of the secondary Hibbil worlds, which gave Uncel concern. But his life was busy with diplomatic assignments, and he saw the immense war machine building all around him, with thousands of factories gearing up to produce armaments and laboratory-bred podships, all necessary for the upcoming attacks on the enemy.

A career diplomat, VV Uncel had always managed to land on his feet whenever the political winds blew, as they invariably did. With the HibAdu Coalition and weapons manufacturing in full swing, he fell into a pattern of just playing his part as a diplomat and as a spy against the Mutatis, without totally understanding what was occurring on his own side. But he had faith that it would all turn out for the best. Mutatis and Humans were the most loathsome of galactic races, and deserved the terrible punishment that was being delivered upon them.

"Another drink, sir?" The Churian was back.

"No." Uncel watched as the prehensile foot extended again, and then took the glax from him. The servant drifted away.

In one of the high points of his career, Ambassador Uncel

had tricked the Mutatis into using Adurian gyrodomes and minigyros, devices that weakened their brains in subtle ways and made them easier to conquer. Afterward, his HibAdu superiors had sent him a laudatory message telling him he had done an excellent job of softening up the enemy for the imminent attack.

Uncel prided himself on an ability to get along with people he did not like, while artfully concealing any antipathies he felt from them. That included not only the Mutati Zultan, but the duplicitous little Hibbil, Pimyt. Though Uncel and Pimyt worked together closely on the Hibbil Cluster Worlds, Uncel had never trusted the furry little devil. Something troubled him about Pimyt's red-tinged eyes, which seemed to conceal too much. While Pimyt professed to know as little as Uncel himself, the Ambassador did not entirely believe him. Pimyt was the sort of person who had schemes within schemes, and fallback positions to protect himself while sacrificing others.

As attaché to the former Doge Lorenzo del Velli, Pimyt had connections to leaders of the Merchant Prince Alliance, and for all Uncel knew he might have spilled the plans to them. Of course, the HibAdus had systems to check on such things, a way of taking cellular samples from Pimyt and others (and even from Uncel), samples that they could read in laboratories to obtain information. Uncel's own father had developed the biotechnology and had been well-rewarded for it. Though VV held no legal rights to the particular patents involved with reading cells, since the patents were considered high-security assets of the state, he recalled how as a child his father had shown him that biological cells contained memories—memories that could be read in order to obtain evidence of a crime or of disloyalty to the government. It was the ultimate police tool, and a key contribution of the Adurians to the HibAdu Coalition.

But Hibbils were crafty. They possessed significant technology of their own, and might even have secret methods of thwarting the cellular lie-detection system of the Adurians. Pimyt was with the Humans now, ostensibly on a clandestine HibAdu assignment. Uncel would like to be a proverbial fly on the wall around that one.

The buzz of conversation intensified around him, and he heard exclamations. Looking up at the speaking balcony, Uncel gasped at the sight of three peculiar figures standing there, all dressed in orange-and-gray robes. HibAdu colors.

From their bodies and facial appearances, he thought two were men and one a woman. They were quite different from any galactic race he had ever seen before, but familiar to him at the same time, in a haunting and disturbing sort of way. A single word came to his mind, one he dared not utter, because he strongly suspected that these were the HibAdu leaders. At long last, they were presenting themselves.

Freaks.

He couldn't help the thought, though he knew it was dangerous. Their heads were of the Adurian insectoid shape, with large, bulbous eyes. But the eyes were pale yellow instead of the darker shades typical of Adurians, while their heads and exposed hands had Hibbil features. All three leaders were fur covered, and they had stunted bone structures. These were laboratory-grown people, horrific hybrids of the two races.

The male freak in the center was the tallest, if he could be called tall. Throughout the reception hall, no one spoke a word, and everyone stiffened up. Uncel felt a shortness of breath, and tried to calm himself. He hoped it was just a joke, something the Adurian lab scientists had cooked up.

"I am High Ruler Coreq," the robed monster at the center said, in a whiny voice that sounded Adurian. Motioning to his left and right, he identified the other male as Premier Enver and the female as Warlord Tarix, and then added, "We are, as many of you have surmised, laboratory-bred, but make no mistake about it. This does not make us inferior to any of you in any way. On the contrary, we are far superior in every way imaginable."

"Gaze upon us and see the future," Premier Enver said. This one sounded more like a Hibbil, with a deeper voice. "One day, when the time is right, an entire race of HibAdus will be created, and there will be no need for any other races to exist."

A chill ran down VV Uncel's spine, and he heard an uneasy murmuring around him.

Warlord Tarix had something to add, in an echoing voice that carried deadly undertones. "Our enemies are on their knees, making their last stands. We have conquered every Human world except for two, and every Mutati world but one." She smiled cruelly, revealing sharp white teeth. "They cannot hold out much longer."

Then, eerily, the three of them spoke in synchronization: "To retain what we have gained, our forces have established impregnable defense systems on every conquered planet. Thanks to Hibbil ingenuity, we have wide-range sensor-guns that sweep considerably more than the areas around pod stations, as the Humans have. Our sensors encompass entire planets. If any unauthorized podship appears, it will be blasted into oblivion."

The triumvirate began to clap, as if for themselves. Everyone in the reception hall joined in, including Ambassador Uncel, but he felt a dark gloom seeping into his soul.

CHAPTER TWENTY-SEVEN

Those who adapt, survive. This basic rule applies to all living things, and to all places they exist in the universe. Biological creatures, being much smaller and weaker than the natural forces of their surroundings, can only control their environments to limited extents. When things change around them, they must change as well. Or die.

—Master Noah Watanabe, *Journal of the Cosmic Sea*

It could have been much worse.

At least that was the first impression Princess Meghina got when the space station stopped tumbling and the gravitonics system went back on. The glax-walled gambling room on the orbiter had righted itself, and was lit with soft illumination coming through the windows. But was it really over? And what in the world had happened?

She crawled out from under the gaming table and assessed the bumps and bruises on her face and body. Around her, others did the same. Some were groaning, but as she saw them move, it didn't look like anyone was seriously injured. Pimyt stood on top of the upside-down gaming table, complaining that one of his hips hurt. His tunic was torn, showing silvery fur on his chest.

Meghina's dagg whined, and scampered over debris to reach her. The large black animal licked her hand, where a bruise was beginning to show.

"Thank you, Orga," she said with a gentle smile. "That makes me feel better already."

"Are you all right?" It was Kobi Akar, the impeccably dressed Salducian diplomat who was one of her immortal companions. He stood over her, looking down with concern in his dark, close-set eyes. Though he had always been nice enough to her, she'd never really liked him that much. There seemed to be an undercurrent to him, something just beneath the surface that was decidedly unpleasant. Exactly what that might be, she had never been certain. But she didn't admire the way he sometimes alluded to getting away with things that others could not, because of his diplomatic immunity. Even so, he could be funny and witty at times, and the others in her elite group of elixir-immortals all seemed to like him.

Typical of his race, Akar was sturdily built, with an oblong head, two small, crablike pincers for hands, and a multi-legged underbody concealed beneath a long robe. The Salducians, while trading partners and military allies of the Merchant Prince Alliance, were a galactic race of their own, and had settled in only a small sector of the galaxy.

"I'm fine," Meghina said. She looked around. "And the others?"

"All minor injuries, it appears."

"That's good." She rose to her feet and gazed out through the clearglax walls in all directions, onto a star-encrusted canvas of space. Looking down along the connected modules of the space station, she noticed large dents that had not been there before, and jagged pieces hanging loosely from sections that were too badly damaged to be saved by airtight emergency doors. Beyond this startling view, she saw something just as unsettling: a brown planet that was obviously not Canopa, where they had been orbiting previously. Sunlight came from behind the orbiter.

An odd, queasy feeling came over her. "Where are we?"

Akar scratched the thin line of hair on his forehead, the last patch of his hairline. "Hard to say."

He was considered handsome by his people, and was reputed to enjoy the company of many mistresses. As for herself, the courtesan Princess Meghina had never found him or any other Salducian male physically attractive, and his quirks and deficiencies were irritating. He looked worried now, but often had a rather artificial smile on his overlarge mouth.

Pimyt limped past her, grimacing in pain from his injured hip. "We need medical packs," he said. He went down a short stairway to the corridor door, and shouted back, "I'll see what I can find."

"This space station is seriously damaged," someone said.

A man's voice came over the onboard com-system. "I am Colonel Truitt of the Red Berets. All passengers, make your way to emergency stations and put on survival suits."

"We're in one of the emergency stations now," Lorenzo said.

Someone activated ceiling hatches, causing nets to drop down slowly, containing life-support suits and emergency supply canisters. Moments later, Red Beret soldiers entered the chamber, opened the nets, and began handing out suits. The emergency doors for this module, which were supposed to be airtight, were leaking.

"But there are immortals among us," said Prince Okkco, a nobleman with wavy white hair. "They do not need life support."

"Everyone puts on a suit," Lorenzo said, with a scowl. "No exceptions."

"We are orbiting an unknown planet in an unknown solar system," one of the Red Berets said, looking at the readings on a handheld device.

Another soldier, holding a similar unit, said, "We're still taking astronomical readings, but nothing looks familiar."

In a few minutes, everyone in the chamber including the Red Berets had put on puffy, pale blue survival suits. But they left the faceplates hinged open, since the on-board air systems were still functioning.

More guests and soldiers from other portions of the orbiter entered the wrecked gambling hall, one of the principal emergency stations on the orbiter. Colonel Truitt came in as well, a tall man with a thick mustache. He conferred with Lorenzo and Pimyt.

Presently, Lorenzo announced, "Though we've lost one of our primary shuttles, we still have two in working order. We're going to use one of them to send a scouting party down to that planet, and see what we can find out. Our scanners show it has a breathable atmosphere and moderate temperatures on the surface, so we won't need these suits when we get down there."

"There could still be unknown dangers," Meghina said. "As one of the immortals, I'd like to volunteer to go down with the scouting party."

"No," Lorenzo said. "You're staying here. But I'm going down, and so is Pimyt."

"Why?" Meghina asked.

And Pimyt said, too, almost at the same time: "Why?"

"Because," Lorenzo said, "one of you is my wife, and the other is my attaché, and both of you will do as I command."

In shared reluctance, Meghina and Pimyt nodded.

Then the Salducian diplomat said, "If you want an immortal to go along, I'll do it."

"No, you'd just get in the way," Lorenzo said. He scanned the four Human immortals, and seemed to consider taking one or more of them along instead. Then he looked at Pimyt and said, "Make the necessary arrangements. Add a dozen elite Red Beret guardsmen to the scouting party."

"Fourteen in all, then," the Hibbil said.

"Right."

As she watched her husband take charge of the situation, Meghina felt a renewed surge of attraction for him. He looked rather handsome in this time of crisis, and was displaying courage that she hadn't seen before.

Noticing her looking at him, Lorenzo smiled. But his resolve appeared suddenly shaky. As if to conceal this, he turned and led the others out the door into the corridor.

When the shuttle dropped down through the atmosphere, Pimyt saw predominantly brown hues on the planet, from horizon to horizon. The world had grayish-brown mountains and formations of rock in other muted colors, but he saw no evidence of water or plants.

He heard one of the guardsmen comment on the same thing.

Looking at them, Pimyt said, "If the air's breathable there must be water and plants somewhere."

"Maybe our instruments are wrong," one of the guardsmen said. A lieutenant with gold stripes on his shoulder, Eden Rista was the highest-ranking Red Beret soldier in the party.

"Instruments are still showing good oxygen levels," another guardsman said, as he stood at a console. They were only a few hundred meters above the surface. The shuttle slowed, fired retro-rockets, and set down on a wide expanse of rock.

Four guardsmen went through an airlock and stepped outside, leaving the rest of the party on the shuttle. As Pimyt watched through a porthole, the men performed several tests, using handheld instruments. Then they swung aside the faceplates on their suits, and gave the all-clear signal.

Now the entire party disembarked, and climbed down from the rock onto an expanse of dry, dusty earth. The air was a little cool, even in direct sunlight. That didn't bother Pimyt, but his companions wore jackets.

Moving off by himself, Lieutenant Rista held a ground-penetrating radar unit.

"Network of subterranean waterways down there," he reported. "Average depth around thirty meters."

"So, there is water here, after all," Pimyt said. Looking at Lorenzo, he added, "If you want, sir, I could bring a hibbamatic down here and build something to dig, and to explore the waterways."

"For what purpose?" Lorenzo asked.

"We're in an unknown region, on an unknown planet," the Hibbil said. "Maybe we should take soil, rock, and water samples. Comparing the data with galactic exploration records, it could give us information on where we are."

"Let's do it," the former Doge said.

An hour later, they had the hibbamatic set up on the ground. Pimyt made several settings on the machine, then began feeding cartridges of raw materials into the hopper on top.

In a short while, the little Hibbil stood at a new black machine, which he had assembled from components that the hibbamatic produced. The glistening machine was around the size of a small passenger car, except it had a seat on top, and handlebars.

"This thing is dual purpose," he said. "Watch."

Pimyt touched a button, and cutters began grinding on the bottom, tearing into the soil. Then he climbed onto the seat and plopped himself there, while holding onto the handlebars. The mechanisms started digging, and in short order it had produced a tunnel sloping down into the ground.

The tunnel had just enough headroom for the others to follow down the slope, on foot. At the bottom, Lorenzo found Pimyt on a flat section of rock inside a low-ceilinged rock cavern, by the edge of a stream. The Hibbil knelt beside the black machine, with lights on the unit illuminating the silvery, luminous surface of the cavern and the underground waterway. Pimyt was making adjustments. As he did so, the seat and handlebars melted into the surface of the machine, and like a shapeshifter it enlarged and morphed into a teardrop form, with a windshield on the fat end.

"Four-man mini-sub," Pimyt reported. "Perfect for underwater exploration."

"Clever," Lorenzo said, walking around the gleaming black boat. "But what does this have to do with taking soil, rock, and water samples?"

"Very little, perhaps," Pimyt admitted, "but where there's water there's life. Or so the saying goes. Undoubtedly there are organisms in the water, but we're looking for something more substantial. If anyone lives on this planet, we might find them beneath the surface."

"Follow the water," Lorenzo said.

"Precisely. And with instruments, we can always get back here."

"Very well, but for only a couple of hours, at most. If we don't find any evidence of meaningful life, we take the samples and go back to the orbiter."

Pimyt nodded.

A number of the guardsmen were older, and said they had experience with a variety of machines. Lieutenant Rista designated two men to go in the sub. The other men lowered the machine into the water, where it bobbed on the surface. Climbing inside the sub, the two guardsmen familiarized themselves with the controls, taking the boat underwater and back up again. The twin engines purred smoothly.

Using a handheld unit, Lorenzo sent a comlink message up to the orbiter, informing them where the landing party was, and what they were doing.

"I should go," Pimyt said, to Lorenzo. "If necessary, I can operate the sub, too. I've been watching them and listening in, and it looks easy enough to handle. How about you, sir? Want to take a little submarine ride?"

"Are you sure it's safe?" Lorenzo asked. He shut off his com-link unit, replaced it in a holder at his belt.

Pimyt grinned. "Absolutely not."

With a grimace, Lorenzo climbed into the four-man craft and took one of the two aft seats, in the narrowest section of the teardrop hull. Pimyt followed, and sat in the remaining seat directly behind him, while the two guardsmen sat side by side ahead of them, in the pilot and copilot chairs behind the windshield.

Slowly, the mini-sub proceeded downstream, casting a power-ful headlight to illuminate the watery tunnel ahead, through murky darkness. At first they made their way on the surface of the water, like an ordinary motor-propelled boat.

"Low rock overhang ahead," the pilot announced. He was much thinner and shorter than his companion, and proved to be entirely bald as well when he removed his cap and stuffed it in a uniform pocket.

"The water is deep enough to submerge," the larger soldier said, reading an instrument panel.

"OK," the pilot said. "Here we go." He submerged the vessel, and they proceeded to the other side of the overhang, where they surfaced again. But only for a short distance. The waterway widened considerably, but across the entire width the ceiling dipped so low that they had to submerge again.

As they proceeded underwater, the big soldier looked back at Lorenzo and said, "Quite an adventure we're on, sir."

"I'm not afraid," the former Doge said, "not at all. I've seen much worse than this."

But Pimyt heard fear in his voice, and this amused him. He'd never liked Lorenzo, and secretly enjoyed seeing him suffer. The Hibbil had other feelings as well, of a more aggressive nature. In his mind, he savored the possibilities.

Suddenly he felt the mini-sub's speed increase dramatically, a strong thrust forward. Moments afterward, a warning buzzer went off.

The pilot swore loudly, and slammed the engines into hard reverse.

Chapter Twenty-Eight

Effective leadership is primarily a matter of striking a pose and causing others to see you in a favorable light. It is all about perception. If you appear to be in full command, others are assured, and will follow you. If you appear to be unsteady or fearful, they will scurry away from you like insects from a burning structure.

—Doge Paolantonio IV, private comments

"So you're the great Noah Watanabe?" The palace reception hall echoed with her words, and with her condescending tone.

Though he had never met the young woman before, Noah recognized her instantly from holophotos he had seen. Tall and blonde, Princess Annyette appeared to be around twenty and very businesslike, in a white pants suit and understated gold jewelry. Her hair was closely cropped, more the cut of a man than of a woman. Just behind her stood her six younger sisters, all blonde and similarly attired, but in clothing of different colors. The youngest appeared to be around twelve years of age.

In deference to the rank that Annyette still retained on Siriki (and in what remained of the Merchant Prince Alliance), Noah bowed to her. He had a small entourage of uniformed MPA officers and soldiers with him, along with his rotund adjutant, Subi Danvar.

In the faces and bone structures of the seven princesses, Noah detected resemblances to both Princess Meghina and to

Lorenzo del Velli, the royal couple who for years had been thought to be her birth parents. That changed when the famous courtesan confessed publicly that she was not Human at all, but was instead a Mutati, one of the loathsome shapeshifters. Lorenzo del Velli had continued to protect his wife, and much of the public continued to support her, agreeing that she was really more Human than Mutati in her thoughts and loyalties, no matter her unfortunate genetics. But the revelation of Meghina's true identity meant that she could not possibly have borne Human children sired by Lorenzo. Obviously, in her attempts to deceive him and the public, she had selected the birth parents of her "daughters" carefully, because the girls standing before Noah looked perfect in all respects, and even carried themselves with a certain royal hauteur.

"I have never claimed to be great," he responded in a respectful tone. "Not in any sense of the word. On the contrary, I see myself as exceedingly small in a very large universe."

"Which means I am even smaller?" she said, arching her eyebrows.

"I didn't mean that at all." He smiled. "I'm sorry, but I was told that the palace is unoccupied, that you and your sisters prefer to live elsewhere on Siriki, in your own royal quarters."

"The HibAdu attacks changed all of that. We have gathered here at the keep for safety, with our own forces." She nodded toward her gold-uniformed guards that stood at attention around the room, all of them eying Noah's men suspiciously.

"Your castle keep is renowned. You have made a wise decision."

"I'm glad you think so."

Noah shifted on his feet. "Of course, I will make alternate arrangements for myself and my officers."

With a broad, almost friendly smile, Annyette said, "Not necessary. You are my guests and allies."

"And friends," Noah added. "Then you can accommodate some of us in the keep?"

"No more than three hundred."

"Most generous. Now, if you could have someone show us the quarters, we are anxious to set things up. I presume there are meeting halls we could use?"

"Of course."

In what appeared to be a complete about-face, Annyette actually became friendly. For Noah and his top officers, she insisted that they accept accommodations on the most secure lower floors of the keep, near her own suites and those of her sisters. She also arranged for protected meeting chambers, and even proved to Subi Danvar's satisfaction that the suites and chambers were safe from eavesdroppers.

Afterward, at a quick and spartan meal with his officers and aides, Noah laid out plans for the following day. Only half of the force he had brought with him had landed on Siriki, where they were setting up bases around the planet. The rest of the Aopoddae warships and smaller fighter craft patrolled the skies and orbital space, constantly on the alert for any HibAdu threat.

That evening, Noah retired to his quarters, just down the corridor from Princess Annyette. But in the entryway to his suite, while he was bidding good evening to Subi, the adjutant suddenly flashed a military hand communication to him—a brief flicker of the fingers that contained a private message: "Remain alert. Perhaps it's only a reaction to the food, but my gut is starting to act up."

With a blink of his eyes, Noah acknowledged, and entered the opulent suite. For half an hour, he sat in a hard chair facing the door, with his ion pistol on his lap. Then, over his mobile comlink transceiver, he received a coded click-message from

Subi: "I double-checked security. Stomach feeling a little better."

Subi was still perfecting the security, but Noah knew it was his adjutant's nature to be overly cautious, and he appreciated that about him. It was just Subi being Subi, Noah assured himself.

Keeping his sidearm with him, Noah crawled into bed. Then, after adjusting the mattress controls to their firmest setting, he lay awake in the darkness, worrying. Many uncertainties crowded his mind for attention as he lay on his back, and his mind scanned them, pausing on each topic of concern for varying lengths of time. Gradually, his thoughts drifted to the skin changes on his arms and torso, how those areas had become rough to the touch and darker, like a smaller version of podship skin. With his hands, which had not changed yet, he felt the coarse skin on his chest, and traced the limits of the metamorphosis to one side, under the left arm. He heaved a deep sigh of resignation. Whatever was happening to him had at least slowed, and he was thankful for that. Thus far, though he had considered it many times, he had not consulted a doctor. None of them would know what he had anyway.

I am like no other person who was ever born, he thought.

Gradually the pockets of worry emptied their contents, and he drifted off to sleep. Noah dreamed about many of the women he had known in his life. In the cloud of his consciousness he heard the voices of his mother, Eunicia, and of his sister in her frail, manipulative way calling his name. Noah had loved his mother dearly and had been as devastated as his father when she died in a grid-plane crash. In contrast, his twin sister, Francella, had not seemed to care about her one way or the other. She'd only been concerned about her own needs, which prevented her from seeing anything outside herself clearly.

Now, even though he tried to prevent it, Noah saw Francella's twisted, angry face and heard her unwelcome tones as she ranted at him in a way that made him want to be anywhere else in the universe except with her. Suddenly, a more pleasant voice intervened—that of Tesh Kori, murmuring to him that she had loved him from the moment she first set eyes on him. In the peculiar chimera of his dream he thought this rang true, but he also knew that she had never actually said that to him. She seemed to care for him deeply in a way that Noah had never experienced from anyone else, but their relationship remained largely unfulfilled. Even the one sexual liaison they'd shared had been surreal and dreamlike, though she had insisted afterward that it actually had occurred.

It was like that now, as he heard other female voices close by—voices that did not seem to be coming from mouths, but instead seemed to be carried in another realm. One of them said in a discomforting tone, "After this, Watanabe, you'll sleep even more peacefully."

As if shocked out of his dream, Noah came to full awareness and opened his eyes. In the darkness, his fingers found the handle and trigger button of the ion pistol.

Across the room, he saw shadows moving. Four Human shapes, coming toward him stealthily, not making a sound, not saying anything. His finger tightened on the trigger, ready to press down. But he hesitated, uncertain of the meaning of the words he had just heard, or if this was really happening. Besides, he had proven numerous times in the past that he could not be physically harmed, at least not easily.

The corridor burst open, and the blue light of puissant pistol fire filled the room. The shadowy figures, all slender and dressed in black, dropped to the floor with anguished cries. Noah rolled off the bed on the opposite side, and crawled around for a better view.

He saw Subi Danvar just inside the doorway, with a steady

stream of MPA soldiers pouring into the room. "Secure the premises," Subi barked. "Noah? You okay?"

"I'm fine. What the hell happened?" He rose to his feet and looked at the carnage on the floor.

Princess Annyette, in a hooded black leotard, lay wounded, beside three of her sisters, also dressed in black, and motionless. Purple fluid pooled around them on the marbelite tiles and Sirikan carpets, and poison-tipped daggers lay near their hands.

"Mutatis!" Noah said.

The Annyette simulacrum looked up at him and contorted her face in hatred. Noah heard words from her clearly, but in the alternate realm that he knew Subi and the others could not hear. Her mouth did not move as she said to Noah, "Maybe we didn't get you this time, but there will be many more like us to test the limits of your mortality. You will never be able to close your eyes again."

The words meshed with what he heard in his dream-fugue. Had she whispered the earlier threat, or had he read her mind?

Then, as if giving way to an irresistible force, her body turned into a fleshy pudding, devoid of all Human qualities. Her companions, for whatever reason, remained in Human form, but bled the telltale purple of the shapeshifter race.

"Our men rescued the real sisters from a compound where they were being held," Subi said. "As for these, they've taken their story with them."

"And Hari'Adab is supposed to be our ally?" Noah said.

"I was thinking the same thing," Subi said. "We're rounding up everyone on the palace grounds now, and will force them to submit to testing. We're also searching every corner with heat sensors, looking for any living beings. This security sweep will be much more thorough than I was able to do before."

"I guess no one is ever above suspicion," Noah said. "Except for you, my friend. You have Parais d'Olor?"

"She's the first one we took into custody."

"Good. Get an immediate report off to Doge Anton, and tell him to check carefully on the boyfriend's activities. Already, Hari'Adab is being monitored, and it's a good thing we made that decision. Now, we must dig even deeper."

Subi saluted stiffly, and went about his tasks, after leaving a new guard detail to accompany Noah.

Unable to remain in his suite while the entire palace was undergoing searches and tests, Noah felt a need to be alone for a few minutes. He sensed something intruding on his thoughts, and needed to collect himself, in an attempt to assess whatever was occurring.

On impulse, he hurried up a narrow back stairway that led to the top levels of the fortresslike core of the structure. On top of the keep, he at first looked down at the ornamental gardens, which were illuminated in bright lights while his forces bustled about in their duties.

Gazing up at the night sky, he found himself unable to perceive much detail, because of the glow of lights from the ground. Then, gradually, the noises of his troops and the effect of the illumination diminished, so that he could make out star systems and the pinpoint lights of his own ships as they patrolled the air and orbital space.

At any moment, the HibAdus could break through from deep space and mount a full-scale attack on Siriki. But Noah Watanabe continued to sense something else out there that was even more perilous, and which had not yet been considered. Something that would dwarf every other danger that he or his allies had faced.

I must be ready, Noah told himself. *But for what?*

Like a man awaiting a signal from God, he stood there for minute after minute, gazing heavenward. Nothing came to him, and he felt very alone.

Almost fifteen minutes passed. Finally, knowing he needed to tend to important military duties involving the Sirikan sector, he hurried downstairs. At least he would accomplish what he could, what he knew. It was a degree of control over his surroundings, albeit a small one.

Chapter Twenty-Nine

If there ever was a time to *not* sleep, this is it. Against all barriers, physical or mental and internal or external, we must press on, reaching deep into the reservoir of our collective racial strength. There will be time enough for rest later, if anything remains of the galaxy.

—First Elder Kre'n, to departing repair teams

Out of his podship, Eshaz stood alone on a floating asteroid, having allowed his craft to drift nearby in the vacuum of space, without any Tulyan at the controls. The podship, *Agryt*, remained in telepathic contact with him in the wordless manner of such relationships, and Eshaz had every confidence that the vessel would do its part, and would remain close by. Some of the other vessels in his repair team were visible around the sector, with some of them like dots to his naked eye, and others beyond the range of his vision. But Eshaz and *Agryt* knew where all of them were telepathically, and what they were doing.

Almost a million years ago, Eshaz had piloted podships to uncounted sectors of the known galaxy, and in the normal course of his duties he had seen all manner of star systems, nebulas, asteroid belts, comets, and other heavenly formations. In those halcyon days the trips had been frequent, at a time when the Tulyan race led their fabled existence of maintaining the galactic infrastructure in the manner that the Sublime Creator originally intended. It had been Eshaz's duty to deliver a single onboard caretaking crew to various destinations. Caretaking ships and crews operated in a more predictable fashion in those days. There had been many vessels, and an air of responsibility that caused everyone to perform excellent work, without the sense of dire urgency that all Tulyans felt now.

To Eshaz, it all seemed to spiral downward when the free will granted to all galactic races altered the Sublime Creator's grand plan. Then, in a terrible series of strikes with telepathic weapons, the Parviis had taken the entire podship fleet away from the Tulyans, a loss that continued for hundreds of thousands of years. The Dark Epoch.

Now, at long last, the Liberator fleet had made a successful attack on the Parvii Fold, and podships had been returned to their rightful custodians. As a result, the excited Eshaz had an opportunity to make much more of a difference than he ever had before, even in those long-ago days when he had been so satisfied with his life and fulfilled an important ecological niche for the interconnected galaxy.

Based upon his experience and qualifications, Eshaz was being entrusted to command one of the larger repair teams. In that position he would employ his skills as part of the larger Tulyan project—in coordination with many other teams—to repair the wounded, dying galaxy. Certainly the industrious Tulyans faced a daunting task, and Eshaz realized that he and his crew could accomplish only a limited amount. All of the Tulyan teams, large and small, would need to work rapidly and efficiently, moving from one trouble spot to the next, following prioritized astronomical charts and work schedules that had been provided for them by the Council of Elders. These charts and schedules were constantly being updated, as conditions required.

Under Eshaz's sphere of responsibility, if he completed the first tier of emergency repairs, he was to move on to the next, and the next, and the next. It would require a great deal of stamina for his crews to keep going without any meaningful rest, but Eshaz—and everyone with him—had vowed to do their parts. . . .

The asteroid on which the dedicated Tulyan stood, which normally might be expected to drift or hurtle through the cosmos, was at the moment hung up on barely perceptible strands of torn and disintegrating Timeweb webbing. He knew from Tulyan laboratory reports that this was exactly the sort of damage that had been caused—or at least exacerbated—by the undercarriages of HibAdu lab-pods as they sped along the galactic infrastructure. He hoped that Noah, Anton, and Hari were having military success against the careless, predatory HibAdus, and that they were able to destroy or ground the artificial podships, preventing them from causing such widespread ecological damage.

All of the Tulyan repair teams, spread as they were around the galaxy, were exposed to HibAdu interference and possible attacks. The Tulyans had conventional and telepathic weaponry on all of their own podships, but against such formidable fighters as the HibAdus, that might prove inadequate. Thus far, Eshaz had not seen any sign of them, though other teams had reported to the starcloud that they saw HibAdu scouts, and large-scale military movements against other targets, focusing on Human and Mutati star systems. To this point, the HibAdu military forces had not gone after the Tulyan repair teams, but the Tulyans were constantly on the alert.

Now, standing on the asteroid, Eshaz opened his hands and scattered green dust onto the problem area. Then, extending his clenched fists upward, he uttered an ancient incantation designed to cure this defect.

As he waited to see if the treatment would work, Eshaz felt like an artist on a scaffold, a Michelangelo of sorts, but working on the ceiling of the galaxy instead of in the Sistine Chapel of Lost Earth. Moments passed, and to his satisfaction the asteroid began to break free, and with his alternate vision he saw the web strands reattaching themselves, healing. One task completed among many.

Agryt drifted close by, parallel to the motion of the asteroid. Eshaz leaped onto the back of the podship, and then dropped down through a hatch.

These were days without end, of moving from one crisis spot to the next, for as long as the Tulyans could sustain themselves to complete the immense tasks they had undertaken. Eshaz felt part of a larger whole, of a larger importance. He felt no fatigue and knew he never would, not as long as he maintained his focus.

Like a patient on a vast hospital bed, the galaxy kept breathing fitfully. Eshaz only hoped it was not a deathbed.

CHAPTER THIRTY

Many take credit for successes, but are nowhere to be found when it is time to assess blame.

—Anonymous

The Eye of the Swarm could not determine when or where his race had slipped onto the path of disaster, or how much he might have contributed to it personally. After the initial shock of loss, he had tried to diminish his personal responsibility for what had gone wrong, convincing himself that he had only done what other leaders before him would have done.

But he'd realized quickly that this was utter foolishness. To correct the present situation, he first had to fully admit his own culpability, and then find a way to resurrect ancient Parvii glories. As long as his people lived and were capable of breeding, the restoration of his fallen race remained a possibility, albeit a faint one.

The aftereffects of the cataclysm were all around him now, and apparent to anyone. His once-magnificent Parvii swarms—decillions of individuals—now amounted to fewer than one hundred and ninety-four thousand.

But after creating the telepathic bubble in which the remaining population could huddle without detection from outside, there had been some welcome signs of improvement. The death rate had slowed, and inside the comparative warmth of the invisible enclosure one of the latent breeding specialists was returning to consciousness at this very moment and was expected to join Yurtii, the latent war priest who had recently become aware of his ancient identity. In these two and in the five remaining latents, the future of the Parvii race hung. His people needed to fight back, but to accomplish that they first needed their numbers to increase dramatically.

And something more occurred to him now. It was important. *Next time, I will divide the swarms into independent telepathic divisions,* Woldn thought. *That could help prevent the massive die-off that we experienced. Of course, it will mean sharing my power—or at least delegating some of it—but perhaps that is important to do.*

Increasingly, it seemed to him that the old ways, while revered and magical in the collective memories of his people, might not always be best. The Parviis, he realized, had been in a long and gradual decline, and the results of their cumulative weakness now placed them on the brink of extinction.

Like a parent observing the birth of a child, Woldn watched a naked boy emerge from the protected cluster of Parviis at the core of the swarm. It was not a new birth, at least not in the physical sense, but mentally and spiritually it was entirely new. And entirely old. Through their telepathic linkage, Woldn learned the ancient name of the breeding specialist that was coming back to consciousness: *Imho.*

Again, as with the war priest Yurtii earlier, the name was at first unfamiliar to Woldn, meaning that this was not one of the most famous of the ancients. But it was someone of significance, anyway, a highly valued breeding expert.

Looking at Woldn, the child blinked his eyes and said, "Knowledge is power, but only if used properly. Otherwise, it can be a curse." His slender body trembled slightly.

"Already you are wiser than I," Woldn said with a smile. He paused, sensing an ancient stirring in the minds of the other latent breeding specialists, like psychic creatures coming out of a long hibernation.

But the other latent war priest, huddled with them, had no ancient thoughts. So far, he was only a modern boy. At least he was holding steady physically. For a time his host body had declined precipitously. But then, on the verge of death, he had rallied. Perhaps—and Woldn had no proof of this—it was because an ancient being wanted to come back. Maybe it would be one of the great war priests, as Yurtii had suggested.

"I feel the flow," Imho said, "breeding data surging into my mind, a flood of it." He paused, and his face filled with a beatific reverie.

One of the older females flew close to the boy. She wrapped a warm blue cloak around him, then guided him over to where Yurtii looked on. Woldn dared to feel a surge of hope. The two of them were of different specializations, but in ancient times war priests and breeding specialists had worked closely together, albeit in much larger numbers.

For the Parviis, the present challenge was all about numbers, and about developing them as rapidly as possible. More bodies and minds meant more power, for only in multitudes could the devastatingly violent telepathic weapons of old be resurrected.

Breeding and war, with each specialization feeding necessarily upon the other. Historically it had been true with many races, and so too with the Parviis. It was a nice balance of life and death, an exquisite concept, and truly beautiful in the application.

With renewed determination, Woldn probed telepathically to the core of the clustered Parviis, to the four latent breeding specialists and the one latent war priest there.

At long last, the second war priest began to stir, along with the other breeding specialists. . . .

CHAPTER THIRTY-ONE

We are each of us only seconds away from committing violence.

—Ancient Saying

Moments before the emergency on the mini-sub, the Hibbil had been staring at patterns of freckles and moles on the left side of Lorenzo del Velli's face, visible in cabin illumination whenever the gray-haired old man turned his head. Seated behind him, Pimyt realized that he had never noticed the patterns previously, but as the boat proceeded through murky underwater darkness, he became fixated on them.

His red-eyed gaze moved upward, along the side of the man's face and back down again. A hand came into view as Lorenzo gestured with it while speaking to one of the two Red Beret soldiers seated at the front, the larger man who was not piloting the sub. Lorenzo's hand had more flesh-fat than the Hibbil had noticed previously, and he felt saliva building in his mouth. An involuntary, anticipatory response that Pimyt had usually suppressed before, trying to put such primal urges out of his mind. But now, in this remote subterranean region of an unnamed planet, new possibilities seemed open to him. Actions he had not dared to seriously consider before, whenever he and Lorenzo interacted over the years.

Prior to the recent turn of events on the space station, Pimyt had been focused inward, on the schemes of the HibAdu

Coalition and on the important role he played in them. In conjunction with that, he'd been forced to deal with the constant demands of this difficult Human nobleman, doing so in a manner that would keep Lorenzo from noticing the Hibbil's true intentions. Playing his part with consummate skill, Pimyt had remained near the important merchant prince, poised to take him prisoner the moment the Coalition was ready to make their move.

Now, for all Pimyt knew, HibAdu forces had already made their attacks on merchant prince and shapeshifter planets. Just before the space station hurtled into this unknown realm, his military leaders had been saying that an important announcement was imminent. If the attacks had been made, or were underway now, certain opportunities might already be available to him. His gaze moved to the two soldiers at the front, especially to the heavyset one on the right who was talking with Lorenzo. Pimyt visualized blood gushing from the severed arteries of all three Humans, and their startled eyes as they looked at the vicious Hibbil and wondered what was happening to them.

I'm much faster than they realize, Pimyt thought. *In the blink of an eye, I could kill all of them.*

The moisture buildup in his mouth increased, but he forced control over himself, having second thoughts that he might not be able to pilot the sub adequately in this underground waterway. His carnivorous pleasures would have to wait. He smiled to himself, though. It had been fun letting his imagination run for a while.

Suddenly Pimyt became aware of the mini-sub shooting forward, and the engines being thrown into reverse. The pilot issued a volley of curses. Through the windshield, Pimyt saw filtered light ahead, and realized that they were back on the surface of the water again, with a very high cavern ceiling above them.

"Waterfall!" the soldier in front of him shouted.

The engines surged and tugged, but the vessel kept going forward, caught in a powerful current. The sound of the engines intensified and increased in pitch, until finally they seemed to catch hold of something. The sub went backward slowly, and veered to one side, toward the bank. On this section, the stream had become a river, and was considerably wider than their embarkation point.

As the pilot guided the craft toward a low shelf of rock on one side, Pimyt gazed in astonishment at a huge subterranean cavern that dwarfed the waterfall and the tiny vessel. The cavern appeared to be illuminated from within, with eerie, pale blue light coming from crystalline walls and stalactite deposits that hung like icicles from above. Across the waterway he saw what looked like another waterfall drop-off, undoubtedly tumbling like the nearer one into a pool somewhere far below.

The mini-sub slid up onto the rock shelf, and came to a safe stop. Relieved for the moment, they all got out of the vessel and walked around in the strange blue illumination, looking up at the luminous ceiling in wonder, gasping in awe at something they'd never seen before.

Abruptly, the rock shook around them, and stalactites began to fall from the ceiling, crashing around them on the rocky floor and splashing into the water. "Quick!" Pimyt yelled. "Back in the sub, or we'll be trapped here!"

As they ran for the vessel, a stalactite smashed down on the larger Red Beret soldier, crushing him to death. Dodging and leaping over debris, the three others hurried back to the sub. They slid the craft back into the water and boarded. Within moments, the hatch was closed and they were underway, submerging as far as they could and going back the way they had come.

To Pimyt, the return trip seemed interminable. Chunks of rock kept falling into the water, as if an enemy was dropping depth charges from above, trying to hit them. The pilot had to take evasive maneuvers, but one of the pieces glanced off the hull, sending them off course. Still, he recovered quickly, and they continued on.

Finally, the pilot confirmed their location from the instruments and surfaced at the embarkation point, in the narrow stretch of waterway. With the ground still shaking, the desperate trio—with Pimyt in the lead—scrambled out and ran up the ramp of dirt to the surface.

The Hibbil was considerably faster than his companions, which elicited a breathless reprimand from Lorenzo: "Slow down, Pimyt . . . and make sure I get out!"

Pimyt ignored him, but heard the soldier say, "I'll help you, Sire." The slender Red Beret had remained back with the merchant prince.

Sputtering in anger, Lorenzo continued up the slope.

When all three of them were at the top, the former Doge started into a harangue at Pimyt, but fell silent when the ground shook even harder, and the hole closed behind them. Over at the landing site, the shuttle hovered just above the ground, awaiting the return of the exploration team.

The shaking intensified, but the shuttle set down on the ground again anyway, where it rocked and threatened to topple over. Six soldiers jumped out and helped Lorenzo, Pimyt, and the submarine pilot onto the shuttle. Without further delay, the craft lifted into the sky.

Gazing out a porthole, Pimyt felt the engines running roughly, so that the pilot had to rev them higher to keep going up. He watched the ground shudder and change shape below. And above, where they were headed, Pimyt saw the lights of the space station flickering on and off.

Then, in a bright green flash, the space station disappeared.

CHAPTER THIRTY-TWO

The universe is the brain of God.
                    —Ancient Saying

"You boys keep your eyes open, all right?" Subi Danvar said. "Noah is worried about you." The adjutant had taken time away from his busy schedule to see Dux and Acey off as they prepared to leave the palace grounds.

"We can take care of ourselves," Acey said, sticking out his chin with determination. He and his cousin wore variweather coats that were adaptable to temperature and weather changes, and small backpacks.

They waited by the main entry gate, where Red Beret robots stood guard. Nearby, other robots and Humans looked on, waiting to talk with Subi.

The rotund man frowned. He looked up as a squadron of MPA patrol aircraft flew overhead, then said, "I'm sending someone with you. All of us think a lot of you, so we've assigned one of our machines to accompany you."

He gestured, and a small, dull brown robot approached, with green and yellow lights flashing around its faceplate. Dux noticed that some of the lights weren't working, and saw a number of dents on the body. That didn't necessarily mean anything, or it could suggest a lack of recent servicing.

"This is Kekur," Subi said. "He served with great distinction under Jimu, and he will be of great use to you."

"Is he armed?" Dux asked, noting compartments on the robot's body, where weapons might be carried.

"Of course," Subi said. "To avoid calling attention to him, he bears no military markings or indications, but he is in fact a soldier."

"We can take care of ourselves," Acey said. "We don't need a metal bodyguard."

"To the contrary, we have intelligence information that Hib-Adu remnants are still on Siriki. They're hiding out, waiting to be found by their comrades, or waiting to regroup."

"We can scout around for you, then," Dux said.

The adjutant nodded. "Right. You're still on duty. Transmit messages to us through the robot."

"I am your servant," Kekur said.

"So we're spies now," Dux said.

Acey grunted, a sound that Dux recognized as agreement.

When the robot arrived, Acey flipped open a control panel on its chest. Apparently he had noticed the same potential deficiencies as Dux. Then he said, "Okay, this will give me something to tinker with when I'm bored. I always have a few tools with me."

"I don't need any adjustment," Kekur said. The lights on his faceplate blinked faster, but some of them were still out.

"Everything will be fine as long as you follow our commands," Acey said.

"I am your servant," Kekur repeated.

"There are certain things he won't do," Subi said.

"Such as?" Dux asked.

"He has one of our enhanced security programs, so he won't follow risky commands, anything that, in his estimation, could put the two of you in increased danger."

"What if we want to override him?" Acey asked.

"Not possible," Kekur said.

"Can we still do what *we* want?" Dux asked Subi.

The robot answered. "As your servant, I may not be able to prevent you from heading into danger, but I would warn you before taking countermeasures. Then, if you insist on being foolhardy, I will do whatever I can to protect you."

"You must do so without trying to block us," Acey said with a grin.

"Only if possible," Kekur said. The faceplate lights dimmed, then went off as his transitional programming settled down.

"I guess Noah doesn't think we can do much to help," Acey said. Staring out the window of the hoverbus, he brushed a hand through his bristly black hair. "I didn't think he'd agree to let us go so easily. I mean, if we were key people, he would have begged us to stay."

Seated beside him, Dux said, "You're the one who said we're just a couple of kids and no one will miss us. Besides, we must have some value, or they wouldn't have sent Kekur to watch out for us."

The robot was seated across the aisle from them. A handful of Sirikan citizens sat in other seats, chatting nervously about difficulties they had been experiencing since the HibAdus first attacked.

"Well, cousin," Dux said, "we are young, and we have been a bit flighty in the past, jumping from one galactic adventure to another."

"We returned to the Guardians, didn't we? That means we have some staying power after all."

Dux smiled. "You surprise me, Acey. You're talking like I do." He nudged the shorter, more muscular boy. "Maybe I should play your part from now on—the aggressive one, the one who's always getting us into trouble. You can be the cerebral one."

"This time it was your idea, cousin."

Dux felt a little guilty about making the special request to see their grandmother, since the boys wanted to contribute what they could to the war effort. But they had to find out if she was all right. The old woman lived in the back country, without modern conveniences. They had no way to contact her without going to see her. She was a feisty old bird, though. . . .

"Say," Acey said. "What are you smiling about?"

"Was I? Uh, I was just thinking about the time Grandmamá chased us around her yard with a stick."

"I remember, because we accidentally ran over her vegetable garden with that aircar we stole. Boy, was she mad!"

"*We* stole? You were driving, Acey, and it was your idea to steal it. I was trying to get you to slow down and take it back."

"Nobody slows me down, buddy."

"Just wait 'til Grandmamá gets ahold of you."

Acey grimaced. "You've got a point there."

Noah stood in an opulent library that contained shimmering holobooks on simulated shelves, the personal collection of Princess Meghina. While waiting for Subi Danvar and his top military officers to report for a meeting, he scanned the titles. To his surprise, several of them were about environmental issues, and he recognized a number of the titles. A large number of other books were about animal welfare.

He recalled seeing the famous courtesan more than six months ago on the pod station where he was taken prisoner by Red Berets. Meghina had tried to prevent Francella from shooting him. The few times he had met the Princess, she had been kind to him. Now, in one of her private rooms, he felt her gentleness, her concern for the environment, for animals, and the compassion she had showed toward him.

Only half conscious of what he was doing, Noah rubbed the back of his neck, beneath the collar where his skin had been getting thick and rough. For several days now the areas of coarse skin had slowed their expansion, and thus far they had not appeared anywhere that people could easily notice. Just the day before, he had finally confided in Subi Danvar about his condition, and the adjutant had suggested that he see a doctor. Noah had refused, saying he was too busy for that, and swore him to secrecy. . . .

In the library, time seemed to slow around Noah, and his thoughts drifted. He envisioned himself out in space, at first inside a podship as it sped along a podway, a strand of galactic webbing. Then, as moments passed, he felt the irregular skin seem to cover his entire body. Presently his face merged into the flesh of the podship, and appeared on the prow of the vessel. With his own eyes and the optic sensors on the hull of the podship, he saw far into the galaxy. He was back in Timeweb.

This metamorphosis felt supremely comfortable to him, and very familiar. As moments passed, questions seeped into his mind, and he wondered if he had always been this ancient podship. If he was the oldest of spacefaring creatures, perhaps that explained why—even in Human form—he had come up with the concept of galactic ecology, of planets and star systems interconnected in one large environment.

As he surged through space, Noah suddenly felt himself buffeted, so that he could hardly remain on the podway infrastructure. He slowed way down, and then came to a stop in space.

A timestorm is coming, he thought, with a sudden awareness of information that had not been available to him previously. Timeweb didn't seem so alien to him anymore. He was part of it, and it was part of him.

Space warped and wavered around the podship, an immense flexing back and forth. Noah did all he could to remain on the webbing. Just ahead, a planet came into view, and its name surfaced in his consciousness: Yaree. It was one of the unaligned worlds, where numerous galactic races coexisted.

Beyond the planet, a jagged hole appeared in space, a spot of black-blackness, so intensely dark that it was readily visible to him. Gradually the hole shifted, grew larger, and he saw a bright flash of green light inside it.

As he stared, transfixed, Noah detected an illuminated object coming toward him from the hole in space, going at a very high rate of speed. As it came into his visual range, he realized in amazement what it was.

EcoStation! The orbital facility that had once been his, and which Doge Lorenzo had commandeered for his own purposes.

As if drawn by a magnet, the space station rushed toward Noah at an apparent speed that should have torn it apart. But it held together and drew closer. Entranced, Noah watched it, unable to move out of the way.

Just when the space station seemed about to slam into him, it suddenly slowed and floated in space, not far away. The facility, though largely intact, was badly damaged, as if it was an ocean-going vessel that had survived a hurricane. All of its modules were dented and some had split open, spilling loose contents and other parts out into the weightless void, along with bodies. Concerned, Noah guided his podship-self in that direction, to do what he could. But something resisted his forward movement and reduced his speed, like a powerful current going against him.

I think the space station was in the undergalaxy and now it's back, Noah thought, as he made slow headway.

But he realized that he knew very little about the adjacent galaxy, only that timeholes in the membrane between the two realms provided occasional glimpses. And he recalled an earlier vision, in which he had seen a small Parvii swarm hiding in the other galaxy, near the bolt hole they had used to escape from their sacred fold. Assuming the vision had been accurate, he had always wondered what had happened to them.

Now, as he drew near the space station and its widening debris field, the timehole sealed over behind them, and vanished from view. Then everything became hazy, just a wash of gray-blackness in all directions.

Noah blinked his eyes, and found himself back on Siriki, standing in the private library. He watched as Subi Danvar and other uniformed officers filed into the room for their scheduled meeting.

I'm not going crazy, Noah told himself. He had been through such paranormal shifts before, and although they never felt entirely comfortable to him, he was getting more used to them.

But he was still left with an uncountable number of unanswered questions.

CHAPTER THIRTY-THREE

War is like a lover. It lures you, embraces you, and rejects you. It lifts you up and tears you down—and just when you think you can stand no more of it, you plunge back into the fray.

—General Nirella del Velli, Supreme General of the MPA

Upon arriving at Canopa at the head of a fleet of twelve thousand podships, Doge Anton had seen Lorenzo del Velli's space station vanish into space, in a bright burst of green. One of the Tulyans with the fleet reported that it went into a time-hole.

More than a week had passed since then, during which the unopposed Liberator forces solidified their military hold on the planet. For this critical mission, the young leader had selected the best fighters and warships, and every soldier was anxious to go into battle against the enemy.

"The silence is weird," Nirella said. She and her husband stood on the bridge of the flagship *Webdancer,* looking out into orbital space and down at the world below. In the time they'd been here, there had been very few HibAdu sightings. Less than a hundred Hibbils and Adurians had been captured, and only a handful of small military aircraft. There had been no sightings of enemy lab-pods at all, though many were reported to have been in the Canopa system before the arrival of Anton's rescue force.

It was very unsettling to him. The HibAdus had used an immense fleet of podships to attack and conquer almost every Human and Mutati world. But where were all of those vessels now? He had been exchanging urgent messages with Noah at Siriki and with the robot Jimu at Dij—messages that were relayed through Tulyan webtalkers. Aside from a brief battle at Siriki when Noah arrived, the conditions were much the same at all three planets. Very few HibAdu sightings at all, and only a few hundred enemy soldiers captured in all.

At distant Dij, Human military officers and the robot Jimu were keeping a close watch over Hari'Adab, and despite the Mutati troubles on Siriki they reported no reason to suspect the Mutati leader of any form of deception. Without his knowledge, other Mutatis had schemed to assassinate Noah. Arriving at the only unconquered Mutati world, the Emir had been greeted by his people as a returning hero. They had staged parades and other accolades for him, but in a public broadcast he had asked them not to waste their energies in such frivolous ceremonies.

"We need to remain on constant alert," Hari'Adab had told them in a speech broadcast to every corner of the planet. "We can never let our guard down again."

For the moment, the three military forces were in holding patterns, ready to defend each of their remaining worlds, and awaiting further commands from Doge Anton about when to move on to other worlds and attempt to take them back from the Coalition.

Now, as Anton stood with Nirella, she said to him, "You and I are married, but I don't know if we'll ever get our lives back, at least not the way they used to be. It's the same with the MPA and Mutati worlds: even if we get them all back, they can never be what they once were, can never have the peace and serenity they once enjoyed."

"The enemy is waiting for us out there," Anton said, as he

gazed into space. "But where?"

He noticed a flare of anger on her face, which he knew was because he had not responded to her personal observation. Then she said, "Hard to say. Our scout ships are out, but they haven't found anything yet."

"We could be sitting ducks here," he said. "It hard to know the right thing to do. With the size of their forces, we don't dare break up our fleet any more. We're strongest here, and at Siriki, and at Dij. For some reason, the HibAdus couldn't conquer any of those worlds before, and now—with all the reinforcements we brought in—it will be even harder."

"You're being optimistic. They were just spread too thin, and are gathering again. I'm afraid they did this to draw us in. Like a spider with three webs."

"Could be, but we've discussed the possibilities, the odds, the options. I think the HibAdus know we commandeered more than a hundred and twenty thousand podships from the Parviis, and—if the HibAdus are watching all three of these planets—they're only seeing a total of twenty-four thousand podships. They could be wondering where the other ninety-six thousand are."

The General half smiled. "I hope you're right, and they think we're laying a trap for them, waiting to pounce with a bigger force."

"So we each wait, and wonder."

CHAPTER THIRTY-FOUR

Just as our galaxy is linked by an invisible web, so is it with our individual lives. From birth to death, we interact with one another in complex ways, never seeing the intricate strands woven around us.

—Tesh Kori, ruminations on the meaning of galactic life

Throughout the immense structure, stationary machines hummed, whirred, and clicked as they produced new instruments, robots, and robotic components. The factory had once been owned by the famous inventor Jacopo Nehr, but following his death it was no longer the property of any Human.

From his place of concealment, the tiny sentient robot identified the sounds, and knew exactly what was going on out on the floor, even though he could not see anything at all. He was immersed in darkness.

Ipsy recalled being told that Nehr had taken extra care in the design of the facility, and had refused to proceed with ground breaking or construction until the production line schematics and computerized projections were absolutely perfect. For months, Nehr had worked with industrial architects, production line designers, and robotics technicians, but they had been unable to meet his exacting standards for the production lines. He required that the lines operate at extremely high rates of speed, producing items quickly, but always of the highest quality.

One of the biggest problems facing him had been that

computer projections told him he would have to slow the lines down to get the quality of finished items that he wanted. Stubbornly, he had refused to accept this. The lines had to be fast, and everything that came out of the factory had to be absolutely perfect. He required the finest materials, with tolerances and efficiencies that the experts said were impossible.

Even though Nehr's name was tainted now, he had once been something of a fabled figure to the sentient machines. And according to legend, after months of working on the details of the factory and wrangling about how to get it functioning, Nehr had gone to bed one night feeling angry and frustrated. Three hours later, he'd sat straight up and started reciting the details, as if from a robotics program. Fortunately, he'd had the foresight to rig video recording machines up in all of the places he frequented. Even in his bedroom.

In a trancelike state, the inventor had dictated the whole thing, and had even made detailed drawings on an electronic note pad. Everything had flowed, and it had all been brilliantly correct, down to the smallest detail. Afterward, with his modifications, the computer projections showed that the manufacturing process would meet every one of his exacting standards. Soon after that, construction had proceeded and Nehr's factories became the most efficient ever devised.

For a time, as long as he held political and economic power, Nehr and his legal teams had controlled where and when the factories would be built, and all were under his ownership. However, based on what Ipsy had learned about the HibAdu Coalition from eavesdropping on a pair of Hibbils, he had now run a probability program. It told him that the Hibbils and their Adurian allies had undoubtedly constructed numerous major factories like this one elsewhere, secretly using Nehr's methods to produce war materiel. The death of the inventor would have made the task even easier.

In his dark cocoon, the robot couldn't wait to get back into action. The weapon-control box in which the little robot concealed himself was sitting on a shelf in a warehouse section designated for emergency-only replacement parts, and this particular panel might not be needed at all for a long time. Other panels like it were not breaking down in HibAdu warships, so it would take a miracle for Ipsy to make himself useful to Humans now.

During the time he had spent inside the panel, he had completed a number of additional repairs to his own internal mechanisms, so that his principal functions now worked reasonably well. But that didn't mean he could escape.

The panel had been tightly sealed from the outside, and he couldn't get out. Trapped, he could only crawl around inside.

Chapter Thirty-Five

I've always thought that there are degrees of goodness in all things, and degrees of badness, and that virtually every situation is a combination of the two. This is not to say that I am some sort of Pollyanna, that I live in a bubble of naïveté. Rather, it means that I try to see even the smallest glimmer of hope in the worst of circumstances, and the tiniest glimmer of virtue in the most vile of people. It helps me to cope.

—Princess Meghina of Siriki, private journals

This time, it was much worse.

Earlier, when the space station tumbled through the void into another star system, there had been only a few deaths, and most of the occupants had survived. Now, as Princess Meghina made her way through the corridors and rooms, she had to hold onto safety railings, since the gravitonics system was weak, and her feet floated just above the deck. It was freezing cold, with hardly any oxygen in the air, but in her augmented physical state she did not shiver, and had no trouble breathing.

Though much of the lighting system still worked, damage to the station was extensive, with gaping holes into space. Bodies of Humans and other races were strewn around the interior, floating and bumping into one another. She had to push her way through them, one horror after another—past the death stares of people she had known as patrons of The Pleasure

Palace, or as servants. In corridors and rooms, there were bodies in disarray, bouncing around in the vacuum.

Her pet dagg was missing, and the more death she encountered, the more she feared the worst for him. As she hurried around, she called his name in increasing desperation, "Orga! Orga!"

But he didn't appear, didn't bark. Meghina felt too numb to cry.

Sometimes through glax floor plates and windows, she got views past broken clouds of a gray-blue planet, far below the space station. Occasionally, something would glint down there in pockets of sunlight, silvery flashes suggesting that there might be manmade structures or other objects there. It gave her some hope, some *connectedness* to living things. But to exactly what, she did not know.

After searching one module deck and shouting for anyone who might remain alive, she encountered no one. There were still many more modules and decks to search, but she was likely to encounter even more fatalities in the other areas, which were much more densely inhabited than this one, where she and Lorenzo had apartments and other facilities for their private enjoyment. The very thought of the catastrophe nearly overwhelmed her, but she drew strength within, and continued on. She was sure that thousands of passengers had died from lack of oxygen, or had been hurtled to their deaths into deep space.

Gradually, the soles of her shoes began to touch the deck, and at the end of one corridor she found a new module where the gravity system functioned better, an area that contained no bodies. As she entered the module, however, the main door to the corridor slammed shut behind her, and she couldn't get it back open. The wall controls didn't function when she tapped the pressure pads, or when she tried to use override commands.

She was cut off from the rest of the space station.

"Can anyone hear me?" she shouted in desperation. "Is anyone alive?"

But Princess Meghina sensed that she was all alone, and very likely the last survivor onboard. With her elixir-enhanced physical condition, she did not need oxygen to breathe, and could not die. But what a terrible fate this would be for her, like a prisoner condemned to solitary confinement for eternity.

She stared out one of the large viewing windows into space, but saw only floating death out there. Grimly, she sat on a window seat, positioning herself so that she didn't have to look through any of the windows at the macabre graveyard outside. It was a sea of death out there. She wondered how much it had to do with strange rumors she had heard about cosmic deterioration, somehow tied to what Noah Watanabe and his radical environmentalists referred to as galactic ecology, some sort of connectivity between wide-ranging star systems. Though she had no reason to dislike Noah, and rather admired him for his independence, many of his ideas had always sounded far-fetched to her. But what if he was right after all? What else could explain the wild, perilous trips this space station had taken through space?

From her earliest years, Princess Meghina had been immersed in currents of change. Born a shapeshifter, she had not liked her natural Mutati form, and had always longed to be Human instead. In her early teens she had altered her bodily appearance to look the way she preferred, the guise of a beautiful blonde Human woman. Despite intense pressures from Mutatis, she kept the alteration in place for so long that her cellular structure actually locked into that appearance. Afterward, she could not have changed back, or into anything else, if she had wanted to. But that was no trouble from her perspective; she had always hated being a Mutati anyway.

Shunned by her family and Mutati society, she had escaped in one of the regularly scheduled podships that used to travel among the star systems, and she had gradually merged into Human civilization on the planet of Siriki, without revealing who she really was. Her new life had presented challenges. Wanting to start out at the same approximate age she had been as a Mutati—thirteen years old—she'd had to apply makeup carefully in order to take years off the age she had chosen to make herself look, which was of a Human woman of around thirty.

Fortunately, she had selected a beautiful, though neutral, face that, with a little clever application of skin tints and other products, could easily conceal its apparent age. Rather like that of a doll. Perhaps from her background as a shapeshifter who was accustomed to modifying her appearance, she proved to have a flair for applying treatments to her skin, and for selecting hair styles and clothes that made her look like a teenager. At a glittering costume ball, she met the powerful Doge Lorenzo del Velli, and soon he succumbed to her considerable charms. She became his consort, and he made her a Princess of the Realm. Then—only a short time after they met—he married her.

In that lofty and enviable position, Princess Meghina of Siriki had become one of the most powerful noblewomen in the Merchant Prince Alliance, even though she was not actually Human. Through clever subterfuge, she had falsified a series of pregnancies, making it look as if she had given birth to seven daughters. In reality, she had obtained each of the Human babies through surrogates, and a carefully woven tapestry of lies and payoffs.

Ultimately, Meghina found herself immersed in even more changes, after she consumed an elixir and gained immortality—as did the four Humans and the Salducian. In that widely publicized event, she and the others became famous and were considered the luckiest of people in the galaxy, like lottery winners. But through intrigues against her by Francella Watanabe and others, Meghina's hidden identity became known to the public. This had tilted the political balance against Lorenzo, and he had been forced out of office. Through it all, he had shown strength that she hadn't known he had, and he'd remained loyal and protective toward her. He had also adapted to a life of business instead of politics, focusing on constructing and promoting The Pleasure Palace, his orbital gambling casino.

In return, Meghina had remained devoted to him. Of course she'd still had her dalliances with other noblemen, and he'd done the same with an assortment of wealthy ladies. It was all part of the social circles in which the two of them ran. But they developed a new sense of understanding between them, and a mutual respect.

Now as she sat in her confined module, she worried about Lorenzo. He'd gone down to an unknown world to explore it, and had not returned. While he was gone, everything went upside down, and the space station had vaulted through space to yet another planet in another unknown solar system.

Hours passed in her confinement. Finally, hearing a thump behind her, she hesitated at first, not wanting to look at something grisly, a body out there bumping up against the space station. Then she heard another thump, followed by what sounded like knocking on the window plate.

Trembling, Meghina stood, and turning slowly, she looked through the window. To her amazement, she saw five people outside, their faces illuminated by lights from the space station. All of them wore jet packs but no spacesuits, and she quickly figured out why. These were the other elixir-immortals, including the Salducian, Kobi Akar, and a young Human woman she'd always liked, Betha Neider.

Meghina felt a surge of hope, but shouted, "I can't get out!"

At first they looked perplexed. Then one of the Humans—a

corpulent man named Llew Jarro, nodded and mouthed the words, "I understand."

Soon his companions understood as well. They went away for several moments, then returned with a long girder that had broken loose from the space station. It looked odd for them to be handling such a large object, but they moved it around like an oversized toothpick in the weightlessness of space. After taking it several hundred meters from the space station, they turned on their jet packs to full power, shooting blue light from them, and surged toward Meghina at a high rate of speed.

Almost instinctively, though perhaps she didn't need to, Meghina ducked out of the way. The beam slammed into the window and made a spider web crack in the glax, but did not penetrate. Back they went for another try, and another, and yet another. In zero gravity, she thought they might be moving the stranded space station. Finally, they broke through the window, creating an opening that was large enough for Meghina to swim through, into space.

For several moments, she floated and swam out there in the noiseless void. At first it was colder to her than in the space station, but as moments passed, it did not bother her at all. Except for light from the station it was dark where they were, with the sun hidden by the planet.

Then Jarro gave her a jet pack. "Manned maneuvering unit," he explained as he helped her into it. His words made no sound to her ears, but she read his lips.

The Salducian pointed down at the planet with one of his crablike hands, and then rocketed toward it, leaving a streak of blue light behind him. His five companions followed.

As they entered the atmosphere, Meghina began to hear sounds and saw orange sparks of heat dancing around her, but felt none of it, due to an electronic shield generated by the jet pack. When they penetrated the cloud layer, Meghina made out the twinkling lights of a city below, with bridges across a river and large buildings. From the unique layout she realized that this was without question the city of Okk, capital of the unaligned world of Yaree. In what seemed like only one of her incarnations, she had traveled widely as a "Human" noble-woman, both on her own and with Lorenzo. In one of their business trips together, they had led a trade delegation to this mineral-rich world, to set up a commercial arrangement. The local ruler, a tall Ilkian named Wan Haqro, had been an attrac-tive humanoid, with piercing blue eyes. He was not, however, a merchant prince, and by strict custom did not qualify for her attentions as a courtesan.

Now, to her alarm she saw the blue light of Akar's MMU pack flicker off below her as his power pack failed, and he began to drop like a stone. Then the same thing happened to Jarro, and to the others. Meghina's jet pack was the last to shut off. In a matter of moments, all six of them were tumbling toward the planet, in free fall.

The last thought Meghina had before blacking out was that this would be a true test of their immortality.

They crashed into buildings, hit motor vehicles and trees, and slammed into the ground. The carnage of their broken bod-ies was spread over portions of a four-block area.

CHAPTER THIRTY-SIX

Events occurred in the past that we cannot begin to imagine.

—Anonymous

Away from the Parvii Fold, Woldn was out of his comfort zone. As he led his small swarm out onto the podways, he was very nervous. Less than a hundred and ninety-four thousand individuals remained in his entire race, a proud people that once counted their numbers in the decillions. Not so long ago, Parvii swarms had been in every sector of the known galaxy, and the Eye of the Swarm had been in telepathic contact with them. They had been his distant eyes and ears, constantly reporting to him. Now he felt like a blind, deaf man, stumbling around in a vast chamber of stars, never knowing where his enemies or other perils were.

He knew it would be safer to remain back at the telepathic bubble, where all five breeding specialist latents had come to life and were beginning their important work of increasing the population. But Woldn had moved the bubble to a remote galactic sector, stationing only a small number of guards inside with the breeding specialists, who had come back to awareness along with the two war priests. The breeding specialists were already using genetic materials to produce future generations of Parviis. Before leaving, Woldn had been pleased to see three thousand Parvii embryos in incubation. Only an infinitesimal number by the standards of his race, but a beginning nonetheless.

It had been necessary to go back to the oldest of methods, all but starting over as a race. As part of that ancient formula for survival and advancement of the species, he needed podships, even if he could only capture a few and build from there.

Now Woldn stationed his mini-swarm along one of the main podway routes, waiting for ships to pass this way, so that he could overwhelm and capture them. He had just enough followers to commandeer one ship at a time, and when the first one was safely tucked away, they could move on to another, and another. His near-term goals were humble, but he had to make the effort. He could not just stand by and watch his race go extinct.

In the two millennia of his lifetime, Woldn had flown with his swarms to the farthest reaches of the known galaxy. In those days, Parviis had controlled a vast fleet of podships, a virtual monopoly that made them the most powerful and influential of all galactic races. The coin of the Parvii realm had not been monetary; rather it had been the extent of their domination over other galactic civilizations, and the degree that those peoples depended upon them for podship service throughout the galaxy.

Now, however, the Eye of the Swarm found himself at the bottom of a spiral that had been spinning out of control. As much as Woldn hated to admit it, Noah Watanabe and the Tulyans had been right: the galactic infrastructure *had* been crumbling, decaying moment by moment. In the unique past position of the Parviis, swarming and piloting podships, Woldn's people had seen the subtle signs of decomposition for centuries, but had not wanted to admit what was really happening. Because to admit it meant only one thing: that they needed to allow the Tulyans to go back to their ancient tasks of maintaining the galaxy, of using their arcane methods to keep everything going behind the scenes. The Parvii leader had hoped it was just a natural cycle, and that it would eventually reverse itself. But the hoped-for reversal had not taken place.

Long ago, eons before Woldn was ever incubated and born, an ancient Eye of the Swarm scored a huge military victory against the Tulyans, and took the podship fleet away from them. In that single event, more than one hundred thousand sentient Aopoddae fell into the Parvii domain. Assuming the mantle of leadership long afterward, Woldn had just continued the old ways, using the might and power of the swarms to keep the podships going on their regular routes. He and other Parvii leaders before him had always considered themselves generous for continuing this tradition, providing it free of charge to all races—except Tulyans had been monitored in their travels and kept from regaining the ships.

But other races think of us as selfish, Woldn thought. *They misunderstand us.*

"Podship coming," one of his followers said, transmitting the thought to him from close range. It was Vorlik, one of the two resurrected war priests. Though he'd reclaimed his old knowledge later than the other war priest (Yurtii), this one was the most famous of the pair. Vorlik had been among the most ferocious and successful of the ancients, and with each passing moment he seemed to increase in aggressiveness and hatred of outside races.

Now, through his Parviis, Woldn heard the Aopoddae coming. He sent the signal for readiness. He could tell that it was a strong wild pod, one that had never been captured.

At precisely the right moment, more than one hundred and ninety thousand Parviis swarmed around the podship as it sped along. For several seconds, the Parviis kept up, but they didn't have the energy to continue or to penetrate into the sectoid chamber, and they soon fell back without the prize.

To Woldn's dismay, only a few of his people even got neuro-toxin stingers into the thick hull of the podship, and the effect had not slowed the big, dumb creature at all. It just kept going.

Even with this failure, Woldn reminded himself that his people were recovering. In concert, they could fire telepathic energy blasts—not very large ones, but perhaps enough to stop a podship. However, Woldn hesitated to use that technique. He didn't want to harm or kill any of the sentient spacecraft, and also feared setting off a reaction among all of the Aopoddae that would make them harder to capture. No, he should only utilize the traditional ways, pursuing podships at high rates of speed and using neurotoxins.

The Parviis waited for another ship. Hours passed. It wasn't like the old days, when podships were constantly going this way and that. Finally one appeared, and again the tiny humanoids gave chase. This time, they did just as poorly. Their stingers, which had always drugged podships in the past, weren't having any effect at all, and the flying speed of the Parviis—always faster than podships before—barely enabled them to keep up, and for only short distances.

In addition to the practical importance of recapturing podships, Woldn had gone on this hunt with another motiva-tion. He had hoped to restore the confidence of his people and reduce their collective stress. But there had been an opposite ef-fect. He sensed fear and panic in the ranks.

The Eye of the Swarm was deeply troubled, knowing his race must find a way to recuperate faster, or it would vanish entirely—a complete colony die-off. Too many galactic perils could kill them all if they weren't strong.

He searched his memory, and—telepathically—the minds of everyone in the swarm. According to the secret knowledge of his people, known only to the most elite groups, the Parviis of ancient times had some sort of a connection with the Adurians. He did not know the details, nor did any of his followers. All information was lost in the dusty archives of Parvii racial memory. But he'd been thinking about going to see the Adurians, in an effort to find out what, if anything, they knew. This podway had been selected with that idea in mind; it was on the way to the Adurian homeworld.

As Woldn hovered in space, looking in dismay at the swarm, he became aware of two strong intellects, so close to him that their brain waves lapped against his own thoughts and almost penetrated them against his will.

Turning, he saw both of the war priests dressed in the black robes of their cult, the stocky man Vorlik and the hairless boy Yurtii. They trembled in anger as they hovered there, demanding entrance into his thoughts. Secretly, he thought they might break through even without his permission, an unsettling realization. Nothing like that had ever happened to him before, and he found the possibility irritating, almost unnerving.

In the airless, soundless void, Vorlik's lips moved as he transmitted his thoughts to Woldn. It was one of the Parvii methods of speaking in soundless space. "You summoned us?" Vorlik said.

"No."

"We sensed an urgency in your energy waves," Yurtii said. "Something you are about to do."

"How do you know that?"

"We are war priests. For the survival of our species, we sense danger."

"Danger? My thoughts are not dangerous!"

"That depends on what they are," Vorlik said. A stocky Parvii with a ruddy, elfin face, he looked very worried.

"Well if you must know, I intend to go and visit the Adurians, to learn more about the ancient connection between our races."

"That old rumor," Yurtii said, his words edged in scorn. "To what purpose do you seek this information?"

"Do you have any details on this in your own memory archives?" Woldn asked.

The two war priests shook their heads.

"Then we'll go and find it another way."

"That is not a good idea," Vorlik said. He scowled.

"Why do you say that?"

"It is our instinct," Yurtii said.

"Well, my instinct says otherwise, and I am the Eye of the Swarm. I have a strong feeling that the path to our salvation goes through the Adurian homeworld."

"Are you sure it isn't the path to our destruction?" Vorlik asked.

"Do not be insubordinate!" Woldn transmitted a psychic command to the swarm, and instantly they grouped into a formation, ready to follow him wherever he led them. The two war priests, after hesitating for several moments, joined them.

A flicker of doubt passed through Woldn's mind, but he suppressed it, and concealed it from the others.

Like flying insects, they sped along the podway. Seconds later, the Parviis darkened a patch of sky over the main Adurian world, and dropped down into the largest city, a sprawling, dusty metropolis. Having flown over the area numerous times, Woldn knew the way, even though he'd never set down on the planet before.

As the swarm hovered over the huge capital rotunda, Woldn heard alarm sirens and klaxons going off.

He led the others through open windows and vents in the rotunda, streaking past startled dignitaries and workers, who looked up at them and pointed. The immense central chamber was filled with the insectoid Adurians, who were having some sort of a government meeting. One of them had been giving a speech to the gathering. But he stopped, and stared in alarm at the swarm covering the dome and the high, ornamental ceiling.

Separating from the others, Woldn flew down to the speaker, and—hovering like a bee—he spoke into a microphone on his lapel. "I am the Eye of the Swarm," he said, "leader of the Parvii race. We come in peace."

"And why have you come in peace?" the speaker asked. A wiry insectoid, he glared at Woldn with bulbous eyes. An electronic nameplate on the lapel of his suit read *VV UNCEL*.

"In ancient times, Parviis and Adurians worked closely together," Woldn said. "I have come to discuss ways that we might do so again."

"In *ancient* times?" Uncel said. "What are you talking about?"

"It is part of our oral tradition," Woldn said. "Long ago, our races worked together."

"In what ways?" asked one of the Adurians out in the audience.

"Swat him like a fly!" someone shouted.

"Details are sketchy," Woldn said, ignoring the threat. "Nonexistent, I must admit. I thought that someone here might have the answer."

"Is this just curiosity?" Uncel asked, "or is what we hear true, that the Humans and Tulyans gave you a good thrashing?"

"That is true, I must admit. But look how we bypassed your defensive systems to get in here. We can slip into places where other galactic races cannot go. Despite our reduced strength, we Parviis still have unique powers."

"That may be," Uncel said, nodding. He pursed his lips, seemed to be thinking.

Another Adurian male stepped up to the podium. Deferring to him, Uncel stepped to one side. "I am Chief of Security," this one said. Looking up, he shouted, "All of you are under arrest."

Woldn heard mechanical noises, and before he could do anything, metallic plates slid over all windows and doors of the chamber. Only a few thousand of his sentries remained outside.

"How dare you?" Woldn shouted.

"How dare you come here uninvited?" a peculiar female voice echoed, through speakers all around the chamber. "I am Warlord Tarix, and your fate rests in my hands."

"I stated our purpose honestly," Woldn said. Panic filled him. The security chief swatted at him with an open hand, but Woldn flew beyond his reach.

"Bring in the bug spray," someone yelled.

Laughter pealed through the assemblage.

Flying as high as he could in the huge dome, Woldn rejoined thousands of his followers there, and hovered between his two war priests. "Our telepathic weapons are not strong enough to deal with them," Woldn said to them, keeping his voice low.

"Not like before," Yurtii said. "We aren't ready for a big fight yet."

"We told you not to come here," Vorlik said.

"Don't lecture me!"

Vorlik glowered down at the Adurians who were looking up at them and pointing. Then he said, "Maybe we should concentrate our energy and knock a few of them down, as a display of power."

"I don't think so," Woldn said. "That could only provoke them to extreme violence, and we don't want that."

Unknown to the frustrated, enraged Parviis, the Adurians in the chamber had been discussing their own involvement in the Hib-Adu Coalition, a military organization that was totally unknown to Woldn or his minions. Overseeing the meeting from their tintplax private boxes around the chamber, the HibAdu triumvirate—Coreq, Enver, and Tarix—had been surprised at the ease of entry by the Parvii swarm, and by their contention that an ancient relationship existed between Parviis and Adurians.

Any ancient connection between these races, if it ever existed, had been lost a long, long time ago. Nonetheless, seeing the potential value of the Parviis to the HibAdu cause—as spies or as swarms to capture natural podships—the triumvirate ordered the Adurian scientists to investigate Woldn's claim. . . .

CHAPTER THIRTY-SEVEN

> How do we measure the accomplishments of our lives? By
> this do we measure our happiness, or our despair.
>
> —Anton Glavine, *Reflections*

At his palatial military headquarters on Siriki, Noah was at
times put off by the grandiosity around him. Knowing that
some people lived quite primitively in the back country on this
world, it seemed strange to him that anyone could live this way,
in such contrasting fashion. He'd observed similar disparities
on other merchant prince planets, of course, but never had he
seen any royal residence more spectacular than the Golden
Palace.

By all accounts, though (including his own personal
observation), Princess Meghina seemed to be a good person,
and caring in her own way. She'd tried to help Noah in the
past, and at her private zoo she kept rescued animals that had
previously been at risk, and some endangered as species. There
were even a number of animals here from Lost Earth and other
planets that no longer existed.

In all, Noah could not say with any certainty that the famous
courtesan was profligate or selfish. Certainly, the rumors of her
extravagant monetary demands on the former Doge had seemed
to be of that nature, since she constantly sought to have new
additions put on the palace. And this afternoon, as Noah walked
through the south wing of the structure and made his way out

to the manicured grounds, he found plenty of evidence of construction activities—work that had been halted when the HibAdus made their presence known. But he suspected that much of that had been for show, because it was expected of her, and that she had not sought to improve her image by publicizing her worthwhile activities.

Beyond a stand of Sirikan elms, he barely saw one of the conventional fences of her large zoo, and a giraffe reaching up to eat something from a tree. From that direction, he also heard simian-like jungle sounds, and the loud chattering of birds.

In recent days, some of the palace contractors had begun filtering back to the security gates, asking if they could resume their work. Subi Danvar had accepted some of them, after running them through checks and tests, confirming their loyalty. He had also coordinated the talents of those who passed his rigid screening process, focusing their labors toward military installations instead of what they'd been doing previously. Now they were armoring buildings, improving underground bunkers, and setting up layers of defense.

Trying to be an optimist, Noah wanted to think the best about Princess Meghina, and now he worried about her welfare. According to intelligence reports, she and the other five "immortals" who had benefited from Francella's Elixir of Life had been on the space station that he'd seen making wild trips through space. The last time he saw the station, it appeared to be seriously damaged, making him wonder if anyone could have possibly survived such tremendous perils, or if anyone remained onboard.

He scowled, remembering an APB nehrcom report that sat on his desk concerning the Salducian diplomat in her group of immortals, Kobi Akar. A woman had filed a formal charge that he'd molested her twelve-year-old daughter. According to her claim, the crime occurred on the space station, while it orbited

Canopa. The woman had been a kitchen employee of Doge Lorenzo's gambling casino, living there in servant's quarters with the girl. If the charge against the Salducian was true, and he was still alive, Noah hoped justice could still be served on him.

On distant Yaree, crowds gathered around the main hospital, awaiting word on the remarkable visitors. This was a melting-pot world, so a wide variety of races mingled together in the street and blocked traffic, even Humans and fleshy Mutatis standing side by side. Here, the races generally got along quite well. There were exceptions, fights and murders involving personality disputes and crimes, but usually they had nothing to do with race.

Like gods who lost their ability to fly, the visitors had fallen from the sky three nights ago. Sirens screaming and lights flashing, emergency vehicles had rushed to the various sites of impact. Medical crews had recovered the bloody, horribly broken bodies—all of which had remained remarkably intact, despite the great heights from which they had fallen. That had been one of the first oddities that anyone noticed. But there had been more to come.

At first, they had all appeared to be dead, and had been taken to the morgue. Then, in spectacular fashion, all six of them had come back to life on the slabs. Looking more dead than alive, they had sat up one by one like zombies, and looked around. Impossibly, the corpses then began to shamble around the morgue and to reshape their appearances, repairing broken bones, facial damage, and grievous head wounds. Cameras recorded much of it, and millions of Yareens had seen it on holocasts.

Hospital gowns soon replaced the victims' own clothing, and gradually their wounds had begun to heal even more. Word had it that their improvements had little or nothing to do with medical attention. Rather, it was something that came from inside their bodies, from their cellular structure. Four of the "space people," as they were being called, seemed to be Human, while one was a Salducian. Yet another—a blonde female—appeared to be Human, but had bled Mutati purple. That, along with the fact that there were six members of the group, gave the authorities clues and suspicions about their identities, and some of the populace arrived at the same conclusion.

In the crowd, names were murmured, and one in particular. "Princess Meghina of Siriki . . ." Could it possibly be her? The name of Noah Watanabe was also mentioned as a possibility for one of the men, because he was rumored to have achieved immortality, though perhaps in a slightly different fashion from the others. But if Noah was among them, there should be seven, not six.

Beneath a warm midday sun, a hospital spokesman stood at the top of the main entrance stairway, preparing to address the tightly packed crowd. A rotund Kichi man with a thick white beard, he adjusted a microphone on his lapel, cleared his throat.

"I am pleased to report that all six of the patients are recovering well. They are eating and walking normally, and almost all of their injuries have healed." He paused. "It is as many of us suspected. These are the people who consumed a wondrous elixir that made them virtually indestructible. One of them is indeed Princess Meghina of Siriki."

"And Noah Watanabe?" someone shouted.

"He is not with them. One of the Humans in the group, however, confirmed something we have heard in the past—that Noah's blood runs in their veins, from the elixir they consumed. An elixir that was prepared from his own blood."

The crowd murmured. Truly, no one on the planet had ever

received visitors of this nature. This would be written of in the history holos for centuries to come.

The government of Yaree was fiercely independent and militaristic. The people were also insular and xenophobic despite their racial mixture, identifying themselves as Yareens above anything else. They did not trust outsiders, or outside cultures. The Hib-Adus, apparently knowing how tough they were, had not even tried to attack them. In an out-of-the-way sector of the galaxy, Yaree was also virtually off the MPA and Mutati Kingdom radar screens.

The Prime Leader of the planet, Wan Haqro, had remembered meeting Princess Meghina during her earlier visit with a trade delegation. This time, the tall Ilkian man greeted her in the austere sitting room outside her hospital room. "I have arranged for you to leave immediately," he told her, after refusing her invitation to sit and speak with her.

"I do not wish to leave yet," she said, rising to her feet. She wore an elegant green brocade dress now, which had been brought to her. "There are matters to attend to on the space station." She nodded toward the ceiling, indicating the general direction of the damaged orbiter.

"We will tend to all of that," Haqro said, tersely. "You will depart tomorrow."

Her voice became chilly. "Headed where? By what manner of transport?"

"To your homeworld, Siriki. I do this as a courtesy."

Hearing the destination, she arched her eyebrows in surprise.

"It is quite simple to get you there, really," he said. "We have a number of laboratory-produced podships that we purchased from an Adurian on the black market, and we are using them to run our own trade routes. You have heard of the war, of course?"

"Of course. Humans and Mutatis have been at each other's

throats for a long time."

"I do not speak of that. From what I understand, you may have been out of the information loop for a good while. While you were away, a secret alliance of Hibbils and Adurians attacked all Human and Mutati worlds, and conquered the vast majority of them. Only Siriki and one other planet remain in the Merchant Prince Alliance, while the Mutati Kingdom has a single remaining planet."

"My God!" she said.

"To counter the aggression, your merchant princes have formed an alliance with Mutatis and with Tulyans."

"This is indeed surprising. You are aligned with our enemies, then? The Adurians?"

"Certainly not. We are neutral, and will trade with anyone. It is only because of a business relationship that I return you to Siriki on an Adurian-made ship."

"If what you say is true, I must leave immediately."

"It is already arranged, My Lady." The Ilkian bowed stiffly, and left.

In a matter of hours, Princess Meghina and her five companions stepped off a Yareen lab-pod, onto Sirikan soil. Moments before, there had been a tense stand-off in the skies over Siriki, when the podship entered its airspace. Fortunately, the Yareen pilot had state-of-the-art communications equipment aboard, and with it he identified the passengers, and the purpose of the arrival.

For a few moments, Meghina and the other immortals had wondered if they would have to arrive there the same way they'd set down on Yaree, falling out of the sky. But that had proved unnecessary, and the landing had gone well. Now, looking up, she saw that the lab-pod was being blocked from takeoff by military craft that hovered overhead.

A throng of officers and soldiers, in both MPA and Guardian uniforms, stood waiting for her on the landing pad. As Meghina reached the bottom of the egress ramp, soldiers rushed past her and boarded the lab-pod.

"See here!" the Yareen pilot exclaimed as he was led out of the ship. "You can't treat me in this manner." He and a dozen other Yareen citizens of varying races were taken into custody.

From the midst of officers on the landing pad, Noah Watanabe marched forward, in a green-and-brown Guardian uniform. "Hold them for questioning," he ordered, "and take this ship in for analysis."

Coming face to face with Meghina, he said, "Welcome home, Princess."

"Thank you."

"We found it necessary to occupy your palace for our headquarters. You will note other changes as well."

"I have heard about the war. I am here to help."

"Good." He looked past her. Seeing a Salducian among those who had disembarked from the lab-pod, he pointed to him and asked, "Is that Kobi Akar?"

"It is."

"Then I will have to place him under arrest."

She raised her eyebrows. "For what?"

Noah told her, and as he spoke, her face darkened. "I've wondered about him," she said. "Very well. But who shall judge him?"

"It is a Canopan charge. I suspect that they will want him to be brought back on the next military flight."

She nodded. "I see."

Speaking to an aide, Noah ordered the diplomat's arrest, then stood with Meghina and watched while it was carried out. As he was being taken into custody, the Salducian shouted protestations and threats of political repercussions. Finally two

MPA soldiers gained control over him, and led him away.

As Noah walked with Meghina toward a waiting hovercar, he said, "There are other serious problems, Princess. This morning, we received a report of a mountaintop breaking off and disappearing into space in a green flash of light."

"Here on Siriki?" she asked, her voice alarmed.

"Unfortunately, yes, and we're getting emergency nehrcom messages about bizarre events on Canopa as well. On both planets, land is breaking off and disappearing—a mountaintop here, a peninsula there, an island. . . . Some scientists and curious citizens who went to investigate have disappeared, too, or have reported seeing green flashes as huge chunks of dirt and rock vanish. More disturbances are occurring in deep oceans and lakes . . . and water levels are fluctuating wildly." He paused, and his breath came in shallow bursts, as if he were running from something, at least in his mind. "So far on Siriki, it is only happening in remote regions, but we are on the alert here, too."

"What is causing it?"

"I have much to tell you, dear Lady. The entire galaxy is in chaos, and what we are experiencing here is just part of it. On a more personal note, two of my most loyal young Guardians—a pair of teenage cousins—are in the danger zone on Siriki. We're sending a rescue mission to find them. Hopefully, still alive."

Gesturing back at her companions, Meghina said, "I have much to tell you, as well. We are the six immortals who took the elixir. For what it's worth, we seem to be indestructible."

"I have the same condition," Noah said, "and I'm not sure what good it does against the tremendous odds we all face."

"To live forever might not be the best thing," she said, somberly.

CHAPTER THIRTY-EIGHT

We are dispatching web repair crews to each galactic
disaster zone as quickly as possible. It is an overwhelming
task, but through all of this adversity we must maintain a
positive face, especially when interacting with our allies. It
would not be in our interest—nor that of any other galactic
race—for us to spread pessimism.
             —Confidential dispatch, Tulyan Council of Elders

In his natural fleshy state, the Mutati left his private quarters on
the flagship and made his way forward. There was a matter he
needed to take care of.

Hari'Adab had not been pleased with a number of things,
among them the fact that he and his girlfriend Parais had been
forcibly separated. Though Doge Anton had seemed pleasant
enough in their meetings, he had nonetheless ordered this action against the two lovers. On one level, Hari understood the
decision, since Humans and Mutatis had long been mortal
enemies. But on another, more personal level, he hated it, and
despised the Humans who had done it to him. Not hatred in
the psychotic, destructive sense his father had felt, but the young
Doge's action showed a lack of respect for Hari's status as the
Mutati leader, and a lack of trust.

There had also been the matter of the fake daughters of
Princess Meghina, the Mutati infiltrators. Hari had not known
about that in advance, and could only surmise that it was a plan

his father had set in motion before his death—or which some hard-core Mutati fanatics had fostered afterward. Both he and Parais had proved their innocence in the matter, and had been restored to a degree of freedom, although it still involved strict controls and oversight.

He sighed. In the present circumstance, Humans and Tulyans had the upper hand, and perhaps it should be that way. His own father, and a long line of Zultans before him, had caused a lot of damage . . . and that could not be repaired overnight.

On the regular courier trips between Dij and Canopa, at least, Hari and Parais had been permitted to exchange personal messages . . . transmittals that were undoubtedly checked by censors and xenocryptologists. At least she had reported signs of progress, because Noah Watanabe had said on several occasions that he trusted her, and that he would talk to Doge Anton about getting her assignments that were befitting of her station and her talents.

That was something, anyway.

The Emir took a gray, black-veined stairway to an upper level. It always amazed him to see the living spaceship around him, with its slightly pulsing walls and protruding surfaces, and the way it sometimes altered itself to fit the needs of the passengers.

Initially, Hari had been irritated by the presence of the "military chaperones" that were sent along with him on the mission to Dij. There had been moments of stress whenever he tried to assert himself with them, testing the limits of his freedom and authority. A number of Human MPA military officers had been assigned to him, including mid-level chetens, starcaps, and even two vice-generals, but for the most part they seemed to cooperate with him. To an extent. They often had to go off somewhere by themselves and obtain permission to follow "orders" that Hari gave to them, but invariably they came back and agreed to do as he wished, with only a few minor modifications.

In the weeks they had been together on this mission, Hari had gotten to know, and like, many of the officers and soldiers. The robots, however, were a different matter, and quite irritating. Nothing he wanted done about them could be handled through the Human officers. Everything had to go through the captain of the sentient machines, a black, patched-together robot named Jimu. That one seemed to have more than one screw loose, and to make matters worse, he reported directly to Doge Anton. Having been assigned to Hari's flagship, Jimu was always there, studying Hari with glowing yellow eyes that alternately dimmed and brightened in a peculiar, unsettling fashion. Usually, Hari tried not to think about him, but that was not always possible. Jimu had a peculiar way of insinuating himself into situations.

It was happening right now, in fact, as Hari and the robot stood face to face on the command bridge of the flagship.

"Now see here," the Emir said. "I don't deserve to be treated this way."

"You are a Mutati." The mechanical words were delivered in a particularly flat tone, even for a robot.

"I want to inspect other worlds now," Hari said. It was the subject of their latest dispute, a debate that had been going on all morning. "We'll leave half the force to watch over Dij, and take the rest with us."

"The fleet cannot be divided."

"But I'm making perfect sense. I discussed it with Vice-General Dressen, and he seemed to agree with my assessment."

"I assume he explained the line of authority to you?"

"Yes, yes. Technically he outranks you, but on this mission you report directly to Doge Anton, just as he does."

"And I have been ordered that the fleet is not to be divided.

If the Vice-General disagrees with that, he can take it up with the Doge himself."

"He already has, as you well know—and the Doge is taking your side, though I can't figure out why. But if you would only listen to reason. My idea is our best course of action."

"You are a Mutati."

"Damn you, stop saying that! We are allies now, so the racial tag means nothing."

"The fleet cannot be divided."

"All right, damn it! Then I want to take all of it to other worlds, on an inspection tour. There's obviously no action for us here."

"The enemy watches our every move, and responds."

"Dij already held out against them. We're not needed here anyway."

The robot's eyes flashed. "It's not known how large a force the enemy committed to Dij in the last battle. You could be making a tactical mistake."

"There are many other important Mutati worlds that I'm concerned about. I must do whatever is necessary to rescue them."

"This can be done, if the fleet is kept intact."

"Yes, yes. By nightfall, I want to set course for Uhadeen, one of our most important military strongholds. Apparently it has fallen, but I intend to change that."

"By nightfall," the robot agreed. "We leave nothing behind."

After they departed, one day passed. Then, in a lightning military strike, Dij fell to a massive onslaught of HibAdu forces.

Ambassador VV Uncel received the good news—transmitted by HibAdu nehrcom—while he was on the Adurian homeworld, submitting yet another report to his superiors. Now he crossed the marbelite floor of the spaceport at a brisk pace. Through the glax of double doors ahead, he saw a lab-pod sitting on the landing field, ready to take him to Dij for an inspection tour. A number of Hibbils and Adurians were boarding it. He crowded onboard with them, and found a seat that had been reserved for him at the front of the passenger compartment. The food-service machines were better in this section than those at the rear, as were the seats and lavatory accommodations.

Getting up, he obtained a Vanadian pear from one of the machines and then returned to his seat. The lab-pod engines whined to life.

As he munched on the crispy fruit, Uncel considered the rapid pace of activity surrounding the war effort. His own Hib-Adu leaders were most peculiar, indeed. A triumvirate of freaks who didn't reveal their identities until two weeks ago. Ambassador VV Uncel shuddered at the thought of the horrific hybrids created in a genetics laboratory, and at the thought of what might happen to him if they ever read the recent memories in his cells. Thus far, it had only happened once, at the onset of the Coalition. He had been positive in those days, and somewhat naive, he realized in hindsight.

Ever since the beginning of this alliance between Hibbils and Adurians, Uncel had been curious about who was running everything. Many times he'd wondered why they were conceal-ing themselves from him, when his years of loyal service and social status should have allowed him entrance to their inner circle. In a peculiar, disturbing fashion, all of his orders had been sent to him through intermediaries. Never in person, and never was he ever treated with the respect he so richly deserved.

But Uncel was a professional, through and through. He never complained to anyone about being kept at a distance by his superiors, about only being told pieces of information and never knowing the complete picture, never knowing the really important things. Year after year he just continued to do his job efficiently, everything the freaks, through intermediaries, had ordered him to do.

Now, though, he worried that the brains of the triumvirate were as abnormal as their appearance. How could leaders be created in a laboratory? Didn't that make someone else their boss? Who could that possibly be? A genetic scientist, or group of them?

One of the three monstrosities—Premier Enver—had suggested that a new race of bizarre laboratory-bred creatures might be created. Hybrid "HibAdus," produced from the genetic stock of Hibbils and Adurians. Previously, the name HibAdu had only meant a somewhat arcane political entity to Uncel. Now it referred to something entirely different. Something decidedly darker.

Not that Uncel considered himself any sort of a moral icon. Morality and ethics were concepts he didn't think about much at all. His primary concerns, in order, were himself and the political structure that supported the lifestyle to which he'd grown accustomed. With his niche seemingly secure, he had kept going, doing whatever he was told. But now, with the talk of creating a new race of freaks—how soon?—he felt an army of worry marching through his brain, making more and more inroads, like little guerrilla attacks. He didn't want to think about such things.

As the lab-pod went into hover mode and prepared to set down in the main city on Dij, the Ambassador gazed out the window at blackened hulks of buildings and military equipment. With a soft bump, the craft set down on a charred landing pad, near the bodies of Mutati soldiers that lay in disarray, their flesh melted away. These defenders, while a stubborn and resourceful lot, had finally been defeated by Adurian personnel bombs that had incinerated them. Now carrion birds picked at the grisly remains.

Wrinkling his nose at the odor, Uncel walked past the bodies. On the landing field he noticed other lab-pods on the ground, with each of the vessels disgorging hundreds of Hibbil and Adurian passengers—military and civilian. Everyone was heading for the nearby city, taking a wide conveyor walkway that had either not been damaged in the attack or which had been repaired afterward.

Disembarking at the central square, the Ambassador paused to watch his Hibbil allies devouring Mutati flesh. He'd heard about such disgusting practices, of course, but had never seen them firsthand. Curious, he moved closer, as did other Adurian onlookers. Then, surprisingly, some of the Adurian soldiers joined in, tasting the flesh of their dead enemies.

"Come on, Ambassador!" a Hibbil soldier shouted. "Get some for yourself! The meat is sweet!"

Grudgingly, like a person tasting an unusual food for the first time, the diplomat waded in, stepping over purple puddles of Mutati blood. A Hibbil soldier handed him a dripping slab of fatty flesh.

At first, Uncel just nibbled at the corner, and found it surprisingly succulent and not repulsive. Delicious, he decided, with another nibble, and he didn't mind the odor anymore. Soon he had devoured the entire morsel and was reaching down to rip off bigger chunks for himself. All around him, the diners grinned and grunted to each other, with purple goo dripping down their chins and all over their clothes.

Already, Uncel found himself developing a taste for the fleshy meat, and he even pushed some of the other people out of the way to get more for himself.

That evening, at a banquet where Mutati flesh was prepared according to gourmet standards, Uncel learned details of biological weapons that he'd only previously heard about as rumors. On Dij and other conquered planets—to make them easier to rule by reducing their populations—the HibAdus had unleashed bioweapons that either killed or permanently sedated Humans and Mutatis. A variety of weapons and delivery systems were employed, the most deadly of which were plague bombs, which were dropped from lab-pods and detonated in mid-air, spreading their spores over entire planets.

Billions of the enemy had been infected, though the resourceful Humans had eventually developed antidotes for their own race. Thus far, the Mutatis had been far less fortunate.

Far across the galaxy, a Hibbil workman stood on a motoladder, having elevated it to its highest setting so that he could see one of the top shelves in the warehouse. Reaching to the back of the shelf, he slid a dusty weapon-control box forward and examined it. An engraved code told him the date of manufacture and certain quality control details.

"Did you think we forgot about you?" he asked, talking to the unit as if it were alive. "Have you been hiding back there, trying to stay out of battle? Well, there's been a malfunction in one of the front-line units, and you're finally going to get your chance to prove yourself."

Using a robotic arm on the ladder, the worker moved the heavy panel box down to the floor of the warehouse and piled it with a number of other replacement components that were going to be installed in HibAdu warships.

Inside the unit, a little robot heard the words, but said nothing, and did not make a sound.

At last, Ipsy thought. *I'm going to get my chance!*

CHAPTER THIRTY-NINE

"Everything we experience is through a series of individual and social filters, from our day-to-day activities to our perception of the universe. No matter the circumstance, what we see is never the same as what any other person sees. There can be similarities and overlaps, but it is never identical."

—Master Noah Watanabe, classroom instruction

Doge Anton and a number of his key military officers were holding a late night strategy session at his headquarters on Canopa. They met on the top floor of the tallest building in the Valley of the Princes. They had not yet heard the bad news about Dij.

"I don't like this waiting game," General Nirella said. She paced the floor in front of a bank of windows. Beyond her, Anton saw the glittering lights of the corporate buildings in the valley, and the cliff-hanging structures of Rainbow City in the distance.

"We need to hit them hard," Keftenant Swen said. He was one of the youngest, most aggressive officers.

"But where?" one of the other officers said. "Our intelligence reports show that they have large forces stationed at each of the conquered planets, and there seems no limit to the forces they can bring to battle."

"That's because they're growing podships in labs," Nirella

said. "The Tulyans hunting wild podships can't keep up; we can't increase our fleet at the pace the HibAdus can."

"Maybe we should figure out how they're doing it and set up our own program," Swen said.

"Look into it," Anton said.

As the meeting continued, the Doge sat uneasily at the head of the table, watching everyone and listening to the exchange of ideas and comments. There were fourteen men and women in the conference room, and many could not seem to remain in their seats. They kept getting up and walking around, as if itching for some real military action.

"Good God!" Nirella exclaimed. She had her face pressed against the glax, looking out at something.

Everyone hurried over to look, including Anton.

The sky over Rainbow City looked like it was spouting green flames. Anton first thought the strange illumination might be an aurora borealis, but it was not positioned over the northern pole of the planet. Using a handheld magnaviewer, he detected a hole in space, emitting what appeared to be green exhaust.

"Get me a satellite report!" Anton shouted.

Two minutes later, a female Tulyan passed through security and strode heavily into the conference room. Doge Anton recognized her as Zigzia, one of the webtalkers who specialized in communicating via the web strands in space. "The satellite report is coming, as you ordered, but there is more you need to know."

"Something to do with Timeweb?" Nirella asked.

"Yes, General," Zigzia said. She looked worriedly in the direction of the fiery green sky. "We need to evacuate the building immediately."

"What?" Anton said.

"There's a timehole up there, Sire. It's getting closer, on a direct course for the valley. It could recede, or could suck this whole building into it, and a lot more."

Astonished, Anton stared at the unnatural sky, and he knew she was right. "Do it!" he barked.

As they hurried out into the corridor, alarm klaxons sounded. The building rumbled, and an eerie green light permeated everything.

"To the roof!" Nirella said.

Running as fast as they could, Anton, Nirella, Zigzia, and all of the others boarded two grid planes, which took off within seconds after all of them were aboard. The pilots hit the jets, and the aircraft shot into the sky at low angles, away from the approaching timehole. Anton held Nirella's hand. They sat side by side, with electronic safety restraints holding them in. Turbulence shook the plane, but it kept flying.

Behind them, the entire Valley of the Princes glowed green. Then, like particles drawn by a magnet, buildings and whole chunks of land exploded into the green sky and disappeared into the insatiable maw of the timehole.

Suddenly, inexplicably, the sky was no longer green, and the night sky over the valley looked almost completely normal, with glittering stars against a dark cosmic ceiling.

Seated beside Anton, his wife read a telebeam message that appeared over the ring on her hand. "More bad news," the female officer said. "The last Mutati world has fallen to the HibAdus. We've lost Dij."

"What about the fleet we sent with the Mutati Emir?"

"Safe," Nirella said. "Hari'Adab wanted to break it up and take a portion of it to other Mutati worlds, but Jimu prevented that."

"Under our orders," Anton said. "Good, good. Where are they now?"

"Deep space in the Mutati Sector, or should I say the *former* Mutati Sector."

"That's some positive news at least. I want them to come back here right away. All six thousand podships."

"Right." She sent the telebeam command, then read another incoming message. "A little more good news, Doge. Substantial elements of the original Mutati fleet have been found in space. They escaped the HibAdus, and have been hiding out. Eclectic solar sailers and other conventional spacecraft, but they're loaded with armaments. Jimu says they're loading stuff into the podships and bringing it back."

"We can use it all."

"Interesting," she said, "how our podships enlarge themselves as necessary to accommodate the additional cargoes. Handy, aren't they?"

"That they are. And Siriki?"

"All quiet there, Sire. And they know about Dij. Do you want to reconsider the podships we assigned to Siriki, and bring them back as well?"

He shook his head. "No. It's not apples and apples, is it? I mean, the HibAdus didn't hit Dij hard until *after* our forces left. Maybe our presence on Siriki inhibits them."

"It's a guessing game, isn't it? We make a move and they make theirs."

Leaning forward, Anton said to the pilot, "Take us to my flagship."

At the heavily fortified palace keep on Siriki, Noah absorbed the stream of emergency courier reports from command headquarters on Canopa. The galactic-ecology situation there was bad, but the loss of Dij was dire news, and suggested that Siriki could be the next target of a massive HibAdu assault, taking out the easier targets first. Noah had his own forces on the highest state of alert, but this was nothing new. At his direction, Subi Danvar had instituted that from the very first day they arrived on Siriki. In orbital space, in the atmosphere, and on the ground, all was in readiness—to the extent possible.

Intending to keep an appointment with Princess Meghina, Noah hurried outside. It was a sunny afternoon, and he walked briskly along a crushed brick path that led to her private zoo.

He found her supervising as handlers unloaded exotic animals from a hoverplane and put them in cages. Dressed in black jeans and a short-sleeve gray sweatshirt, the attractive woman did not look like a princess or a courtesan. Her blonde hair was secured in a simple ponytail.

Seeing him, she said, "These animals just came in from one of our remote islands, where there has been destructive activity. They were panicked. I wish we could take them to another planet where it's safer. For that matter, I wish all of us could go somewhere safe." She looked long at Noah. "But there's no such place, is there?"

"I'm afraid not, but so far Siriki has been spared the horrors suffered by other worlds." He looked apprehensively at the sky, half expecting HibAdu warships to appear at any time. "I've assigned a new guard force to protect you," he said. "At any given moment, they can get you immediately into an emergency escape craft."

"I've seen them following me everywhere," she said, nodding her head in the direction of uniformed Human and robotic soldiers on the path. "You needn't worry about me so much, though. I'm pretty tough."

"I know you are, but I feel responsible for you now." He shuffled his feet. "Look, I want to tell you how much I appreciate the kindness you showed me when my sister was behaving so badly."

"Was she ever any other way?"

"I know you didn't like her, and she gave you good reason to feel that way. You tried to keep her from shooting me, and I know you made other attempts to help me behind the scenes. You also took food to my nephew Anton when he was imprisoned by Doge Lorenzo."

"I'm afraid I wasn't that great an advocate for either of you," she said, with a rueful smile. "Fortunately for you, though, you have your own built-in cellular survival kit."

"And so do you."

"Mmmm, but from what I hear, your special talents are not limited to the ability to physically regenerate yourself. In that area, we might be comparable, but I don't have the far-ranging psychic powers you enjoy."

"I wouldn't call it enjoyable. The powers seem to come and go. Sometimes I can get into a paranormal realm of my own volition, and sometimes I can't. There appear to be numerous ways in, but I haven't figured them out."

"Timeweb," she said. "I've heard about it. Is it as beautiful as they say? A faint green filigree extending all across the cosmos?"

"I can't put it into words," he said.

Meghina excused herself for a moment, to speak with one of the handlers, a woman who was trying to feed raw meat to a caged Sirikan tiger. Noah knew something of the rare, endangered species. It tugged at his heart to see that the orange-and-black animal was emaciated and bruised. It appeared listless, more interested in going to sleep than eating.

When she returned to Noah, she said, "Did you hear about the incredible ride I took in The Pleasure Palace? And about Lorenzo? He's still missing." Her eyes glistened with sadness.

"I'm sorry that's happened to you. As for the orbiter, I still think of it as EcoStation."

She wiped a tear from her eye. "Yes, it is rightfully yours, but I'm afraid it's severely damaged. I rode it God only knows how far—through one of those timeholes and back out."

"Yes, I saw some of that with my . . . special vision."

"What's left of your EcoStation is orbiting the planet of Ya-ree. The orbiter is severely damaged. Some of the modules may still be sealed or partially sealed, but I'm not sure. It's taken quite a beating in its travels."

Noah narrowed his gaze. "The pilot of the lab-pod that we confiscated told us a little about Yaree. It's an unaligned world in a remote galactic sector, a melting pot of various races. Humans, Mutatis, and other races working side by side."

"Sort of a utopia that way, though it's not the most scenic spot I've ever visited. The planet is mineral rich, and its rulers are clever traders, dealing in all sorts of goods. With the cessation of regular podship travel, their business activities have been severely curtailed, but they are an industrious people, and militarily quite strong. So far, the HibAdus have not attacked them. The Yareens say they wouldn't dare."

"Will they join us militarily?"

"I didn't ask, but they might."

"I'm going to look into it—we need all the help we can get," Noah paused, envisioning EcoStation as it used to be, when he conducted Guardian classes onboard, teaching eager young students about his concept of galactic ecology. Maybe it could be that again, and more.

"If we can repair EcoStation," he added, "it could be used for military purposes, as an observation platform for relaying information to Doge Anton."

"It would be easier to build a new space station," she said.

"But it wouldn't be the same," Noah said.

CHAPTER FORTY

We are each alone in this universe.
The multitudes around us only conceal this fact.
—Anonymous, from Lost Earth

In a different context, another universe, it seemed to Lorenzo del Velli, that the Hibbil had been respectful, and—though feisty and combative at times—always deferential when confronted by his superior. In those better days, Pimyt had been his Royal Attaché, both during and after Lorenzo's reign as Doge of the Merchant Prince Alliance.

Now, it was all quite different.

His space station was gone, inexplicably! Standing on the ground by the landed shuttle, Lorenzo still had trouble believing it, or comprehending where The Pleasure Palace gambling casino was. Weeks had passed, and he'd been forced to sleep on the deck of the shuttle with the others. As a result, he had sore muscles and bones (including a painful hip from lying on his side), and his stomach kept rumbling. He despised the emergency rations and strange local plants they'd been eating. Totally unsuited to a nobleman of his station and lineage.

Each day Lorenzo and his companions—Pimyt and the eleven surviving Red Beret soldiers—had been searching orbital space around the unnamed, unknown planet. The ion engines kept running roughly, and were giving all of them considerable concern. There'd been no sign of The Pleasure Palace at all, not even a real clue as to its whereabouts.

Around an hour ago, as the shuttle landed yet again, Pimyt had offered a theory. Lorenzo had been inspecting himself in the bathroom mirror, noticing that his own aged face was worry-worn. The door had been ajar, and Pimyt had pushed it open. The temerity of the creature!

Lorenzo, unhappy at this affront and still displeased with him for running up the slope ahead of him and hardly looking back, had glowered at the furry little alien. But, for the sake of harmony, the merchant prince had held back a stream of invectives that he had in mind.

As Lorenzo pushed his way out of the small room, Pimyt said, "We have experienced but one of many unusual occurrences all across space. You and I have seen the reports, Lorenzo, and we've heard the rumors. Something is seriously amiss in all galactic sectors."

"I get the feeling we're not even in the known galaxy anymore," the former Doge then said. He rubbed a spot on his forehead nervously, a place he had already made red and rough.

"Let's see you get out of this one, Lorenzo. What political strings can you pull now?"

Lorenzo swore and made a menacing step toward the smaller being, but had second thoughts when he saw the Hibbil's glowing red eyes, so the Human just glared at him instead. . . .

Later that afternoon they moved the shuttle to the other side of the planet, to a clearing at the center of the most peculiar jungle any of them had ever seen. The trees and other plant forms, while living and supple, were entirely gray-brown. One of the Red Berets thought it might be an unusual form of photosynthesis, peculiar to this solar system. Though warm at times and providing reasonable illumination, the yellowish sun had a constant grayish tone around the edges—as if from a lens, or a peculiar solar cloud.

Yes, everything was quite different now.

Disheveled and dirty, Lorenzo had not washed properly since arriving on this unnamed planet. He stood at the main hatch of the shuttle, watching several of the Red Berets venture into the jungle. A few minutes earlier, Pimyt had gone in that direction as well.

Behind Lorenzo, the slender Red Beret who had piloted the mini-sub stood attentively, awaiting instructions from his superior. The man removed his red cap for a moment, smoothed it and put it back on.

"What is your name?" Lorenzo asked, noting no insignia of rank on his uniform. Just a common guard, apparently, although he had been through intensive security screening, like the others.

"Kenjie Ishop, Sire," he said.

"Well, Ishop, I appreciate your loyalty and attention to my needs. I'm going to take a walk, and while I'm gone I want you to watch over this shuttle. Don't follow instructions from anyone else until you hear from me."

"Yes, Sire. Would you like me to go with you? There could be unknown dangers out there."

Lorenzo's eyes flashed at him. "As if our situation could get any worse, you mean? No thanks, I'll go on my own." The nobleman grabbed a copy of the *Scienscroll* off a shelf, and slipped it into a clearplax carrying bag. The ground was wet and spongy from a recent rain.

The guard unclipped a small black device from a bulkhead, and handed it to Lorenzo. "This is a locator beacon for your safety, Sire. If you get lost in the strange terrain, it will enable us to find you, and it will also enable you to find your way back to the shuttle. It has a range of more than a hundred kilometers."

"A bit more than I planned to walk today," Lorenzo said with a smile. He examined the device and its touchpad controls.

The guard nodded, and showed him how to work the directional features. Then he said, "See that orange circle? If you flip open the cap over it, you have an energy-burst weapon, capable of bringing down any animal that might try to come after you. Just touch the red button and fire."

"Thank you."

"I'll take care of everything here, Sire."

"I know you will. I'm counting on you."

Lorenzo took a different route into the jungle from those he'd seen the others take. He had in mind sitting somewhere alone with the quasi-religious book and searching it for appropriate passages, as he occasionally liked to do. Perhaps he could find a dry rock, in a warm patch of sunlight.

There were no trails in this area that he could make out, suggesting a paucity of animals, or a complete lack of them. But he did find a relatively clear area that sloped slightly downward, as from water runoff. Leafy trees leaned in on each side, making a canopy overhead, through which filtered sunlight passed.

As he proceeded, Lorenzo kept one hand on the *Scienscroll* bag and the other in his jacket pocket, over the weapon. Only rarely did he have to move thick leaves or branches out of the way. Just ahead, he saw the sunny rock he'd hoped for.

As he neared the rock, he found a dry, warm place to sit that also had a back rest. He also noticed a small, quiet pool of water nearby, beneath a rock overhang that must have kept them from noticing it when they were in the air. Sitting on the hard, dry surface, it pleased Lorenzo that the contours were relatively comfortable, almost as if a simple chair had been constructed just for him.

Removing the book from the bag, he read for a while, but only superficially. Nothing really caught his interest.

But he did have something else with him. Unzipping a pocket

of his coat, he removed a small padded medical kit that he had obtained from the CorpOne medical laboratory, back on Canopa. He opened it and examined the contents: a plax vial of red-wine-colored fluid and a dermex injector.

It was a vial of the Elixir of Life, which the crazed Francella Watanabe had developed, using the blood of her brother, Noah. She had sought eternal life, but had only obtained the opposite, an eternity of darkness. Earlier, using the public as guinea pigs to see how effective the product was, she had sold more than two hundred thousand doses. In the vast majority of cases, the elixir had shown no effect at all. But there had been a handful of successes—Princess Meghina, the Salducian diplomat Kobi Akar, four others, and perhaps Noah, too—but by a slightly different route.

After Francella's death, Lorenzo had come into possession of this vial, but he'd never used it. She had died horribly after consuming the substance, albeit in massive quantities. In addition, there had been recent reports of other elixir consumers coming down with painful, rare diseases and dying. Lorenzo had heard of several hundred cases, and Dr. Bichette had told him that there could be more, as what he called "delayed medical reactions" set in.

Touching the cool surface of the vial, Lorenzo considered his options. Unquestionably, consuming it could make his life more interesting in this boring place. But conceivably, a large percentage—or even all—of the people who had taken the elixir would eventually suffer unpleasant deaths.

Not quite ready to take the chance, he closed the kit and replaced it in his pocket.

Feeling quite sleepy, Lorenzo leaned back and closed his eyes, intending to do so for just a few moments. Since falling from power he'd been through a terrible ordeal, and had been feeling increasingly tired. It was comparatively warm here, and almost comfortable. Perhaps he could forget his troubles for a few minutes. . . .

Pimyt had been trailing him at a distance, keeping out of sight, making hardly any sounds. The furry, disheveled Hibbil crept closer and watched the former MPA leader as his head lolled to one side and he drifted off to sleep. Long minutes passed, and as he drew even closer, Pimyt heard the foolish Human snoring.

The Hibbil was far from his people, but he could still sense their collective pulse, and their awakened appetites. He sniffed the air, moved closer.

Chapter Forty-One

There are uncounted secrets in this universe.
The vast majority of them will never be revealed.
—Parvii Inspiration

Webdancer floated in the midst of other sentient vessels, all with their space anchors activated. Inside the warmth of the podship's sectoid chamber, Tesh lay supine on the deck, staring up at the iridescent green ceiling.

The Parvii woman knew that in the officers' conference room on the deck below her, Doge Anton, his officers, and a number of Tulyans were discussing web conditions in the Canopa region. After the big upheaval in the Valley of the Princes, the timehole near the planet seemed to have settled down, but everyone knew it could flare up at any moment, without warning. Now a Tulyan repair team was high above the planet, working to keep that from happening.

Anton had just begun a meeting, after concluding an even more important session with Hari'Adab, who had just returned with his fleet after the loss of Dij. From listening in on part of the earlier meeting, Tesh knew that the news from the Emir had not been all bad, because he had also brought back a sizable additional force of Mutati warships, soldiers, and military supplies, which he had retrieved from hiding places around the huge sector that had formerly been the dominion of the Mutatis.

With so many important events occurring that required Tesh's attention, she really saw no good time to do anything as personal as she was about to do now, and she felt some guilt about even thinking about such a matter. But she needed to do this anyway, had to move forward so that her mind could be clear for other things. Helping her a bit, Doge Anton was occupied and didn't need her for a while, so barring any new catastrophe Tesh might have enough time to do what she had in mind. She only needed a few moments of intense concentration.

In her natural minuscule form, the sectoid chamber seemed quite large, the relative size of a typical passenger compartment to a normal Human, perhaps. When she first took control of the vessel, this core chamber had been substantially smaller. But gradually, as the war progressed and as *Webdancer* became more important to the Liberator fleet, the ship had grown bigger, of its own volition. Now it was at least twice the size of any other podship in the fleet.

Though Tesh never conversed with *Webdancer* in words, because they utilized different forms of language, she still thought she understood some of the motivations of the great ship. The two of them had a wordless connection, on a higher level than the superficiality of any spoken tongue.

Tesh was more than seven hundred years old—a mere youngster by galactic standards, and she realized that she still had a great deal to learn. Even so, beyond her knowledge of the Aopoddae, she knew other significant things that were perhaps even more arcane.

In her comparative youth six centuries ago, Tesh had befriended a retired breeding specialist at the Parvii Fold, a slender old woman who took her into her confidence. Old Astar had wanted the younger Parvii to become a breeding specialist like herself, a rare opportunity presented to a "commonblood" such as Tesh. At the time, the profession was dying out, she said, not considered necessary anymore. Astar was the only remaining one, and she had not practiced her craft for more than a millennium.

She explained that in the Parvii race, there used to be more than one way to pursue some of the most important professions. In the case of breeding specialists, most came from particular genetic lines, but historically there had been exceptions, notable commonbloods who displayed special talents that enabled them to join the elite group. Tesh had been one of those extraordinary people who had been noticed.

For Astar, it had been unusual for her to open up to anyone, for she had always been known as an insular person, filled with secret knowledge. From the beginning of their relationship, Tesh had told her that she didn't want to become a breeding specialist, because that was not the direction in which her heart pointed her. Besides, there would be extreme political difficulties if she were to make the attempt. Instead, the young woman had always wanted to pilot podships across vast expanses of space. It had felt like her calling, a glamorous career that consumed much of her imagination. Astar had been disappointed, but had said she accepted the decision. Even so, it took a long time before she gave up trying to get Tesh to change her mind.

One day, when it was clear that Tesh would not accept the calling, and that the old woman did not have long to live, a highly unusual event occurred. In the years since then, Tesh had thought of it often.

The two of them had been flying side by side, at a slow speed because of Astar's declining health. They reached a foldcave, and once inside, the old woman said it would give them complete security from the telepathic probes of the Eye of the Swarm. There, standing in the small natural chamber, illuminated in low gray light, Astar said, "I have thought long and hard on this, and there is something I want to bequeath to you, a special gift that will help you in times of great need. I would be criticized for doing so, but I went through secret channels and consulted a Tulyan timeseer about you."

For several moments, the airless cave seemed to contain another presence, a thing that the old woman had not yet said. Finally, Astar continued, her voice quavering. "The timeseer told me that a unique future lies in store for you, Tesh, unlike anything that has ever happened to a member of the Parvii race."

"I only want to be a podship pilot."

The slender woman placed a wrinkled hand on Tesh's shoulder. "I know, dear, but something more is available to you, something far greater. Throughout history, there have been occasions when our women and men have fallen in love with members of other races."

"I have heard this."

"Then you have also heard that it is impossible for a Parvii to breed with another galactic race. Even though we can engage in sexual acts with them, no children can result."

"Yes."

"Well, that is not strictly true. There are certain methods. Offspring have in fact been conceived from such unions. Not many, but it has happened. A few thousand perhaps, over millions of years. Some of the children were hunted down and killed as monstrosities by various Eyes of the Swarm, but others escaped and lived out their lives as fugitives. In your case, you are destined to face such a breeding conundrum. And it will be unlike any of the other examples. The alien male you meet will be exceptional, perhaps even godlike."

"I'm not sure if I like the sound of this."

"When you encounter this person, you will know. At first, you will have doubts about whether he can possibly be the one who has been foretold, and you may even discount what I am telling you now as nonsense. You will think he is an ordinary alien male, and will discover that sexual acts with him are pleasurable, though perhaps not fantastic. But after you are intimate with him, a certainty will seep into your awareness, and you will know that you must bear his child. Increasingly, this will consume your thoughts."

"And what will my child be like?" Tesh's heart had raced as she asked the question.

"Ordinary in appearance, but anything but ordinary inside. The gender has not been revealed to me, nor have specifics about the life your child will lead. Throughout the history of all races there have been special children who have accomplished great things, such as Sanji the Tulyan and Jesus Christ the Human. Your child could very well be on that scale."

"You have omitted mention of any great or legendary Parvii."

"And with good reason, Tesh. I hate to say this, but our race has been making terrible mistakes for a long time, grievous errors that have had widespread consequences. I know you want to be a podship pilot—perhaps for the glamour of it—but I have long wondered if that is our true calling as a race. Certainly it is not the honorable pursuit our leaders make it out to be."

Astar paused. Presently, looking into Tesh's eyes, the wrinkled breeding specialist said, "I suspect you're wondering how I can keep such blasphemous thoughts away from the telepathic probes of the Eye of the Swarm. Let me just say that there are ways. And perhaps it is wishful thinking on my part, but I think your child just might be part of the solution, a way for us to alter the course of Parvii destiny. I sense goodness in you, Tesh. Otherwise, I would not be saying such things to you."

Placing her own hand on the old woman's face, Tesh said, "I believe you."

After that, Astar revealed things about the intricacies of the Parvii female body, and described specific methods that could be used to become pregnant with the child of an alien, and how to conceal certain thoughts from Woldn. Then the old woman made Tesh repeat it all back to her, in detail. The younger woman got it right the first time.

"Never forget what I have taught you," Astar said, in the most solemn and ominous of voices.

"I won't. I promise."

"There are so many more things I would like to tell you, Tesh, but I don't have the energy to do so, and perhaps it would not be right anyway. Know and understand, though, that you will face great, undetermined dangers in taking the path I have outlined. You will be bearing a forbidden child, considered a horror by our people. But our people are *wrong.*"

Weakened by the exertion of the flight and all she had to say, the old woman slumped to the floor of the foldcave. Tesh eased her down, and sat on the hard surface, holding Astar's head on her own lap.

Looking up into Tesh's face, the aged woman smiled. Then her facial expression became stony and she said, "There is one more thing I must tell you. I don't have the specifics, but long ago, in the early days of the galaxy. . . ." Astar coughed, struggled to speak.

Tesh comforted her, but couldn't help wanting to know what the old woman had to say.

Finally, Astar said, "What I am about to tell you is all I know about a particular subject, and that is not very much. It is a fact known to all breeding specialists, but it is only a fragment of information. Long ago, so distant in time that it has been all but erased from our memories, the Parvii race had a connection with another galactic race."

"The Tulyans," Tesh said. "We defeated them in battle, took the podships away from them."

"Not that type of connection, child. No, not that at all. Something entirely different and more cooperative in nature."

She sighed. "Oh, if we only knew more than that morsel of information, and more than the name of the race!"

In Tesh's arms, the old woman trembled, and then said, "I speak of an important connection between Parviis and Adurians. What it is, I do not know, and the races seem so different. But there are similarities that are apparent to one in my profession."

"Both races have extensive breeding knowledge?"

"Precisely." The smile returned, though a wary one. "With the specialized knowledge I have imparted, you are now a limited breeding specialist, with just enough information to navigate your own remarkable future. I wish you all of the good things in life, for you and your unusual family."

"Thank you."

The old woman closed her eyes, and against Tesh's fingertips she felt Astar's pulse slowing. The younger woman turned away, crying.

Nearly an hour passed. Finally, the aged breeding specialist slipped away, into her own eternity. . . .

Now, in the privacy of the sectoid chamber, Tesh had been using a combination of things she knew about the internal workings of her own body—the things that every Parvii woman knew, along with the secret knowledge that Astar had shared with her. Already, she had used the additional information to protect something precious that Noah had given to her, something she had been concealing within her body for two months.

Reaching under the side of her collar, Tesh touched a place on her skin that she knew was a tiny, dark mark, beneath which lay the implanted med-tech device that operated her body's magnification system. This time, though, instead of rubbing the spot to activate the magnifier and enlarge the appearance of her body, she held a forefinger there for several moments, until she felt another feature of the med-tech unit click on.

Over Tesh's head, a hologram appeared, a full-color, life-size videocam of the interior of her body. Using the technology, she conducted her own private medical examination. Along with the projected images in front of her eyes, data flowed into her brain, telling her the exact condition of every organ, every muscle, and every cell—even every atom and subatomic particle, if she chose to analyze them in detail. Barring an accident, she could expect to live for almost fifteen hundred additional years. So far, this was an analysis that any Parvii could accomplish.

But that was not what Tesh was looking for.

Taking a deep breath, she activated one of the hidden features of the system that Astar had revealed to her centuries ago. This went beyond what Tesh had already done to her body as a result of Astar's teachings, the keeping and preserving of Noah's gift within her. That only allowed her time to think, to consider possibilities and decide if she wanted to go on to the next stage. Now, she was certain.

Staring into the hologram, Tesh felt a beam of bright light wash over her, causing her to shiver in anticipation. Her vision became foggy and unfocused, and her mind seemed to expand outward, into a luminous green cosmos that stretched into infinity. And far away in that realm of apparent space, in the place that Astar had told her how to reach, Tesh saw an opening, like a tunnel in the universe. But she knew this was inside her own body instead, a special feature of the embedded medical apparatus. She hesitated, felt her metabolism quicken, and then plunged psychically into the tunnel.

In a matter of moments, Tesh emerged on the other side, in a tiny, colorless chamber of her own body. And there she saw what she sought: a sac of the alien cellular material that she had been storing in her body, ever since her sexual encounter with Noah Watanabe.

Again, she hesitated. But she knew the decision no longer hung in the balance. She had gone this far, and needed to continue.

Carefully, mentally adjusting the med-tech device in the precise manner that Astar had revealed to her, Tesh opened the sac and let Noah's sperm flow through her body, bypassing the racial firewalls that had been designed to prevent breeding between Parviis and any other ethnic group.

Now she felt Noah with her again, his physical closeness and warmth, as if they were making love once more. The rapture she shared with him was even more intense than it had been previously, wave upon wave of pleasure building to a grand climax in her mind and body. Finally, as after a great storm, the fury of passion subsided and she lay there in the green luminescence, completely sated.

Having done this, Tesh no longer felt alone, and that gave her some comfort. But she sensed grave perils ahead. To face them, she would need to reach deep for all the strength she could muster, and for all the strength she could draw from others. She knew absolutely that she had to attempt this difficult path, no matter where it took her . . . and her child.

And no matter how anyone felt about it. Even Noah.

CHAPTER FORTY-TWO

Time is a measuring stick, but it goes in a circle.
                                        —Tulyan observation

As Eshaz continued to lead his ecological repair team around the galaxy, he thought he must be one of the busiest Tulyans alive. He not only had to coordinate the work assignments of his caretakers, but he liked to get involved personally, and perform some of the important web repair tasks himself. A number of his team members wondered how he could possibly do so much, and to that inquiry, Eshaz invariably had a simple reply: "I don't sleep anymore."

It was an exaggeration, but not much of one. He slept only a couple of hours a day now, and somehow he kept going anyway. Humans would have said their adrenaline was causing it, or caffeine, or one of the designer drugs that kept them awake. In Eshaz's case, it was sheer desperation. He knew he would never again face such an important challenge. The responsibility of managing five hundred podships and the Tulyans aboard them weighed heavily on him. He felt up to the challenge, but knew when it was completed, if he ever got back to his beloved Tulyan Starcloud, he wanted to sleep for a month straight.

At the moment, he was performing yet another duty, having merged into the flesh of the lead podship, *Agryt,* in order to pilot it and lead the repair fleet across the galaxy. They were just leaving the Tarbu Gap, a sacred and secret Tulyan region whose location was concealed from the prying eyes and telepathic probes of outsiders by electrical disturbances.

Ahead, if he kept on this route, lay the fabled Wild Pod Zone. He wished he could go there as he had in the past, but knew that was impossible. It was now in the Hibbil Sector.

Through visual sensors on the hull of the pod, combined with his own enhanced eyes, Eshaz saw far out into space, to the dim dwarf stars of that region, white or brown in color. But even if he was able to go there, he suspected it would not be the same as the past. In all likelihood there were dangerous galactic conditions there, things that needed the attention of his expert team. To him, the threat of military action by the HibAdus didn't seem any worse than some of the other dangers around the galaxy. It seemed like a matter of priorities, that he should just barrel ahead and try to complete as many repairs in that sector as he could. But the Council of Elders had forbidden him from going there. They were keeping part of the Liberator fleet to perform military operations to enforce the web repairs that were needed, and perhaps at this very moment other Tulyans were conducting operations in that region. If he went against orders, he could compromise their efforts.

My superiors know better than I, he thought.

Grudgingly, Eshaz changed course sharply, and headed for yet another star system, in a different sector. The other podships followed. One by one, he was completing the tasks on his list. In only a few minutes, he would be in the next work zone, unless he had to take an alternate route due to web conditions.

In his lifetime of nearly a million years, Eshaz had seen many things, and had done many things. He had been a renowned and talented timeseer, among a small number in all of the Tulyan Starcloud who could see portions of the future. It had always been an imperfect talent, affected and limited by cosmic conditions and by other factors that were largely unknown to him. In one of his most distasteful assignments, the Council had ordered him to perform timeseeing duties for Woldn and the Parviis—an unusual cooperative arrangement between the races that existed before the latest hostilities. The attempt had not gone well, and as a result Woldn had not been pleased. But Eshaz had been painfully honest with him; he really had not been able to provide the information sought by the Parvii leader.

Sometimes—both under assignment and on his own—Eshaz had tried to visualize other specific futures. Prime among them, he had endeavored to discern the path lying ahead of the most remarkable of all Humans, Noah Watanabe . . . the galactic ecologist, Timeweb traveler, and immortal. Against all odds, this Human might outlive the most ancient of Tulyans. Remarkable, indeed. And, though Noah denied it, he might be the messiah foretold in Tulyan legends.

But each time that Eshaz had made the effort to focus his timeseeing abilities on Noah, he had encountered only chaos around the man, a cosmic, veiling murkiness that prevented any intrusion. The more he had tried to probe, the more Eshaz had found himself with a ferocious headache, so he had gradually given up the effort. Some things were truly impossible.

Now as he sped along the webway, Eshaz attempted something that seemed even more broad than focusing on Noah's life. Mulling it over, however, he realized that it was something that stemmed from Noah, or at least from something Noah had said—and this might add to the difficulties of timeseeing.

With his far-seeing eyes, Eshaz gazed beyond the physical reality of the galaxy around him, into an alternate dimension that was connected to the web of time. Having already commanded his podship to follow a particular course, he could take a few moments to make this new attempt.

For a good distance, the ethereal realm opened up to him and he saw where Timeweb was connected to the substance and mass of the known galaxy, and where many of the Tulyan care-taking repair teams had either completed important work or were continuing with it.

And far, far beyond that, he peered into the place where all things were heading with each passing moment, an inexorable flow of time and destiny from countless directions. Like streams and currents. *There!* he thought, feeling a surge of excitement, but one that was tinged in dread. He focused, or tried to.

Something dark and amorphous lay in the future of all living beings in the galaxy, blocking all paths, preventing any way around it. But what? As he attempted to see farther into the lens of time, his corporeal limitations intruded, and he felt the worst headache of his entire life. And Eshaz knew that if he pressed forward, he would create such pain and such internal cellular damage that he could die.

This risk did not matter to him, not with so much at stake. As a consequence, he pressed on with his own form of psychic timeseeing, looking with the specially attuned eyes that he had received as a gift with his birth. *The pain!* Sharp lances surged into his awareness.

But he refused to back off.

Less than a minute passed, though it seemed like much longer to Eshaz, as in the compression of a dream . . . or a nightmare. Finally, something kicked him out, hard, and he landed back in the reality of the podship speeding through space.

Moments later, *Agryt* reached the destination that Eshaz had provided, and slowed down. The rest of the Aopoddae behind did the same. All of their pilots and crews awaited Eshaz's further instructions. He wondered what his own face must look like on the prow of the vessel.

He didn't feel in any condition to guide the team. His head screamed in pain. Then, as moments passed he felt the discomfort diminishing, and he realized that *Agryt* was comforting him, using some unfathomable Aopoddae method to bring a foolish Tulyan back to awareness and function.

Presently, Eshaz felt fully restored, and grateful to his symbiotic companion. But he was left with a certainty that troubled him above all others.

Noah had been right. There really *was* a great and towering danger out there—more than any of the galactic races had ever encountered before—and to complicate the situation even more, no one could identify it.

CHAPTER FORTY-THREE

In this universe of wondrous possibilities, certain constants exist, and all of them are linked to the symbiosis of science and religion. These two divisions of the Ultimate Truth are—in the basic analysis—one and the same, and their respective subparts contribute to the whole.

—*Scienscroll*, 1 Eth 77

With Princess Meghina right behind him, Noah negotiated a spiral, rock stairway that led down to the ancient dungeons of the palace. Bright lights illuminated the way, so that they could walk more safely on the uneven, stained surface—stairs that had been worn down in places by the passage of many feet. It was early morning.

"As you know, it was pretty dark down here before," he said, "so we added more lighting."

"My palace has a long history," she said, "much of it unsavory. I'm afraid there were torture chambers down here centuries ago."

"We found some evidence of that. No machines, but there were still shackles on the walls."

Noah pushed open a heavy iron door, revealing a corridor lined with glowing orange, electronic containment cells. His officers had converted this to a military gaol, always necessary to confine fighters and a limited number of others who needed to be taken into custody. And, though it was not large or crowded with prisoners today, it became, nonetheless, quite noisy as they approached a cell on the far end.

"Finally!" the Salducian diplomat shouted as he jumped up from a cot. His normally impeccable gray suit was wrinkled and soiled, and at the knees of some of his numerous legs the fabric was torn and bloody, with visible wounds. Glaring through the containment field at Noah, he then shifted his gaze to the Princess. At that point his demeanor changed, and in a pleasant tone he said to her, "Thank you for coming to get me out. I have spent a most uncomfortable night."

"I'm not here for that," she said.

"What?" Confusion moved across Kobi Akar's oblong face. His crab-pincer hands flexed back and forth behind the containment field, as if looking for something to grab onto and rip apart. Looking at Noah, he asked, "Are you attempting to assert military jurisdiction over me?"

"No," Noah said. "Your confinement is presently military, since that offers the best security. However, the jurisdiction is civilian. As soon as possible, you will be transferred to Canopan authorities."

"In the midst of a war? What outrage is this? I want a lawyer!"

"You will have access to lawyers on Canopa," Noah said.

"This is outrageous!"

"It is the law," Noah said. "A serious charge has been placed against you."

In an indignant tone, the Salducian said, "One of the guards mentioned something about sex with a minor girl. It's a complete lie!"

"You will have your opportunity to prove that. Reportedly it occurred on the orbital gambling casino, over Canopa."

"It's all a monstrous fabrication, designed to extort payment out of me. However, just for the sake of argument, I ask you: How can there be any Canopan civilian jurisdiction over an orbiter that is in space? That falls under intergalactic law, not planetary law."

"We don't know the particulars," Meghina said, "only that the Office of the Doge has ordered you to Canopa."

"It's all a waste of time, you know," Akar said. He scuttled backward, and sagged wearily onto the cot. "Whatever the jurisdiction, I have diplomatic immunity."

"And the courts will determine if you abused it," Noah said.

"Abused it? In this matter, that is not legal terminology. Obviously, I know the law and you don't."

"I'm not here to debate you."

"I asked Noah to bring me to check on your physical condition," the Princess said. "Are you being fed well, Mr. Akar? Have you received treatment for your injuries?" She looked down at his bloodied legs that draped over the side of the cot.

"The food is unfit for roachrats," he replied. "And as for my injuries, that is an additional matter. My lawyers will prefer charges for mistreatment of a prisoner."

"I viewed the surveillance file on you," Noah said. "You injured yourself when you fell on the stairs."

"I was pushed!"

"That isn't what the evidence shows."

"I shall send you better food and a doctor," Meghina said, stiffly. Then, without another word, she turned and left, with Noah behind her.

"What are they going to do?" Akar shouted after them, "Give me a life sentence?" He cackled, delighted at his own dark humor.

"That is not up to us," Noah said, over his shoulder. "We are only holding you for other authorities."

"I have a long list of grievances!" Akar shouted after them. "You'll both hear from my lawyers!"

"On that, at least, I believe you," Noah yelled back, as he and

Meghina went through the heavy iron door.

"What's that supposed to mean?"

In response, Noah slammed the door shut.

"A charming man, but I never entirely trusted him," Meghina said. "That doesn't mean he's guilty, though."

Noah couldn't help but agree, though soon—after completing the transfer to Canopa—the matter would be out of his hands.

Sometimes, Noah dreaded going to sleep. In his military duties, he spent long hours attending to important tasks, so by the end of each day he invariably felt tired enough to drift off. But so many problems kept churning through his mind that he found it difficult to leave them unresolved. So much seemed beyond his ability to fix or even to understand. At times, he wished he knew less than he did, or at least that he had been exposed to less.

The mysteries of Timeweb were at the very top of his list.

It awed him to think of the incredible galactic web that connected everything in a manner that most galactic races could not detect, a structure that had existed for millions and millions of years. During all of that time, it had been strong enough to hold everything together, but now, after so much abuse and neglect, it was falling apart. Reports from the Tulyan caretaker teams indicated some progress in completing repairs, and a number of the most heavily damaged areas had been improved. But there were also ongoing reports of new timeholes needing attention and entire galactic sectors in peril, so the Tulyan Elders needed to constantly adjust their priorities and plans.

As First Elder Kre'n had said, it was like the triage method of assessing the injuries of soldiers on a vast galactic battlefield, except in this case Timeweb was a single entity, with many widespread wounds.

Humankind is a single organism, Noah thought, as he made his way to his private quarters in the keep. *In fact, all races are a single organism. And all races are linked to Timeweb.*

He felt his thoughts stretching beyond prior levels of understanding or connection.

Suddenly, in the corridor he dropped to his knees, and a green darkness pervaded his consciousness. In the background, he heard guards asking if he was all right.

Noah was conscious of remaining on his knees, and of people all around him. Some of them touched him, and he heard their distant voices asking if they should help him to lie down. Someone summoned a doctor, and Noah wondered if it would be the same doctor that would attend to the Salducian. An odd, throwaway thought that intruded on others of much more importance.

Priorities, he thought. Life was about assigning priorities, and acting upon them. He wasn't sure if he had heard that somewhere, or if he had figured it out himself. Another throwaway thought.

Then, with all of the commotion around him, Noah became an island unto himself, and voices drifted away around him. He recalled the horrible death of his sister, the way she aged too rapidly and died looking like a haggard old woman, and probably in terrible pain. Certainly, she suffered from a horrendous anguish of the soul. Noah thought back to the last time he saw her, when she stabbed him with a dermex needle, claiming it contained her own tainted blood. Even though doctors subsequently assured him that she had not infected him—and Noah seemed to have his own brand of immortality—he still worried about it occasionally.

So much information to discard. So many details that only clogged his mind and made it work inefficiently, details that intruded like guerrilla fighters and then retreated, only to irritate him over and over again. Concerning Francella, he didn't want to think about her bad side, though that was almost all he'd ever seen of her. Instead, he tried to remember the few comparatively pleasant times they had shared (mostly as children), occasions when they almost seemed like normal siblings.

My life has been anything but normal, he thought. *And hers, in its own horrific way, was far from normal as well.*

The Human condition seemed to cover a broad range of purported normalcy. But he realized that at its very core each Human relationship contained an inevitable element of dysfunction, and that people—the optimistic types—tried to put a positive cast on problems, making them seem less significant than they actually were.

Noah had always tried to be an optimist himself, even when the obstacles against that state of mind seemed insurmountable. Now, more than ever in his lifetime, and he was quite certain—more than ever in the history of the galaxy—the obstacles were greater than ever.

Like a great flood waiting to break through holes in a dike, chaos threatened to inundate everything in the known galaxy, ruining eons of cosmic evolution, changing everything for the worse. The Tulyans were like little Dutch boys running around putting their fingers in the holes. But there seemed to be many more timeholes than there were caretakers to fix them.

He felt the dark seepage of pessimism enter his awareness, and fought to push it back.

At the moment, he sensed someone carrying him, but that part didn't matter. He cried out, and felt the flood of an abrupt vision that took over his consciousness. Suddenly, he found himself thinking with Francella's mind and seeing through her eyes. Startling! But fascinating. He didn't fight the sensations. It didn't seem like one of the doors to Timeweb; it seemed like something else. . . .

It was a gloomy, rainy day on Canopa, and Francella was at CorpOne headquarters with their father, Prince Saito Watanabe.

"You know," the old man said as they stood by the rain-swept window, "I might have been wrong all my life about industrial pollution and waste, so maybe I should change after all, as Noah has been preaching to me—even if it means dismantling every business operation my company has. Maybe I should turn operation of the company over to your brother and let him clean things up from the inside."

"He can only destroy CorpOne!" she shouted back, her voice cracking. "Noah has never cared about this company or this family! How can you say such a thing?"

"You will accept whatever I decide," the old merchant prince said. "If I have been wrong in the past, I must make amends." He looked at her with rheumy old eyes. "And you must make amends, too. For a long time, I have noticed how you never reach out to Noah, never seem capable of seeing anything good about him. Why is that? I never wanted the two of you to grow so far apart."

He extended a hand to touch her shoulder affectionately, but she pushed it away.

They argued for a while, father and daughter, with far more than the normal associated emotions. Finally Francella went away by herself, to her own island of warped consciousness. She felt extremely upset at what the old tycoon had said to her. In her office her thoughts went wild, and she smashed things around her.

It was a turning point in her life. Always before, she had imagined doing terrible things, even worse than the financial indiscretions she had long committed against her company and her family. Now, for the first time, she actively plotted to kill her father and blame it on Noah.

As the images faded and Noah found himself in his own apartment with a doctor tending to him, he was left wondering if he had experienced an accurate vision of her thoughts, something transmitted by her blood—which she had injected so violently into his bloodstream. They had been born fraternal twins, and perhaps the injection had intensified a paranormal connection they'd already had.

"He's breathing hard," the doctor said.

Through bleary eyes, Noah saw an elderly man with white hair. Noah tried to calm his own pulse, but became conscious of it roaring in his ears as blood pumped wildly through his veins.

Could their father's death really have occurred the way he had just envisioned it? Noah was stunned, but somehow it all seemed to fit.

He felt medications taking effect, and heard the voices drift away again, but this time he blacked out.

CHAPTER FORTY-FOUR

Each breath we attempt to take is an adventure into the unknown.

—Ancient Saying

So much had happened, and of such grave and far-reaching significance, that Princess Meghina had not had time to grieve for her lost dagg, Orga, or for the many citizens of Siriki who had died in the HibAdu onslaught. Many had been her friends and associates. Sadly, she had to face the fact that portions of her past were gone, and irretrievable. Even her once-magnificent Golden Palace was looking worn and tired, from its conversion into a military headquarters for the Liberator forces.

She didn't object to the use of her opulent home for that noble purpose, so her sadness was tempered by the stark realities that faced everyone now. There were two grave threats—the HibAdus, and the declining infrastructure of the galaxy. She'd even heard rumors that the Tulyans and Noah thought there might be yet another great peril "out there" somewhere, but whenever she had asked any of them about it, she had received only vague responses. Even Noah, who had a reputation for being concise and direct, had evaded her question. She came away with the feeling that the people around her were bordering on paranoia, and perhaps a quiet hysteria, constantly feeling that terrible things were about to happen.

It was mid-afternoon on a cloudy day, and Meghina found

herself in an improbable place, standing on the edge of a high cliff with Llew Jarro, Betha Neider, Dougal Netzer, and Paltrow. All of them were the "elixir-immortals," but missing the Salducian diplomat, who was being transferred as a prisoner to Canopa later that day. The five of them were still on the palace grounds, and had gone up in a tram. The high perch had always been a favorite place for Meghina to go, often by herself, and sometimes with one of her rare pet animals.

"We form an exclusive little club, you know," said the corpulent Jarro. He stood with his back to the precipice, facing the others. "I thought you might be interested in learning what I have been discovering about our . . . special condition."

"Not that we're afraid of heights or anything," Paltrow said, with a little snicker. "But I'll ask again: Why have you brought us to this cliff?"

A thick, buxom woman, Paltrow nonetheless didn't appear to have an ounce of fat on her. She looked to have trained for sporting activities of some sort in the past, but was close-mouthed about her personal history, except to say that she was only too happy to "leave it in the dust," including her own birth name. With her immortality, she had not only assumed a new body, but a new name of her choosing. Despite the enigma around the woman, Meghina rather liked her, and didn't sense anything shadowy about her. Not what the Princess had sensed—accurately, in all likelihood—about Kobi Akar.

"Some things are best demonstrated rather than described," Jarro said. "I'm about to jump off this cliff. Not to kill myself, of course, because that is an impossibility. I've been coming up here on my own, and have gone off several times."

Meghina glanced over the edge, and felt a little tug at her stomach, a touch of queasiness. It was a long way down. According to Sirikan legend, two star-crossed lovers had committed suicide from this place, long ago. Through a grove of trees, the Princess saw some of the fences and buildings of her private zoo, and beyond that, a meadow that had been converted to a landing field for conventional military aircraft, and for occasional podships.

Jarro took a half step backward, toward the edge, and barely maintained his footing. "We've all heard of the horrors that Noah Watanabe experienced at the hands of his sister, how she kept hacking him up, and his body kept regenerating. From our experience at Yaree, it is clear that we share some of that remarkable ability. We could fall off here, and eventually recover."

"That's true enough," old Dougal Netzer said. A scowl formed on the artist's creased, ruddy face. "It wouldn't be good, though, if we were all trapped in a rock slide. We still have our muscular limitations."

"I hadn't thought of that," Jarro said, "but the rocks seem stable enough here."

"You're not a geologist," the old man said.

"You're right."

"A timehole could open up, too, and start some sort of an upheaval."

"You do have an imagination," Jarro said. "But that could happen anywhere, not just here. I guess we could all decide to remain separate if we're worried about that. However, I think we have more to learn from each other. I've jumped off this cliff eight times now, and . . ."

"You've used up your nine lives, then," Betha Neider quipped, "counting your fall at Yaree."

"Usually you are a delightful young woman," Jarro said, "but your inexperience can cause you to be facetious at times. This is one of those occasions. No, Betha, I have many more lives than the proverbial allocation, as do we all. I was about to say, each time I've done the jump, I've recovered faster than the time before. At first, it was hours before I could get up and walk back to the palace. The last time, it was a matter of minutes."

"This promises to be a delightful day," Betha said, undeterred. "You'll walk back and have dinner, while we lay splattered at the base of the cliff, until we get up in the darkness and stumble around like zombies."

"I'm talking about self-improvement," Jarro said, glaring at her. "If any of you prefer, you can ride the tram to the bottom. As for me, I have an alternate means of transportation." He backed up and leaped off backward, tumbling into the air. "See you at the bottom!"

After a few seconds, Meghina heard the sickening thump of his body when it struck the ground, far below. She looked over the edge, but couldn't make out where he had hit. A couple of minutes later she saw something moving down there, and heard a distant voice that carried all the way up the cliff face: "Come on in! The water's fine!"

"See you guys in Zombieland," Betha said, as she leaped off head first. Paltrow followed her, leaving Meghina and old Dougal on the high perch. "I can't have girls showing me up," the artist said, with a shrug. Then he followed the others.

For several moments, the Princess stood on the edge of the precipice, looking down. So far, only one person moved down there, whom she presumed to be Llew Jarro. It seemed most untidy and undignified to her to add herself to the splattered flesh and broken bones at the base of the cliff, and a wayward thought occurred to her: What if animals from the woods came and started eating the bodies? Maybe they wouldn't finish the bodies off before they started regenerating, not even with the help of carrion birds, but it gave her pause. Besides, she was not in the mood to make herself the subject of a scientific experiment, especially an impromptu one. In the midst of a huge galactic war, with so many concerns on her mind, she could not afford to be foolish or capricious. She shouldn't even have come up here with the others, not without finding out what Jarro wanted.

And by title, she remained the civilian leader of this planet, requiring that she behave with decorum.

Jarro, and perhaps some of the others, might not agree with her feelings, but that didn't matter to her. She had heard somewhere that true leadership was not a popularity contest.

Summoning a different sort of courage than her companions had displayed, Princess Meghina boarded the tram, and rode it down. She would send palace guards and doctors to attend to her friends.

That evening, with the necessary transfer documents completed, two MPA marshals escorted their high-security prisoner onto a podship for the flight to Canopa. The electronically cuffed Salducian was not cooperative, and as they entered the passenger compartment he tried to kick one of the officers—both of whom were burly Human men. They stepped out of the way easily, and shoved him roughly onto a bench, then activated a shimmering containment field to keep him there.

"You'll lose your careers for this!" Kobi Akar shouted, as he struggled unsuccessfully to break free.

"Oh, do you hear that, Iktar? We're really worried, aren't we?"

"Yeah," said the other, as the diplomat glared at them. "Maybe we should turn this guy loose, or 'accidentally' let him escape. That would really look good in our personnel files, wouldn't it?"

"Sure would. Our salaries would be doubled right away, and we'd be promoted."

The one called Iktar sat on a nearby bench, and said, "Too bad we're having trouble with the restraint controls. I just can't seem to get them to open up."

"Yeah, they are temperamental, aren't they? Like our famous prisoner here."

Kobi Akar shouted obscenities at them in two languages, until they set the controls to prevent his mouth from moving. After that, he could only grunt—and each time he even did that, he received an electric shock. Soon, glowering crazily, he settled down.

Because of poor podway conditions, the flight took more than an hour and a half. Finally, they reached the pod station over Canopa and docked. The prisoner was transferred to a shuttle.

But as the shuttle descended over Canopa, a glowing green hole suddenly opened in the sky—just large enough to swallow the craft before closing afterward. Witnesses on the ground and in space reported seeing a small timehole for a few seconds before it vanished, taking the ship and passengers with it.

CHAPTER FORTY-FIVE

"We have no superiors—not even those who created us."
> —High Ruler Coreq, remarks to the other
> two members of the HibAdu triumvirate

He was shorter than the typical Adurian and taller than most Hibbils, with features of each race. His oversized, pale yellow eyes took in everything around him as he passed through security doors and strutted into the laboratory complex. The odors of flesh and strong chemicals permeated the air, as Adurian scientists and research technicians went about their tasks at spotless, gleaming work stations. All of them wore sealed body suits and helmets to prevent contaminating the genetic samples they were handling, while electronic bio-barriers kept any visitor at a safe distance. Complex machines hummed and throbbed. Concise, technical words filled the air as staff members discussed their experiments.

The yellow-suited Adurian workers seemed to hardly give the hybrid any notice as he passed by, but he knew they were watching him peripherally, and fearfully. In the past, some of their predecessors in these labs had even called him a freak and other improper terms, but never to his face. No matter, High Ruler Coreq always found out who they were from cellular-memory readings and had them eliminated. Permanently. Those who were left now seemed to be relatively stable, though they always needed to be monitored, and checked. There was another problem with them at the moment, however. They did not want to perform a particular task that the triumvirate had ordered them to do—the one involving the Parviis.

Coreq considered the Adurians weaklings, only good for limited, assigned functions. When the time was right, he and his triumvirate would orchestrate the breeding of an entirely new hybrid race, one that would kill or enslave all other sentients in the galaxy.

By the standards of most galactic races, the High Ruler was still quite young, having not yet passed his fifteenth birth marker. But that only accounted for his physical self, part Hibbil and part Adurian, bred under optimal laboratory conditions. Inside his mind—the part that mattered much more than the external appearance—he was exceedingly old, because the wisdom and violence of the ancients had been infused into him, but not in any random or cluttered manner. He had their cellular memories, but only those that mattered for the success of the galactic-wide military force that his triumvirate led.

I am first among equals, he thought, thinking of his two companions.

It was Coreq's own observation, but an apt one. The others— Premier Enver and Warlord Tarix—deferred to him on virtually all matters of importance. Sometimes this surprised him whenever they were discussing military or security matters, since Tarix knew considerably more about those subjects than Coreq did. But Tarix always phrased her statements with exquisite care, so that she was the adviser and Coreq the decision maker.

Even so, Coreq didn't entirely trust her, or Enver, either. He always suspected they were plotting against him, planning to take over at the first opportunity. But the High Ruler was no fool. Wherever he went, he had his personal retinue of elite robot guards close behind, and robotic security agents checking the route ahead. Tiny biomachines tasted his food and beverages for poisons, and even flew in front to test the air he was about to breathe. He'd thought of everything. Some of them hovered above him now, still taking readings and sending audible electronic signals to him, while others went further ahead, to scout where he intended to go.

Presently he left one lab section and entered the large central chamber, where some of the most famous experiments were conducted. It always gave him a rush coming in here, because he and his two HibAdu cohorts had been created at these very lab stations, had taken their first breaths here.

Ahead, Coreq saw a flurry of biomachines in the air, like a horde of insects. He heard their high-pitched exchanges and reports as they confirmed the area was safe for the High Ruler to enter. Because of their tiny size, the units reminded him of Parviis, but the comparison did not go much beyond that. Coreq could control these biomachines with an implanted transmitter in his own brain, while Parviis required a different sort of attention.

For the moment, Coreq's aides had arranged for Woldn and his followers to occupy all of the observation galleries around the central chamber, where they clustered on the other side against the thick glax, and peered into the huge laboratory. Security sensors reported more than one hundred and sixty thousand of the tiny aliens there, packed into the enclosures.

Though the High Ruler had tried to secure the galleries and prevent the escape of the pesky visitors, the tiny humanoids had a form of collective paranoia, in which Woldn kept them in a state of hyper alertness, constantly checking and maintaining routes of escape. Obviously, it was a survival mechanism and Coreq would have found it interesting, had he not wanted to dominate these creatures and take them into custody. But, to keep the situation calm and under control, he had been forced to back off, leaving some escape routes open.

Woldn had presented twenty volunteer Parviis to the Adurian scientists for dissection and detailed analysis. This reflected the purpose of the Parvii leader's visit: to investigate a possible ancient connection between Adurians and Parviis. Seventeen days ago, upon first hearing this claim from his private box in the assembly hall, Coreq had almost dismissed the notion out of hand, since his enhanced and focused memories carried no reference to such a connection. But—via an intercom that connected the leaders' private boxes—Warlord Tarix and Premier Enver had convinced him otherwise. Enver said he had a faint but undocumented sensation that the contention might very well be true. While no data actually existed in the Premier's conscious memory, not even a discernible fragment, he said it was important sometimes to follow through on sensory feelings. He and Tarix had recommended that they look into the matter, so Coreq had agreed.

And, although the Adurian scientists had been reluctant to say much, Coreq knew they were fearful of this line of inquiry. It had to do with an odd psychosis of their tunnel-minded race, in which—despite great successes in genetics and bioengineering—they were afraid of their own collective past, and ashamed of it. According to legend, terrible things had happened to them as a race long ago, and their collective humiliation had caused them to stop talking about such matters, and to gradually try to forget them. Even so, fragments of the past remained in their consciousness, of lost wars and planets destroyed. The details were vague, however, despite the fact that the Adurians had the ability to track genetic memories back for thousands of generations. It seemed logical to Coreq that some Adurians must have gone privately into the cellular archives and learned the full truth, but if so they were not talking about it—and thus far he had been unable to discover anything through the ongoing police methods of reading the cells of citizens.

In the days since Coreq had ordered the new investigation, highly agitated Adurian scientists had been delving further into the genetic memories of their own people, and of the twenty Parviis from the swarm, seeking information, some common ground. The old data did not come through clearly, but clues were surfacing along genetic paths that the researchers followed backward, using complicated techniques. The scientists did this with both races, and as ancient memories came back they were processed, converted to data, and projected onto screens.

Now, on a large wall screen of the central chamber, the lab technicians displayed two side-by-side composite projections, one for the combined memory cells of each race. Images sped up and slowed, as the experts searched for connections, for similarities. As Coreq stood looking up at the screen, the Parvii side showed views of deep space, of suns, planets, and swirling nebulas in a hypnotic array of colors and shapes.

To the left of it, the Adurian side was much more limited in astronomical scope, showing trips through space, but comparatively more images of the Adurian homeworld itself. Coreq recognized his own capital city, always bustling in its various stages of historical development, and he saw yellow-suited scientists that worked long ago, looking very much like their modern counterparts.

Now the present laboratory manager—an old Adurian with a pointed chin—pushed back the hood of his suit and joined Coreq. "I wish you had not asked us to research this matter, sir, for it has put my staff on the verge of a nervous breakdown. They are holding together as well as possible, but I am worried about them."

"Don't ever come to me with such drivel," Coreq said. "My time is valuable, and if you're not careful, your time will be limited."

"I have already enjoyed a long and productive life, but I do not wish to displease you. In addition, High Ruler, I must admit that I am finding the ancient lab procedures intriguing as they are revealed to us, though many of them would be of little interest to you. There is . . . Wait! I just saw something."

Though Coreq normally cared little about names, he had remembered the name of this particular scientist, because he had been on the team that grew the three triumvirate leaders in this very laboratory. He called himself Bashpor, and might need to be dealt with eventually because of his arrogance, even though he had never been proven disloyal. For the moment, at least, he remained useful.

From a high-caste family, Bashpor and his team had initially tried to exert control over the HibAdu triumvirate. That had soon proved impossible, because the hybrids were so dominating and powerful, so the Bashpor group had slipped into what appeared to be a subservient position. And, while they were not entirely pleased with this, Coreq had the surveillance reports to prove that they had formed no conspiracy against the triumvirate, and that they held considerable emotional affection for their three laboratory creations.

Of utmost importance, from all appearances the galactic aims of the top Hibbil and Adurian scientists and of the HibAdu hybrids matched: Eliminate the Merchant Prince Alliance and the Mutati Kingdom. Thus far, the military successes had been gratifying, but a great deal of work remained to be completed, mopping up the remaining—and significant—resistance forces.

With a wave of his hand, Bashpor stopped the Adurian screen images from moving, and backed them up. Then, as the scientist enhanced the image of a table at the rear of the long-ago laboratory, Coreq saw what looked like tiny humanoids inside a clearglax enclosure. It took several seconds, but with more enhancement and enlargement, the images came into focus.

"Parviis?" the High Ruler asked.

"It would appear so, Your Eminence. I'll do more checking, but it looks to me like we created them in our laboratories."

Around him, Coreq heard the Parviis clamoring inside the observation galleries. A microphone clicked on, and Woldn asked, "That's the proof, isn't it?"

"It is a possible indication," the lab manager said, transmitting to him. "We shall investigate it further."

"I was right!" Woldn shouted, with his small voice made large by the lab's sound amplification system.

Later that day, the HibAdu leaders received a more complete report from the lab manager.

Inside a sleek office suite, High Ruler Coreq sat at a wide, polished desk, with Premier Enver on one side of him, and Warlord Tarix on the other. They stared blankly with their overlarge, pale yellow eyes, and listened.

"An intriguing tableau has emerged," Bashpor said. "Now that I've opened my mind to it, I must admit that it is very interesting." He paced back and forth in front of the big desk. "In ancient times, we Adurians were even more involved in biotechnology than we are now. Content with our present scientific and societal conditions, we never thought to delve so far back in our genetic history."

"Not content," Coreq said. "Fearful is more like it. But continue."

The old Adurian paused, and looked at the three. "We have always believed that the future is a more interesting domain."

"Undoubtedly that is one of the reasons that you created us," Tarix said, her oddly-echoing voice reverberating through the room. Her long white teeth glistened, which she liked to display to throw terror into underlings. At the moment, it had its effect on Bashpor, as he could not hold gazes with her. To avoid that uncomfortable position, he resumed pacing.

"In ancient days, we were engaged in countless wars, some of which did not go well for us. In modern times we knew that had occurred, but only in general. Here's a specific detail that rises above others: Long ago, we created two galactic races in our laboratories."

Coreq leaned forward. "*Two?* One was the Parviis, I assume?"

"Correct. The other has no name, but they are even smaller than Parviis, and have a domain that is quite surprising and intriguing. For want of a better term I shall refer to them as sub-biologicals, or sub-bios. Mmmm. They are nano-creatures, so I shall call them Nanos instead. Yes. In the most unlikely of all places, the Nanos live *inside* the galactic webbing, the structure that Tulyans and Parviis call Timeweb."

"I think we should call them Webbies instead of Nanos," Enver said. Sometimes he said off-the-wall things, focusing on irrelevant points. Just the same, Coreq thought the name that Enver suggested was preferable, so he nodded.

"Very well," Bashpor said. "Regarding their exact function, we don't know how to test any hypothesis, but we think the . . . Webbies . . . may explain how Tulyans are said to communicate across vast distances over the galactic infrastructure. If that is the case, the infinitely small creatures might also have something to do with the nehrcom transmission system of the Humans, a system we have replicated, without really understanding how it works. It is believed to operate through some sort of web-related cosmic frequency. I have more to tell you, much more."

Bashpor increased the speed of his pacing, as if charged with a drug. "Long ago, other galactic races took offense at our laboratory methods, so they went to war with us over them. Among our enemies were the Blippiqs and the Huluvians, and they forced us to abandon our laboratory attempts to create new races. It seems that we went back to doing the forbidden

271

things anyway, however, when we created you three HibAdus. Of course, that doesn't amount to an entire race yet, but I know your professed intentions in that regard."

"*Will* you stop pacing!" Coreq said. "My neck aches from watching you go back and forth."

Looking very nervous, Bashpor slumped into a chair in front of the leaders. Then, not making firm eye contact with them, he continued to speak. "In those long-ago days, the other galactic societies considered our experiments dangerous and unethical—which led to the hostilities. After using their war machines and forcing treaties on us to shut down that phase of our researches, the Blippiqs and Huluvians made attempts to eradicate the entire Parvii race. This proved unsuccessful." He paused. "But in response to the threat, the Parviis bred at a high and efficient rate, and soon their aggressive swarms wreaked havoc in the galaxy by taking control of the podship race away from the Tulyans. It seems that we caused a bit of trouble in space, albeit indirectly and unintentionally."

"And we're doing it again," Tarix said. "But this time, no one will stop us. We are no longer mere Adurians. We are *HibAdus.*"

"There is one thing more of particular interest," Bashpor said. "We have long suspected this, but now we have the proof, having followed the genetic markings back in time and unraveled the details: Genetic mutations of the Parviis led to the abhorrent Human race."

"Good reason to wipe out both races," Tarix said, leaving a long, eerie echo at the conclusion of her words.

Awaiting word from the triumvirate, Woldn felt a change of pressure in the linked observation galleries. He exchanged telepathic alarm signals with his followers. All of them went into a frenzy as those stationed at the perimeters, in the ducts, and at all previously unsealed areas sent information to him. Outside the dome, the sentries he had positioned relayed additional information. With all of this data, the Eye of the Swarm knew the Adurians were making a more concerted and overt effort to seal the galleries and prevent escape.

"We reject your offer of close cooperation between Adurians and Parviis," Coreq said, his voice booming over the speaker system.

"And I reject your rejection!" Woldn shouted back.

Ever-wary and prepared for this, Woldn knew exactly where the weakest Adurian security points were—and where he should focus the telepathic attention of his swarm. Though not yet at their full mental or physical powers, he and his followers had been growing collectively stronger, and they had telepathic detonators that functioned passably well. He led his swarm through a heating duct system, blasting everything out of the way in mini-detonations. Soon they found themselves in free space.

Woldn determined their course for the return voyage across the galaxy. Moments later, at the head of the small swarm, he vowed, "This Adurian insult shall not go unanswered!"

But he wondered who—and what—that odd creature in the laboratory had been. It looked male, as well as part Adurian and part Hibbil. A horrific combination of genes, from the look of it. Certainly it should have been a failed experiment, but the creature looked to be in charge of the entire operation.

Woldn had never seen anything like it. The very sight of the monster had given him chills.

Chapter Forty-Six

Appearances can be deceiving. Despite its bulky, fleshy form, a Mutati adult in its natural state weighs only half as much as a typical Human of the same age. Aeromutatis— the aviary version of the shapeshifter race—are just as light, but have stronger frames, so that they can fly other Mutatis on their backs, generally one at a time.

—MPA autopsy and interview results on Mutati prisoners

By taking interconnected hoverbus and airgrid plane routes, Dux, Acey, and the robot had been able to travel thousands of kilometers, getting them to Xisto, considered the last of the Sirikan frontier towns. In reality, there were other villages and towns in the back country beyond, but they did not have any form of public transportation.

When the boys and the small brown robot disembarked in the central square of Xisto, it was late morning. Dux and Acey had been eating sandwiches and any other quick food they could find, to keep going. Their passage and other expenses were all being paid by the unobtrusive-looking robot, from a compartment full of local funds that he carried. None of the townspeople even gave the trio a second glance; there were numerous other robots on the streets and visible in shops, performing a variety of tasks.

Unofficially, this was a personal trip to see the boys' grandmother. Officially, it was a military mission, to see if there were any HibAdu elements in the hinterlands. So far, other scouts had found no trace of them.

Acey said he knew his way around, since he'd been to this town before, with Grandma Zelk. "We want to go that way," he said, pointing toward a dirt road that led north.

They began walking, and within the hour picked up a ride from a flatbed hovertruck driver who talked cheerfully about his ranch and children. The teenagers rode with him inside the cab, while Kekur held onto a railing in the back. Later that afternoon they caught a ride from another farmer, this time on a motocart laden with fruits and vegetables. The people were quite friendly, just as the boys remembered. That night, they slept in an abandoned, ramshackle barn, while the robot kept guard over them.

The next afternoon, they got even luckier. For a modest charge, paid by Kekur, a young woman gave them a ride of five hundred kilometers in her crop-duster plane. On the way the boys ogled the attractive redhead and flirted with her. She had nice legs and a good figure that she didn't mind showing off to them. But nothing came of the encounter, and at dusk she circled over a small meadow near a river, preparing to set down in hover mode.

In the low light, none of them noticed a camouflaged encampment on the opposite river bank. Suddenly, beams of blue light hit the wings of the aircraft, sending it spinning toward the ground.

"What the hell?" the pilot shouted.

"HibAdu forces," Kekur reported. "I am notifying command headquarters."

The pilot fought for control against the blue beams, and for a few moments she got the craft flying again, on an escape route. Then a blast of light penetrated the cabin and hit her in the head, killing her instantly. Descending fast, the plane ripped off the top of a tree and then skimmed over the ground, ready to go down hard.

Neither the boys nor the robot noticed a large white bird circling high overhead. . . .

After the party left, Noah and Doge Anton had decided to send even more protection for them, so they'd told Parais d'Olor to follow, and to do what she could to keep them safe. Now she watched helplessly as the crop-duster plane landed roughly and skidded to a stop. She saw movement inside. One of the doors opened and the boys tumbled out, followed by the robot. They were on the side away from the HibAdu camp, so maybe the soldiers wouldn't see them.

Flying in a streak toward the crash site, Parais landed. Except for some bumps and bruises the boys were on their feet and looked all right to her.

"Parais!" Dux said. "What are you doing here?"

"Noah sent me," she said. "We need to move quickly."

Knowing she had no time to waste, Parais ripped free broken tree branches that the aircraft had snagged, and scooped up chunks of disturbed soil. Then she embraced the pile of material in her wings until it all glowed orange and melted into her body, making her into a larger and darker bird. Gradually, the glow subsided.

In absorbing so much organic matter at once, however, the shapeshifter risked compromising her complex internal chemistry, which could result in cellular damage and even death. Bravely and privately, she accepted the risk anyway, since she needed to carry three passengers on her back. With their dense bone structures, Humans were heavier than the Mutatis she typically carried, such as Hari. And that little robot probably weighed as much as the boys combined.

"I sent a distress call to headquarters," Kekur said, "with the coordinates of this enemy force."

"Good," Parais said. She heard soldiers running toward them, shouting commands to each other.

With the transfer of mass complete, the bird looked like a giant black eagle. "Jump on my back and hold onto my feather mane," she said.

Acey got on first, followed by Dux and the robot. In the early evening light, all were shadowy shapes on the bird's back.

As the bird got underway Dux shivered in fear, and from the chill wind that cut through his jacket and trousers. He held onto Acey, and behind Dux, Kekur held onto him. At first, Parais flew low over the ground, away from the troops. Finally, with powerful strokes of her massive wings, she lifted into the sky in a great upward arc.

Looking back, Dux saw spotlights illuminate the crash site. But he and his companions were safe, lifting high into the air where the HibAdus could no longer see or harm them.

"I'd better take you back to headquarters," Parais shouted back.

"No!" Acey shouted.

Just behind him on the eagle's back, Dux said, "We appreciate your help, Parais, but we need to check on our grandmother. We've come all this way to do that, and we don't want to turn back now. Please, fly us to her."

For several moments, the bird kept flapping in the same direction. Presently she asked, "Which direction?"

"To the right," Dux said, "beyond those mountains."

She changed course. As they flew past the peaks he had designated, an orange moon rose on the horizon, illuminating the way. Though the air was cold, the mountains were not extensive, and presently they saw a valley just ahead.

"She lives on the other side of that valley," Acey shouted.

The air became warmer. Below, Dux made out the simple

farms and fields of the Barani tribe, in this remote region where he and Acey had spent much of their childhood. Dim lights illuminated the windows of some of the small homes. But soon he saw that all was not well down there.

As they crossed the valley and passed over a small river, the orange moon cast enough illumination for Dux to see heavy destruction of the landscape, leaving its once-distinctive lakes and gnarled hills barely recognizable. Some of the land was broken, as if from seismic activity, and the stream where he and Acey had fished as boys was much wider now, having flooded many of the homesteads.

Nonetheless, the teenagers were still able to find the familiar ramshackle cabin of their grandmother, on cleared ground partway up a slope. The cabin was dark as they landed in a front yard that was cluttered with old household articles and rusty flying machines.

"Grandma doesn't like surprises," Acey said, keeping his voice low. "I'd better go ahead on my own and let her know we're here."

"God, I hope she's all right," Dux said. He waited with the robot and the shapeshifter, watching as Acey climbed a rickety stairway and rapped on the front door, shouting to identify himself. Dux saw a light go on inside, and then the door opened, casting more light across the cluttered yard.

Dux felt a rush of joy, and ran toward the cabin.

"I knew you were too ornery to get killed, Grandmamá," Acey said to the old woman, using a Barani term of endearment that she liked, but did not use in referring to herself. Dux caught up to them, and the boys hugged her.

"We brought along a couple of friends," Dux said, motioning back toward the shadows.

Small and deeply wrinkled, Grandma Zelk squinted to see. "Well, tell them to show their faces." A superstitious woman who spoke unusual dialects, she had a stooped posture and wore a long embroidered dress with large pockets. At her waist hung a stained pouch, with compartments full of her favorite folk medicines. Despite her years, she was tough and wiry-thin from climbing around in the hills, and had always bragged that she could out-hike any man.

When many members of her tribe were enslaved for not paying taxes to Doge Lorenzo, she was not included, since she hid in the backwoods and survived off the land until her pursuers went away. They wouldn't have wanted to catch up with the old woman anyway. At her waist she also wore her customary handgun in a holster, a weapon that she called her "equalizer"—to be used against any authority figure who might try to apprehend her.

"One of my friends is a robot," Dux said. "And you should know that the other is a . . . shapeshifter."

"A Mutati," Acey said, "but a good one. She's big, too, and flew us here on her back."

"I don't trust Mutatis," the old woman said, her voice a low, dangerous growl. "The robot can come in, but not the shapeshifter."

Dux hurried back to explain the situation to Parais, who stood with her wings tucked in against her sides. She had grown so large that she was bigger than a Tulyan. "That's all right," she said, in a voice that sounded very tired. "I have a coat of feathers to keep me warm. I'll just find a place out here to sleep."

"I'm sorry," Dux said.

"I might not be able to get through that doorway anyway. Besides, I see a nice thick canopy of trees to sleep in, and that's something I have grown accustomed to over the years, from long flights taken around my homeworld of Dij." She gestured with her beak, showing where she planned to be.

"We'll check back with you in the morning," Dux promised. Looking up, he saw that the sky was clear. Maybe it wouldn't rain during the night, but surely it would get colder than it was now. He shivered in a slight breeze from the mountains, but the bird didn't seem to feel it.

"Okay," Parais said. Her voice was weak and didn't sound good to him, but he assumed she would be better after she had rested.

He joined the others inside, where Grandma Zelk lit a log in the rock fireplace. As she puttered around, preparing tea, she spoke of the spirit world, and especially of Zehbu, the ancient god who was said to live within the molten core of Siriki.

"Interesting data," Kekur said. He stood by the fireplace as if warming himself there, though he should not have needed to.

"Some people think it's a lot of silliness," Acey said to the robot.

"Not necessarily," the robot said. "In my data banks I have similar stories from other star systems. Conclusion: Your god is a common legend that might very well have a basis in fact."

The old lady nodded, and said to Acey, "Don't make Zehbu angry, boy, or he'll get you for sure."

"I wasn't talking about myself," the young man said. "I was talking about some people."

"Well those 'some people' better not be around here," she said. "That's for sure. And don't you boys come around here with any foolish outsider ideas."

"We aren't, Grandmamá," Dux said. "We came because we're worried about you. We saw a lot of damage in the valley."

"The planet's got a sickness," the old woman said. She lifted a teapot from the stove, and poured three cups.

Dux held back saying what he'd heard, that the troubles were caused by something that went far beyond Siriki. A disintegrating galactic web and timeholes. His grandmother was stubborn, and would not take any interest in such stories, except to reject them out of hand. Acey kept the information to himself as well.

"Timeholes," the robot said.

"Eh?" Grandma Zelk said.

"She doesn't want to hear any nonsense," Dux said to Kekur. "Do not speak unless we give you permission."

The robot fell silent.

"I tried giving that order to you boys when you were only knee high," the stooped woman said. "Dux, you kept quiet, but Acey—I never could get you to shut up."

"I'm the same as I always was," Acey said. "And we're happy to see that you are, too."

Perched on a low cedar bough, Parais felt sharp lances of pain all over her body, and a deep fatigue that seemed to draw her down into it like quicksand.

Struggling for life, gasping for air, she knew that she needed to find a way to reduce her body mass quickly, or she would die. But she had used up a great deal of energy taking on the additional mass and flying here, and now she felt too weak to go through the necessary recovery steps.

Her eyes flickered shut.

CHAPTER FORTY-SEVEN

"Noah has invariably tried to see the positive side of things, despite extreme difficulties. It's one of the things I love about him. I haven't been able to see Noah for a while, but I've been told that he seems to be growing increasingly darker . . . as if he is losing some sort of an internal battle."

—Tesh Kori, remarks to Eshaz

Accompanied by men and women in MPA and Guardian uniforms, Tesh boarded a podship at the Canopa pod station, and found a bench seat at the rear. She did not like to magnify herself and ride as a passenger in one of the sentient vessels as she was doing now, but if she wanted to get to Siriki quickly, this was the only choice she had. Doge Anton, while permitting her to visit Noah in this manner, had forbidden her to take her own podship, *Webdancer,* on such a mission.

She thought back on the conversation she'd had with the youthful Doge that morning, and of the child growing in her womb.

"Think of what you're asking," Anton had said to her. They were standing in the tower of an airgrid station on Canopa, where the Liberators were setting up one of their ground bases. "*Webdancer* is my flagship. I can't have it flitting around the galaxy on personal missions. What is it you want to discuss with Noah anyway?"

"As I said, sir, it is a personal mission and I'll only be gone a few hours. The round-trip flight shouldn't take long, and allowing for the time to . . ."

"My answer is the same. No."

Tesh had looked away, at airgrid planes landing and taking off on the field, using their vertical take-off and landing systems.

"You and I were once close," Anton had said, "but it was not our fate to remain together for our entire lives. Or, I should say for *my* entire lifetime, in view of your longevity." He glanced over at his wife, Nirella (who was out of earshot), and exchanged smiles with her. "I'm happy with the choice I made," he added, "even though you forced it by leaving me."

"I prefer to say we drifted apart," she said.

"If I'd been paying attention, I would have noticed that you had a wandering eye. I took you away from Doctor Bichette, and in turn Noah spirited you away from me."

"Noah and I have no relationship," she said, bristling.

"Only because there hasn't been time," Anton said. "I've seen the way the two of you look at each other, the way you act around one another. There's electricity in the air, even when you argue. Anyone can see it."

"I won't deny that. All right, I'll leave *Webdancer* here."

"Leave the sectoid chamber unsealed, so a Tulyan pilot can operate the vessel if necessary."

After a moment's hesitation, Tesh nodded. "Unsealed it will be."

Now the other podship was loaded with passengers, only around twenty for this trip. The vessel taxied out of the orbital station and prepared to engage with the podways. Tesh saw a burst of green light outside, and then a dimmer, barely perceptible green hue out in space as the vessel sped along one of the strands of Timeweb.

This particular flight was part of a military procedure that General Nirella had established: regular courier runs linking

Canopa and Siriki, using designated podships. Since both planets were among the original merchant prince worlds, they still had functioning nehrcom stations at each, a technology that could have been used for communication. However, the Humans now knew that the cross-space communication system had been compromised by Jacopo Nehr's treacherous brother Gio, who had revealed the secret of the operation to the Mutatis almost a year ago. The Mutatis had, in turn, revealed what they knew to the Adurians. While some of the MPA leaders had suspected that the technology had been leaked for some time now, they now knew details of how it happened—information that had been provided voluntarily by their new allies, Hari'Adab and the Mutatis.

It was early evening on a moonlit night when Tesh rode the shuttle down from the pod station and landed on Siriki. The Golden Palace, which she had seen lit up in past visits, was now blacked out for military purposes, as was most of the planet. With modern infratech systems, she knew darkness only provided limited concealment benefits, so she wondered why the authorities didn't just blaze all the lights they had, as a means of flaunting, and of aggravating the enemy. Maybe that was the answer; maybe they didn't want to provoke the emotions of their foe. At least not yet.

Emotions, she thought. *That's why I'm here.*

Having sent a comlink message down from the pod station, she hoped it had gotten through to Noah. She waited at the main entrance of the terminal. For just twenty minutes, but it seemed like an eternity, as Humans, robots, and Tulyans looked at her in peculiar ways. Around her, everyone seemed to have their lives organized with military precision, but hers was anything but that.

Finally, when she was about to give up and go in search of him, he arrived in an MPA staff car, driven by a robot. One of the rear doors slid open. Not even getting out, Noah leaned through the opening and said, "Get in. I can only talk for a little while."

"Perhaps we should make it some other time."

"No. With my schedule, it's always something." An interior light brightened, so that she could see him better. Noah hadn't shaven in a couple of days, and his eyes looked tired. His curly, reddish hair was mussed. He smiled disarmingly, and this broke her momentary anger.

"I suppose that's understandable." She sat beside him, and the door closed behind her. The interior light dimmed.

"What is it?" Noah said, as the car made its way back toward the palace, without visible headlights.

"Aren't you glad to see me? It's been too long."

"Of course. It's just that there's a lot going on here. I was about to leave for Yaree, but something important came up and I've been forced to change my plans. EcoStation is orbiting that planet, so I wanted to check on it. The unaligned Yareens are potential military allies, too."

"Sure, EcoStation. I worked for you on the orbiter, remember? But how did it get to Yaree?"

"It's one of the things I want to investigate. I still hope to go, but later. Until I can get there, I'm sending a recon team of Tulyans, diplomats, and military officers."

"What made you change your plans?"

"You remember Acey and Dux?"

"Sure."

Noah went on to tell her where the teenagers had gone, and how the robot Kekur had sent a distress call that they were under HibAdu attack in the back country. "We're organizing a rescue-and-attack squadron right now," he said. "I'm going with it."

"But you have so many other responsibilities. Surely you can delegate that one."

"HibAdus are a priority. Besides, those boys may not always be near, but they're Guardians through and through. I've always seen them as future leaders, after they finish sowing their wild oats. And as for you, Tesh, I'm always glad to see you. From the moment I met you, I knew you were a . . . special case."

"You make me sound like a fugitive from a nut house."

"In this war, aren't we all?"

"I suppose. Look, I don't need much of your time. I have to get back to my own duties, piloting Anton's flagship."

"Pull over there," Noah said, reaching forward and pointing so that the driver could see what he wanted.

Noah and Tesh got out in a shadowy garden area, where pathways and a pond were illuminated in moonlight.

"Here," Noah said, handing a pair of night-vision glasses to her. "I don't think you'll need these with the natural lighting, but just in case."

"Thanks." She tucked them into a pocket of her jacket, as he did with his own pair. "It's kind of heavenly out here tonight, and maybe that's a sign."

"A sign?" he said.

"Just the observation of a hopelessly romantic female."

"You're anything but hopelessly romantic." Noah leaned down and kissed her affectionately on the lips, then grasped her hand and led her toward the pond. His grip was warm and strong, and she felt his steady pulse against her magnified skin.

"Since we don't have much time, I'm going to be very direct," Tesh said.

"Normally we men prefer that, but coming from you, I'm not so certain I want to hear it. I've never been able to figure you out, or what we mean to each other."

"Odd that you'd say that, because I've been stewing over the same thing. There hasn't been enough time for us, has there?"

"No." He kissed her again, longer this time, before they continued on the walkway. The moon reflected on the pond, an image broken by a wooden boardwalk that led to a small island at the center.

As they walked along the creaking boardwalk, Tesh said, "From the beginning, I knew something about you, too. Or should I say, about *us*. Sparks were always there between us, a physical passion that neither of us could deny. As a Parvii, I've lived a lot longer than you, and I've had more . . . relationships, as your Human women like to call them. From the beginning, I couldn't stop thinking about you, Noah. I'm sorry to be so direct, but the war forces my words, compresses our lives."

"That's all right." He led her to a bench on the island, and they sat down, still holding hands, to gaze out on the reflections of the pond.

"We had our one time together. You thought it was only a dream since you were with me through Timeweb, but it actually happened."

"Two months ago, right?"

"Sixty-eight days," she said, with a hard stare at him.

During all that time, until just a few days ago, Tesh had been carrying his seed within her, until she finally made her decision about what to do. Now she felt their child growing inside, and she wondered how to tell him, what to say. She needed to choose her words carefully. This was no ordinary man, and she could not predict how he would respond if he knew.

Unsure if she should tell him at all, and especially now, she hesitated. Noah was a busy, important man.

"As complicated as our lives have been," she said, "neither of us have had time to explore the real potential of our relationship."

"I have to admit, I've always found you intriguing," he said. Looking at her intently, he said, "This is going to sound like a line, but whenever I look into your pretty green eyes, I see a universe of stars and planets, a universe of possibilities. I see the past and the future in you. You are one woman, and you are all women who have ever lived. I love the depths of you."

"That was quite a mouthful. You can see the color of my eyes, even in this light?"

"Do you think I would forget what you look like?"

She kissed him, and asked, "Did you just tell me that you love me, or that you love all women in general? Do you only love the 'depths of me,' or do you love all of me?"

"That's a complex question." He grinned as he considered how to reply.

While she held his left hand, her fingers wandered inside his sleeve, and she felt rough skin on his wrist and forearm. Odd. It must be the scars of an injury he hadn't told her about yet. Not wanting to make him uncomfortable, she quickly withdrew.

Just then, they heard voices, and on the far side of the pond—away from the palace—Tesh saw dark figures in the moonlight. Five Human shapes, moving furtively through the garden.

Noah put on his night-vision glasses, and so did she.

"It's . . ." Tesh hesitated. "One of them looks like Princess Meghina. Is she here?"

"Yes. She's led an interesting life."

"Look," Tesh said. "They're moving strangely, going in a circle. What are they doing?"

"I don't know."

Rising to his feet, Noah went back on the boardwalk the way they had come, moving slowly and keeping to the side, where the boards squeaked less.

Following him, Tesh did the same. So far, she had not gotten to say what she'd intended, and now she might not get the opportunity. As they left the magical, moonlit island, it seemed to her that a spell had been broken. She sighed. Maybe it was for the best. For his own safety, Noah needed to keep his full attention on his important duties. That was the case with her, too, and she wondered if she should have waited longer before commencing her pregnancy.

What's done is for the best, she thought. *If I had waited, it might never have happened.* And it needed to happen. Tesh was sure of that.

She followed him to a stand of high shrubbery, and they peered through an opening in it. . . .

Princess Meghina had been feeling peculiar, and almost giddy. For her, always conscious of her duties and of making the proper impression on others, this was most unusual. But around the other immortals, especially now that Kobi Akar was gone, she'd been feeling more comfortable. After jumping off the cliff, her companions had all healed at varying rates, and they were fine now. Meghina still didn't think she would ever make that leap.

She wanted to maintain her dignity, but she also wanted to be part of this special group, a group that was elite in its own, ineffable way. Not that living forever was a sign of status, or of some bonus that the gods had given to them. At least she didn't see it that way. Sometimes she almost felt it was a curse, a burden that she and the others had to bear. The Salducian diplomat had failed in his responsibilities, and now he was paying the price for it. He would spend a long time incarcerated, a long time being miserable. Of course, they couldn't give him a life sentence, because that would never end, and he had not committed a crime that warranted the death sentence. He was a unique prisoner. No doubt about it.

Now she held hands with Betha Neider on one side and Paltrow on the other, and all of them were linked in a circle with Llew Jarro and Dougal Netzer, circling in the moonlight, circling and dancing.

On one level, the one that was most obvious to her, this all seemed silly, and almost a cliché. But they weren't *dancing* in the moonlight, not exactly. It was more an improvised thing for them to do together in this private place where they could let off some of the pressures and behave in an impulsive, childlike manner. But this wasn't childlike, she quickly realized. As they moved around and around, it occurred to her that they were doing something very important.

Stupid thoughts. On a superficial level, Meghina felt silly. But deeper, where it really mattered much more, she felt quite different. This was their shared destiny.

Our destiny to spin in circles? One side of her asked a question of the other. And the other side did not answer. It just kept compelling her to go around and around in the garden.

Looking on, Tesh and Noah heard the scuffing and stepping of feet as Meghina and her companions continued their strange amusement. To Tesh, it looked like some sort of weird religious ritual, and she wondered if they would strip off their clothes next and paint themselves blue, as the ancients of Lost Earth used to do. With her military glasses, she saw the garden in full color, and the dark clothing of the circling people.

"Do you think they're drunk?" she whispered. Then, from the direction of the zoo, she heard an animal roar.

"They're drunk on something," he whispered back. "Can't say what, though."

"Shall we join them?"

"I . . ." When Noah hesitated, she noticed a peculiar expression on his face as he watched Meghina and the others. One of longing, she thought, and fascination. Then he said, "I'll go, but you stay here."

"Why? They aren't dangerous."

"Maybe I shouldn't go, either."

"You're not making sense."

"I . . . I feel like they're tugging at me, wanting me to be with them. But I feel something else, too, telling me not to. I . . . Uh, on second thought, I think we should both stay here."

"That was a confusing answer."

He fell silent.

Tesh felt her own conflicting sensations. Noah always had good instincts. It was one of the things that made her comfortable being around him. He seemed like a protective force to her. But now she wondered why he was behaving this way.

Princess Meghina glanced in their direction, as if she had heard something. Tesh froze, seeing the eerie glint of moonlight in the inquisitive, questing eyes. A chill ran down her back, as she felt a rush of fear. But the Princess soon looked away, and never stopped circling with the others. Faster and faster they whirled in a bizarre dance. And, as if in concert with them, animals in the zoo roared, chattered, and called out in high, agitated pitches.

At that moment, a faint green mist encompassed the five people, a mist that thickened and grew more green as moments passed, until Tesh could no longer see the dancers. The sounds diminished, and finally faded away entirely.

Presently the mist cleared, and the people were gone. Tesh saw only a moonlit garden, as if the whole scene had been an apparition.

Moving with caution, Noah led the way around the shrubbery, to the place where they had seen the strange activity.

On the ground, they found five heaps of clothing arranged in a circle. It looked like a magic trick. But as Tesh lifted the heap that had been Princess Meghina's black gown, she gasped.

Tesh saw a moonlit hole in the ground, with something jammed down into it, out of reach. Thinking Meghina was trapped in the hole, Noah used a comlink to call for help.

While waiting, he and Tesh dug desperately with their hands, widening the opening. Finally Noah touched whatever was in there, but it only crumbled. Within minutes, uniformed soldiers burst onto the scene, and they began digging with autoshovels.

Beneath each pile of clothing, they found a hole. And inside every hole, only the husks of four Humans and one Mutati—like exoskeletons—with nothing inside.

CHAPTER FORTY-EIGHT

Each sentient creature has a mental list of things to worry about. The lists are of varying lengths and of varying significance. It has been observed, though, that the thing that gets you will not even be on your list.

—Anne Jules, child philosopher of Lost Earth

Several times during the night, Dux had awakened and worried about the brave Mutati outside. Now, as he stirred yet again and opened his eyes, he wondered if he should go out and check on her. That might disturb everyone, though. He recalled that his grandmother was a light sleeper, and cantankerous if she didn't get her rest.

Dux and his cousin slept on thin pads that Grandma Zelk had laid out for them on the floor of the small cabin. In the shadows only a couple of meters away, he saw the robot sitting by the dying embers of the fireplace. Kekur was a peculiar sentient machine, but he did seem dedicated to his duties. One of the yellow lights around his faceplate pulsed slowly. Undoubtedly, he was monitoring his surroundings, standing sentry over the boys.

Once more, Dux drifted off to an uneasy sleep. . . .

In the morning, when he heard the old lady clattering around in the kitchen, Dux dressed hurriedly and went outside. A chill wind stabbed into his bones, and he closed his jacket.

Just ahead, he saw Parais perched on a low cedar bough that

drooped under her weight, almost all the way to the ground. He hurried to her side. Behind him, he heard his grandmother calling his name, but he ignored her for the moment.

The Mutati opened one large eye, and Dux was shocked to see that it was a sickly shade of yellow, with purple veins through it. Her posture was bad and she leaned, as if about to tumble off the branch.

"Parais," he said. "Are you all right?"

"Took on too much mass," she said. "Must expel it, but I'm so tired. My avicular chemistry has been warring with the increased organic material that I absorbed." Her voice grew increasingly faint as she continued. "Just before dawn, I tried . . . tried to shed my body of the excess, but only stirred up my insides more, making me feel worse. I'll try again later."

"Are you sure you should do that?"

"Maybe. There are methods I've learned from other aeromutatis." She looked up into the gray, foggy sky. "Perhaps the sun will come out, and give me new energy."

Turning toward the cabin, Dux saw the old woman on the porch, with her hands on her hips. She did not look pleased, but at the moment he didn't care about that.

He ran to her and said, "Grandmamá, we must help the Mutati. She saved our lives and risked her own. Can you give her a folk medicine?"

The wrinkled woman scowled. "You say she's a good Mutati, eh? Maybe she's fooled you, and the minute she's stronger she'll kill us all."

Acey was in the cabin doorway now, with the robot behind him. "Parais wouldn't do that," Acey said. "She could have killed us many times before. We all trust her."

"The Mutati needs help," Kekur said.

The prior evening, Dux had told the robot not to speak without permission, so this gave him a moment's pause. He decided not to scold him, however. Maybe Kekur's internal programming had determined that it was a military priority to revive the Mutati.

"My healing powder might work on her," Grandma Zelk said, touching the pouch at her waist, "but I hate to waste it on a shapeshifter. With all of the sickness in the ground around here, I've been sprinkling it on problem areas, trying to heal Zehbu."

"Living planet organism to the Barani tribe of Siriki," Kekur said. "Zehbu is linked to larger galactic-god entity Buko. A variation on the Tulyan deity Ubuqqo, one of many versions of the ultimate divinity. All unsubstantiated folk tales."

"Don't make me come after you with a stick," the old woman said to the robot.

The yellow lights blinked around Kekur's faceplate, but he had the good sense not to respond.

"Sadly, my supply of healing powder is diminishing," Grandma Zelk said. "My powder came from my ancestors before me, who got it from Zehbu, along with the obligation to use it properly. Just a grain or two a decade was all Siriki needed in the past to remain healthy, but the required amount has increased dramatically."

"Don't waste your . . . healing powder on me," Parais said, barely getting the words out. "Use it for a larger purpose."

"The shapeshifter makes sense," the old woman said, patting her small bag. "Look, boys, have you ever seen my pouch so flat? This is all I have left. Zehbu has been too sick to produce any more of it, and I'm afraid the downward cycle is irreversible."

As if punctuating her comments, Dux felt the ground tremble underfoot.

"No place is safe anymore," she said. Her face darkened, and gripping the pouch tightly, she turned and strode up a rocky slope. The boys followed, as did the robot. She kept up her legendary brisk pace, and as they climbed Dux was surprised that he didn't hear a flow of water coming from up there, where the mountain stream ran down into the valley.

They reached a rock promontory where they could look down on the stream. Though it was late spring in the Sirikan back country and the water had always flowed swiftly in the past, it was nothing like that now, only a weak, trickling rivulet.

Bowing her head, the old woman said, "This water is one of the arteries of the living planet-god. You see how it is."

"Yes," Dux said. Somehow, the old superstitions and legends about Zehbu and the larger galactic entity Buko had always seemed true to him. The concepts seemed linked to the galactic ecology theories espoused by Noah Watanabe.

Hearing a noise behind them, Dux saw the large black eagle Parais fly in, struggling to flap her wings. She managed to alight on an evergreen tree branch, which sagged under her weight. He thought she might look a little smaller than before, so perhaps she had managed to shed some of her mass. Or, it was only his wishful thinking. She still didn't look well.

Noticing the shapeshifter, Grandma Zelk scowled at it. Her fingers rested on the handle of her powerful handgun, then moved away.

"Zehbu is displeased with the sins of mankind," the old woman said, "so he seeks vengeance on the inhabitants of the planet." Her voice became eerie and shuddering as she added, "None of us are safe anymore."

She brought out a smaller, yellowing pouch from the larger one at her waist. Dux had seen it before. It was her special "healing powder," a green dust that reminded him of a similar-looking substance that he'd seen Eshaz sprinkle on the ground of Canopa once, during a momentary lapse when the Tulyan had not seen him watching. Dux wondered now if the substances might be related, and perhaps even identical.

Grandma Zelk opened the little pouch carefully, and for several moments she stared into it. But for some reason she did not reach in and sprinkle any of the contents around. Instead she tilted her head slightly, as if listening for something.

At that moment the ground shook violently for several seconds, and everyone struggled to maintain their footing. Acey hurried to his grandmother to help her, but she stood on her own and shook him off. Dux heard a distant roar, and was shocked to see the stream hiss below them, and turn to glowing red. Moment by moment, it became a heavier flow.

"Magma," Kekur said, in a mechanical, matter-of-fact tone that seemed out of place for the emergency. But after that he said, "I am reporting this rupture of the planetary crust to headquarters."

The glowing river flowed surprisingly fast, a powerful torrent heading for the valley floor below. Then, filling the old stream channel, the molten material began rising toward Dux and his companions, climbing the banks several meters a minute and causing trees and loose rocks to tumble into it.

Abruptly, a deep crack appeared in the hillside close to their feet and some of the lava began to flow into it.

"We'd better get out of here," Acey said, again reaching for his grandmother.

But the rail-thin old lady would hear none of it, and held her ground. "I'm staying," she said.

Dux saw a pool of hot magma perhaps fifty meters down slope from them, and he felt the heat. A queer sensation filled his brain, as if part of it had cracked off with the debris and fallen into the chasm.

Grandma Zelk opened her little pouch of healing powder and scattered a pinch of it toward the lava. As if by magic, a little breeze caught the powder and lifted it into the molten material, where it sparked and disappeared. "That is all I can do," she said, closing the pouch. "It is no use to throw more in." Her voice trailed off and she began murmuring incantations, as if to further ward off the evil spirits.

As long moments passed, Dux detected no noticeable effect on the flow.

Finally, behind him he heard a squeal of pain, and saw that Parais had tried to fly to them, but had fallen to the rocky surface, where she lay in a pile of feathers, struggling to breathe.

CHAPTER FORTY-NINE

*I can think of no more admirable trait than loyalty. It is the
bond of honor that holds together relationships at all levels.
The great leader can only fulfill his vision if he obtains the
undying allegiance of his followers.*

—*In the Words of the Master,* by Subi Danvar

Having already dispatched an attack squadron to confront the
HibAdu force that Kekur had reported in the back country,
Noah prepared to depart for the same region himself—an area
where Kekur was also reporting tremors and the eruption of
underground magma.

A military gridjet awaited Noah at the palace landing field,
along with another squadron. In his office moments ago, he had
dispatched a courier message to Doge Anton, reporting the
situation to him. It had been a long night, and Noah had only
been able to grab two hours of restless sleep, which he had
forced on himself with a dermex, something that he didn't like
to do. But it had provided him with a deep slumber, and he did
not feel overly tired at the moment.

Before leaving for the back country, Noah stopped by the
garden area where Meghina and her companions had disappeared the night before. As he stepped out of the hovercar, a
moist morning fog hung in the air, brightened by filtered
sunlight.

He walked around the high shrubbery and saw soldiers using

ground penetrating scanners and other equipment, trying to determine what had happened. The area had been excavated, creating a large single hole where there had previously been five smaller ones. In a patch of sunlight off to one side, two of Noah's officers and a Tulyan woman investigated the exoskeletons that had been removed from the holes. They lay in pieces on a ground tarp, but enough remained of their structures to show that they had once been four Humans and a Mutati, and that their original bone structures had been altered in death to thin, dry crusts.

Of all the strange things Noah had seen and experienced in his lifetime, what he had witnessed last night had been the most peculiar. And not just because of what he saw. While watching the whirling dancers, he had felt a powerful urge to join them, and an even stronger urge *not* to, because it would be dangerous to do so. He had hesitated, and then had followed the more compelling instinct, which proved to be right.

Where had Meghina and her companions gone? Would Noah have gone with them? All of them, and Noah as well, were immortals. Now he sensed that the compulsion to join them had something to do with the never-ending quality of life he shared with them. They had been drawn into something, but he—perhaps because he had a slightly different and perhaps stronger form of the condition—had been able to resist.

But what did I resist? And did I do the right thing? Suddenly, he wasn't certain.

Glancing at his wristchron, he knew he had to board the gridjet. Even so, he took a few moments and walked over to the exoskeletons. He'd seen them during the night when they were dug out, and now they seemed to confirm that it had not all been a nightmare, and that it had really happened.

The Tulyan woman looked at him, and said, "They vanished into five tiny timeholes that opened up and then closed afterward. Like little cosmic jaws."

"Maybe we'd be safer getting off this planet," one of the two officers said. He was Keftenant Ett Jahoki, a young man from a long tradition of military officers who had served with distinction in the Merchant Prince Alliance.

"No place is safe," the Tulyan said, her voice ominous. "Time-holes tear through spacecraft, too."

"But aren't podships safer?"

"True enough. They do sense cosmic disturbances and often are able to go around them, but I think Master Watanabe here would prefer to hold this planet and attempt to remedy the problems here."

"You're absolutely right," Noah said to the Tulyan. "What is your name?"

"Iffika," she said. "My good friend Eshaz has told me many good things about you."

"Thank you. But five tiny timeholes here? All in such close proximity?"

"Infrastructure defects take varying, surprising forms. We have seen similar things occur around the galaxy. I have tested this site carefully for telltale signs. There is no question about what happened."

"But where did Meghina and the others go? Where did the timeholes take them?"

"They were all immortal, so wherever they are I suspect they're still alive. Unless the physical impact on them was so severe that it demolished their cells to such a degree that they could not regenerate."

Noah emitted a long whistle. "I've gotta get going," he said.

Minutes later, as he boarded the red-and-gold gridjet, he thought about the special purpose of this trip. Kekur's additional report of tectonic activity in the back country could refer to timehole activity, and Noah wanted to see it firsthand, accompanied by another Tulyan expert who could analyze what was going on. Even in the midst of galaxy-spanning chaos, some geologic upheavals were still considered normal. But Noah wanted to be sure. He also wanted to check on the welfare of Dux, Acey, and Kekur, along with the independent old woman.

Making the situation even more complicated, there were Hib-Adus to be dealt with.

In the rugged Sirikan back country, it was midday. Overhead, the sky had darkened, as if forewarning a downturn in the weather.

Hours ago, Grandma Zelk had scattered a pinch of her healing powder onto the magma river, and in that time there had been some apparent effect, a slowing of the flow. Now she sat on a high rock staring down at the molten material and murmuring trancelike incantations to Zehbu, while holding the small pouch in her hands. The level of the lava had risen closer, and now was perhaps ten meters below her. Remaining with her, Dux, Acey, and Kekur had all expressed concern that they should leave, that it was not safe to stay.

But the old woman would hear none of it, and the boys didn't want to risk her health by forcing her to leave. She knew this country better than anyone, and had a right to remain if that was what she wanted. Her fate had become theirs.

Behind them, the Mutati bird lay on a flat stone. Since landing there, she had been taking measures to reduce her bodily mass, which she said she needed to do in order to remain alive. Every once in a while, Parais would glow orange and pieces of her body would peel off. Then she would adjust her form slightly, and the flesh and feathers would regenerate, as they were doing now.

So far she had shed only a small portion of her mass, and earlier she had told Dux it was a slow and painful process—and that she needed to get rid of more. "I won't go all the way back to my previous size," she'd said. "I want to remain large enough to carry two of you at a time."

"We can get out of here on our own," Acey had said.

"Perhaps, and perhaps not," she'd said in a gentle voice. "I suspect the latter." Then, she had grimaced from the internal pain and had concentrated inward.

Looking back at her now, Dux noticed that her feathers had lightened slightly in hue, so that they were no longer a rich black, but were instead more of a charcoal hue, with patches of dark gray.

He heard his grandmother's incantations louder beside him, and then she stood up. Holding the small pouch over her head, she shouted, "Zehbu, son of Buko, I implore you! Save this world!"

At that moment, the magma bubbled and smoked, and fingerlings of molten red material rose toward her, as if the planet god was reaching out to take her.

"Grandma, we've got to leave," Dux said. But, as she had done earlier with Acey, she pulled away. She had a beatific expression on her wrinkled face.

Despite the old woman's stubbornness, Dux was just about to grab her and force her to safety. At the last possible moment the lava fingers changed course, and—flowing quickly—they encircled the rocky promontory where he and his companions were. In a matter of moments, before anyone could do anything, they found themselves on an island, with lava flowing all around them. Dux felt the heat even more than before, and smelled sulfur, as if demons below were causing the upheaval.

The lava rose again, this time all around. Higher and higher. Feeling a wave of panic, Dux saw the Mutati standing up on her bird legs. Her eyes were still a sickly yellow, veined in purple, and she looked unsteady, in no condition to fly any of them to safety. Even if Parais could lift off, she might not be strong enough for passengers. . . .

Aboard the gridjet, Noah's pilot flew toward the coordinates that had been provided by Kekur. Just ahead, he saw the gridplanes and 'copters of his other squadron engaged in aerial dogfights against the orange-and-gray aircraft of HibAdu forces. On the ground, soldiers on each side faced off. He saw the HibAdu encampment in flames, but its soldiers were still fighting fiercely.

"Let's help out," Noah said.

His pilot nodded, and the small plane streaked into battle, firing blasts of white-hot energy at the enemy. The other ships with him followed.

Dux felt a jolt that knocked him down. To his horror, the rock under Grandma Zelk cracked with a loud report, and she tumbled into the lava. Her body hit the red-hot flow with a sickening thud and a hiss of steam, then vanished. Only her pouch of healing powder remained behind.

"Come on!" Parais shouted. "Get on my back!"

Grief-stricken, Dux grabbed the pouch and ran with Acey to the bird. As they were climbing on, Parais said, "I think I've found the right balance of mass and strength, and I feel a little better. I think I can fly, but no guarantees."

"Just like life," Acey said grimly.

She flapped her wings slowly, and began to lift off ever so slightly from the rocky deathtrap, like a heavily loaded cargo plane. Up they went, slowly and steadily. They passed through a pocket of very hot air that nearly took Dux's breath away. Moments later, higher, the air grew cooler and more breathable.

Looking back at the rock promontory below, he saw the loyal robot Kekur standing motionless, awaiting his fate.

"Drop us off and go back for him," Acey said, saying what Dux was already thinking.

But the living lava had another idea. Burning bright red, it swept over the rock and took Kekur with it.

CHAPTER FIFTY

In desperate times, desperate measures are required.

—Parvii Inspiration

Accompanied by two war priests and a small Parvii guard force, the Eye of the Swarm flew over a planet that glittered in varying hues, an ever-changing effect caused by solar conditions and the movement of glassy dust through the atmosphere. Once a favored site for galactic tourists and for the development of a machine army, the world had since fallen into complete disuse. With no regularly scheduled podships to bring anyone back, it was perfect for his needs.

Ignem.

The resurrection of this remote planet's importance would run parallel to the reawakening of the Parvii race. Soon he would have billions and billions of Parviis to set up military defenses here. Or, he could find another similar planet for his purposes. For what he had in mind, he only needed Ignem for a matter of days. Certainly, no one would disturb him in that time. High overhead in the orbital ring, there were still a few hundred machines at the Inn of the White Sun, but they were not expected to be any problem. They had no means of space travel, and even their shuttles for reaching the planet were slow and easily thwarted.

Woldn had come to believe in contingency plans. It was not something he had been particularly good at in the past when things were going well for the Parviis, but recently—in his hours of shame and despair—he had found himself reaching out, trying new things. Sprinkling seeds for the reawakening of his race.

For some time now, his breeding specialists had been operating a new propagation program inside the telepathic bubble, which Woldn had concealed far from Ignem in a dark, remote region of the galaxy where there were no suns or planets, and no other races were likely to interfere with his plans. Thousands of Parvii embryos had already been born, and more in incubation were about to be born. It was a steady, proven process.

But something even larger and more important had occurred, and this would involve Ignem. It would be a second, and potentially much larger, crucible for forging new life. . . .

Weeks ago, when Woldn and most of his swarm were on the Adurian homeworld, he had dispatched tiny spies to gather information from the entire laboratory complex. For millennia, it had been widely known that the Adurians operated the most advanced biological research and development facilities in the galaxy. But the products of those labs were not always known, since operations were kept under the tightest security. Even so, during his visit, Woldn had taken measures to find out what they were up to.

And he had accomplished that goal like a magician. The skill of misdirection.

While the Adurian leaders were focused on Woldn and his swarm in the observation galleries, his tiny spies were entering secret lab areas through the smallest openings, where they gathered data and transmitted it telepathically to the Eye of the Swarm. Not really understanding what they were looking at, the Parvii infiltrators were like little videorecorders, collecting information and sending it out for compilation and analysis. Even Woldn had not comprehended what they'd provided to him, so he'd taken it back to the five breeding specialists at the telepathic bubble.

The breeding specialists had been astounded by what they learned. Inside the bubble, hovering near the incubating Parvii embryos, they had met with Woldn. One of the breeding specialists, Qryst, had spoken for the others.

"The new information is exceedingly complex," he said. "Even with years of study, we might never understand all of it. But some important facts have emerged. First, that strange leader you saw is a hybrid of Hibbil and Adurian genes, one of only three that they created in the laboratory. Three that lived, I should say."

"And one of them is a leader? It looks like he at least runs the laboratory, and I suspect he's even more important than that."

"It seems backward, doesn't it? Growing leaders in a bio-lab. And yet, that appears to be what they did. But beyond that, we have learned something even more important, at least for our purposes."

"Yes?" Woldn felt his metabolism accelerate, and he heard it buzz around him.

"Although the Adurians have developed many methods of breeding, some of their incubation methods run parallel with ours. It is in this area that we focused our attention, trying to build on what we already know. The effort has required the mental probes of all five of us in concert, utilizing every bit of Parvii genetic knowledge that we have. And finally, I am pleased to report, we have something that is extremely useful."

"What is it? Get to the point, please!"

"The Adurians have a very clever, and very basic, incubation generator that produces births in a much larger number, and at a greater speed, than we ever dreamed possible. It is so simple that I'm surprised we didn't think of it ourselves. But of course, with the historical successes of the Parviis, we didn't need to, did we? We grew lazy, and complacent."

One of the other breeding specialists, Jeed, interjected. "On the other hand, our predecessors may have investigated this method and discarded it because of its inherent problems."

Woldn felt a sudden letdown.

"Nothing insurmountable," Qryst said.

"But it is something we must pay close attention to," Jeed insisted. "It seems that the incubation generators cause birth defects in a significant percentage of the embryos. We can produce many more Parviis with this method, but it must be done carefully, with strict quality control, segregation, and disposal procedures."

"What percentage will have defects?"

"As much as one in eighteen. We might get it as low as one in thirty, but I don't think we can do much better than that."

"There are methods of analyzing the embryos for defects," Qryst said, "so that we can get rid of them before birth."

"Of course, a small number of defective embryos will slip past any screening," Jeed said. He seemed to be the pessimist of the two. "Some of the hardier defective embryos will adapt for their own survival, so we will need to keep adapting ourselves."

"And the percentage of defects that get through?" Woldn asked, not sure how he felt about all of this new information.

"Very low," Qryst said. "Perhaps ten in a billion."

"I don't suppose I want to know what sort of defects they might have," Woldn said.

Qryst smiled. "Minor problems, for the most part."

"Theoretically," Jeed said.

"Nothing to worry about," Qryst retorted. "They won't be able to fly through space, or they will be slower, or they won't have telepathic abilities. We'll soon find them even if they are born."

Now, remembering all of this, Woldn led his guard swarm down toward the glassy surface of the planet. They passed through the red dust of a volcano, and entered a lava tube.

In his newfound system of developing contingency plans, Woldn had set up two distinct Parvii breeding programs, and had assigned breeding specialists to each. The initial program, the traditional one, would continue back in the telepathic bubble, under the direction of Imho and two other breeding specialists. This was the tried-and-true method, the way that his race had always bred. Assisting Imho in the bubble would be the pessimistic Jeed, and another breeding specialist, Sosk. As the reincarnated versions of past breeding specialists, the three of them were expected to be steady, predictable performers.

Here on Ignem, the new Adurian-inspired breeding program (and by far the most exciting of the two) was under the direction of Qryst, since he had shown such enthusiasm for the concept of incubation generators. To Woldn, he seemed like the sort of positive personality who would find ways around problems, a scientist who would keep the program going, despite difficulties. Assisting him would be Ruttin, a breeding specialist who in ancient times had been brilliant but erratic. Woldn expected Qryst, equally brilliant but more emotionally stable, to keep him in line.

Qryst and Ruttin had been on Ignem for only a short time, setting up the cutting-edge program. Already they were reporting excellent progress, and were about to combine their efforts with those of the war priests.

Inside the warm lava tubes of the volcanic planet, tens of billions of Parviis were breeding, using the laboratory methods of the Adurians. The Parviis were massing to attack again, breeding much faster than they could under natural conditions. In the past, a machine army had formed on the surface of Ignem, and had gone off to fight for the merchant princes.

Now a far more powerful force would emerge, one that would smash all opponents into oblivion.

CHAPTER FIFTY-ONE

The great unknown is a lure and a terror. Simultaneously it beckons and threatens us, and we find ourselves unable to resist the temptation. We simply *must* walk down those creaking stairs into the dark cellar.

—Ancient observation

On the unnamed planet in the unknown solar system, Pimyt scurried along a now-familiar path through the gray jungle. A morning fog hung low and moistened the fur on his face as he moved through it. He was the first one in the party to rise today, and had gone for a walk so that he could think, and settle his nerves.

The stranded group had even more problems than they had initially imagined. Something in the air had eroded the engines of the shuttle, so that the craft no longer flew at all. It was only good for a shelter, and already they were out of the packaged meals they had brought with them. That left only the local plants that they could gather from the jungle, most of which had minimal food value. No one had expected to remain away from the space station for so long.

Despite the obstacles, they had developed a routine in the weeks that they had been here. Every morning, seven or eight Red Berets would go out on foot on hunting and gathering expeditions, while three or four would remain with the shuttle, guarding it and performing other tasks. The highest-ranking guardsman among them, Lieutenant Eden Rista, had some scientific training, so he set up a work station in the shuttle where he performed tests on plants to confirm that they were potentially edible, with worthwhile nutrients.

Lorenzo acted as if he was in charge of the operation himself, but Pimyt and a number of the soldiers only tolerated him. As time passed, the aged merchant prince was getting more irritable and difficult to tolerate. Among other things, he kept complaining about the limited number of items they had on their menu. Part of that had to do with the genetic unsuitability of far-planet microbiology, the fact that Humans and other races were not able to eat and digest extremely alien foods. That was a problem here, so the soldiers had performed tests on various plants and had used customized additives to make them edible.

Many of the gray-brown native plants had proved to be either toxic or impossible to eat, either because of their stringy texture or bitter flavors. But a number of greenish roots were moderately tasty when cooked, and some of the plants could be dried and ground up to create seasonings. They also found an area of soft stones near the pool of water where Lorenzo often sat to read the *Scienscroll*, stones that could be scraped and mashed into fine particles that were the equivalent of salt. Oddly, they found no animal life at all, not even insects or creatures crawling in the soil. It was, to a degree, a sterile environment for everything except plants, which gave them pause and put them constantly on the alert for poisons in their food and drink.

The pool of water contained organic and mineral contaminants, but after digging several test holes into the subterranean rivers, they found water that proved drinkable without boiling or other treatment.

In this environment Lorenzo only proved his inadequacies. Though he didn't mind getting dirty, he did not display any skills or knowledge to help the group. He was just *there,* and often in the way. Among the soldiers, only Eden Rista and Kenjie Ishop seemed to kowtow to him. Both worked on the food—Rista doing the tests and Ishop the preparation and cooking. The others did as the fussy merchant prince ordered, but Pimyt had heard them grumbling about it privately, when Lorenzo was out of earshot.

Like a broken holorecording, Lorenzo had been complaining about the limited menu, and insisted that the Red Berets bring in something new every day for analysis and testing. Each afternoon, he would await their return from the jungle, and would ask, in an edgy voice, "What did you find for me today? Anything interesting?" And the plant or mineral would go to Rista to look it over and perform tests on it.

Even with the discomforts and annoyances, the group was getting by. Ishop even had a talent for music, and had constructed a stringed instrument that sounded surprisingly good, using plant fibers for strings and a hollowed-out tuber root for the sounding box. Ishop was a nice-enough fellow. He'd even learned the words of an old Hibbil ballad from Pimyt, and sang it passably well.

But for Pimyt that had only been to pass the time. Essentially, he had been treading water, waiting for someone to come and rescue them. He wished he knew what was happening on the war front. Whatever it was, his own contribution had disappeared altogether. The HibAdu leaders had probably already forgotten about him, after only a few weeks.

Originally he had been brought into the HibAdu conspiracy because of his closeness to the merchant prince leader, Doge Lorenzo. Pimyt had accompanied Lorenzo after his fall from political power, when Lorenzo still had considerable influence as a wealthy merchant prince. But now, neither Pimyt nor Lorenzo had any power at all. They had only this tiny group of thirteen survivors, with no hopes or prospects for the future. There weren't even any females here. Doomed, they could only die off in this forgotten place, one by one.

Pimyt grinned ferally as a recurring thought surfaced. He could make things more pleasurable around here anyway. At least for a time. He didn't think he could face one more meal without meat protein.

The night before, they had all gotten drunk on an alcoholic beverage that one of the soldiers had brewed using roots and brown berries. The liquid had been a sickly color, but had tasted reasonably good, especially after a few drinks of it. His companions were sleeping it off now. After losing a bet to Pimyt about who could drink the most, Lorenzo had stumbled out of the shuttle and announced that he was going to sleep "somewhere else." No one could talk him out of it, so one of the soldiers, Kenjie Ishop, had helped the former Doge construct a makeshift bed at the edge of the jungle. Then Ishop and the others had gone back inside the shuttle, where they all slept on thin mats or on the hard deck.

Reaching the clearing, Pimyt saw the shuttle. The silvery craft sat silently, with no lights on inside or activity visible through the portholes or front windshield. Moisture dripped down the windows and the solar array that the crew had left open.

Perhaps a hundred meters away, the Hibbil found Lorenzo sleeping on the ground, on a bed of branches and broad leaves, snoring loudly.

The furry little man crept closer, and stared down at the once-powerful merchant prince. "Lorenzo the Magnificent" was nothing now, would never see his former trappings of power and wealth. Like the other Humans, he had a scruffy, dirty beard. His clothes were damp, but he was too stupidly drunk to have noticed.

Humans are such ugly creatures, Pimyt thought. Personally, he had always preferred the fat, fleshy meat of Mutatis. Human meat was tougher, chewier, and too sweet. But this time it would have to do.

The little Hibbil moved closer.

Hearing a noise, Lorenzo awakened. He looked around and sat up. "Whah? What am I doing out here?"

"You insisted on sleeping outside," Pimyt said. He felt the hunger mounting inside, and knew his red eyes must be glowing brightly, like hot little coals in his face. He narrowed the eyelids to slits. Saliva built up in his mouth.

"I did?" The ex-Doge shivered, and tried to stand. But his legs buckled under him.

Plopping back down on the leafy bed, he said, "Look what my life has become. At one time I ruled the vast Human universe and dispatched merchant ships to the farthest reaches of my realm. I was wealthy beyond belief. Now I am trapped on the most remote, worthless planet imaginable. It's all your fault, you know, Pimyt."

The eye slits widened. "No, it isn't. Anyway, fault is a meaningless word that doesn't matter out here. In this place there are no rules, no conditions, no social mores or niceties."

For the first time, Lorenzo seemed to notice Pimyt's eyes. "Why are you looking at me like that?" Fear crept over the Human's face.

To the Hibbil, it didn't matter what the fallen man was saying. Pimyt's eyes had taken on an untamed cast and he no longer thought of being a Royal Attaché, a member of the Hib-Adu Coalition, or anything like that. He thought only of satisfying his hunger.

With a sudden move, the Hibbil bared his sharp teeth and lunged for Lorenzo's white, wrinkled throat, taking the Human down and tearing into his flesh. It happened so quickly that the hapless prey hardly had time to emit a squeal.

On all fours, Pimyt fed on the corpse, and felt great. Then his teeth struck something hard and foreign, causing him to examine what it was. Clothing had been no obstacle; he'd just shredded his way through it and swallowed. But not this. Holding the object in one hand, he saw it was a dermex in a small padded case. Inside the case, he saw a vial of red fluid that looked like Human blood. Interesting. He would get to that later. For now, he was enjoying the flesh.

At a noise, he paused and looked toward the shuttle, with blood and tissue dripping from his furry chin.

One of the Red Beret soldiers awakened, then went to the main hatch and looked out. Confused at the sight of the Hibbil in a feeding frenzy, he hesitated for a moment too long. With inhuman speed and strength, Pimyt bolted toward him and attacked, then surged inside and killed the sleeping or awakening soldiers one after the other before they could get their weapons, before they knew what was happening to them. It helped him that they'd been drinking alcohol the night before, which made them groggy and slow.

He ripped all of them apart and tasted their meat . . . one sample after the other. Though not the finest quality of flesh, organs, and bones, it was perhaps the best meal he'd ever had. He had been so hungry!

When he reached his fill, he considered what to do next, and then remembered the vial of red fluid by the body of Lorenzo. Covered in blood, he bounded out of the shuttle and across the clearing.

Examining the dermex and the vial, Pimyt wondered why Lorenzo had been carrying these things with him. Opening the top of the vial, he sniffed. It had definite elements of Human blood, but had a color that was more like wine. He didn't see any purpose in wondering why Lorenzo had it.

Tossing the dermex aside, Pimyt swallowed the vial's

contents. *Delicious!* It was like a fine aperitif after a big meal.

Then, sitting on the ground beside the corpse, he was pleased to see carrion birds circling overhead. So, there were living creatures on this planet after all, and they'd come out of their places of concealment.

The clever Hibbil started to think about laying traps for them, using pieces of the corpses as bait.

A sudden swoon came over him, as from lightheadedness, and he felt fire coursing through the veins of his body, energizing him. *Fantastic!* His pleasure mounted.

He heard a loud crashing. Without warning, the shuttle tumbled over and vanished. Green light came from a hole in the ground, giving an eerie cast to the foggy air.

Eh? Intensely curious, Pimyt went over to look down into the hole. With nothing to lose, he didn't feel any fear. As the blood-soaked Hibbil stood on the edge, he rubbed his full belly and looked down into a chasm so deep that he didn't think it had a bottom.

Drawn by a sudden compulsion, he inched closer to the edge, then lost his footing and tumbled into the hole. Through the green light he plunged, into an abyss that gave him a feeling of euphoria. But gradually something seemed to change, and he had the distinct sensation that he was going in the other direction, back the way he had just come. How could that be? Moments later, he realized he was right, as he vaulted out of the hole and over the encampment where he'd slaughtered Lorenzo and the others.

Soon he left all that behind as well, and found himself drifting slowly through a vast, starry universe. Inexplicably, he could breathe out there. The green light had faded entirely, but there was a source of faint, colorless illumination in this place. He saw something ahead. Drifting toward it, Pimyt was amazed to see the faces of Princess Meghina and four of her immortal companions, floating in space. Three women and two men.

At first the Hibbil could not make out the bodies of the people, only their huge, out-of-scale faces. As moments passed the visages began to bend, as if they were on banners fluttering in a breeze, and their features became distorted.

Then Pimyt saw their bodies, stygian black and barely discernible—immense, multilegged creatures coming toward him with bizarre Human faces. He tried to scream in terror, but in the void he heard no sound.

Silently, ominously, they closed in on him. . . .

CHAPTER FIFTY-TWO

"In conquering almost every Human and Mutati world, the HibAdus used a nasty trick—which we figured out by checking and rechecking all remaining parts that the Hibbils made for us when we thought they were our allies. And there it was: a tiny, ingeniously designed computer chip that functioned perfectly during testing but didn't hold up to further scrutiny. In the midst of battle, the chip detected the presence of attacking HibAdu warships, which in turn instantly shut down the firing mechanisms of the defenders' artillery pieces. If undiscovered, we Liberators would have been destroyed in our first big engagement. Now, let the enemy wonder if we have spotted their ruse."

—General Nirella del Velli, speech to her officers

From a military perspective, Doge Anton and General Nirella did not consider the loss of Dij entirely bad. Their feelings had nothing to do with any past enmity toward shapeshifters. Rather, they were pleased that Hari'Adab had managed to locate a large number of Mutati warships, soldiers, and military supplies around the former Mutati Sector, and that he had returned safely to Canopa with a much more powerful force than he had when he left.

Now Anton and Nirella sat inside a gourd-shaped officers' yacht as its robot pilot guided them slowly through an airless moorage basin containing the newly arrived podships. A number of the sentient vessels disgorged conventional Mutati craft, which were going into moorage and defensive positions around the larger ships, far above Canopa. In times past, seeing so many of these Mutati vessels would have been cause for alarm. But not now. Humans and Mutatis—along with Tulyans—were in alliance against the most deadly enemy any of them had ever faced.

The yacht took a position on the perimeter of the moorage basin. Then, at a signal from General Nirella, hundreds of podships separated from the others, forming a procession heading out to space. This was the first wave of them.

Within the hour, three hundred podships—a small portion of the force that had been allocated to the Mutati leader—would depart for Siriki on a new assignment—at the request of Emir Hari'Adab. The new operation would be under joint Human and Mutati command, and the shapeshifter Emir was being permitted to accompany them, so that he could personally check on the welfare of his lady friend, Parais d'Olor. A disturbing report from the Sirikan back country suggested that she could be in grave physical danger.

The lead ship accelerated with Hari'Adab aboard, and in a bright burst of green it was the first to vanish into the cosmic web. The others followed, and in tight military precision one split space every three seconds. . . .

With two passengers on its back, the dark bird beat its wings rhythmically, and lifted slowly into the air. Holding onto the mane of feathers behind Parais' neck, Dux thought she was slightly smaller now, but not that much. She seemed stronger, but he heard her wheezing as she exerted herself.

In the midday sky, gray clouds sagged above them, as if pregnant with water and about to release their contents. So far, though, Dux felt no moisture in the air, just a warm updraft. It was not a comforting warmth, though, coming as it did from the lava-flooded valley and woodlands below, the remote area where he, Acey, and their grandmother had spent many happy years. Now it was fast disappearing. Here and there some of the homesteads on higher ground held out, but gradually all of them were being inundated. Dux hoped that some people were able to escape, and he felt considerable survivor's guilt for having gotten away himself.

From the left, he heard what he thought were the sounds of battle, loud percussive thumps and explosions. Looking in that direction—approximately where they had been shot down earlier in the crop-duster plane—he saw bright bursts of blue and orange beyond tree-lined hills. Now, as Parais rose higher, Dux saw an aerial dogfight, and one fighter craft shot down the other. From this distance he couldn't make out military markings, but he assumed it was a force sent by Noah to root out the Hib-Adus that Kekur had reported there.

Suddenly he felt a shudder in the bird, and saw the wings slow their beating, and then stop. The aeromutati lost altitude, slowly at first, and then faster as she had difficulty keeping her wings spread. Intermittently finding strength, she would attempt to use the wings again, but she couldn't sustain the effort.

"Hold on!" Parais shouted. Dux couldn't grip her any harder, and even his normally courageous cousin shivered in fear as he held onto Dux.

Increasingly, as the shapeshifter's wings threatened to completely tuck themselves against her body, she began to fall like a feathered rock, only intermittently getting the wings out a little. Somehow she managed to keep herself upright, or the boys might have fallen off. Below, trees were fast approaching.

Shuddering and groaning, Parais extended her wings, and at the last possible moment she was able to regain her aerodynamics and glide. As seconds passed, however, she continued to lose altitude. They were away from the flow of lava but too near the battle zone for comfort. Dux heard the sounds of fighting even louder than before, and saw a red-and-gold MPA gridjet speed overhead.

Skimming the tops of evergreen trees, Parais barely cleared them. Finally, over a small meadow her strength gave out, and she drifted down for a bumpy landing. As she hit the ground, her passengers tumbled off.

Scrambling to his feet, Dux assessed his new bumps and bruises, as did Acey near him.

"Now we've survived two crashes around here," Acey said.

The boys hurried to check on Parais, who lay on the ground breathing hard, with one wing tucked and the other half extended. Though she didn't say anything, she clearly wanted to fold her other wing in, so Dux and Acey helped her accomplish this.

After several deep, gasping breaths, she said, "Thank you." Her eyes were open, and though they looked better than before, they still had a sickly yellow cast to them, with small purple veins running through them more visibly than ever.

"Look!" Acey husked in a low voice. He pointed toward the woods.

Through an opening in the trees, they saw an orange-and-gray aircraft. It was sleek, had a pointed nose, and—from the number of portholes on the side behind the cockpit—the craft looked large enough to carry at least ten passengers.

"HibAdu ship!" Acey said.

Out in the meadow the three of them were exposed, but so far the HibAdus did not seem to have noticed them. At least no one was bursting out of the woods and running toward them, or firing at them.

Moving as quickly and silently as they could, Dux and Acey

helped Parais walk into the cover of trees, perhaps a hundred meters from the ship. From there, they watched for several long minutes, detecting no activity around the vessel.

"Could be an escape craft," Acey said. "Stashed here for officers. It looks fast. See those jet tubes on the sides? I'll bet that baby can scoot. I don't see any guards, but you can bet they'll be back pretty quick."

"Are you thinking what I'm thinking?" Dux asked. He grinned. "I don't even need to ask that question." Looking at Parais, he said to her, "Acey and I are soldiers, and we need to either steal that ship or sabotage it."

"I understand," she said, her voice raspy.

"Do you want to stay here or go with us?" Dux asked, as he stroked the feathers on her back.

"If I'm not too much of a burden, I'd like to go with you."

"After what you did for us," Acey said, "you're no burden at all." He looked toward the sleek craft. "Let's go."

They were slowed by having to help Parais walk toward the ship, and they found it easier to go back out to the edge of the meadow with her. Agonizingly long minutes passed, and finally they made it to the rear of the vessel. Still no sign of anyone, not even any robotic guards. On the back side of the hull, a ramp was down.

The boys assisted Parais up the ramp, and Dux found her a spot on the aft deck of the passenger cabin, where she plopped down unceremoniously. Acey had hurried to the cockpit, and Dux heard him up there muttering to himself as he tried to figure out the controls. He hit a toggle, and the engines surged on. They made a high-pitched whine that irritated Dux's ears.

Hurry, hurry, he thought.

But he heard angry shouts. Looking out a porthole, Dux saw three HibAdu soldiers running toward them. Two Adurians and a Hibbil.

"Get the ramp up and take off!" Dux shouted. "We've been spotted!"

"I'm trying, dammit!"

Seeing a handgun in a holster on the bulkhead, Dux grabbed the weapon. His thoughts accelerated, and he remembered Acey showing him how to operate a similar one earlier. Touching a pad on the barrel, he caused the energy chamber on top to glow yellow.

Just as Acey got the ship to move off the ground a little, one of the insectoid Adurians ran up the ramp and burst into the passenger cabin. Dux hit him in the chest with an energy burst, and the soldier dropped. The other Adurian and the Hibbil got on before Dux could get off another shot, and they jumped behind a half-bulkhead, just inside the passenger compartment.

The ramp closed with a loud click, and the craft lifted into the air. As the engines whined louder, the ship went faster. Suddenly they shot up into the sky at an angle, and it was all Dux could do to keep from falling backward. The Hibbil lost his footing and tumbled past Dux, into the aft section.

Dux wanted to fire at him, but by the time he regained his footing, he saw Parais attacking the Hibbil, tearing at him with beak and talons. The furry little alien screamed in pain, so it looked as if the shapeshifter had found enough strength to deal with him. At least, Dux hoped so. He didn't want to shoot in that direction and risk hitting her.

Having lost track of the Adurian, Dux crept forward around the seats. Just ahead, he heard the Adurian say something from the cockpit, but Dux couldn't see him. "Turn this ship around and land!" the soldier said in a whiny voice. "Now!"

"No!" Acey shouted.

Now Dux saw the barrel of a gun around the bulkhead, a weapon that was pointed at Acey. Dux couldn't get a good angle to shoot at him. From behind he heard a sudden shot, and then Parais cried out, as if she'd been hit. But she kept attacking the Hibbil.

"I've got my hand on the self-destruct button," Acey said, glancing back at the Adurian. "Put down your weapon, or I'm going to put all of us down."

Deciding to help Parais first, Dux hurried aft, watching all the while in case the Adurian spotted him. In the small rear section he found a bleeding, badly injured Parais battling the much smaller but still deadly Hibbil. She had managed to knock his weapon away and it was wedged out of reach, but the Hibbil was by no means defenseless, and he was very fast. Bleeding badly himself, he kept getting around her beak and talons and ripping into her flesh with his sharp teeth.

Even in her weakened, injured condition, with purple blood soaking her feathers, Parais had some cellular regeneration ability as a shapeshifter. The Hibbil, with no such ability, finally fell back on the deck from his injuries. As he tried to get back on his feet, Parais drove a sharp talon through his chest, like a spike into his heart. He stopped moving, but Parais had expended almost all of her energy. To Dux's horror, her cellular structure started to break down in front of his eyes. Pieces of flesh and feathers sloughed off onto the deck, in a purple mass of goo.

Then, giving him some hope, he saw a substantially smaller version of Parais stabilize her shape.

Just then the ship lurched, and Dux heard Acey shout, "Have a nice trip!"

The Adurian screamed, and through a porthole Dux watched him tumble out of the aircraft.

Running forward, Dux saw to his amazement that Acey had found another hatch door, this one for the cockpit, and he had skillfully opened it just as he steered the ship sharply in the opposite direction, causing the Adurian to fall out.

"Nice move," Dux said. He told Acey about the other two enemy soldiers, then added, "We each got one of the bad guys, but we need to get Parais some medical attention. She's having trouble back there."

Acey set course for the headquarters at the Golden Palace, while Dux went back to do what he could for Parais. She was only around half as big as she had been when she carried the boys and Kekur on her back. One of her wings was badly torn and she didn't seem able to regenerate its cellular configuration. All over her body and on her once-beautiful face, open wounds oozed purple.

Barely alive, the brave Mutati slumped to the deck, quivering and shaking. Dux found her a blanket and massaged her back gently, where it didn't seem to cause her pain. She looked at him thankfully, but he felt helpless.

"Hang on," he said in a soothing voice.

Chapter Fifty-Three

Maturity is not something that can be given to you, or which you can gain by simply growing older. It is something you must *earn,* through the harsh lessons of personal experience.

—Subi Danvar

"Siriki below," the robot soldier reported to a group of Human and Mutati officers who stood on a cargo deck of the Aopoddae flagship. One of the shapeshifters sneezed from an allergic reaction to Humans, but he smiled and adjusted a tiny medical booster on his wrist, which enhanced the allergy protector implanted in his body.

Anxious to board the shuttle, Hari'Adab stood at the forefront of the group. Unlike most of his race, he had never felt a physical aversion toward Humans, and neither had his girlfriend, Parais. He had always wondered how much of it was psychosomatic, based upon stress, mass hysteria, or the power of suggestion.

Now he tried to be patient. Looking through a filmy viewing window, he watched a shuttle approach to take them down to the planet. Somewhere down there on the blue-green world, his precious Parais was in trouble, and he desperately wanted to get to her. He hoped and prayed that she was still alive, and that she would recover.

"Shuttle two minutes away," the robot said. Slender and

compact, the sentient machine had a neckless head, and arms that were kept in compartments and only appeared when needed. At the moment, one of the arms was saluting in an awkward fashion, while his mechanical face looked at no one in particular.

Hari sighed. As a Mutati, he naturally gloried in the marvels of flesh and the creative possibilities that a shapeshifting body could assume. Just looking at this robot (or any other one), and seeing the rigid physical structure—the manufactured, non-biological components—he was always struck by the inferiority of machines and their distinct limitations. As far as he was concerned, their artificial intelligence did not elevate them in the least. It was a synthetic thing, and unnatural.

He knew he should not be thinking this way, that it touched on the feelings of racial superiority that Mutati leaders had long felt, especially in comparison with Humans. Some people considered sentient machines a separate galactic race, though this seemed like quite a stretch to Hari. Even Noah Watanabe, whom Hari greatly respected, was reported to hold that opinion. As evidence of that, he was said to point to the example of his machine leader and trusted adviser, Thinker.

Considering it more, Hari wondered if he could really dispute that position. After watching the irritating robot Jimu in action, with all of his clever maneuverings, there certainly seemed to be a spark of life there . . . albeit an irritating one. The loyalty of sentient robots to Humans was legendary, and so pervasive that it seemed to go beyond anything that could have been programmed into them. Jimu was watching Hari now, from a mezzanine over the cargo deck.

The cargo door opened, and Hari hurried through an airlock into the shuttle. It seemed to take forever for the other passengers to load, though he knew it was less than ten minutes.

But every minute and every second away from Parais tormented his heart.

When it came to mechanical things, Acey had always been a quick study. Almost a year ago he and Dux had been on a treasure-hunting crew among a motley bunch of rowdies, many of whom had had experience working on conventional space-ships. When their craft broke down, the teenage Acey had helped figure out the problem, just one of many instances in which he had proved himself capable.

Now Acey had done it again, though it might not be enough to save Parais. Under pressure from three attacking soldiers, he had figured out the operation of the sleek HibAdu craft and had flown it away. The vessel sped over mountains, lakes, and forests, while Dux remained in the aft section, tending to the grievously wounded Mutati. Though she had fought valiantly for survival, she seemed to have been shot in a vital place, one that her already destabilized condition had prevented her from healing. From what he had heard, a Mutati could often survive terrible wounds by changing its cellular structure around and finding new body forms. But this seemed different. She'd been wounded when she was already weak from the problem of having taken on too much mass.

Clearly, her condition was worsening. During the flight Parais had been devolving in a frightening way, as her body was losing its distinctive features and becoming a quivering mass of salmon-colored flesh. Moments ago, her eyes had slipped back inside the fatty cellular structure, but Dux had not been repulsed, and had not moved away from her at all. He kept talking to her in a soothing voice, using her name and massaging where her shoulders and back used to be. The pulse of her flesh was slowing, but occasionally—as if in direct response to his words or touch—she would revive. Then, moments later, she would fade again. He only knew that he had to keep trying, letting her know that someone cared about her.

In his pocket he had Grandma Zelk's pouch of healing powder, and he had considered sprinkling some of it on the Mutati. But he had hesitated, not wanting to risk doing anything that could worsen her condition, or even cause her death.

Through a porthole Dux saw the glittering spires of the Golden Palace nearing, and the military compound that had grown up around it. Having established comlink contact a half hour ago, Acey now circled the landing field, waiting his turn after a shuttle that was setting down. Dux allowed himself to feel a surge of hope.

A minute later he heard the welcome, reassuring voice of Noah Watanabe over the comlink: "Okay, Acey. Bring her in next to the shuttle. We have doctors waiting for your patient."

As Acey went into hover mode and landed, Dux saw at least a hundred Humans and Mutatis standing on the groundpad. With the engines whining down, the hatch and ramp of the HibAdu craft opened.

Mutatis rushed on board first, and it soon became apparent that they were a medical team. Having shapeshifted into various modes of appearance, all wore pale blue uniforms. Dux stayed out of their way, and watched as they carried Parais down the ramp on a metalloy stretcher to a waiting ambulance.

Noah Watanabe and a robed Mutati hurried along with them. Having seen holophotos of the Mutati before, Dux knew it was the shapeshifter leader, Hari'Adab.

Noah and the Emir shook hands. Then the somber Mutati climbed into the ambulance with Parais, and the vehicle sped off.

Seeing Acey and Dux leave the HibAdu aircraft, Noah went to them. "Good to see you boys," he said, giving each of them a hearty hug. "You'll get commendations for this." His freckled face darkened. "Sorry to hear about your grandmother. Terrible conditions in the back country."

"Thanks," Acey said. "We lost Kekur, too."

"I know. A fine robot, that one."

Taking one of his staff cars, Noah accompanied the teenagers back to their barracks on the palace grounds. On the way he told them about a wounded HibAdu lab-pod that had been found on Siriki, having been hit by ion-cannon fire.

"I just got back from seeing it," Noah said. "Some of my aides wanted to kill it because of the damage such podships cause to the galactic infrastructure. I couldn't do that, though. It's defective, but it's still a living creature. Eshaz is here on a brief stopover, and he said it might be revived with a green dust that he carries around with him, but he didn't recommend doing that."

Dux thought of the healing powder in his own pocket, but said nothing about it. Soon he would give it to Noah or Eshaz, but first it was something that he only wanted to show to Acey. It was all they had left that had belonged to Grandmamá.

Noah sighed. "Maybe it would be better to put the creature out of its misery, after all. We can't ever let it fly again, and would have to keep it pinned down. I guess I know what has to be done."

"These are unusual times," Dux said. "I never would have thought we'd fly a HibAdu ship here, trying to save a Mutati."

"That makes me think of an ancient curse from Lost Earth," Noah said, shaking his head in dismay. " 'May you live in interesting times.' " Then he looked at Dux and Acey, and added, "Well men, that's where we are now."

One of his words did not go unnoticed by either of the cousins. Exchanging glances, each of them knew they were *men* now.

CHAPTER FIFTY-FOUR

"We Humans are easily susceptible to stress. From my observation, the root causes seem clear: Stress is derived from a lack of perceived control over conditions around you. To a great extent this operates on a personal level, on situations impacting the individual. If you can gain a measure of control over those things, reducing their negative impact on you, it will reduce your stress. Think of disease, or financial matters, or relationships. It is simple to think of stress in this way, but not so easy in the application. We are Humans after all, and far from perfect in anything we attempt. Realize, too, that our collective anxiety as Guardians is potentially great, because we are going to war against ecological damage. Not an easy thing to control, but like soldiers, we must find comfort in our just purpose, and serenity in the knowledge that we are doing our best."

—Master Noah Watanabe, speech to
the last graduating class on EcoStation

In his apartment at the keep, Noah prepared to leave for Yaree, the trip that had been interrupted by the battle on Siriki and the Parais d'Olor matter. His breakfast sat half-eaten on a coffee table, near a dirty pouch of green dust that Dux Hannah had given him . . . purportedly a strange "healing powder" that had belonged to his grandmother. Eshaz had already examined it, and said it was similar to the substance that Tulyans used to remedy small timeholes.

Quickly, Noah tossed the pouch and a stack of holofiles into a briefcase, then snapped it shut. These were old-format research reports about Yaree and their customs that he'd found in the palace library. Meghina had a lot of books and files in there, gleaned from her travels around the galaxy in happier times. Noah also had three reports from the recon team that he'd sent to Yaree—one for each day they'd been there. These were on new-format holofiles, which he converted to telebeam storage files and kept in his signet ring. He could convert the older files, too, but there would be a longer conversion process, and he wanted to get going.

Noah's thoughts churned as he hurried out into the corridor. He walked briskly, with aides signaling to each other as they accompanied him, making last-minute arrangements. His whole life felt rushed now, as if he couldn't get a handle on it, and it was not in his control.

A wayward memory intruded. Upon seeing how he could regenerate his body after a serious injury, a doctor once said to Noah, "You'll live forever. You have time in your pocket."

Perhaps that was true, or perhaps not. A pocket—like the galaxy itself—could have holes in it.

Without any doubt, he believed that his enhanced cellular capabilities were linked to Timeweb, but that paranormal realm had proven to be volatile and elusive. It only allowed him to enter it on *its* own terms, not on his. But if he was connected to the web, and the infrastructure was deteriorating, couldn't that mean that he would eventually lose his immortality as well? He thought so, and that any serious future injury he sustained could prove to be fatal.

His lack of understanding troubled him deeply, but he

remembered the calming exercises he had taught to his galactic ecology students. Inwardly, even as he evolved physically, he took a long mental breath, and felt a little better. As moments passed, one merging into the next, his stormy continent of worries diminished to a small tropical island, with warm, gentle waves lapping against the shore. But the trick only lasted temporarily, and in his mind he envisioned storm clouds approaching over the sea.

Complete control. Such an elusive, impossible concept.

Yaree was in a galactic sector that had displayed severe time-hole activity. It was also a planet with an unpredictable leadership. He hoped he could learn something in Meghina's holofiles about how to deal with those people. He knew the Yareens had rich mineral deposits and that they had a long history of independence as savvy galactic traders. For centuries they had been excellent businessmen, so he would probably need to make them an offer that was economically attractive to them.

He didn't like thinking in such terms. In the present state of the galaxy, with the HibAdus running rampant and not caring what irreparable damage they were causing with their military acts and their ecologically harmful lab-pods, he needed people who were capable of answering to a higher calling than money. First he would try to appeal to Yareen morals and see if they would respond to the galactic emergency on that basis. Even better, if they could be convinced of the severity of the ecological crisis, they might pitch in for their own survival.

Noah was taking an escort of only three armed podships on the trip. With such a small force, he hoped to avoid being noticed by the HibAdus, slipping under their scanners. He thought it likely that this would work, because he had earlier sent a reconnaissance mission to Yaree with that number of ships, and there had been scores of courier flights, all without incident. His advisers had objected to the light escort, but he'd prevailed over them with an argument they could not dispute—his instincts told him to go to Yaree in that manner. He'd grown to rely on visceral feelings to a considerable extent; on more than one occasion, they had proven their value to him, going all the way back to his childhood.

As part of his plan, Noah left the bulk of his fleet at Siriki, along with Hari's reinforcements. All were ready to respond if he needed them, but because of poor podway conditions, the Tulyans were estimating that the trip would take more than an hour each way. This meant that it would require more than twice that long to get reinforcements to Yaree if necessary, assuming a courier could make the return trip and sound the alarm. It also meant, however, that he now had a little time to review the holofiles in his briefcase before arriving at his destination.

After instructing his aides to leave him alone, he secluded himself in his office on the podship, and began examining the documents. Using a projector, he floated five holofiles at a time in the air, and moved from file to file.

Almost oblivious to the fact that his ship was splitting space and gaining speed, he learned from the documents that the Yareens had a potential weakness, something he might be able to exploit if necessary. Though he would first appeal to their morality and need to survive, if those attempts failed he had a contingency plan.

As recently as a couple of years ago, the Yareens had been addicted to nobo, a hallucinogenic tree root that only grew in the rain forests of Canopa, so it had to be imported from there. Of little significance anywhere else in the galaxy, nobo was in high demand on Yaree, where it was burned in religious rites in elaborate ceremonies that were said to ward off evil spirits. If their stockpiles were low, and if they didn't have access to podships, Noah thought he could gain considerable leverage with them.

But first, he would inspect EcoStation and the galactic conditions nearby, receiving the latest information from the experts on his recon team.

With Noah's three podships moored in orbital space, he rode a tube-shaped transport ship over to the orbital position of Eco-Station. The facility was ragged and torn open, in such horrible condition that most people would think it was not worth restoring. Even so, Noah wanted to recover it, for the inspirational value it would offer. In view of the ongoing war and other crises, he would not file a formal salvage claim for the space station. Instead, he would just take charge of it, without the filing of any documents. Someday Lorenzo del Velli might surface again and make preposterous legal demands. If necessary, Noah would deal with such a challenge when the time came. For now, he had other priorities.

The transport ship locked onto a docking port of the orbiter, and Noah noticed that the hulls of the modules glowed faintly green. He didn't know why, and it gave him some trepidation. Double doors slid open with a grinding noise.

Passing through an airlock, he was greeted by the dented black robot Jimu and four other soldier robots. With a crisp salute, Jimu stepped forward and said, "Fantastic to see you again, sir. Everything is in readiness for your inspection."

"First I want a full report on what happened to this station. Wait a minute, what are you doing here? I thought you were keeping tabs on Hari'Adab."

"I was, sir, but he complained that I was getting on his nerves, so others were assigned to him—a couple of robots with better personalities than mine. I just arrived before you did. The Tulyans received your comlink message and are ready to provide the information you desire. I will take you to the meeting chamber."

Looking around, Noah saw the evidence of recent repairs to the hull of this module, to make it airtight. He heard loud machinery noises, and saw robots at work restoring one of the other docking ports.

"Heat and life-support systems are functional in some modules," Jimu said, as he handed a survival suit to Noah. "You'd better get into this, because we'll be passing through airless sections. I've made sure that we can walk through most modules safely, but some are ripped apart, and clinging to the framework of the space station by the barest structural components."

Noah put on the suit, but left the face piece open in the helmeted top. The suit was transparent flexplax, and squeaked a little as he followed Jimu to a lift.

"We've sealed some modules where there are bodies of Red Berets who were stationed here, and the bodies of gambling patrons. They were all caught by surprise when something tore the station apart."

"I've heard," Noah said. "Princess Meghina told me some of the horrific details."

The lift door closed, and the car rose, noisily and slowly.

"Has she been found, sir?" This robot had an excess of personality at times, but Noah had never found him overly annoying. Jimu had a history of dedicated service, and had accomplished a great deal for the Liberator cause. He was one of only a handful of sentient machines who could be spoken of in the same breath with the name of Thinker.

"Sadly, no."

They stepped out of the lift, onto an uneven, badly dented deck. Ahead, Noah saw hundreds of motionless robots. Although an unrepaired hole remained in the ceiling, the sentient machines still stood erectly and didn't disappear into space, held in place by the onboard gravitonics system. They did not appear to be damaged.

"I know each of these robots well," Jimu said. "I used to be in charge of Red Beret machines here, you know. These were among the units I was reproducing as worker variants instead of fighters. They performed office, janitorial, construction, and food service duties."

Noah scowled. "When you worked for Doge Lorenzo."

"Before I knew any better, until I joined you and Thinker."

Jimu stepped close to the front row of robots, touched one of the faceplates. "These machines are all deactivated," he said, "locked down so that they cannot energize themselves. After I led a mass defection, taking most of the fighting machines to join your Guardians, Lorenzo had these shut off—to play it safe."

"And they just left them here?"

"As far as I can tell. In another module I've reactivated sixty-two machines and put them to work. I've given each of them a name. I now prefer to make the robots more personal to each other and connected to their unit, instead of using typical machine codes. This way, it seems more Human to me."

Noah followed Jimu through two modules, then boarded another lift with him. On an upper level, the Guardian leader found more robots working, and a small Tulyan woman speaking with them. He recognized her as Zigzia, the webtalker who had sent cross-space messages for him in the past.

"Better connect your breathing apparatus," Jimu said. "We'll be going through some modules that have no air. We've got an emergency gravitonics system working in most modules, but you'll notice some difference. We're only doing the emergency repairs you ordered, but there's still a lot of work to do, depending upon what you decide to do with the station."

Spotting Noah, Zigzia broke away from her conversation and

joined him, as Jimu led the way into another module, one that was still sealed. Noah almost gagged from the stench, and soon he saw why: bodies and body parts were stacked along the sides of the corridor and in adjoining rooms. Some of the doors to those rooms were damaged or blocked, and didn't close all the way. From earlier reports, Noah knew to expect this, but it was impossible to prepare himself for the gruesome reality. He had told the reconnaissance and robotic-repair teams not to jettison any of the bodies. They deserved proper ceremonies. This, and the identification of the victims, were among many details that still needed attention. He had already set that in motion, and expected a mortuary and burial team to arrive in a few days.

For the moment, though, he needed to find out what had occurred here, and he was anxious to meet with the Tulyan experts.

As Noah looked around at the damaged space station, he couldn't help wondering if it was really worth salvaging. It would be no small task to repair it, which would require time and the allocation of additional robotic assets that might be more appropriately used elsewhere. There was also the problem of transporting it to a more suitable location, either orbiting Canopa or Siriki. That might be accomplished by breaking it up into sections and loading them into podship cargo holds. In one of the earlier reports, Jimu had estimated that this would involve seven or eight sections, and three or four podships to transport them.

But now, seeing EcoStation firsthand, Noah reminded himself of the reason he had ordered the makeshift repairs that were occurring now. His famed School of Galactic Ecology had once been here, filled with classroom and laboratory facilities. This orbiter was much more than machinery, much more than the sum of its tortured modules and shredded parts. It represented something immensely important—a potentially powerful source of inspiration for humankind—proof that the galaxy could survive against all odds, even in the face of warfare and the collapsing infrastructure. Wherever he placed it, EcoStation could become a beacon in the cosmos.

It was very personal for him. Noah had strong feelings for the facility, and a sense that he needed to connect with his past in order to counter the flurry of changes around him, thus reconnecting to a time when he began to call himself and his followers "eco-warriors."

Jimu and Zigzia led him into one of the original school sections that had been converted into a gambling hall. Now it didn't look like either, with overturned, smashed equipment and gaming pieces piled against the walls. "This way, please," the webtalker said, pointing out an improvised divider wall at the center. Entering the hall, Noah found four other Tulyans, seated at a large table.

"Master Watanabe," one of the Tulyans said, rising with his companions and bowing. It was Inyaq Vato, head of the reconnaissance team. "Please, take a seat." He gestured toward the head of the table.

When Noah sat down, the others slipped back into their places along the sides. Jimu and Zigzia stood, looking on.

"Our first assumptions proved to be correct," Vato said. "This space station fell through a timehole into another galaxy. Then, somehow, it was knocked back into this one. On the modular hulls and other parts, there are spectral traces of alien materials, not found anywhere in this galaxy. Telltale signs that it has been someplace else."

"Is that why the hulls glow faintly green now?" Noah asked.

"No," one of the other Tulyans said, a bulky male with wide, slitted eyes. "We treated the space station to make it less susceptible to timeholes, in case any more appear. A film that acts as a repellent."

"Is it like the healing dust I've seen caretakers use?" Noah asked.

"It has some similar properties. This is a liquid variation that adheres to the hull."

While listening to the Tulyans, Noah went to one of the magnaviewers by the window, a double-mirror unit that bathed him in light when he looked through it. First he located his own space-moored podships, six in all, including three that had arrived earlier with the reconnaissance and repair teams. Then, focusing on the surface of the planet Yaree, Noah saw what looked like a Yareen military base on the ground, and considerable activity there. Black military shuttles and other small aircraft taxied across an airfield and took off, one after the other.

Suddenly, orbital space filled with orange-and-gray warships, closing in on EcoStation. Noah pushed Zigzia out of the way, and opened a link to the six Liberator podships that were moored a short distance away.

"Mayday!" Noah shouted.

His podships were already in motion, with five of them going into a defensive formation. In a prearranged maneuver, the sixth sped away and split space in a burst of green light.

"We sent for reinforcements!" an officer shouted over the line.

"Zigzia," Noah said, looking at the Tulyan. "Can you transmit an emergency message to the Tulyan Elders?"

"I can try, but the web isn't in great condition between here and the starcloud, so I'll have to use alternate transmission routes." She thumped heavily out into the corridor. Noah wasn't sure where she would attempt to make the contact, but knew that Tulyans could see the web where others couldn't.

Noah's remaining podships had their space cannons pointed toward the advancing warships, and fired. The HibAdu vessels were all conventional craft, but bristling with weapons. So far he didn't see any of their much larger lab-pods, but suspected they were nearby.

Some of the advancing HibAdu ships burst into flames, but others changed course quickly and sped toward the Liberator vessels at new angles. One of the defending podships exploded, and the four others drew back toward the space station in a last-ditch shielding effort.

But Noah had a sinking, hopeless feeling. He was badly outnumbered, and reinforcements could not possibly arrive in time. . . .

CHAPTER FIFTY-FIVE

Everything in this galaxy is linked to everything
else. Nothing is really detached, no matter how
much it seems to be.
> —Textbook introduction,
> School of Galactic Ecology

Unknown to Noah, the podship that escaped the HibAdu attack was among the oldest and most experienced of the spacefaring Aopoddae. In ancient times the vessel had been known as *Diminian*, and it had been present in the earliest days of the galaxy. Even then, from the outset, there had been problems with the webbing infrastructure—and those conditions bore ominous parallels with those of modern times. The galaxy had been fresh and new in the beginning, but with podship travel and other conditions the infrastructure became worn and frayed rather quickly in many places . . . in the equivalent of only a few thousand years. This was one of the reasons that the first Tulyan caretakers had been dispatched to perform repairs, and afterward for regular maintenance duties.

With seasoning, the webbing actually became stronger and more able to withstand podship travel and other cosmic conditions, but there were always weak points that appeared from time to time, requiring the attention of the expert caretakers. Many of those weak points proved to be chronic, and were among the most difficult to keep in good repair during the current crisis of galactic decay. With his long and perfect memory *Diminian* knew all of this, and knew better than any podship how to take alternate routes. Though he did not communicate in words, he had other means of sensing the emergency of the HibAdu attack on the space station. Thus the return flight to Siriki, which Noah had expected to take an hour or more, required only four minutes.

The Tulyan pilot, having his own means of communicating with both Aopoddae and Humans, delivered the mayday call to Noah's command headquarters. When *Diminian* arrived, Subi Danvar was in orbital space near Siriki, commanding a military exercise involving eight hundred podships and some of the Mutati warships that had been sent from Canopa. For the maneuvers, Acey and Dux were acting as Subi's personal aides on the primary vessel.

Over a comlink, Subi informed all Liberator pilots and officers of the new mission, along with the astronomical coordinates of Yaree and the orbital position of EcoStation. Then he put the just-returned Tulyan pilot on the connection, to provide details for the other pilots on the alternate, but faster, route they needed to take.

When the Tulyan finished giving the information, Subi shouted, "Let's go!" Moments later, he led the armed podships out into space, leaving the Mutati warships and the bulk of the podship fleet behind.

Even with Noah under attack, they could not risk sending more of their military assets to Yaree. Subi and the other officers were under standing orders to maintain a strong defensive position at Siriki, and not to be drawn away. They did not want to repeat what happened to the Mutati planet of Dij and lose another important world.

Back at Siriki, other officers sent *Diminian* and his Tulyan pilot to relay the new information to Doge Anton del Velli in the Canopa sector. They also sent a number of additional podships to Yaree, to act as couriers from the battle zone.

Only minutes after the attack on EcoStation, all Liberator forces in the galaxy went onto full alert. At Canopa, Doge Anton received the mayday call. With additional information on favored routes provided by the Tulyan pilot (from his esoteric connection with *Diminian*), Anton dispatched an additional one thousand podships.

Leaving General Nirella behind with the bulk of the fleet, the young Doge led the second rescue force to Yaree. Some of his officers had questioned his decision to go himself, saying he should delegate it to one of them. But Nirella, outranking all of them, had silenced their comments. "Noah is Anton's uncle, and there has always been a strong bond between them." Smiling stiffly, she had added, "Besides, I'm the better military commander in this marriage. From a strategic standpoint, it's essential that I remain with the bulk of the fleet."

"We've already talked it out," Anton had said, "and I'm on my way."

In the flagship *Webdancer*, Anton now stood on the command bridge, at the forward viewing window. Beside him, the venerable robot Thinker folded open with a small clattering and clicking of metal. Anton was anxious to help Noah, and for this mission he needed the most brilliant of all sentient machines. He also needed the best pilots, and for the flagship that meant Tesh Kori.

As they sped through space, Thinker said, "I know you want to add my military recommendations to those of your officers, but I need to assess the battle before adding anything to what they told you. I agree with them that we must move quickly to protect the space station, since Noah was last reported aboard it. But conditions will undoubtedly be fluid on the battlefield, and he may have moved."

"Assuming he's OK. Noah once told me his 'immortality' might be as fragile as the galactic webbing, or might have been compromised by the tainted blood he got from his sister."

"Our Liberator force from Siriki may already be there."

"I hope they are," Anton said.

"As do I. There is something more. A number of the ships and fighters we have with us now were brought back to Canopa by Hari'Adab, after the loss of Dij. We have Mutati officers and soldiers among us."

"You're not concerned about their loyalty, are you?"

"No, sir. But for the first time in history, Mutati forces are going into battle under Human command."

"That is hardly at the top of my mind," Anton said.

"Nor of mine," Thinker admitted. He whirred for a moment. Then: "My internal programming informs me that I was just making nervous conversation. Like you, I am very worried about Master Noah."

At the Tulyan Starcloud, the Council of Elders received the emergency web transmission from Zigzia. They immediately sought out Eshaz, who was restocking his ships with supplies and assigning fresh caretaking crews for yet another mission.

With a small entourage, Elder Kre'n and Dabiggio rode a space platform through the mists that floated around their fabled planets. In one of the protected moorage basins they found Eshaz's fleet of vessels. All five hundred ships had returned safely, with no reports of HibAdu encounters. But that was about to change.

They docked the platform at a ship that bore no Tulyan face on its prow, but which was known to be the vessel operated personally by Eshaz. Moments later, Eshaz appeared at the main entrance hatch, and then boarded the glax-domed platform.

"We have urgent news from Zigzia," Kre'n said. "She is with Noah Watanabe at Yaree, where they are under attack by Hib-Adu forces. Zigzia said a courier flew to Siriki for reinforcements, but she didn't know when they might arrive."

"We must mount our own military force then," Eshaz said. "How many armed podships can you round up?"

"The fifty with you, and three hundred more," Dabiggio said.

Eshaz formed a scowl on his reptilian face. "Hardly an overwhelming force."

"No," the towering Elder said, "but we can make the force look much larger if we also send the nine thousand caretaker podships we have here, along with the armed podships—everything we have here. They don't contribute much to our starcloud defenses anyway." He looked at Kre'n, awaiting her comment.

"Do it," she commanded. "Our mindlink protects the starcloud."

"And my orders?" Eshaz asked.

"You are in command," Kre'n said.

It all happened quickly. Every podship went out, even if they had only Tulyan pilots aboard, and no passengers or armaments.

As they accelerated onto the podways of deep space, Eshaz and the Tulyan pilots behind him reported feeling bursts of speed unlike any they had ever experienced before. The podships took their own course to Yaree, reaching tachyon speeds but not traveling in anything close to a straight line.

The mysterious Aopoddae seemed to know in advance which sections of podway were in the best condition. . . .

CHAPTER FIFTY-SIX

There is a Tulyan prophecy of the Sublime Creator and the Savior, the bipartite entity who will hold dominion over all aspects of Timeweb. It is said that he will appear one day from the most unlikely of sources, and will determine the course of the universe.

—MPA report on Tulyan motivations and religion

For Subi Danvar, this was unlike any of the military maneuvers he and the other officers had practiced. And for him personally, far more was at stake.

Like fireworks in the air, his eight hundred podships arrived near Yaree in successive bursts of bright green light. Not waiting for even the few minutes that would have been required for all of them to arrive, Subi instead rushed forward with only a handful of support vessels behind him. He saw the space station in orbital space, and near it HibAdu warships battling a defensive force of Liberator podships and smaller craft that had come out of the cargo holds. Though there were hundreds of HibAdu ships attacking, all of them were small, short-range gunships, not lab-pods. The defenders were tenacious, causing problems for the attackers.

It gave the adjutant a feeling of relief to see EcoStation still there, though it was not in good shape. Just then, he saw one of the lower modules explode, a ball of orange that quickly dissipated in the airless vacuum. From his security experience on

EcoStation, he knew that each module had oxygen cutoff systems, lessening the impact of a problem in one area on the rest of the orbiter. Based on the brightness of the explosion, he judged that there had been quite a bit of oxygen in that particular module. He worried about Noah.

As Subi's podship entered the fray with its space cannons blasting, he remembered Noah's supposed immortality. For the loyal adjutant, that did not lessen his concerns. Mirroring Noah's own feelings, Subi doubted if the condition could possibly be absolute, so he was always on the alert for gaps in it, so that he could better protect the Master.

Subi scattered the lead ships in the approaching HibAdu squadron by flying toward them and then veering off at the last moment, while his crew fired space cannons and automatic weapons at them. To keep his lead podship flying the way he wanted, Subi gave orders to a Tulyan with him, who in turn relayed them telepathically to the Tulyan pilot. The responses were almost instantaneous.

Two of Subi's shots struck their mark. Then more gunships exploded as the rest of his podships and smaller fighter craft from the cargo holds joined the battle. But to his dismay he saw more enemy craft advancing, as if from a limitless source of them.

In the distance, from the direction where the enemy was advancing, he saw green flashes in space, and from markings on the vessels he confirmed that they were enemy lab-pods. His heart sank. The HibAdu ships near the space station were only an advance force. They had used just enough firepower to alarm the Liberators, and to lure more of them in.

It was too late for Subi to worry about things like that. He heard his own podship squeal as it was hit. But the sentient spacecraft recovered, and kept responding to Subi's relayed commands. For the moment, he cleared an area around the space station, where he positioned fifty of his own armed podships, all with the faces of their Tulyan pilots on the prows. Then Subi sent the rest of his force smashing through the enemy gunships and some of the newly arrived, larger battleships. He blasted them out of the way, heading toward the more powerful and dangerous lab-pod mother ships in the distance.

But near those vessels he saw many more flashes of green, bright flowers in space. They were not his own podships arriving, because those had already been engaged in the battle. In a matter of seconds, he received confirmation that they were Liberator vessels. To his delight he saw the newly arrived ships surge into battle against the lab-pods and begin to drive them back, even as the HibAdus were trying to disgorge more gunships and larger warships from the holds.

Adjusting the comlink channel to connect with a portable unit that Noah carried, Subi said, "Noah, you there? Are you all right?" In the distance, he saw the space station, with the armed warships Subi had left to protect it. No activity there. But over the comlink, he heard only static in response.

Looking back at the battle scene, he saw the smaller HibAdu craft retreating in disarray, but not making it back to the mother ships, because they were being blasted out of space. Over other communication channels, he heard the excited chatter of his officers and voices of others from additional podships that Doge Anton had dispatched. How many vessels, Subi didn't know, but the combined Liberator force was proving superior, because it chased the HibAdus and made kill after kill. He hoped this was not a trick, designed to lure forces away from Canopa and Siriki.

Over the connections, he heard Doge Anton himself, and the mechanical voice of Thinker, whose brilliant machine intellect was being committed to this important battle. It gave Subi some reassurance that the best minds were being employed for the

Liberator strategies. He also heard them say that thousands of caretaker podships had arrived from the Tulyan Starcloud, vessels that were mostly unarmed, and which Anton had kept away from the center of battle. Eshaz and other Tulyan web technicians were among the new arrivals.

But Subi had another priority, the reason he came here in the first place.

"Prepare to board EcoStation," he announced. "I will dock and go aboard with my soldiers, and I want the twenty closest ships to me to dock, too. We need to search every area of the orbiter to find Master Noah. There are uncertain atmospheric conditions on board, so wear survival suits."

In the midst of the HibAdu fleet, Ipsy remained concealed inside a weapon-control box that had been installed in one of the new lab-pods. He heard the chatter of Hibbil and Adurian officers on the command bridge, and knew that this vessel and others had turned around and fled into space when the battle appeared lost.

This cheered him somewhat, but he would have felt much better if his ship had been in the middle of combat, and the officers had tried to use the weapons activated by this panel.

Even so, he was not without options. When installing the panel on the bridge, the technicians had removed the screws on the back side of the unit, intending to lift off the cover, which was necessary in order to make the electrical connections. With no way to hide from the workers, Ipsy had prepared for the worst.

But the little robot got an important break. Before lifting off the cover, the technicians took a break and left the bridge. Cautiously, Ipsy then pushed the cover aside and peeked out. No one was on the bridge at all, and the ship was not in operation. He transmitted signals, verified that no alarm or videocam system was in operation.

The robot climbed out of the panel box, and replaced the cover. Then he concealed himself in a dead air space behind the main instrument console. A short while later the technicians returned and completed their work.

The following day a pilot and crew took the lab-pod into space and tested the powerful energy cannons. They fired perfectly, and the vessel was brought back in. From his place of concealment, Ipsy heard an officer say something interesting, while they were shutting down the systems. This was not merely an ordinary vessel. Because of damage to the flagship of the HibAdu fleet, this ship was replacing it. The vessel would be under the direct command of the High Ruler.

For the little robot, the stakes were increasing quickly. He had waited for a long time for this opportunity, and didn't want to blow it. Alone during the night, he inspected the main instrument panel, and quietly removed panels and covers to examine the interior layouts of computer boards, circuits, and other components. He didn't need to actually operate the systems to understand how they worked. Just looking at the inner workings and control surfaces was enough for him.

Carefully, he made adjustments to the weapon-control box, hidden settings that no one would notice. If the HibAdus performed any additional tests, the weapons would fire. But something entirely different would occur if Ipsy transmitted an electronic signal into the box. . . .

With the enemy ships routed or destroyed, Tesh received the command for *Webdancer* to approach the space station. From the glowing green sectoid chamber, she guided the sentient vessel in that direction, gazing into near-space through her link with the multiple eyes on the hull.

But something unusual was happening. Unarmed caretaker

ships were swooping past her and gathering closely around EcoStation, so many vessels that she could hardly see the orbiter itself. Just before that, Subi Danvar had sent a comlink message that he was docking with twenty other ships, but many more were massing around the space station now. Something seemed terribly wrong.

Over the connection with Doge Anton, Tesh heard his concerns, and those of Thinker, as they sent comlink messages to the officers on the ships. The replies, which she did not hear directly, must not have helped, because Anton contacted her, through a Tulyan with him.

"Tesh," Anton relayed, "do you know what's going on there?"

"No, sir," she replied.

"Anything on Noah? Is he inside?"

"No one knows."

Ahead, Tesh saw more podships packing themselves around the space station, and now she could no longer see the orbiter at all, just the irregular shape of it. The podships seemed to flow together and become one, like a mottled, gray-and-black cocoon.

Anton ordered *Webdancer* to veer away from the station. But when Tesh followed the command, she felt a tugging coming from the direction of the strange cocoon, as if the massed podships were drawing her vessel toward them. A surge of fear enveloped her, but she was able to guide *Webdancer* away.

In space several kilometers away, Doge Anton gathered the bulk of his podship force. There, Tesh did not feel the magnetic pull of the cocoon.

At a new command center for his own moored ships, Doge Anton and his closest advisers tried to assess the unusual situation. Tesh was asked to leave the sectoid chamber and join them in the main conference room of the flagship, along with Eshaz. No one sat. Instead, everyone stood anxiously near the windows, looking back at the space station, which was shifting into an amorphous form, like a giant alien shapeshifter. Anton's aides, Acey Zelk and Dux Hannah stood near him.

"At least three hundred ships are in that cocoon," the Doge said. "We need to find out what's happening, but I didn't want to rush forward, endangering more of the fleet."

"Subi Danvar is in there looking for Noah," one of the officers said. "But for some reason Subi is no longer responding to us by comlink."

"I don't like this," Anton said, "and I'm worried about a Hib-Adu trick."

"It could be that," Thinker said, "but my projections do not indicate they are capable of controlling podships in that manner. Obviously, the Aopoddae in the cocoon are linked mentally and physically, but for what purpose I cannot determine. One sign of hope: they are all caretaker Aopoddae, except for the ones Subi took in."

Wrinkling his scaly brow, Eshaz said, "I've heard of them forming into cocoons in ancient days, but long before I was born. The reasons were varied."

"And you were born almost a million years ago," Tesh said, trying to envision how long that was. While speaking, she watched the cocoon in the distance. At first, she thought it had stopped morphing, then she wasn't so sure. She thought she saw it move slightly.

"In the earliest days," Eshaz said, "before my time, there were many unique dangers in space. For various reasons, to face different perils, the podships would form themselves into larger units—such as what you see here."

"Could the cocoon be protecting something?" Doge Anton asked. "Could it be Noah?"

"Possibly," Eshaz said. "Protecting important individuals and groups was one of the purposes of conglomerating, but by no means the only one."

"We need to send in our own search team," Anton said.

"But any ship we send could just find itself merged into the others," Tesh said. She spoke of the tugging sensation she had felt through *Webdancer,* and listened while other officers said they had received reports of the same thing.

"Something similar happened to us," Eshaz then said. "In the thousands of ships I brought from the starcloud, my pilots all reported sensations of increased speed on the way, as if an unexpected, sustained wind had sped us to our destination. When we drew within visual range of the space station, we all felt a pull too, as you others have described. It was like magnetism, drawing us toward it. We kept away from the station, as Doge Anton commanded."

"There seems to be an Aopoddae telepathic link that goes beyond the cocooned podships," Anton said. "Far out into space."

"I would like to accompany the search team," Thinker said. "I am only a machine, so death is not a consideration."

"You're not just an ordinary machine," Anton said. "But I do have multiple backup copies of your computer program, so we could rebuild you if necessary. All right. You'll lead the investigating squad."

The Doge then looked around, and spoke to one of the officers, a cheten named J.B. Alcazar. "You coordinate it," he said. "But no Humans go on the mission. Or Mutatis. I want you to use robots."

"We machines could take that as an insult," Thinker said, "but in this special instance we won't. That's why I volunteered. For Noah."

"Don't send another podship in, either," Anton said. "Instead, use a shuttle."

"Can we go?" Dux asked.

"You heard me," the Doge said. "Robots only." His tone offered no discussion.

"An armed shuttle?" Alcazar asked.

"I don't see where firepower would do any good in this situation," Anton said.

"I strongly suggest an unarmed shuttle," Eshaz said, "and remove any smaller weapons that might be onboard. Deactivate all robotic weapons systems, too. You don't want the podships to perceive any threat at all. In their cocoon state, they're on high alert. The smallest thing could trigger a violent reaction. You've heard how individual podships react to forced entry, crushing intruders. It could be like that with the cocoon, but on a much larger scale."

"Make it unarmed," Anton said.

"One more thing," Eshaz said. "At least one Tulyan should go with Thinker. Tulyans and podships have connections that no other races or machines can fathom."

"All right," the Doge said, after a moment's consideration. "I suppose you're volunteering, aren't you?"

"I am."

"What about us?" Acey asked, looking at Eshaz for his support.

"Not this time," Eshaz said. "We need experience and intellect, not youthful exuberance. Do not take that as an insult. It is just fact."

Acey sulked away, but Tesh saw Dux nod in understanding.

Onboard the unarmed shuttle, Thinker at first went into a folded position, to focus on and contemplate the additional data he had been receiving. Standing beside him on the forward observation platform, Eshaz looked at the space station as it loomed larger and larger. On the gray-and-black skin he noticed a steady pulse, as if the cocoon was breathing in the airless void of space.

Presently, Thinker unfolded himself, after having been closed for only a couple of minutes.

Eshaz felt his own pulse quicken when they drew nearer and nearer to the strange amalgamation. As if in synchronicity, the throb of the cocoon increased as well.

A section of podship flesh parted, revealing a docking station beyond. But as he neared it, Eshaz saw that it was not part of the space station. Instead, it was Aopoddae flesh beyond, with docking connections like those he had seen on orbital pod stations.

In trepidation, Eshaz continued forward. He had no other choice.

Back when the HibAdu force first approached, Noah had originally assumed the worst, so over the orbiter's communication channel he had ordered all Humans and Mutatis on the space station into an armored command chamber with him. From that windowless enclosure, Noah and the others had watched the battle on a holoscreen . . . the dramatic ebb and flow of combat.

When the HibAdus had seemed defeated, he'd watched on the projected screen as Subi Danvar's podship connected to the space station, along with a score of others. In near-space just beyond Subi's ship, Noah had seen numerous unarmed caretaker podships—and he'd felt them reaching out to him wordlessly, assuring him that they would protect him and would even respond to his commands. Curiously, Aopoddae names and their biographical details had simultaneously surfaced in Noah's consciousness, like objects bobbing up from deep in the ocean. One of the vessels had been the ancient spacefarer, *Diminian*, who dated back to the earliest days of the galaxy. Most of the others had been nearly as old. Noah found all of it intriguing.

With the battle apparently won, the Mutatis and Humans in the command chamber had streamed out, to greet Subi Danvar and the others. But Noah had remained behind by himself, feeling an odd sense of serenity and a need to be alone. Despite his own history, his part in developing the defensive pod-killer weapons on MPA pod stations, these podships no longer feared him at all. He was confident, as well, that the change went throughout the entire Aopoddae race.

Earlier, out in the airless battlefield, Noah had seen the debris of combat, including bodies floating in orbital space, and podships that he sensed were waiting for him to command them. Summoning his courage, he had reached out with the psychic tentacles of his mind and had drawn the sentient spacecraft in around the space station, where they had combined with the vessels of Subi and the others. . . .

Now Noah felt their protective layer, their cocoon. In addition, he sensed a force far out in the cosmos, one that was separate from him, but one with him at the same moment. And, though he did not yet understand it, Noah knew that he could call upon it whenever he needed. At last, he had a degree of control over the paranormal elements around him. Or was that only his perception? How much—and what—did he really control?

These thoughts agitated him, so he withdrew from them, and floated in the troubled, cosmic sea of his mind.

CHAPTER FIFTY-SEVEN

There is no safe place in this universe.
—Anonymous

From the armored chamber within the cocoon, Noah touched the new rough skin covering his legs and feet. Though he was still Human in all places where it showed to others, the hidden patches beneath his clothing had extended in the last few minutes, and tingled on the surface. He pulled his trousers back on, then slipped into his socks and shoes. He knew he looked normal, like the old Noah. But changes had a way of coming over him unpredictably.

His mind reached out into orbital space, to the battlefield where bodies and the debris of combat drifted. He saw a shuttle approaching—and looking inside, he knew who the passengers were, and that they were coming unarmed.

Eshaz and Thinker. Friends.

But he cautioned himself anyway. Relationships had a nasty habit of changing for the worse. Even Tesh, who cared about him deeply, had expressed concern over his strange powers—and she'd said that before this latest escalation. She was out there now at the fringe of the battlefield, in the sectoid chamber of *Webdancer*. Tesh and the others thought they were beyond the reach of Noah's cocoon, but they were wrong.

Ever the optimist, Noah didn't like to think of negative possibilities, but he knew he had to anyway. As his powers increased, he had to always be wary of people who might not understand them, and what he was going to do with them. Even Noah didn't know what his powers were all about, or the extent of them. He was on a path going somewhere important, but he didn't know the purpose of his journey or the destination. He only knew his own heart and instincts, and had to assume he would not betray them, no matter the physical form he took. It was one of the reasons he felt drawn to EcoStation. In a way that he could not put into words, the orbiter seemed to ground him emotionally and spiritually.

I am an eco-warrior, he thought.

From his earliest moments of consciousness as a small child, Noah had marveled at nature—at leaves, insects and birds, and the animals of the forest near his home on Canopa. He had noticed a symmetry, a regularity, and a beauty to the supposedly more primitive life forms in his immediate vicinity, and he had seen how this contrasted with the way Humans behaved. As a child, it had made him feel out of place and awkwardly conspicuous, as if the various life forms were watching him and ridiculing him.

It was from that core of early existence that Noah had stretched his thoughts as far as he could. In his teens he had come up with the concept of galactic ecology, the idea that remote star systems and planets were linked throughout the heavens and needed to be protected against the avarices and carelessness of Humans and other races.

For most of his life, he had been on an environmental quest, seeking to draw everything in the galaxy together and make perfect sense of it. With his newfound knowledge and powers, no matter how patchy or unpredictable they might be, he had an even greater desire than ever to understand the vastness and minutia of the cosmos, to find ultimate precision and faultlessness. Perfect sense out of chaos.

Bringing himself back to his immediate surroundings, to the augmented flesh that contained his enhanced mind, Noah knew with certainty that he needed to guard himself against all attacks, so that he could continue his incredibly important quest.

And ultimately, Noah fully understood—or sensed—that there were far greater life forms than his own. But he also sensed that not all of them would agree with his beliefs and desires. What if one or more of those outside entities were able to gain an influence over him? He thought that this might have already occurred, explaining to some degree the enhancements and powers he had been given. But he could not be certain. It might also be true that he was like a cosmic magnet, drawing talents and abilities to him so that he could complete his great quest, his galactic-scale mission.

Then, winding his thoughts back to his own Human form and his feelings that he had to protect himself against attack, Noah wondered if he felt this for himself—for his own interests—or if he was instead feeling this on behalf of some outside entity that was shaping him to its desires. Feeling no selfishness at all, he hoped an outside entity was not guiding him, and if it was, that things would turn out well. It seemed to him that Timeweb was a beneficial structure, and that the creator—or creators—of the galactic filigree were . . .

He wasn't sure if the word he had in mind was adequate. *Virtuous.* To be virtuous in the context he was considering it, taking actions for the benefit of the galaxy did not necessarily mean being kind. It could very well involve making difficult, even brutal, decisions.

As he analyzed his thoughts from different angles, Noah could not stand the idea of an outside entity controlling him, pushing him forward and possibly luring him into a trap or making him into a slave, perhaps even for eternity. He needed facts, explanations, but there were none. And now he was farther along on the course of physical and mental changes than ever before. But heading for where? The impetus for all of it was uncertain, as was so much more. He had to stay alert, had to look around the next corner and see what was there.

For all his vision, for all he was and all that he was becoming, Noah Watanabe had a paranormal blind spot that prevented him from seeing an immense timehole that was about to surface near him.

Inside the unseen timehole, in a starless void between two galaxies that was sealed on both ends, a powerful fleet of Hib-Adu lab-pods floated, with their crews in confusion. Minutes before, they had been far across the known galaxy, preparing to attack Canopa, the most powerful remaining merchant prince world. Then, just as they were about to emerge from space over the planet in bursts of green light, they had found themselves somewhere else entirely, in an unknown, uncharted realm. And from that place they could not split space and travel on any galactic webbing, because no cosmic infrastructure existed there. They could only move under backup propulsion systems and send desperate, bewildered communications from ship to ship. The Hibbil and Adurian officers and soldiers didn't know where they were, and couldn't see—or go—beyond the confines of their dark prison.

Aboard the largest and most elegant ship in the HibAdu fleet, High Ruler Coreq sat in the midst of the mounting turmoil of his officers, saying nothing to them in his despair, and not even responding when they addressed him. It had been Coreq's idea to attack Canopa with massive force, and to bask in the glory of certain victory. He had wanted to be there at the forefront, soaking it all in. So he had gone along on the mission, leaving Premier Enver and Warlord Tarix to run things on the Adurian homeworld while he was away.

From the beginning, when he first emerged from an Adurian laboratory, Coreq had known he had a calling that spanned every star system, that God in his perfect wisdom had created him and his two hybrid companions for a purpose. Now he sensed powerful forces at work around him, and that he had not been thwarted in his desire to attack Canopa. Instead, he had been guided in a different direction, toward a far more important target.

Absorbing his surroundings, feeling a sudden flow of energy, he directed his ships to fly in a specific direction that seemed upward to him, though such a direction did not really exist where he was. Nonetheless, he went up, until the fleet could go no farther, until they seemed to bump into an unseen barrier.

As moments passed the barrier grew filmy, with faint lights visible beyond. Then the gossamer substance of the barricade faded entirely, and he saw stars beyond. His fleet surged through, and now he saw something else.

It was a large, amorphous shape, and a fleet of enemy warships beyond. Looking through a scope, he thought the bulky form almost looked like a giant podship with a mottled gray-and-black surface, but it was in a different configuration. He'd never seen anything like it, but he sensed an urgency to destroy it.

Without hesitation, Coreq gave the order to attack. Beside him, a newly installed control panel displayed a series of multicolored lights, showing that it was ready to fire the warship's weapons.

Noah had a brief vision, a burst of thought in which everything blew up around him and his body tumbled into a glowing green timehole. It only took a couple of moments for this to flash in his mind, and then he readied himself for action.

Extreme danger.

In his mind's eye he saw the approaching HibAdu fleet, and finally saw the gaping, green void of the timehole beyond. All around him, he felt the urgency and collective panic of the podships. They shifted and thickened and hardened themselves, but Noah knew it would not be enough.

He also saw *Webdancer* and the rest of the Liberator fleet moving as they perceived the HibAdu threat. Doge Anton's forces activated their weapons and rushed toward the cocooned space station. But they would not get there in time.

Precious seconds ticked by, and Noah looked farther, beyond anything that was happening here, or that might occur in this place. Now his far-seeing eye saw the Tulyan Starcloud and he longed to be there, as if it were a heavenly destination.

On the command bridge of the HibAdu flagship, an Adurian officer touched pressure pads on the weapon-control box to fire the high-energy space cannons. A tremendous volley went out, but from the wrong weapons, at the rear of the ship.

"You idiots!" Coreq shouted. "What are you doing?" He saw HibAdu war-pods behind his vessel explode into orange flowers of light, and other ships taking evasive action.

"Sir, we did everything right," the officer insisted. He pointed. "Look, the panel is showing that we fired the forward cannons."

"I accept no excuses," the High Ruler said. With one powerful hand, he reached out and broke the officer's neck.

From his hiding place behind the instrument console, Ipsy heard officers chattering nervously, saying they didn't know what was wrong, and they still had other ships going after the target. The little robot wished he could do more to stop those attacks, and to destroy the rest of the HibAdu fleet. But at least he had made a difference.

Ipsy realized that he could become a casualty of war with this now-defenseless ship, or he might be discovered in his place of concealment. It shouldn't matter to him one way or the other. Based on the commotion he was hearing out on the bridge, he knew he had made a difference.

But he wanted to do something even bigger. Perhaps he could discover a way . . .

After looking across space for only a few seconds, Noah had shifted focus to his immediate surroundings, and he watched the unfolding battle, the confusion in the attack force and the ships from the rear coming around to the front to take up the assault.

Moments later, he saw HibAdu energy bursts bounce off the skins of the cocoon-linked podships. The approaching Liberator fleet fired back, hitting three lab-pods and blowing them apart. But other enemy ships continued to advance and fire. Noah felt the cocoon weaken, as podships on one side of the space station envelope were injured by the powerful blasts.

Suddenly everything turned brilliant green around Noah, but he knew it was not from an explosion, or from being sucked into the timehole. He blinked his eyes, and EcoStation—with its Aopoddae cocoon—was somewhere else.

Of his own volition, Noah had split space to take a podway shortcut that still existed, despite the decline of the galactic infrastructure. And almost instantaneously, his cocoon emerged from space inside the serene cosmic mists of the starcloud. All around he felt the telepathic probings of Tulyan citizens, some of whom had stronger telepathic powers than others. They probed, and he felt the psychic power of mindlink mounting, as if to attack and destroy the intruder.

Inside the Aopoddae skin around the space station, Noah heard the voices of Tulyan pilots and Liberator fighters who were in the honeycomb of passages and chambers. He heard Thinker talking to Eshaz as they hurried through a dimly illuminated passageway on foot, and he determined that Eshaz was responding to the telepathic probes of his people, telling them that the cocoon structure did not threaten them, or the starcloud.

Oddly, Noah felt simple, almost primitive thoughts mixed with his more complex ruminations. *Eshaz is my friend. Let him through. And Thinker, too.*

With this thought Noah caused a new passageway to open up near the Tulyan and the cerebral robot, allowing them to leave the membrane and enter the space station. Then Noah sent his own clairvoyant signals to Eshaz, guiding him through the modules to his armored chamber.

Around him Noah sensed that the Tulyan probes had faded and that their mindlink weaponry had subsided. The starcloud defenders would not attack. In their own way, the Tulyans had determined the identity of the unusual intruder in their starcloud, and no longer considered it a threat.

Noah also knew what was occurring over Yaree. He could not predict the outcome, but using Timeweb he watched from afar, frustrated that he could not contribute to the fight. . . .

At the vanguard of the Liberator ships, Tesh threw *Webdancer* into the battle first. At their weapons ports, Doge Anton's crew fired space cannons, ion guns, and energy detonators at the HibAdus, as did the other ships in his fleet. In only a few minutes the HibAdus realized they were outgunned and outmaneuvered, and they fell back, trying to save their lab-pods for another day.

But Doge Anton ordered pursuit, and his podships chased and killed hundreds of enemy vessels. Even though they were only going after lab-pods, the Liberator pilots each reported feeling a jolt in the bodies of their own podships when each kill was made. It seemed to be a sympathetic psychic reaction experienced by the Aopoddae. Tesh felt this herself from her connection, but pressed onward. The Liberator podships suffered even in victory, but continued to cooperate with their pilots and crews. . . .

Hearing Eshaz and Thinker at the door, Noah let them in. "Give me a moment," Noah said as they entered.

In his mind's eye, Noah saw the waning battle, *experienced* all of it. And even before the fighting was complete and the remaining HibAdu ships had fled into space, he watched Tulyan caretaker ships take positions over the timehole. Perched there, the Tulyans dropped exploding packets into the opening and murmured their ancient incantations.

Gradually the cosmic hole became smaller and smaller, and presently it was no longer there.

CHAPTER FIFTY-EIGHT

> In the case of Noah Watanabe, the known rules of cellular
> physiology do not apply.
> —Excerpt from CorpOne medical report

"You are something even more unusual now, aren't you?" Eshaz
stood over Noah, looking down at him with slitted, pale gray
eyes.

"Some realities are not fact or science based," Thinker said,
standing beside the Tulyan. "Master Noah, increasingly, I must
place information about you into my alternate data banks."

Noah clasped one of Eshaz's oversized hands, then reached
over and patted his robotic companion on one of his metal
shoulders. "My friends, it is good to see both of you. Very good,
indeed. We have won a great victory at Yaree. It is the beginning
of the end for the HibAdus."

The reptilian man and the robot just stood there, looking at
him.

"Well of course I'm different now," Noah said. "Everyone is
different from moment to moment. That's true of each of you
as well. Even you, Thinker, with your changing data banks."

"Your skin is metamorphosing, isn't it?" Eshaz said. "I sensed
something once when I touched your shirt fabric. It was on one
of your arms." He squinted his slitted eyes, thinking back. "Your
left arm. Through Tesh's connection with *Webdancer* and the
other podships, I learned from her that she actually felt rough

skin under the sleeve on your left arm. Would you like to show it to us?"

"For what purpose?"

"You must trust us," Eshaz said. "Perhaps we can help you."

Noah hesitated, trying to maintain some personal space around himself. Then he sighed, and said, "All right, my friends."

He stripped down to his shorts. All of the skin on his muscular body—with the exception of the neck, head, and hands—had turned gray, with deep veins of black coursing in several directions. "What am I becoming?" Noah asked. "A podship?"

"Accessing alternate data banks," Thinker said, blinking his metal-lidded eyes. Orange lights flashed around his faceplate.

"How did you fly the space station to the starcloud?" Eshaz asked.

"Mmmm. Basically, I envisioned it, and it happened. Beyond that, I'm not sure."

"Interesting," the Tulyan said. Looking around the armored room, he said, "This is your sectoid chamber, then, and from here you control the amalgamated podships?"

Noah grew quiet for a moment, and heard the faint pulse of the cocooned Aopoddae. From this room, he was not in physical contact with their amalgamated flesh, but he was in touch with it in a different manner, and he cared deeply about the creatures. Through the link, he satisfied himself that the injured podships were beginning to heal, benefiting from their connection to their brethren, and from a connection they had with Timeweb.

Finally, Noah answered the question. "This is not a sectoid chamber at all. I just happened to be here during the battle and the flight."

"But the podships have cocooned you for a reason," Eshaz said. "To protect you, obviously."

"Supposedly I am immortal, and if that's true I should not need protecting." Then, remembering another vision he had in which his body tumbled free of the space station into a time-hole, he said, "Perhaps you are right after all. They do offer me some protection. A great deal, actually. I think they enhance my mental abilities, as well. I feel more focused here, calmer and more centered. The podships actually trust me now, Eshaz!"

"Processing new data," the cerebral robot said. "Remarkable information."

"Knock it off, Thinker," Noah said, as he put his clothes back on. "You don't have to announce that you are processing data in order to do it."

The metal-lidded eyes blinked quickly. "No, but I am feeling great excitement and astonishment at what is occurring around me. Programmed emotions, to be certain, but I want to be part of the discussion, sharing the joy of the moment with you. A great victory over the HibAdus and a new journey for Master Noah. Truly, these are epic times!"

Smiling, Noah said, "I recall making you the official historian of the Guardians, and the trustee of my life story. OK, my metal friend, process away."

Meeting Eshaz's gaze, Noah then said, "Everything that occurs here goes beyond this room, doesn't it?"

"Not necessarily," Eshaz said.

"With Thinker here, if I instruct him to do so, he will bury the data somewhere. It could still be subject to detection by an expert investigating his data banks, but if any robot can successfully hide the information it is this one. You are not the same, though, Eshaz. You are linked to all Tulyans and to the Aopoddae."

The reptilian man straightened. "Nonetheless, there are methods of concealing information from the truthing touch and from every other probe. What do you command of me, Master Noah?"

"And what do you command of me, Master Noah?" Thinker said.

"If I wanted either of you to maintain confidentiality about me, I might *request* it, not command it. However, I see no way to keep the secret. It will get out eventually, because the podships cocooning me are linked to other podships, and in turn to their Tulyan pilots. Also to the one Parvii pilot, Tesh. No, it would get out anyway. And maybe it should."

"We would do anything for you, Master Noah," Thinker said.

"I know you would, and I appreciate that." Noah finished dressing, and then said, "Lead the way, Eshaz. We must discuss the situation with the Council of Elders."

"They asked me to tell you that is not necessary. Earlier, they were linked to you telepathically, and they obtained all the information about you that they needed. For the moment, anyway."

"Very well. With their power to probe, they must know I'm turning into a podman."

"Probably," Eshaz said, "but to make certain, I'll let them know on your behalf. First Elder Kre'n also asked me to tell you that she actually permitted your cocoon to enter the starcloud in the first place. Our strongest minds—including her—detected your imminent approach, and opened the way for you."

"Then why did they subject me to such intense scrutiny when I arrived?"

"For extra security purposes."

"Can't hurt, I guess."

Eshaz scratched his side. "The First Elder agrees with you that EcoStation can be an important symbol for the Liberators, and for you as an eco-warrior. It could become a symbol of resistance, inspiring the people of various galactic races."

These remarks only reminded Noah of his own limitations, and of his need to remain humble and respectful during all exchanges with the powerful Tulyan leaders.

"Please be sure to tell them we have a lot of bodies onboard," Noah said. "I'd like the authorization to hold a burial ceremony somewhere in the starcloud."

The Council of Elders gave permission for Noah to conduct a memorial service on the smallest of their three planets, in a flower-filled mountain meadow. The morning after Noah's arrival, they provided transport ships to carry the mourners, along with more than twelve hundred bodies, to the destination.

As Noah boarded one of the ships and it pulled away from the cocoon, he felt a mounting panic, and considered asking the pilot to turn around and take him back. A sensation of dizziness came over him, and he felt weakness in the muscles of his legs, so that he had to hold onto a high railing for support when he stood—even though the flight through the mists was quite smooth.

"Are you all right, Master Noah?" It was Eshaz, reaching out to steady him by the arm. Thinker and Subi Danvar were there, too.

"I'm fine," Noah said. As he had grown accustomed to doing, Noah wore clothing that completely covered the changes in his skin. This time, it was a green-and-brown Guardian uniform and cap.

Gradually, Noah felt a little better. But he came to suspect that it was only a stabilizing effect, and that he had to get used to feeling weaker away from the cocoon. How far he could journey from the amalgamated pods, he didn't know. But he sensed a supportive, healing power here in the starcloud that gave him assurance that he could proceed with the burial ceremony.

When Noah disembarked on the high meadow, walking carefully, he said to Subi, "I am told that you are doing a terrific job in your duties with the fleet. While my Guardians have been merged into the Liberator force, I want you to oversee them in my place, whenever necessary. It seems that I am becoming rather occupied with other matters."

"Yes, Master Noah, I will do that for you, until you are ready to resume your duties. I know how close the Guardians are to your heart."

"Thank you."

On the meadow grass, the entire Council of Elders greeted Noah, dressed in elegant black-and-gold robes. "I'm glad we are able to accommodate your desires," Kre'n said. She shook his hand.

As the big alien woman held his hand, Noah felt the probing of her truthing touch. Another level of Tulyan security, he surmised. But he didn't mind, and allowed her to complete her task. Finally she removed her grasp, and looking at him, she said, "You may indeed be the one spoken of in our legends."

"I doubt if I qualify for any legends," Noah said, with an embarrassed smile.

"More and more of us are agreeing with Eshaz's assessment," she insisted. "He thinks you are the first important member of the Human race in the history of the galaxy."

"Oh, there have been far greater figures than myself," Noah insisted.

"Perhaps not. You are the man who restored the ecological health of numerous merchant prince planets, and then went beyond even that. You are a man of vision. Many of us—myself included—believe that your emergence has triggered the resurgence of the Tulyan race. For the first time in millions of years, we are again dispatching caretaker teams to maintain and repair the web." She paused. "Only time will tell how successful we are."

Wrinkling his brow, Noah considered her comments for a moment, while she awaited his response. He remembered an earlier visit to the Tulyan Council Chamber, when Kre'n first mentioned the legend of a Savior to him. Some of the Elders had looked upon him with a certain reverence at that time, with the notable exception of the big, grumpy one, Dabiggio. Now, it was different. Even Dabiggio seemed to believe.

Presently Noah insisted, "I don't think I'm the Savior spoken of in your legends. I am a mere Human, with a few quirks. However, I wish to do everything possible to make myself worthy of your respect. Admittedly, I do have certain leadership qualities that might prove helpful to others. As Master of the Guardians, I have been able to inspire others to achieve more than they might have without me. At this time, I find myself in a position to accomplish more than ever before. I hope I am not too much more than a man, that I am not evolving into a god of any form, or your Savior. But if anything like that happens, if that is my destination, I shall be prepared to fulfill it."

"Humbly," Kre'n said. "I have already read this in your thoughts."

Noah bowed to her. "Of course."

"We Tulyans do not die often," she said, "and we have always been underpopulated for the size of our starcloud. Consequently, we have plenty of space for burial plots. As we told Eshaz, this will be a single ceremony to include timehole and war victims alike, but there will be individual burials in carefully marked graves. Identities will be indicated if known, and there will be genetic charts for each victim. Later, if any of the family members want the remains sent somewhere else, those requests can be accommodated."

"Thank you. It is very much appreciated." Looking around, he saw gnarled mountaintops at higher elevations, and pristine lakes in a valley beneath the sentinel perches. It looked like someplace in a fairy tale, and the scenery alone seemed to return some of his strength. He stood tall as he accompanied the Elders to a large, flat stone where they all gathered.

Golden sunlight found its way through the mists of the starcloud, and bathed Noah in warmth. On meadows and grassy slopes around the site, he saw many Tulyans in white robes, standing beside coffins and grave sites that had already been dug. In those coffins were a variety of races, people killed onboard the modified space station. Though most of the timehole victims were Human, there were also Blippiqs, Huluvians, Salducians, and other races, including a couple of unidentified Mutatis who might have been spies sent by the vile Zultan, before his son Hari'Adab took control of the race and changed its alliances. Noah thought of the Mutati who had preferred being Human, Princess Meghina of Siriki, and wondered where she and her immortal companions could possibly be now.

Kre'n straightened her own robes, and stood facing the gravesites. Noah heard her words carrying far out on a warm breeze, without the need of electronics. As the Tulyan leader spoke, hundreds of tiny comets appeared high overhead, and sped through the mists separating the planets.

"We stand upon one of the miracles of our wondrous starcloud," Kre'n said to the assemblage, as if in answer to Noah's unspoken question. "This is one of our most sacred transmitting stones, one of the points where our most powerful intellects can stand, and dramatically increase the powers of mindlink. In this day and age, even at this very moment, we cannot afford to let our guard down for a moment."

On the perimeter of the stone, several Tulyan men and women stood with their faces turned skyward, looking in different directions. They appeared to be in trances, but were undoubtedly watching for any approaching danger.

Kre'n continued: "We are honored to dedicate this sacred site to a new purpose, as the first multiracial graveyard on Tulyan soil. We are part of this great and just war and of the interconnected galaxy, and this is one of our contributions. All Tulyans are pleased to do this. In tribute to these dead, many of whom died honorably fighting for the Liberators, we have brought in a comet for each of them."

Looking up, she pointed, and the comets put on a spectacular aerial show, speeding this way and that, swooping down almost to the valley floor and then going back up again, high into the ethereal mists. Then, in the blink of an eye, they were gone, as if the comets had taken the spirits of the dead to some other place.

Noah heard a clapping sound in the air, but didn't see anyone moving their hands to do this. Telepathic clapping? Yes, he decided as he watched the faces of the Tulyans.

Then, looking down at his own hands, which were clasped in front of his body, he saw the gray-black flesh encroaching, moving onto the tops of his wrists. As he absorbed the ongoing ceremony and looked inward at the same time, Noah felt his own self dying. The *old* self. He continued to become something radically different, and found the possibilities both exciting and terrifying.

Whatever was happening to him, Noah wondered how much of it he controlled himself. Earlier, the podships had moved close to the space station without cocooning it at first, making him aware that they were available for him to direct. He had responded by drawing them in around him in a protective fashion, and they had completed their amalgam around EcoStation. It seemed to have been a cooperative, collective effort between himself and them. Now he wondered how much of the changes to his body were of his own volition, and how much could possibly be caused by outside influence.

Focusing hard, he saw the encroaching skin retreat a few centimeters. This told him something. A piece of the puzzle, but not the answer. He allowed the metamorphosis to continue.

I want it, he thought. *With all of its unknown dangers, I want it.*

But for the moment he resisted the urge, and caused the encroaching skin to retreat back under his clothing. This was not the time, or the place, to permit it to flow over his entire body.

"Please say something now," Kre'n said. Placing a hand on Noah's shoulder, she guided him to the spot where she had been standing.

Noah took a deep breath and said, his words carrying out to the assemblage, "Thank you for sharing this special place with me, and with those who are being honored here today. On behalf of the families of the loved ones we are laying to rest, I express their heartfelt appreciation. By courier, I have also been in contact with Doge Anton, and he wants me to pass on his deep gratitude to you as well."

Pausing, Noah looked around, to the gnarled mountain peaks and down to the magical lakes in the valley. Then he said, "Being here, I could almost imagine that there is nothing wrong in the galaxy, that all is in perfect order. But all of us know that this is not the case. Sadly, these dead are the proof of it."

To close the ceremony, Noah asked for a moment of silence. When it was completed, he nodded to Kre'n, who in turn gave a signal to the Tulyans at the grave sites.

Simultaneously, the Tulyans raised their hands, and with their collective psychic energy they lowered the coffins into the ground.

CHAPTER FIFTY-NINE

There are more roads to tragedy than to happiness.
—Ancient observation

As Hari'Adab strode through a corridor on the top floor of the Golden Palace, he hardly noticed the opulence around him, the gilded walls and furnishings, the infinity mirrors, the priceless paintings and statuaries. He had seen such finery before in the Mutati Kingdom, in the palatial residences of his own family. Often in the past he had felt considerable embarrassment for living in luxurious surroundings, considering the impoverished conditions suffered by many of his people. His father (and some of Hari's advisers) had pointed out to him the necessity of a leader acting and looking like a leader, and of displaying the trappings of success to the populace.

So they'd said, and Hari had essentially gone along with the role-playing they espoused, but he had also instituted more programs to help the poor than any leader in Mutati history. And he'd done it with layers of anonymity that prevented most people from knowing his involvement. To him, it made no sense to do things for people and then ask for their adoration in return. He didn't like the equation, just as he'd never liked the thought of praying for himself. For Hari, it was far more important to pray for someone else, just as he had been doing for his beloved Parais.

The Mutati doctors had set up a medical room for the injured

379

aeromutati on the top level of the palace, and they had been tending to her with all known treatments and technology. Since learning of the terrible injury to his lover, the young Emir had been at an emotional nadir. To the extent possible, trying to be vigilant but not interfering, he had overseen her medical care. For two straight days he had hardly left her side, and he was only away briefly now, while they administered treatments that they said would be difficult for him to watch. Parais was experiencing cellular complications that were unique to Mutatis, and she needed surgical procedures to improve the flow of medicines through her body. Hari had tried to stay, but the doctors had prevailed on him, insisting it was best for him, and for the patient. They needed to focus on her, not on his reactions.

Now Hari couldn't wait to get back inside the room. He came to a stop just outside her door, waiting for it to open. They'd said it would only be a half hour, but now it had been nearly two hours. He heard them inside with their instruments and machines, chattering in their arcane medical language. The tones were urgent. Hari felt like bursting inside, but worried about causing harm to Parais.

The HibAdu weapon used on her had been insidious, sending an energy pulse into her body that had expanded and wreaked havoc on her internal organs. In reaction to the violent intrusion, Parais' cellular structure had gone into retreat, fleeing inward to a place where it thought it could best restore the body. Hari only understood this in generalities, but it had long been known that shapeshifter cells had a racial brain and survival instincts that were not under control of the mind of any individual. In taking control away from Parais, the cells had reverted to a state that was even more ancient and basic than the natural fleshy appearance of a typical Mutati. They reverted to a primitive core, which scientists said was similar to the primordial matter that generated the first Mutati life millions and millions of years ago.

Slowly, hesitantly, Hari walked away from the door. Two uniformed MPA soldiers hurried by, carrying message cubes. They entered a room that Hari knew was one of the offices used by Liberator military commanders, including the remaining officers of the Mutati High Command. The day before, Hari had met briefly with them to discuss how they might allocate their combined military assets to recover the conquered worlds of the Mutati Kingdom. They were considering a military offensive that would start with the Emir's own planet Dij, and if success was achieved there, they would move on to others.

Heightening the need for this, there had been sickening rumors of atrocities committed against the Mutati people by the invaders, including gruesome public displays in which Hibbils and Adurians had eaten the flesh of their shapeshifter victims. He hoped these were only rumors, the sort that were common in times of war, but a little voice inside told him they were true. He'd long sensed the resentment felt by Adurians toward Mutatis, and Hibbils were known to be vicious little carnivores. Unfortunately, it all added up.

All of the allied officers and political leaders—including Doge Anton, Hari'Adab, and First Elder Kre'n—wanted to rescue and recover every Human and Mutati planet, but they were also worried about the strange absence of large-scale military activity by the HibAdus against Canopa and Siriki. There had been skirmishes and the recent, relatively small battle in the Sirikan back country, but not much other than that. The two MPA planets were like beacons of hope in the bleak war against the HibAdus. Some of the officers, particularly Subi Danvar, thought that the galactic instabilities that had occurred on both Canopa and Siriki were preventing the HibAdus from mounting full-scale attacks there. There had been extensive geological damage to the Valley of the Princes on Canopa and to remote sections of Siriki, along with other timehole activity in the vicinity of both planets.

There were so many immense concerns going on simultaneously that Hari felt the limitations of anything he could do to improve conditions. According to all estimates, the HibAdus had much larger military forces than the Liberators and their Human, Mutati, and Tulyan elements. In addition, the Tulyans—who were heading up the other "war" against galactic disintegration—were not able to keep up with the deterioration that was continuing.

The Emir heaved a deep sigh, trying to calm himself, and returned to the door to Parais' room. The voices and equipment noises seemed unchanged, a sense that the doctors and their aides were taking efficient, urgent actions.

This section of the Golden Palace was the most heavily fortified, and constituted the keep that had been designed and built to protect its royal inhabitants against outside attack. As far as Hari was concerned, it housed the most important person of all now, Parais d'Olor. But the vicious assault on her had already been made, and he had not been there to protect her.

For that, he had initially blamed Doge Anton, who had kept them apart. But ultimately, Hari came to the realization that it wasn't the Doge's fault after all. There really was no one to blame—at least not anymore—for the long history of enmity between the Human and Mutati races, and the deep distrust that resulted. Even now, with close cooperation between the races, some of the old feelings lingered. There had been fights and name-calling among the soldiers, but cooler heads always prevailed. During moments of frustration, Hari had experienced such feelings of antagonism himself, but had kept them in check.

He felt overwhelmed by all of the details surrounding him, and longed for the halcyon times he had spent with Parais, flying on her avian back to a retreat where they could enjoy each other's company in private. On Dij, they had frequented an isolated beach, where the sun warmed the sands. In his mind now, he tried to remember how it used to be with her, particular details that he wanted to relive, pushing aside the cold realities of the moment. He shivered.

The door to her room opened suddenly, and Hari got out of the way as two Mutati medical attendants hurried past him and down the corridor. Their faces were emotionless, but he knew this was the way of their profession, the need to suppress feelings and keep doing their jobs. A Human doctor followed them, an elderly man who had been allowed to observe, and to offer what limited assistance he could.

"You may come in now," another doctor said from inside the room. A small Mutati male with a narrow mustache, Dr. Wikk motioned toward the bed where Parais lay. Two other doctors left the room.

Summoning his courage, Hari entered. "How is she?"

"Only time will tell. We've adjusted her medications slightly, to reduce the pain. I'll leave you two alone for a few minutes."

Fighting back tears, Hari stood by the mass of quivering flesh and dark feathers on the bed. A copy of *The Holy Writ*—the sacred book of the Mutati people—sat on a table beside her. Unable to speak, Parais barely clung to life. Her facial features were puffy and horribly contorted, and almost unrecognizable. From a medical treatment, her eyes had reemerged from the fatty cellular structure of her face, but they were closed now.

"It might be kinder to put her out of her misery," the doctor said, as he departed.

"What?" In sudden fury, Hari almost lunged at him. Then, in a menacing tone, he said, "You'd better not try anything like that. If you do, I . . . Look, I'm sorry. I know you're just doing your best, and thinking of her suffering."

"I'm sorry." The doctor left, and the door slid shut behind him.

Hari'Adab was alone with Parais again, but not in the way he'd been remembering. The contrasts were so far apart, and the prospects so dismal. As he had done after killing his father, Hari'Adab again contemplated suicide. It would put an end to his suffering. But what about Parais? He couldn't just leave her, and couldn't bear the thought of euthanizing her. At his previous low point, despite the loss of Paradij and all of its inhabitants, she had insisted that Hari live and make himself strong for the sake of the Mutati people. With her loving influence, she had convinced him to spend the rest of his life doing what was right, not only for his own followers but for other galactic races as well.

Now he placed a hand gently on her face. In his mind's eye, Hari envisioned Parais clearly in her various mutations, the way she used to be when she morphed from one beautiful flying creature into another. She favored white feathers then, unlike her present disarrayed condition. The memories were so clear that he could almost imagine the lovely aeromutati back to normal at this very moment. In his memory, they spoke again of having children, and of their many other dreams.

He felt movement under his fingers. Parais opened her eyes and looked at him with her blue eyes, so filled with suffering that it ripped apart his emotions. He was at least heartened to see a glint there, and she seemed to recognize him. But she couldn't speak or hold her eyes open, and soon faded back into her universe of pain.

CHAPTER SIXTY

The Human brain is a gold mine of wondrous possibilities . . . and a cesspool.

—A Saying of Lost Earth

Noah stood by himself in one of the larger chambers of EcoStation, examining a section of bulkhead where podship skin had filled what had once been a large, jagged break in the module. It was his third day back at the Tulyan Starcloud. He detected the approach of visitors through the linked corridors of the cocoon and the space station, and he knew their identities: Doge Anton and a small entourage.

The leader of the Liberators had flown here after the Battle of Yaree, and had announced that he wanted to meet with Noah. But not wanting any interruption, Noah had sent no response. At least the Council of Elders seemed to already know that Noah wanted privacy, from their earlier telepathic probes, and—from a linkage with them—Eshaz knew as well.

He heard Doge Anton enter the chamber behind him, along with Tesh, Thinker, and two Tulyan caretakers. Noah did not have to turn around to see them, but he did so anyway. It would reduce the number of questions they asked of him. For now, in his white, long-sleeve tunic and dark trousers, the rough skin that covered most of his body was not visible to them. His hands, forearms, and head remained normal in appearance.

Tesh stood silently on one side, looking anxiously at Noah.

"I've called a meeting to assess everything," Anton said. The blond, mustachioed man wore a red-and-gold MPA uniform, decked with ribbons. A weapons belt circled his waist. "It will be held on General Nirella's ship this afternoon. I also have a request from Tesh to discuss something with you. She says it's important."

"I am unable to attend your meeting," Noah said. "I'm not feeling up to it at the moment, and don't think I can contribute. At least not yet. I have experienced many changes, many pressures on my mind and body, and I need to recuperate."

Scowling, Anton said, "Very well, but let me know when you are ready. Nirella and I would like your input, your suggestions."

"I can contribute more if you permit me this time alone."

"All right, Noah."

"With no interruptions. Please don't ask me for an explanation, because I'm not sure if I can provide one anyway—but I can see and hear everyone in EcoStation and everyone in the passageways and chambers of the cocoon. Please order them to leave."

Puzzled thoughts played across Anton's face. "You want the Tulyan pilots to leave, too?"

"They are without employment here. The cocoon does not respond to their commands."

"But it does to yours?"

"Yes."

"There is much to grasp here, Noah, but I will defer to your wishes. I will take care of it."

"Thank you."

Then, looking at the Parvii woman, Noah felt a tug of emotion. The cast of her green eyes and the slight trembling of her lips told him she had something important to discuss with him. At least, it was important to *her.* He didn't like having such a thought, because at his core he didn't feel superior to Tesh at all. But he could not take the time or energy to talk with her yet.

"I need more time," Noah said to her. "I will inform you when I'm ready."

Her face showed displeasure, but she said nothing, and left with the others.

Afterward, Noah stared at the podship skin on the bulkhead, and knew the flesh was connected to the cocoon. Reaching out and touching the wall, he felt the regular pulse of the living creature.

In images before his eyes, he also saw Doge Anton and his entourage striding away through a corridor, and saw the evacuation of the space station and of the cocoon—Humans, Tulyans, and robots streaming out into waiting transport ships. With one exception. In what had once been an education module of Eco-Station, a solitary figure stood immobile, with the lights around its faceplate glowing softly. Thinker.

So, the official historian of the Guardians, and the trustee of my life story has decided to defy me.

From his vantage, Noah sensed Thinker going almost entirely silent inside his robotic mechanisms, leaving only a sentry program operating. And, though he had not expected to feel this way, the presence of his friend gave the Guardian leader some comfort.

He thought of concentric circles around himself, starting with the toughness of his own body, the way it could heal and regenerate itself after injuries. Beyond that, as another layer of personal security, he had Thinker, Tesh, and Subi, and everyone else who cared about him. And even more, he had the cocoon, drifting within the protective mindlink of Tulyans in their sacred starcloud.

Am I truly the Savior they speak of in Tulyan legends?

He still did not think so, though he had no evidence one way or the other. Noah suspected, however, that it was not a provable thing, that it might be argued one way or the other.

Maybe I'm just helping the Tulyans save themselves. Maybe they are their own Savior, in a collective sense.

Gods and prophets—they didn't have to be what they were commonly believed to be in Noah's opinion, didn't have to look like their universal depictions. As just two examples among many, he doubted if he would ever see (in any form of sight that he possessed) a bearded old man in the sky or angels with wings. Maybe the supreme deity was more of a collective entity that stretched across the cosmos, like Noah's own concept of galactic ecology.

And, though Noah did not consider himself the center of the universe or even the galaxy, he nonetheless saw himself as the hub of *something*, with those concentric circles around him, radiating outward. At last, he could enter and leave Timeweb of his own volition. This enabled him to remain connected to the galactic web, and to the podship flesh he was touching now.

At his fingertips, Noah felt his own energy flowing outward into the amalgamated Aopoddae flesh, probing all of the arteries, organs, and cells that made up the ancient creatures. They were so complex, and yet so primitive. It made him realize how far afield many of the galactic races had gone with all of their details and complexities, all of their branched-out, hedonistic, disoriented priorities that caused them to wreak such havoc on the galaxy.

He saw that the battle-injured portions of the cocoon had not yet completely healed themselves, that their connection to their brethren and to Timeweb had helped them, but had not been quite enough. And it never would be enough without his involvement.

Noah didn't hold anything back from the Aopoddae. He allowed his energy to flow into the primitive flesh, as if he was Timeweb himself, providing healing nutrients to injured creatures. Once, Eshaz had done that for him, and Noah had made a miraculous recovery. Now, moment by moment, the alien flesh of the cocoon fused and healed at an accelerated rate. All the while, Noah probed and tested carefully, and perfected the cellular repairs. There was no question of trust anymore, no doubts of any kind from the Aopoddae about Noah's motivations. No fear of him. They needed him, and he needed them. It was a symbiotic relationship of extraordinary proportions.

He realized as well that the cocoon protected not only himself, but EcoStation. If Noah's plan unfolded for the space station, the enhanced facility would become an inspiration for all galactic races, a beacon of hope and more of a teaching facility for interstellar ecology than he had ever envisioned before.

Noah felt the podship skin tremble against his own flesh, as the cocoon anticipated what he was going to do next. He allowed the strengthened energy of the cocoon to flow back into him. Noah had healed the collective creature, and at this moment—in its fortified form—he anticipated that it would return the favor. Ultimately, Noah knew he was much more than a human being—physically and spiritually—and he sensed that the Aopoddae could guide him, could enable him to discover the path he should take with his remarkable life, and perhaps give him the tools that he needed.

The inflow was tremendous, and he struggled to absorb it and comprehend. Much of the new Aopoddae data, the vast majority of it, was indecipherable to him. But a limited amount of information, as if passing through a filter system from the Aopoddae language to something he could understand, reached his consciousness.

Noah realized that he was all of the galactic races, inextricably linked to them. He saw the history of sentient life as multiple paths spreading out in his wake, and found the broad routes he had taken in his own genetic history and life that brought him to this exact place and awareness. Countless other events could have occurred instead, events that would have prevented Noah from ever existing, or from ever being needed at all. Events that would not have led to the state of galactic decay in which everyone now found themselves trapped.

And, though Noah could not predict the future, he was able to envision multiple paths of unfolding galactic possibilities extending into future time, radiating outward from him. He could only try to nudge the various races to take the proper paths. He could never force them to do so.

Opening the synapses and paranormal elements of his mind, as if they were pores that he was unplugging, Noah tried to let more data flow in, everything the podships knew. He hungered for all of it. In response, an overwhelming surge of additional information flowed in, a tidal wave of data—much of it in raw, indecipherable form.

Pain!

It was too much, too fast, and the Aopoddae didn't seem to realize it. Or did they? Were they trying to kill him? Was that a last bit of data they would inject into him through the connection? Their confession of guilt, or even a gloating?

He screamed from the unbearable pain. It was not just physical. It went way beyond that.

Parallel realities surrounded him, like the concentric circles. In one of them, he realized that he had fallen to his knees, and that he was still trying to maintain physical contact with the Aopoddae cocoon. In his agony he lost contact, and slumped to the deck.

Noah became aware of needles in his brain, and of data flowing outward, like something removing poisons from his body. Bringing him back from the brink, rescuing him from his foolishness.

Opening his eyes, he saw Thinker kneeling over him, with a tentacle containing an array of needles linking the robot to Noah's skull. An organic interface, Noah realized. The robot had used it on him previously, to download information on Noah's life and genetics. Now he was doing it again, but for a different purpose. Gradually, Noah began to feel better.

"You saved my life," Noah said, as the pain faded. He breathed a sigh of relief.

"Perhaps not," Thinker said. "As we speak, I am analyzing limited elements of the Aopoddae information, even as it is being downloaded into my data banks and sorted. Contrary to your suspicion, the podships did not wish to do you harm. They gambled that you could handle the flood of information, and that you would heal mentally from any adverse effects of it—just as you have proven yourself able to recover from physical injuries."

"But you had to intervene."

"Because I didn't know what else to do. I don't think I caused any damage, and you can certainly reconnect to them and get the data again. However, I have an alternative that might be preferable to you."

The robot disconnected the interface, and it snaked back into his metal body. Noah sat up on the deck, noticed that his hands were different, entirely gray and rough-surfaced now, with veins of black. He felt his face. It had changed as well. He was ready for the complete metamorphosis. The time had arrived.

"What alternative?" Noah asked.

"I expected you would ask," Thinker said. He straightened, looked down at Noah. "Consider me your portable backup. I can adjust the interface, enabling you to search through my data banks at will, making the Aopoddae information available to you in a more palatable form."

"An intriguing offer," Noah said. "Yes, I want you to do that."

"I hasten to add, however, that most of the data is incomprehensible, even to me."

"I found the same thing. If that is true, though, how can you be certain they don't want to do me harm?"

"Good question. My only answer beyond what they have revealed to us is that I do not sense they have aggressive intentions toward you. I know, however, that my instincts in this regard are only programmed into me, and thus are by definition inferior to yours."

"I sense the same thing. The Aopoddae are essentially gentle souls, but dangerous when threatened, if they perceive enemies. Once, they considered me a possible enemy, but that has since been worked out between us. You notice I said between. I believe they are a single organism, a collective organism."

"Each species, each race is like that," Thinker noted. "I think you're saying that the Aopoddae are more closely linked to one another than other galactic races are?"

"That is my belief, but I also believe, in my heart of hearts, that all sentient life forms in the galaxy are ultimately linked to one another. It is a matter of definitions and semantics, and of filters on our thought processes. But it makes sense to me. It's tied to galactic ecology, to the interdependence of all matter in the galaxy, whether sentient or not. One life overall; one ecosystem overall."

"And tied to the concept of God."

"Not a typical comment for a robot," Noah said, with a gentle smile.

"I am not your typical robot."

"No, you aren't."

"I will run decryption programs on the Aopoddae raw data and see what more I can discover. It will not be easy, but . . . Hmmm, just a moment, please." Thinker whirred, and his body jerked, as if in pain. Noah heard something clank inside the mechanism.

Presently, however, the orange lights on the robot's faceplate blinked cheerily, and he announced, "I was overloading too, but I connected to a series of reserve memory cores. It is better now."

"There is probably more that we didn't absorb yet," Noah said. "I broke off the connection."

"Based upon what I'm seeing, Master Noah, I think we'd better try to figure out what we have first before obtaining more."

Noah nodded.

Thinker blinked his metal-lidded eyes. "Why don't we work with the information, sir, and see if we can handle it more safely? Maybe the Aopoddae didn't properly anticipate the danger to you, and we should set up safeguards."

"As usual, your wisdom is impeccable, my friend."

Rising to his feet, Noah looked down at his hands again. *Podship skin.* In a reflected metal surface of the chamber he saw matching changes in his face. He still saw the old Noah in the features, but they were distorted, an amalgam of his Human past and his evolving future.

I am unlike any other creature in the history of the galaxy, he thought.

It was a portion of the Aopoddae data that he *had* understood, and had retained in his mind. People had thought this before about him, and so had Noah himself. But no one had anticipated the degree or scale of the phenomenon, and the continuing changes Noah was undergoing. He suspected that he had not yet reached his final stage of evolution, and that he might continue to metamorphose over the course of an eternal lifetime, without ever reaching stasis.

He found it fantastically exciting, and terrifying at the same time.

CHAPTER SIXTY-ONE

Each life form in this universe—even those that seem most injurious to others—appears for a purpose. It may not always be easy to ascertain that purpose, but if you really search for it—if you drill down—you will find it.
—Master Noah Watanabe, early notes on ecology

The planet was giving birth, but not to its own kind.

Billions of tiny creatures flowed out of lava tubes and swarmed as thick as locusts over Ignem, covering the glassy surface of the world so that it absorbed hardly any light at all. It took on a dull, lifeless appearance, but would recover its jewel-like glitter soon. Woldn did not intend to remain there for long.

Now he led the newborns in maneuvers over the remote planetscape, training and molding them telepathically so that they learned to function under the collective mind of one: that of the Eye of the Swarm. These were simple, preliminary exercises, which most of the Parviis picked up quickly. Some of the individuals straggled as they learned a little slower than the bulk of the others, but within an hour Woldn had them in line, as well.

Utilizing secret methods they had stolen from the Adurian laboratories, Woldn's breeding specialists had instituted the most massive reproduction program in the long history of the Parvii race. The gestation period in the lava tubes was comparable to the traditional method, but the warmth in the tubes and other conditions enabled the breeding specialists to generate exponentially more individuals from the same batch of raw genetic material.

This was a dramatic change from the old days and methods, where there had been distinct limitations. That had not mattered so much in the past, though, because the swarm had always maintained its population equilibrium, and the intermittent infusion of a relatively small number of births had been adequate. In those days, only Parvii leaders and specialists had known the number of their brethren, but it had been vast. Now his race was on the road to recovery. In this batch alone, he counted more than eight hundred and fifty billion individuals. More than enough for what he had in mind.

In the new method, the maturation period following birth would be the same: only a matter of weeks to reach adulthood. During that time, they would be trained here and out in space, building up to increasingly complex maneuvers and techniques. For the next stage, he summoned the war priests.

Vorlik and Yurtii arrived in a matter of moments, having already been with the breeding specialists on Ignem, where they had been watching the progress of the breeding program. Man and boy respectively, they wore the black robes of their cult, raiments that were actually projections around their bodies.

Flying beside Woldn, Vorlik looked down on the hovering, waiting swarm and said, "The breeding specialists report that some of our youngsters already have potent neurotoxin stingers and show excellent potential for working with each other to fire telepathic weapons. They also appear to fly well for their age."

"Yes," Woldn said. "I am always wary of anything new, however. In due course, we will take them out into space and assess their capabilities in capturing podships. I'm worried about training them properly. Natural podships and the artificial lab-pods created by the Adurians could present different challenges."

"But it is especially important for us to test our young swarms in combat. The stresses of warfare will sort the weak from the strong. With our new breeding process, we can replace the losses quickly."

"Perhaps you are right," Woldn said.

"I disagree," the hairless Yurtii said. "I am worried about the capabilities of these swarms. Especially considering how these individuals were bred. It occurs to me now that we might have been lured into the Adurian laboratory so that we would adopt their breeding methods and create Parviis that would one day turn against us."

"Too bad you didn't think of that earlier," Vorlik said with a scowl.

Below them, the naked individuals clustered in groups according to their skin tones, forming divisions in which they were more comfortable. For the time being, Woldn permitted it, because he knew they were still insecure in their extreme youth. But as they grew, he would separate them more and more, so that skin tones would no longer matter to them at all.

"If need be, I could put all of these to death in an instant," Woldn said. "But I have probed them myself—individually and collectively—and there is nothing to raise any alarm signals." He looked at Yurtii and smiled stiffly. "*So far*, that is. You are right to raise a voice of caution, but I agree with Vorlik that we must test the swarms in combat as soon as possible."

"In war it is necessary to take chances," Vorlik said. "That is how wars are won."

"And lost," Yurtii said.

Vorlik frowned. "I'm talking about *calculated* risks, professionally assessed. Don't tell me you don't know what I mean, Yurtii. In your time, you took chances, and achieved military victories.

You could have been even greater, though, if you had been more bold and daring."

"Like yourself?"

"Of course." The mature, stocky man beamed proudly, and Woldn knew he had every right to do so.

But Yurtii still had points to make. "Admittedly, your historical achievements were greater than mine, because you were largely responsible for defeating the Tulyans and taking the podships away from them. However, your quick, glamorous victories in the Tulyan War cannot be compared with the obstacles I had to overcome. My later war in the Far Sector involved complexities that you did not encounter. We each faced different times, differing challenges and conditions. In retrospect, I came to the opinion that I should have proceeded even more carefully than I did on some of my military campaigns. The enemy was resourceful, laid traps for me. I still defeated them, but it was not easy."

"We are an apple and an orange, you and I," Vorlik said. "To borrow a Human phrase."

"No," Woldn said. "You are each of the same ilk, but display different aspects of it from your particular experiences. This is a good balance. I will listen to both of you equally, and render my decisions."

"As you wish," Vorlik said, though he did not look entirely pleased. Given enough provocation, he might even kill Yurtii. But with his own telepathic control over both of them, Woldn knew that should not happen. And even on the remote chance that it did, Vorlik would never get away with it. Already, the breeding specialists had discovered new war-priest latents, and nascent breeding specialists.

Everyone can be replaced and will be replaced if necessary, Woldn thought. *Even me.*

He dispatched the two war priests to perform their training-instruction duties, and notified the swarm to follow them. Then he watched as Vorlik and Yurtii divided the swarm into ten divisions and caused changes, so that all of them appeared to wear pale blue uniforms. Soon the war priests were leading the first two divisions in basic war maneuvers, swoops and streaks of pale blue that went this way and that over the planet, sometimes blocking the sun, and sometimes allowing it to glint off Ignem's glassy surface.

In a short time, many of the trainees changed to what looked like purple uniforms, proof that they had perfected the first phase of their studies. He saw the light blue swarms shift increasingly in hue as the most advanced individuals contributed to the whole and melded themselves into it in the Parvii way. Soon there were two purple divisions, and the war priests began to work with the other divisions, bringing them up to the same standard.

It was still early in their training. Purple would not be their ultimate color. That would be a bright red, suitable for a military force since it was the most common color of blood among the numerous galactic races. Already the young Parviis were displaying significant improvements in style and technique, and soon they could constitute a formidable fighting force.

Wave after wave of them surging into battle, annihilating all enemies in their path. . . .

CHAPTER SIXTY-TWO

In the vast majority of races, the female of the species is more complex than the male—physically and psychologically. Thus, the female should be considered more valuable. But that is not always the case.

—Excerpt, Jimlat report on the galactic races

Noah could walk independently throughout the large, empty space station and its Aopoddae outer layer. He moved with the normal gait of a human being, but knew he must look like a monster, as if some diabolical alien creature had invaded his cellular structure and taken over.

"Just a minute," he said to Thinker, who rattled along beside him. Something in the flat-bodied robot's body had come loose, but he had been so preoccupied with other matters that he had neglected to diagnose and repair it. The sentient machine had been sorting and re-sorting the Aopoddae data in his data banks and in his reserve memory cores, but so far very little of it was decipherable.

Now the two of them stood in front of an ornate corridor mirror that somehow had escaped the destruction wreaked upon the orbiter. It was one of the gaudy decorations that Lorenzo had installed when he had the facility converted into a gambling casino. Lights were on in the corridor. Thinker had figured out how to get them working.

Looking in the reflective glass, Noah saw that his original facial and muscular features were identifiable—he still had a strong chin, aquiline nose, and wide-spaced hazel eyes—but the skin was gray, with streaks of black throughout. It had a rough texture like that of a podship, and portions of it pulsed on the surface. His curly red hair was gone, having been replaced by a clump of reddish flesh on top of his head, in the approximate shape of his former hairstyle. Fine lines in it looked like strands of red hair, but weren't. They were veins.

"My face looks like the prow of a podship, with its pilot immersed into the flesh. The question is, can I fly?"

"You are not a flying craft," Thinker said. "There is no doubt about that. I have seen no undercarriage, no place or way for you to engage with the strands of the podways. No, you are something else entirely. A *podman,* for want of a better word."

"The question is, what comes with my new appearance?"

"That is one of many questions."

"Do you think people will fear me when they see what I look like?"

"They already fear you, Master Noah, in varying degrees. Even Tesh, who cares deeply about you. She's been asking to see you. In fact, she's demanding it now, and says you can't keep ignoring her. She is in a shuttle that is in comlink contact with us at this very moment. I am linked to the comstation by remote. Would you like to hear her, or reply to her?"

"I wonder if she will still consider me attractive," Noah mused. "Of course, she is much older than I am—though she doesn't look it—and she has had past relationships with a variety of galactic races. She told me so. She also said she'd never met anyone like me before."

"An understatement, I'm sure. Especially now."

Noah chuckled. "I see you've developed a sense of humor. I don't recall one when I first met you, but lately you've been different. Did somebody program it into you?"

"Subi Danvar and some of the others thought I was too stiff

and intellectual, so they tweaked my operating systems a bit. I asked them to make certain I would never be inappropriately funny, because I don't wish to irritate you Humans. Therefore, you should find my humor somewhat subdued."

"So far, you're doing fine, my metal friend." Looking at both of them in the mirror, he added, "We're quite an odd pair, aren't we?"

The orange lights around Thinker's faceplate glowed, then went out. "Shall we send for the lady, sir?"

"I wonder if she knows a female robot to bring along. Then we could have a double date."

"You are much funnier than I am, Master Noah. I interpret that as a possible yes?"

"Send for her, then. I'll receive her in the module where I used to have a dining hall for my students. You know where that is?"

"Of course. You've had robots move furnishings and gambling tables out of the way in there."

"Yes, they've set up a smaller dining table for me in there, with chairs and vending machines. Later I want to get the habitat enclosures installed around the eating area again, the miniature forest of dwarf oak and blue-bark Canopa pines, along with the birds and other organisms."

"That will be delightful."

"One day, Thinker, this will be a School of Galactic Ecology again, and much more. I have grand plans for EcoStation."

"I will help you with them."

"Give me thirty minutes before letting Tesh in. I want to spruce myself up."

The robot rattled away, chuckling.

High Ruler Coreq stood on the bridge of his flagship, gazing at the vast armada gathered around him, as the ships moved gracefully in concert, flowing and shifting through the Kandor Section of space like dancers following his choreography. They were practicing battle maneuvers.

He slammed a fist against the thick glax window, and made a vow.

Things would be far different in the next military encounter with the enemy, not like the debacle from which he had been fortunate to escape with his life and a portion of his force. Inexplicably, galactic conditions had interfered, just as he'd been about to split space and emerge over the target world of Canopa. Something bad had happened, and suddenly he'd found himself far away, in a region of unknown coordinates. Holes and traps in the infrastructure had nearly spelled the end of him, but he suspected that the enemy must be having as much trouble with it as he was. They'd just been able to take advantage of him that time. The perilous galactic conditions could not possibly be a weapon of theirs; no one could have a power that immense and far-reaching.

After the incident, Coreq had sent a report back to the Adurian homeworld by courier, providing Premier Enver and Warlord Tarix with as many details as he could—and urging them to step up the production of laboratory-bred podships even more. In addition, he had ordered the bulk of his occupying forces to depart from Human and Mutati worlds and join him here for a final thrust against the so-called Liberators. . . .

Left alone in the corridor, Noah stared in the mirror again, at the rough alien flesh covering his face. He focused on the lump of reddish flesh where his hair used to be, and on the fine veins in the lump. Something shifted in the mass, and he was able to separate out a single strand of curly red hair at the front. Then he separated another, and then hundreds of them, and finally his entire head. With his mind, he commanded how he wanted the hair to be arranged, and it cooperated, down to the last follicle.

However, looking at himself now, with his humanoid face and normal hair, it did not look right at all. He looked like an alien clown.

So he focused on his face, and as moments passed he saw the alien skin fade away, from the forehead down, until the normal, freckled Noah looked back at him, the one everyone expected to see. He did the same with his hands and forearms, completing the visible areas.

Now I've spruced myself up, he thought. And he made his way to the dining hall.

He was not there long when Tesh strode in with a determined look on her face, as if she had finally caught the person she had been chasing. She wore a green skirt and white blouse, which he presumed were projections from her energy field, instead of real apparel. Walking right up to him, Tesh looked closely at his face, and showed confusion on her own.

"Thinker said something to you, didn't he?" Noah asked.

"He told me not to be shocked by your appearance, that's all."

"No details?"

She shook her head, causing her black hair to brush over her shoulders.

Noah frowned. "Shall I put it into words or show you? Mmmm. Words are inadequate, so here goes."

In the blink of an eye, Noah assumed the alien "podman" appearance, including the reddish lump instead of hair.

She gasped and took a step backward. Then, cautiously, she reached out and touched the streaky, gray-black skin on his cheek. "I, I . . . Once, I felt roughness on your forearm, under your shirt. This has been happening gradually?"

He nodded. "Now I seem able to control it at will, though."

"Like a shapeshifter?"

"To an extent. On the surface of my skin, at least."

She narrowed her eyes suspiciously. "There are many forms of shapeshifters in this galaxy: Mutatis, Aopoddae, Parviis. And you are yet another, it seems. I believe you are the first of your kind."

"Oddly, I feel more comfortable this way. The old Noah is gone now."

"But I miss the *old* Noah," she said. "Just when I thought I was getting to know him and care about him, he changed."

"You don't need to fear me," Noah said. "I see in your eyes that you do."

He watched her take a deep, shuddering breath. The emerald green eyes flashed, and she said, "My reasons are more complicated than you assume. There is something important I need to discuss with you."

"I get the feeling I'm not going to like this."

She smiled, but it had a hard edge to it. "That depends."

"On what?"

"On what sort of a . . . *man* . . . you are." She grasped one of his alien hands and said, "Noah, I'm pregnant with your child."

"From the one time when you said we really had sex, when I thought I only imagined it?"

"It was real, and so is our baby."

He jerked his head back. "But you told me once that the galactic races could not interbreed."

To this, she wagged a finger at him like a schoolteacher and said, "As I told you before, Parviis and Humans were once the same race, until they branched off. Technically, they are not entirely separate galactic races. I have in fact heard of a very small percentage of cases in which children have been born. The odds of conceiving a child, however, are extraordinarily low."

"Mmmm, I'm sure you omitted some of those details from me earlier."

"Or, you might not have been listening carefully." She looked at him apprehensively, seemed to be gauging his reactions.

"I guess we're lucky, huh?" He grinned, but wasn't sure how he felt about her condition. He didn't want to make her feel he was not pleased. And even if he wasn't, he promised himself that he would take steps to protect Tesh from now on, and their child. He didn't even consider asking her to terminate the pregnancy. That was out of the question.

"We are lucky." A cast to her eyes revealed to him that she had not yet said certain things, but he decided not to press her.

Instead, Noah asked, "Am I really Human? Was I ever really Human?"

"I think you were when we conceived the child, though I'm not so sure what you have become since then."

"But I was already different then, when we conceived. Eshaz had already healed my injuries by connecting my injured body to the galactic webbing, allowing its nutrients to flow into me. You saw how I could recover afterward from virtually anything."

"Yes, you were different, but apparently not different enough." She patted her belly, but he couldn't see any difference in it. He didn't doubt her pregnancy, though.

"When will you give birth?"

"In a cross-racial situation, that can vary. Anywhere from a few weeks to a few months. I think I will get a sense of it as our child grows in my womb." Her eyes sparkled, and he could tell that she was happy about what was happening inside her body.

Noah held her tightly, and kissed her. She melted into his arms.

When they separated, Noah looked at her and marveled about what an incredible creature *she* was. He had heard somewhere that the Human woman was much more complicated than the male, and he thought this Parvii female must be even more involved than that. At the moment, the pretty brunette looked like a normal-sized Human woman, but that was only because of her magnification system. It was a remarkable technology, one that made her projected skin feel normal to him, even though it was actually an energy field. She told him once that the force field around her made physical acts seem as if her body was really much larger. Apparently this included the process of fertilization.

"What size will our child be?" he asked.

"That is determined by the natural size of the woman, by the dimensions of the womb and birth canal. If I were, instead, a Parvii man and you were a Human woman, the child would be what you would consider normal size."

Wrinkling his forehead, trying to comprehend, Noah did not know how to respond. He was having trouble envisioning a son or daughter that he could hold in the palm of his hand, or which he could carry about in a pocket.

Placing her hands on her hips, she said, "Are you happy with the news?"

"Of course! It just takes some getting used to."

"I know how you feel, then." She ran her fingers over the alien skin and the Human contours of his face. "Your lips are a bit rough now, dear," she said, "so you'll have to be gentle when you kiss me."

"Can't you adjust your magnification system?"

"I could. But I would rather see you show consideration by making your own alterations occasionally, somewhat like shaving off bristle. A woman always likes a man to be considerate. Perhaps you can do it without altering your appearance. I think you're very handsome now."

He smiled. "I really am happy about the news," he said.

"I know you are, Darling."

In all of the past and future paths that Noah had envisioned via his connection with the cocoon, he had not seen any of this. But he knew with certainty—an instinctual feeling—that their child would be important.

CHAPTER SIXTY-THREE

The Sublime Creator designed life and death to go in a circle, a never-ending dance of birth and death. But something has interrupted the sacred process. None of the races—not even the Tulyans—are supposed to be completely immortal.

—Report to the Council of Elders

He lived in a universe of strange, mind-stretching possibilities.

Master Noah entered a large chamber of the orbiter, a room that had once been Lorenzo's Grand Ballroom, a separate, private area of The Pleasure Palace Casino. Now it was a shambles, with wrecked furnishings and shattered plax on the floor, crunching under his feet. A broken mirror showed a distortion of his half-Human form as he walked by.

Almost a year ago, Eshaz had healed Noah by connecting his injured flesh to a defect in the galactic webbing, at a point where a timehole was just beginning to form. Afterward, Noah had displayed miraculous physical capabilities, an ability to recover from traumatic, even grisly, injuries by regenerating the cells of his body. Since then, more things had happened that were even more remarkable. Thinking back now, Noah was coming to believe that he had visualized healing himself, and that it had happened. Somehow, in his intense pain—especially from being hacked up by his sister—he had seen his way through a narrow, treacherous path, and had survived.

It had been a learning experience on an extrasensory journey. But had he actually risen from the dead, like Lazarus of Lost Earth? He was not sure, but knew that stories about him had gotten out, and had contributed to the fear and awe with which many people looked at him, especially those who didn't actually know him personally. It would be even worse from now on because of Noah's appearance, though he knew he could modify his skin to make it look Human. He could visualize it, and it would happen.

Clearly, this ability to imagine and shape went beyond the creation of physical changes in his own body. He had proven that when the cocoon was under attack by HibAdu forces, and he'd transported the space station across the galaxy to the Tulyan Starcloud, after envisioning that heavenly realm in his mind. There had also been times in the past when he had intermittently been able to enter and control podships in a paranormal manner. He presumed that he could do that now if he wished, on an individual podship basis, but he felt no need or desire to do so.

He could even control multiple podships, as he had proven by moving the cocoon through space. It might just be possible for him to gather every podship in the whole galaxy, making him like another version of the Eye of the Swarm, but on a much more grand, and potentially powerful, basis. Noah suspected that his abilities went farther than he dared imagine, and the very thought of the possibilities made him want to slow down. He did not want to leap forward too rapidly, before he was ready.

But the galaxy was in chaos. He could not ignore this fact, could not hide from it. There was no formal training facility where he could learn and polish his unusual craft. He'd had to discover and perfect the highly specialized skills on the job, during times of crisis. Noah had escaped to the starcloud without a moment to spare. But he had been unable to stand and fight, a situation he had found frustrating.

Now the injured portions of the cocoon were healed, though as he looked around the space station itself, he saw that a tremendous amount of restoration work remained to be done. The robots had patched some of the breaks in the hulls, and had completed some basic repairs to the gravity generators, plumbing system, electrical connections, and air circulators. The bodies had been taken away and buried, but on the floor of the Grand Ballroom he still saw splotches of dried blood in both red and purple, evidence of the traumatic deaths that had occurred here.

Peripherally, he noticed Thinker enter the chamber, moving more smoothly and quietly than before. He seemed to have repaired his own loose parts. "I was looking all over for you, Master," he said.

"And Tesh?"

"I escorted her back to *Webdancer*. She's very determined to continue her piloting duties, even with the news of her pregnancy."

Noah bristled. "There are no secrets from you, are there?"

"As your authorized biographer, I require such information. I think Tesh rather likes me, and I feel the same about her. I asked her if everything was all right, and she told me about the baby."

"Maybe you'd like to marry her and take my place."

"Oh! I could never do that, Master." He paused. "I just came to let you know she is safe."

"Thank you."

"Would you like me to leave you alone?"

"No, you might as well observe what I'm about to do firsthand. I thought I would do a little cleaning up around here."

"You mean for exercise? Wouldn't you like me to send for

robots to do it?"

"We'll see," Noah said.

The windows of this ballroom had once looked out on the planet Canopa, and on the twinkling vastness of space. Now they were covered by the podship skin of the cocoon. Noah found a place where the windowplax had been broken away, and which was now covered over and sealed by the amalgamated Aopoddae. Walking over there, he looked more closely, and touched the mottled gray-and-black skin. This time, he did not seek or permit the inflow of raw Aopoddae data. Instead, he had something else in mind, something he hoped would help him on the journey to understand the podship race.

The cocoon flesh softened to his touch. He let go, and the flesh oozed back into the ballroom in a thin film, flowing down the outer wall and onto the floor, where it pooled around Noah's feet. With his free hand, he pointed to the overturned and broken furnishings, to the dried blood, to the dents and breaks in the walls and windows. More alien cellular material flowed out of the break in the plax where he had touched it, and covered the floor. Thinker scrambled out into the corridor, but kept looking in through the doorway.

All around Noah, objects began to change as they were touched by the podship flesh. Everything became gray and veiny black, and just as he had anticipated, new forms began to take shape—a central platform, and rows of chairs extending outward from it. He had always wondered how podships altered the internal configurations of their vessels, and now he was experiencing it directly as the amalgamated creature created an auditorium for him. It looked like another version of a room that might be onboard a podship.

"Marvelous!" Thinker exclaimed from the corridor.

"You're witnessing the rebirth of EcoStation," Noah said. "In the future it will again be a school for galactic ecologists, but on a much larger scale than it ever was before, as an inspiration for all races to restore and maintain the ecological health of the galaxy. Like me, the space station is evolving."

"Don't forget me," Thinker said, as Noah freed himself from the liquefied flesh and joined him in the corridor. "I've evolved too," the robot insisted.

"We're all doing it together," Noah said. He strode to the next large area of the space station, Lorenzo's former Audience Chamber. Utilizing podship flesh from another break in the hull, Noah soon created an Astronomical Projection Chamber, in which he would demonstrate the motions and connectivity of star systems, planets, and other cosmic bodies. Compliantly, the Aopoddae formed the basic enclosure according to his specifications, and much of the furnishings—all attached to the expanding cocoon. When circumstances permitted it, Noah would later bring in the technological devices. But this was the framework he wanted, the canvas on which he would paint his eco-picture.

For the rest of the day, he and Thinker moved from module to module and chamber to chamber, where Noah put himself in direct contact with the podship flesh and made the alterations he wanted. In the process, he was restoring EcoStation, bringing it back from its own near-death. He realized as he did this that he could just envision the whole project at once, but he didn't want to speed it up. There were subtleties in the control he exerted over the alien flesh. He and the cocooned Aopoddae were getting to know one another, learning how to work together, making the procedures more efficient.

When the work was nearly complete, Noah and the robot stood inside one of the new classroom modules, where Noah had set up the raw framework of learning stations for his students. Looking around with a degree of satisfaction, he realized, *I am learning at my own school.* And he knew this was as it should be. Even the wisest and most accomplished people still had many things to learn. That held true for robots, too, as they continually updated their data banks, always advancing their operating systems and memory cores.

During the restoration of EcoStation, Thinker had been adding new observations to his data banks. Noah had kept the cerebral robot with him for this, and for other reasons. This intelligent machine was the smartest of them all, an excellent and faithful adviser. And, though Noah was not intentionally allowing new Aopoddae data to flow into him, he remained concerned about making a serious mistake, perhaps through some communication problem. At least Thinker was always nearby if necessary, to relieve any overload on Noah's brain. But would that be enough? He wasn't sure, but it gave him concern. Maybe something like that, the overwhelming power of the psychic flow, could actually kill him. And if Noah died, he could not advance, could not achieve what he needed to do.

Sensing something, he touched the podship flesh at a learning station desk, then used the multiple eyes of the creatures to gaze far out into space. Something was approaching fast, bearing down on the Tulyan Starcloud. He looked closer. It was a Parvii swarm, the biggest one he had ever seen. Somehow, they had regenerated and were coming back in force.

He sensed a disturbance in the starcloud as the mindlinked Tulyans detected the approaching danger from their mortal enemy. The immense swarm neared at high speed, and split into divisions that veered out to the sides, to attack from different directions.

They struck with stunning speed. Blue bursts of energy came from the center of each swarm. Telepathic artillery. Some of their shots hit the thick skin of the cocoon, and Noah heard the pain of the amalgamated podships.

He turned the unarmed cocoon around and retreated into the starcloud. Mindlink opened and let him in, like a cosmic gate. It shut behind him, then guided him to a safer position. Moments later, he saw comets and meteors streak by him in eerie silence, heading out against the swarms. Hundreds of armed Liberator podships also surged out to join the battle, ships that had been assigned to protect the starcloud and the caretaking crews that came and went. Noah wanted to contribute to the effort, but could only watch.

Frustrated, he turned to Thinker and asked, "How are you doing at deciphering the Aopoddae data? It's important."

"I know, and I have been able to decipher a few additional fragments," the robot said. "In the midst of all the other data, I found an even more heavily encrypted section, like an armored core of data. I don't know if I can ever get into that part. The podships still harbor doubts about you concerning the release of this particular information, uncertainties about whether or not you are a person they can fully trust."

"Keep trying to find out what it is," Noah said.

He touched a nearby bulkhead, and through a Timeweb link he saw the raging battle. At least he could access the paranormal dimension at will now. He watched the swarms dive forward into the onslaught of defensive weapons that the Tulyans threw at them. To his dismay, he saw mindlink seem to weaken. Holes in it opened up, and tiny invaders surged through.

But Noah soon saw that it was a Tulyan trap. Any swarms that got through mindlink soon detonated in puffs of white, while other swarms beyond the starcloud fled from the pursuing comets and meteors. Noah estimated that the Parviis lost half their force before they turned and retreated into space.

He knew they would be back, and probably in even greater numbers the next time. Somehow they had regenerated their population at an incredible rate.

CHAPTER SIXTY-FOUR

Most legends are designed to fit the needs of those in
power. But there have been notable historical exceptions,
and they can be the most significant of all.
>   —Finding of the Galactic Study Group,
>   subcommittee on religion

A bleak, gray sky hung over the Golden Palace.

In the medical room on the top floor, Hari'Adab's mood
matched the weather. When not attending to his duties as the
Mutati ruler, he spent every available moment at Parais' side. It
occurred to him now, as he looked at the quivering mass of
flesh and dark feathers on the bed, that this remarkable aeromutati was really his top *professional* priority. It wasn't just
personal, because he was nothing as an Emir without her guidance and love. Now and then he'd been attending the military
strategy meetings with Mutatis, Humans, and Tulyans, but he
had not really been *there*. He had not been all that he should be
in the high position he held, all that his people deserved.

As Parais faded, so did he, along with all of his abilities to
lead and inspire others. He knew he should step aside, and in
effect he had done exactly that, because he had been turning
over more and more command duties and decisions to Kajor
Yerto Bhaleen. It seemed ironic to Hari that he—always a
pacifist at heart—would come to rely so heavily on a military
officer. At one time, he never would have considered such an

action. But that had been before he faced the stark realities of command that were arrayed before him now, with the extreme pressures of political and military responsibility weighed against his personal and emotional needs.

I am only a Mutati, he thought. *A bunch of feelings and desires in a cellular package.* As a shapeshifter, Hari knew he could alter his appearance, making himself look carefree and happy, but it would only be the thinnest veneer. He wouldn't waste his time doing that, so he'd only been modifying his cellular structure occasionally in small and customary ways, to keep his same basic appearance while not permitting the cells to lock into any one position. His mind and heart, though, the engine of his soul, were shutting down, preparing to lock everything into death.

On the surface, he was dressed differently today. For the strategy meeting he'd just left, he had worn a gold-and-black dress uniform, which he still had on. Having received intelligence information on the location of the main HibAdu fleet, Doge Anton and the officers were planning a major military assault. The meeting was still going on, down the corridor. He heard the clamor of their voices, through open doors. That morning there had been some disagreements—different war philosophies between Humans and Mutatis. But Hari expected the participants to iron them out. The spirit of cooperation among all of the allies—Human, Mutati, and Tulyan—was very strong.

For some time now the Liberators had been sending podships to neutral worlds around the galaxy, rounding up Humans and Mutatis who happened to be living there . . . calling for volunteers and specialists. Many of the Mutatis were proving to be particularly valuable, since they could disguise themselves as any race, even as Hibbils and Adurians. That was how the Liberators had now learned the location of the enemy fleet—in

417

the distant Kandor Sector.

Hari knew his ceremonial uniform gave him a more official and commanding appearance, and in part he had chosen it today for that very reason. But he had another. The costume included a ceremonial sword—the same one he'd almost used after the disastrous destruction of Paradij, when he had intended to kill himself for his culpability in that matter. He'd placed the point of the weapon against his belly, and had been ready to fall on it. But Parais had knocked the sword away, saving his life and telling him he needed to live for the sake of the Mutati people, preventing another fanatic like his father from ruling.

This time, she could not save him. The sword and its scabbard lay on the table by the bed, beside Parais' personal copy of the sacred Mutati book, *The Holy Writ*. After his failed suicide attempt, the two of them had placed their hands on that very book and shared a prayer.

But this he had not shared with her, his vow: If she died, he would follow her soon afterward.

Hari knew he could only lead his people with Parais at his side, and he had only continued to hold the titular title of Emir in the hope that she would recover. Gazing upon her now, feeling the faint, weakening pulse of her skin, he was losing all hope. Increasingly, he found himself unable to think of anything but a bleak future.

With each passing day, Parais looked less and less recognizable. Only when she occasionally emerged from her pain and looked at him with those gentle blue eyes could he ever confirm it was her. She had done that the evening before, but now the eyes had sunken back into the flesh, and he had only a vague sense of where they were. Tragically, she was almost entirely unidentifiable, with only a ghost of her facial features remaining, as if they had been scoured off.

Removing the sword from its scabbard, Hari touched his

finger to the sharp blade. Purple blood trickled from his skin and dripped on the floor.

In a few seconds he could be dead. So easy, so inviting.

But he almost heard her scolding words. That would be the easy course, she'd say, the coward's way out. Death was always easier than life from a personal standpoint, but for those who remained behind after the event, it was much more difficult.

Hari'Adab rose to his feet. Ponderously, he resheathed the sword and clipped it onto his belt.

For Parais, I will take the more difficult path. I will live. For her, and for my people.

And he vowed to never again reach this state of personal despair, not even if she died. If Parais' life ever meant anything—and it *did*—he had to follow her wishes. She would want him to be strong.

On the bed, he saw the hulk breathing, but barely. He tried to distance himself from his darkest feelings, told himself that he had to.

I shall not be selfish, he thought.

Then he realized that he was still, in a way, actually being selfish, since he was also concerned about his legacy, what future generations of his people would think of him. He had already killed billions of Mutatis, the unwanted collateral effect of assassinating his own father. His people had died accidentally, to be certain, a terrible mistake. But in the process—and Hari struggled once more to convince himself of this—he had saved trillions more across the entire Mutati Sector. His father had been a complete madman. Everyone with any brains knew that.

Feeling stronger now, Hari returned to the meeting. The participants fell silent as he entered. Holding his head high, the Emir strode across the room and sat next to Doge Anton.

"How is Parais?" Anton asked.

"The same. Thank you for asking." Looking around the room,

Hari added, "I'm sorry if I was distracted before. I'm ready to perform my duties more fully now. Parais is with me here." Fighting back his emotions, he patted his own chest, over his heart.

"That's good," Anton said, "but know this. We share your pain."

"Thank you."

The military discussions resumed. General Nirella and Kajor Bhaleen got into a disagreement over military strategy, over how much force should be applied in the initial assault against the HibAdus. Nirella wanted to keep major assets in reserve, to protect the planets and star systems they now held, but Bhaleen disagreed.

"What use is it to hold onto what little we have?" he asked. "Two Human planets, plus Yaree and the Tulyan Starcloud. The Tulyans just held off a large Parvii assault, so they're proving their own defensive capabilities. If only their mindlink was strong away from the starcloud, we could spread them around. But mindlink weakens dramatically in other galactic sectors, so I agree that the Tulyan defenders are most effective remaining where they are. But if we're ever going to succeed in this war, we need to hit the enemy with all the other forces we have, and make them hurt. At last, we have solid information that the main HibAdu fleet is in the Kandor Sector. There is not a moment to spare."

"For what it's worth, I agree." The rotund Subi Danvar, one of Noah Watanabe's representatives at the meeting, stood up. "I've spent my life thinking about security, trying to protect what we have and where we are. But what point is that if our diluted forces cause us to lose everything anyway? I say we throw everything we have at the bastards, and not to just hurt them. We need to *annihilate* them!"

A clamor of disagreement arose in the room. Gradually, the

advocates of a more aggressive approach drowned out the others. Doge Anton and Hari'Adab both stayed out of it, watching and listening.

Then Anton rose and stood by Subi and the other officers, Human and Mutati, who had gathered around Kajor Bhaleen, to support his position. "What is a military force for, if not to attack?" the Doge asked.

The rationale of his words still left room for debate, but the opponents of massive force had no more wind in their sails. Grudgingly, General Nirella stood and went to her husband's side.

"There is one thing more," Hari'Adab said. He remained seated. "From now on, the forces of the Mutati Kingdom will be named the Parais Division. She will be the inspiration for me, and for my fighters. I'm going into battle with them."

"She will be an inspiration for all of us," Doge Anton said. "Before we're finished, we'll emancipate *all* Human and Mutati planets, and free our people that have been enslaved. The Hibbils and Adurians will regret ever turning against us with their traitorous schemes!"

Clapping and cheering carried across the floor. Hari hoped that Parais could hear it, and that she would find the strength to hold on.

CHAPTER SIXTY-FIVE

The Eye of the Swarm appears to have a new method of breeding Parviis that enables him to breed large masses of his people quickly. We don't know the details, but this much seems clear: The young swarms are not able to generate sufficient telepathic power for the weapons they need. The multi-input weapons fire, but have diminished impact. Perhaps that will improve with time when the swarms mature. But as they progress, so must we, to counteract and destroy them. Complacency is our biggest enemy of all.

> —Report to the Tulyan Council of Elders

In the reconstructed student dining hall, Noah touched the podship skin that covered a window opening. As he did so, the surface became filmy, so that he could see through it, as if it were a porthole on a podship. He let go, and the window remained.

He had again moved the cocoon out into space, just beyond the misty starcloud, because he wanted to perform his own experiments there, not interfering with the mindlink defensive system. Through the window, he saw Tulyans and elements of the Liberator fleet performing battle maneuvers in the sunlight, coordinating mindlink telepathic weapons and the firepower of armed podships.

All of the key leaders and most of the podships were at the starcloud now, for critical preparations. On an emergency basis,

General Nirella had obtained the cooperation of the Tulyan Council to arm much more of the caretaking fleet than the original allotments. With the cooperation not only of the Tulyans but of the mysterious Aopoddae, this conversion was accomplished in a matter of days. The military force under Anton's command now amounted to more than one hundred and ten thousand podships, with the remainder assigned to the most crucial web caretaking duties.

Noah saw Eshaz speed by, his face on the prow of a vessel he was piloting. Then Noah recognized *Webdancer* with only its normal Aopoddae look, meaning that Tesh was in the sectoid chamber, guiding the vessel in her Parvii way. In view of what she had told him about her pregnancy, he wished she would discontinue her dangerous military duties, at least until the baby was born.

She wouldn't, though. He'd tried to convince her himself, and had even asked others to make the effort. They'd all come back with the same answer: An adamant *no*. Her voice filled with emotion, she had told Noah and Anton that the whole cause of the Liberators was at risk, not just one fetus. And it was hard to argue with her. She was one of the very best pilots, and her skills were needed for the upcoming attack against the HibAdus in the Kandor Sector, the most important battle that Humans, Mutatis, or Tulyans had ever fought.

The combined Liberator force needed to commit every available resource to the fight—and they needed to attack as soon as possible—before the HibAdu Coalition could produce too many more laboratory-bred warships. But against the immense military power the enemy already had, no one knew if victory was achievable.

The Liberator leaders only knew that they had to make the monumental effort.

★ ★ ★ ★ ★

Taking a break from war maneuvers, Tesh stood in the passenger compartment of *Webdancer,* looking out on a series of scaled-down comet attacks that the Tulyans were using to destroy large holo-simulations of enemy warships that the Liberators were projecting into space. The projections moved in a variety of attack formations, so that the Tulyans had to constantly adapt and adjust. In other maneuvers nearby, General Nirella led armed podships in simulated battles. Later in the day there would be joint operations, involving Liberator and Tulyan forces against the theoretical enemy.

Tesh had noticed that *Webdancer* was even larger than before, with more interior chambers, as the intelligent podship had sensed that even more space and amenities were needed to accommodate its use as a flagship. Moments before, she and Anton had been engaged in an uncomfortable conversation. A year ago they had been lovers, but both of them knew that could never happen again, and neither of them wanted to resume the old relationship. They had taken alternate paths, had new loves in their lives. But the conversation had still slipped back to some of the old times they had enjoyed together, and there had been moments of awkward silence in which each of them remembered, but said little. Now Anton was getting coffee from a wall-mounted machine.

He returned and handed her a cup of the naturally white, Huluvian beverage. "Thanks," she said.

Their conversation shifted to the war maneuvers outside, and Anton said, "Look at the way the podships move gracefully through space. They're so smooth and fast. I often wonder what it would be like to have a conversation with one of them."

"I've wondered the same thing," she said, "even though every Parvii knows it is an impossibility. For millions of years our race was linked to them, and yet it seems like we never truly understood them—at least not beyond a surface comprehension of us as the master and the Aopoddae as our servants. Podships were just there, and we guided them on regular routes, from star system to star system. I doubt if even the Eye of the Swarm ever really knew in a deep sense what it was all about. He only did what his predecessors had always done under our dominion, and the whole system continued."

"Until now."

"Yes, until now. I think it's right for my people to give up the podships, but the galaxy is in such chaos. If I can contribute to the Liberator cause—just one Parvii woman—I'll bet there are others of my race who would be willing to help as well. If only Woldn would release them from his hold."

"That will never happen. You were lucky to get away."

Tesh held the cup under her nose, and inhaled the warm, aromatic steam. She sipped. This was good, imported coffee that the Liberators had obtained, the only coffee she'd ever found that actually tasted as good as it smelled.

"You know," Tesh said, "watching these podships, I'm reminded of something Noah said to me once, about the poetry of the name *Webdancer*. He said it evokes romantic images of all the Aopoddae—that they're all webdancers, negotiating the slender, delicate strands of the galactic infrastructure."

"Yes, it is like that, isn't it?"

"But any one of the podships—or many more of them in a mass catastrophe—can fall off the damaged webbing and tumble into oblivion. It's like dancing on the edge of a sword, as they used to say on Lost Earth."

Noah heard Thinker nearby, whirring as he processed data. In order to intensify his focus he had folded himself shut . . . and had been that way for almost half an hour now.

Noah considered tapping on the robot's flat metal body to ask him a question, but reconsidered. He didn't want to interrupt the mechanical genius in the midst of a critical analysis.

Presently, Thinker opened, with a soft click of metal parts as they shifted and locked into new positions.

"Anything?" Noah asked.

"I think I've gotten what I can, and that's only what I told you before. The armored memory core remains impenetrable. I've tried everything possible. It just won't open for me."

"Not for you. But what about for me? Can you link me to the core and allow my mind to probe, and enter it?"

Hesitation, and whirring. Then: "The Aopoddae trust you more than before, but not completely. I don't think they entirely trust me, either, perhaps because I am not biological, or perhaps due to my connection to you. I'm afraid if we get too aggressive trying to obtain the information, the data will go into permanent lockdown."

"Originally, the Aopoddae let the data flow into my brain," Noah said. "I think you need to give it back to me."

"The overload could kill you."

"How much data is in the armored memory core?"

"I can only estimate. Based on bulk storage space, I think it's around fifteen percent of the whole."

"Can you transfer the armored core to me? Only that, and no more?"

"I think so. But the data count could be exponentially greater than I estimated, if they compressed it. Even if you find a way of opening it, the surge could be too much for you to handle."

"We live in dangerous times," Noah said. "I want you to do it."

"Are you sure?"

"We want them to trust us, don't we? I need to be vulnerable to them."

"And the rest of their data?"

"Keep it, for now. Let's prioritize this, and try it in increments. If I open the armored core, and the Aopoddae fully trust us, maybe I can download it back to you, unencrypted."

"You make it sound so easy."

"I always try to be optimistic," Noah said, with a wry smile.

The organic interface snaked out of Thinker's body. Just before it connected to Noah's skull, he closed his eyes. He felt the powerful inflow of raw data, filling the cells and synapses of his brain. The process took more than a minute, and during that time, he saw only images of blackness. No color or light at all. It occurred to Noah that he might reach out into Timeweb and perhaps escape the terror he was feeling, the stygian darkness. But that could interrupt the flow and damage the information. So he remained focused and motionless, a cup to be filled.

"It is finished," Thinker finally announced. "And irretrievably erased from my own data systems."

Opening his eyes, Noah didn't feel any different.

In the past, he had been able to stretch his mind across the cosmos, taking fantastic journeys through space. Now he tried to do the opposite, and probed inward, looking for the armored core and the key that would open its door.

But nothing happened.

CHAPTER SIXTY-SIX

There is one certainty to military combat: Wars, and the
battles that comprise them, never go entirely as planned.
—General Nirella del Velli

Later in the day Noah paced nervously inside the shuttle, refusing to take a seat beside Tesh. She had just brought him a message from Doge Anton.

"He didn't say what he wants?" The podman passed a gray-
skinned hand over the reddish lump of skin on top of his head,
as if he actually had hair there to smooth out. As usual, he felt
weaker away from the cocoon, but he kept pacing anyway, trying not to reach out and grab anything for balance. For the
most part he was successful in this regard, so perhaps it was a
learning experience.

Tesh pursed her lips. She sat near Thinker, who had bent his
own flat body to fit onto one of the benches—something he did
on occasion to test his working parts, or to act like a biological
person. "No," she said, "but I suspect it's important. He is the
Doge, after all, and we're about to head off into battle."

"He's probably wondering where I fit in. I sent him a message yesterday, telling him I should remain here at the starcloud.
My interests—and talents—are more akin to those of the Tulyans and their web restoration work, instead of open warfare.
The cocoon is almost entirely composed of unarmed caretaker

podships. They're useless in combat. I had to turn tail and run from battle." Grimacing, Noah added, "I hated doing that. I wanted to fight, wanted to blow the HibAdus out of space. But I didn't have any way to do it."

"Maybe Anton has some way of arming the cocoon," she said. "I heard him and Nirella speculating about that, wondering if it could be turned into a battle station."

"That would just make it a bigger target."

"Perhaps you're right."

As Noah stepped off the shuttle onto the flagship, he was greeted by Subi Danvar. "Right this way, Master," he said. "Anton is waiting for you in his private office." Looking at Thinker and Tesh, he added, "He wants to see Noah alone."

Following the rotund adjutant through the main corridor of the vessel, Noah was struck by how much larger the ship was now, with many more rooms and side corridors than before. Even though he had psychically guided the cocoon to make changes to the space station—and the massed Aopoddae had cooperated with him—he still didn't understand how they did it.

But he thought he understood *why*. Though their motives were not as easy to figure out as those of other races, Noah thought the podships were acting to protect and enhance the integrity of the galaxy. It had nothing to do with politics or personalities, and everything to do with galactic ecology. He believed now that he had been born with the destiny to be one of the leaders of this cause, and that destiny had guided him along a path that led him to this very place. Whether destiny translated into connecting him with a higher sentient power, he was not certain, and he thought he might never determine that answer. As far as he knew, destiny just existed . . . it was an element to the cosmos that kept things going. It could not be ignored, or eluded.

And if Anton wanted to turn EcoStation into a battle station, Noah could try to help in the effort. He wasn't afraid of combat himself, and wanted to do everything possible to advance the Liberator cause. But the podships had their own collective mind, and might not cooperate.

"Right through there, sir," Subi said, pointing to an open doorway.

Noah continued on his own, with his mind racing, wondering. Maybe the Liberator commanders wanted the cocoon podships back as individual craft, to arm them separately and send them into battle.

Yes, that could be it, he thought. *They think I've been dithering, getting in the way of the war effort.* But his instincts told him that he needed to do everything possible to protect the integrity of the cocoon, and that it should never revert to its former parts.

"Noah!" Anton said. The young Doge bounded across his office and gave him a hearty handshake. Then he stood back and assessed Noah's gray skin, streaked in black. "I've heard about your metamorphosis, of course, and VR images have been brought to me, but seeing you in person is quite different."

"VR images?"

"Yes. Thinker said you wouldn't mind." Anton held onto Noah's rough-skinned right hand, then released it.

"No, I suppose I don't. He does work for you and for me. Look, I think I know what this is about, why you called me here." Noah took a seat across from the desk, while Anton slipped into his own chair.

"You know, eh?" To Noah's surprise, the mustachioed merchant prince looked amused, not nearly as tense as he might be before the upcoming military adventure.

"You're wondering where I fit in, and how I can contribute to the war effort."

"Oh, you've already contributed far beyond the call of duty, Uncle Noah."

"You don't think I've been wasting my time in the cocoon?"

Anton laughed. "In this galaxy, with all the strange events that are occurring? Are you kidding? I say, if you can figure the Aopoddae out, it will help all of us. Maybe you're in there generating a superweapon, for all I know."

"If I were doing that, Thinker would have told you."

"Ah, but you are on a different plane from the rest of us, Noah. You can accomplish things no one else can imagine. I'm sure you could conceal things from the robot."

"Not from his organic probe, though. It's his form of the truthing touch. No, I don't have a superweapon in the cocoon. I wish I did, but I don't."

"Well, wishes do come true. Keep wishing, and maybe it will happen. We could sure use more firepower. But that is not why I asked you to come here."

Doge Anton fiddled with a pen, spinning it around on the desktop. Then he continued. "I'm intrigued by the way you got from Yaree to the Tulyan Starcloud." He snapped his fingers. "Like that. Even with all of the web damage. But how?"

"Some of the podships in my cocoon are among the oldest in the galaxy, and they know alternate routes, shortcuts across space."

"I'm aware of the alternate routes Diminian found, and which his pilot showed to us—dropping travel time to a matter of minutes, going around damaged web sections. But you accomplished something even faster, didn't you? Noah, you just visualized the starcloud, right? And the cocoon went there immediately?"

"That's about right."

"Can you show the rest of the fleet how to do that? Speed is always an asset in warfare, and I want every advantage we can get."

"I don't know exactly how it works, but I'm sure the podships do—the cocoon. My connection with the Aopoddae seems to be a work in progress, but I could give it a try." He didn't mention the unopened, armored core of data in his brain, knew Thinker would reveal its existence anyway, if he hadn't done so already.

"All right. Let's run some preliminary tests. You get in the cocoon and see if you can get it to lead the others. Think of guerrilla warfare, on a scale never before seen. Ideally, I'd like to have my whole fleet appear out of nowhere, attack the Hib-Adus, and then disappear. We could then keep hitting them from different angles, and vanishing before they could mount an attack. No matter how big their entire force is, we could whittle it down, hopefully faster than they can reproduce lab-pods."

"Sounds good to me."

The two of them worked out more details. Then Noah rose to his feet and bowed to his nephew.

"Please," Anton said, coming around the desk and shaking Noah's hand again. "Only do that when someone is looking. Here, we are family. More than that, we are friends."

"In what seems like a prior lifetime, I had a similar arrangement with my adjutant, Subi. He was not allowed to insult me in front of others. Only in private."

"We shall do that, too," Anton said, as he accompanied Noah to the door. "Private insults, only."

"You're in a surprisingly chipper mood," Noah said.

"Because I think we're going to win." The young Doge paused, and grinned. "In fact, I *visualized* it."

The next morning the combined fleet was ready to go into battle, with the exception of one final detail.

Noah and Thinker strode into what had once been the Grand Ballroom of Lorenzo's Pleasure Palace, a chamber that Noah had transformed into an auditorium for his future School of Galactic Ecology.

"I might as well try it from here as anywhere else," Noah said, as they walked up the steps to the central platform. "Let's see what sort of a magic show we can put on."

"Very well," Thinker said. "I shall be your audience." He went back down the stairs and bent his metal body, so that he could sit in one of the front-row seats.

"You and the whole fleet. All right, here goes."

Kneeling on the floor, Noah pressed the palms of both hands against the podship flesh that covered everything, like a blanket of gray, black-streaked snow.

He and Doge Anton had agreed on galactic destinations, so Noah visualized Yaree, where they had won their battle against the HibAdus. It seemed like a safe destination now, where the Liberators had joint defensive operations with the Yareens. Hours ago, Anton had dispatched courier ships there (and to Canopa and Siriki) to notify them of last-minute war maneuvers that could take place in their vicinities.

Feeling a link to Timeweb, Noah saw far across space to the Yareen star system and its central planet, framed against the faint green filigree of the cosmic web. Simultaneously, he expanded his far-reaching eye, so that he also saw where he was now, just outside the Tulyan Starcloud with the Liberator fleet. And, just as he was expanding outward, so too did he delve deep into his own psyche and to the linkage he shared with the cocoon.

Show them the way, Noah thought, wondering if the secret of nearly instantaneous travel lay inside the armored core of data that Thinker had passed on to him. *We lead, and they will follow.*

A burst of green light filled his consciousness, and he felt the slightest sensation of movement. Looking again, Noah saw that EcoStation was now in a geostationary orbit over the blue-green planet Yaree, and thousands of armed podships were with him.

Then he noticed that it was not the entire Liberator fleet, but still a significant portion of it, which he determined was around thirty thousand ships. Less than a quarter of the total. *Webdancer* was with him, and other familiar podships. The older ones, mostly, including *Diminian*. Many of the younger Aopoddae had not made the journey, perhaps because they were confused back where they had been left. But a large number of older podships remained behind with them as well.

Noah made the effort again. This time, he visualized returning to the rest of the fleet, and in a matter of moments he made the leap across space. Then, assessing the results, he saw that all of the ships that had gone to Yaree had returned with him.

Next, he visualized Siriki, and after that, Canopa. With each gigantic leap across space, a handful of the younger podships figured out how to do it, and joined the pack. The majority of them, however, were having difficulty learning the method, and some of the older Aopoddae didn't even seem to make the effort. A number of the younger ships got lost for a while, and had to find their way back to the original jump-off point. A handful were still out there in space, and had not been accounted for. . . .

Finally, retrieving the bulk of the fleet and bringing it back to the Tulyan Starcloud, Anton and Noah had another meeting in the Doge's flagship office.

"Mixed results," Noah said. "With time, we might make it work, but I know what you're thinking. We don't have time."

Anton scowled. "We can do the guerrilla attacks with twenty-five percent of the fleet, but my generals—who were initially supportive—are now saying that we should hit the HibAdus with everything we've got, the whole fleet. Our best Tulyan scouts say it will take two hours to get to the Kandor Sector the conventional way, due to rough podways and no good shortcuts of any kind."

"To me, it still makes sense to hit them with guerrilla attacks. Even twenty-five percent is still a lot of ships, a lot of firepower."

"My generals say otherwise. If we don't reduce the number of enemy ships fast enough, they're afraid the HibAdus can dramatically increase the manufacture of lab-pods in response, and overwhelm us. We have the intelligence reports, and we're going back to Plan A, what we've been building up for all along. I just had a wild idea that something else might work."

"It was worth trying. All right, think of it this way. The exercises were not wasted. If we get in a jam, we can still evacuate thirty thousand ships quickly."

"And leave the rest to be slaughtered?"

"No, many of the other podships could still break away into space and join up with us again. Think of me as an escape hatch, a desperation plan to be used only in the event of a dire emergency, if all seems to be lost."

"All right. I'll set that up as a last resort. But we need to be in close contact all through the battle. We'll take the two-hour route to Kandor, and I want you at the rear of the fleet with my own division. We'll have redundant communication to stay in touch with you—comlink and Tulyan webtalkers."

Supreme General Nirella del Velli—commanding the combined Liberator fleet—divided into four divisions—Andromeda, Borealis, Corona, and Parais. The latter three, all smaller than the core Andromeda Division, went out to holding positions just outside the Kandor Sector, while the core division took up a position at the rear, with Doge Anton and Noah. Most of the Mutati fighters and support equipment were with Hari'Adab in the Parais Division, inspired by the brave aeromutati who still clung to life on Siriki.

Then, from those three forward divisions, twenty-one scout ships were dispatched into regions that were near the last-reported position of the main body of the HibAdu fleet—but not so close that the scouts would be detected. It required twenty-one of the best Tulyan pilots, and—through wartime testing procedures—it was determined that one of them was Eshaz, who had been assigned to the Borealis Division.

Having received a different assignment from that of his cousin, Dux Hannah was aboard Eshaz's scout ship, which separated from the other scouts and sped through space alone. Their craft entered the Vindi Lightway, an atmosphere-encased asteroid belt that was illuminated by miniature suns, each of them looking like a small, bright moon. Taking different routes, the other scout ships were probing different areas near the Kandor Sector.

Onboard the cocoon, Noah went into a deep "timetrance," a term he had developed for particularly vivid journeys into Timeweb. Though he had not anticipated this, he now found himself able to see through the eyes of the distant scout podships—and he saw the Kandor Sector, a region of nebulas and blue stars visible in the distance.

Concentrating as the scouts closed in, taking carefully developed routes, Noah was able to magnify the images seen by the podships. The planets and suns came into focus, and—beyond a veil of nebula dust—he saw a multi-level armada of lab-pods so immense that it looked like a huge dead sun.

But there were blind spots now. Previously he had been able to peer inside some of the pseudo podships in the HibAdu force, and he had seen Hibbils operating navigations units inside them, and soldiers in the cargo holds. The enemy might have found a way to veil the interiors from him since then, or web conditions were preventing the reach of his mind into the enemy vessels. He also could not see through the eyes on the hulls of the lab-pods.

Noah wondered about the enemy ships, how similar they were to their natural cousins. The Tulyans had inspected two of them back at the starcloud, and had found startling cellular similarities—along with differences in the undercarriages that caused damage to podways when they traveled over them. The lab-pods also seemed to be substantially out of contact with natural podships—although the natural pods had shown slightly averse reactions when participating in attacks on their faux versions. Maybe this lack of contact had something to do with Noah's blind spots.

The armada was much larger than any of the figures he had heard. There must be more than a million armed lab-pods there! As he watched, the immense layered formation began to shift in eerie synchronization. Large sections broke away and spread outward in all directions. The maneuver was almost hypnotic. It looked choreographed, a dangerous thing of beauty.

Emerging from the trance, Noah transmitted an urgent warning to Doge Anton.

CHAPTER SIXTY-SEVEN

Throughout military history, there have been instances of determined, inspired warriors winning the day, despite the immense odds against them. We hasten to add that such examples are quite rare. Overwhelming force usually prevails.

—Report to General Nirella, by officers
formerly in the Mutati High Command

The command bridge of the flagship was a buzz of activity, of robots and junior officers at their consoles and bustling from station to station, preparing for battle. Standing at the forward viewing area, Doge Anton stared tersely ahead, looking through a deep-space magnaviewer—one of several round units attached to the windowplax. Beside him, General Nirella did the same.

"I don't see anything yet," he said.

"We will," she said.

Moments ago, they had received urgent transmissions from their scout ships and from Noah. The HibAdu fleet was vastly larger than earlier intelligence reports had indicated, and it was in motion.

"Maybe they're only performing a practice maneuver," Anton suggested.

"Whatever they're doing, I don't like it."

"Do you think we should fall back and regroup?"

"Not yet. Hold on. Another transmission coming in from

Noah." She adjusted her ear-set.

"I'm getting it, too, but it's filled with static."

Neither of them could understand what he was transmitting. Noah was in his cocoon at the rear of the main Andromeda Division, but despite the distance he had earlier reported getting a clear view of the enemy armada. Anton could not begin to understand the powers of his uncle. They seemed to change constantly, and Noah had often said himself that they were unpredictable. The young Doge only knew that he trusted him completely, and so did every fighter in the Liberator force.

Anton motioned to a Tulyan, who was also in contact with Noah's cocoon via the specialized method of the reptilian race. On each end, experienced webtalkers in the Liberator fleet found creative ways to touch the cosmic web, and in turn they relayed messages to other Tulyans in the warships. Because of the relays and changing galactic conditions, it sometimes took a little longer than the military comlink system, but it was often more clear and reliable.

In his comlink ear-set, Anton began to hear sentence fragments from Noah. "HibAdu force . . . shifting direction . . . large portion is . . ." The Doge couldn't get any more.

Moments later, a small Tulyan woman hurried over and said, "Noah reports that the bulk of the HibAdu force is heading toward us. Speed moderate but steady. Portions of the enemy fleet keep breaking off and then returning. Noah thinks they've spotted us."

Now Anton saw the armada, coming toward him like an immense cloud of interstellar dust, with sunlight glinting off portions of it. He sucked in a deep breath. "Do we stand and fight or regroup and save what we can for another day? Maybe we should reconsider guerrilla attacks. They're much larger than we thought anyway."

"We still have time to fall back on that," Nirella said. "All the podships that can follow Noah through galactic shortcuts are with us in the Andromeda Division. But first we need to probe our foe and see what his tactics are, how mobile he is, and how responsive he is to changes on the battlefield. Maybe we can discover a weakness, or force him into a mistake."

"I know," Anton said glumly. "We've gone over all this."

"Yes we have, and we have some tricks up our sleeve."

Anton didn't like the fact that a large portion of his main division was comparatively safer than the other three portions of the fleet, with access to an escape hatch through space that they didn't have. But it made perfect military sense. Aside from the probing, the Liberators had a fallback position in Noah Watanabe, enabling them to survive and fight again. Anton and his generals had studied the options, and another consideration had come into play: Despite Noah's purported immortality, the military experts were concerned about risking him unnecessarily. He was extremely valuable, and had arcane powers that even he did not understand. He must be protected, and for now he seemed best suited to remain at the rear of the fleet.

Leaning over to study a console screen, Nirella said, "Spectral scanners report that some of the HibAdu activity is illusion, that not all of the ships breaking away from the main force are really doing that. Some of them are projections of warships, similar to the ones we use in war games."

"How much of the main force is real?"

"Unfortunately, more than half of it. You could override me, Anton, but I don't think we should retreat yet. Parais Division has their space mines ready to go, and with luck we'll get results from them. The HibAdus may have their tricks, but we have some of our own. They might even be operating under the false assumption that we didn't discover their sabotage attempt on our space artillery pieces, or other sabotage attempts we've found."

Anton nodded. "The tiny computer chip that Hibbils made when we thought they were our allies. But are the HibAdus foolish enough to think we wouldn't go back and check all of those parts and replace them if necessary?"

"They might be overconfident. The Hibbils and Adurians had their secret coalition going for years undetected."

"True enough. That means we probably have not discovered all of their tricks."

"Agreed. But we still have some nasty surprises for them."

"All right, we stand and fight." Looking at the console, Doge Anton saw the Parais Division out in front of the others now, with the brave Mutatis in that force plunging into battle before anyone else—according to plan. Hari'Adab had wanted it that way.

Inside the enemy flagship, Ipsy watched from a place of concealment behind the main instrument console. He had rigged an ingenious method by which he could look around the command bridge unnoticed, using the various console screens as remote viewing windows.

Now he watched High Ruler Coreq hurrying back and forth from battle station to battle station, making sure his officers and technicians were doing what he had commanded. Coreq had set up the projected warships to make his force look even larger, and he was also coordinating the movements of the actual warships. At times the hideous hybrid would stand at the center of the bridge and wave his arms this way or that. In response, large sections of the armada would shift position. Moments ago, he had done that, drawing most of the divisions together into a central force.

"Beautiful!" he had exclaimed. "Perfect!" He was like a choreographer, setting things in motion around him.

Now, however, he stopped gesturing, and scowled. His

oversized, pale yellow eyes looked around dangerously. Something was bothering him. He focused on a young Adurian officer, who had not yet brought up a battlefield report that Coreq had ordered.

With a sudden movement, Coreq hit the man so hard in the head that his skull broke open and fleshy pieces of brain splattered on the console. "Clean this up and get me another officer!" the HibAdu leader screamed. Then he returned to his favored position at the center of the bridge.

The High Ruler extended his arms forward, bent the elbows outward, and joined the fingertips of both hands in a wide "vee" shape. The armada was moving forward in that formation, covering a broad swath of space with its invincible ships. To Ipsy, he seemed like a madman.

The industrious little robot had developed several plans of what he might do. As conditions developed, he had to select the proper moment, and take just the right measure. He was a choreographer, too, and everything needed to go perfectly. He could not wait too long, but couldn't move precipitously, either.

The HibAdus had taken measures to block Ipsy, or any other would-be saboteur, from tampering with the weapon-control box on this ship. The unit had been replaced, and had been sealed so that an intruder could no longer gain access to it without drawing attention to himself. As a consequence, whatever Ipsy did would have to be different from the last trick he pulled. But he still had options. His internal programs constantly reviewed them and perfected them.

Able to deactivate videocam and other security systems by transmitting electronic signals, Ipsy had used the privacy to make secret adjustments to the ship's systems that should prove interesting if he ever activated them. All the while, he left no sign that he had ever been there.

He had even made enhancements to his own mechanical

body and brain—self-improvements, he called them. Thinking of this and all of his preparations, he smiled to himself, a feature of his internal programming that did not show on his metal face.

General Nirella sent Hari'Adab's force directly at the main body of the enemy fleet, and then readied the Borealis and Corona divisions to make flank attacks. Watching the action unfold, Doge Anton felt like an ancient military officer on a hill, observing a slaughter that was about to occur on the battlefield.

Moving from the magnaviewer to the console, he saw the inspired Parais Division surge forward—a force of thousands of armed podships that looked painfully small in comparison with the enemy. For the moment, the HibAdus seemed content to advance at a steady speed, drawing most of their force together.

"Why don't they divide up more?" he asked.

"They don't think they have to," Nirella said. "Look on the spectral scanner. They're not even using the holo-warships anymore. Now that they see what we have—less than a quarter of their armada—they think they can run over us like a juggernaut."

"I hope they're wrong."

"So do I."

Then Anton saw sunlight flash increasingly off the hulls of the advancing HibAdu force. The intensity increased dramatically, and became so bright that he had to look away.

"That ruse was old a long time ago," Nirella said. "We're ready for it."

At a gun station in the Parais Division, Acey Zelk saw the blinding flashes, and heard the sharp command of the Mutati officer on this level. "Solar mirrors," the shapeshifter said. "Fire on them the way we practiced."

Acey had trained for this, as had all of the other gunners on-board with him, at their stations along the hull of the podship. Firing away with long-range projectiles, he saw some of his shots hit their mark, opening dark spots in the enemy fleet. Other Liberator ships did the same, and had a similar effect.

"Good shooting, Acey," the officer shouted. "The rest of you, see if you can do as well as this young Human!"

Acey kept firing and hitting, while the target continued to draw closer and closer. He saw other podships in his division firing alternate weapons, space cannons with purple beams of light—heat rays. Many of those shots were slipping past the surprisingly tough solar mirrors, penetrating the hulls of some lab-pods and destroying them.

He heard the Mutati officer say that the Borealis and Corona divisions were also engaging the enemy, making flank attacks.

Following commands, Acey reset his space cannon to fire heat rays. Now his shots, and those of his companions, penetrated deeper, causing more damage. But it all seemed like throwing pebbles at a hippophant. The monster just kept coming, knocking the debris of its own damaged ships out of the way.

Through his magnaviewer, Doge Anton del Velli saw the Borealis and Corona divisions draw together around the Parais Division. Then they reversed course en masse and sped back toward a holding position, with the immensely larger HibAdu armada still advancing toward the center, heading right for the Andromeda Division.

Glancing at the console, he saw the readings that confirmed what Kajor Bhaleen of the Mutati High Command had planned. As the Liberator divisions retreated, they cast thousands of electronically cloaked space mines behind them . . . a Mutati trick.

"The HibAdus are speeding up," one of the junior officers shouted, "anticipating a big kill."

"Perfect," General Nirella said. "That will make our stingers hurt more."

Moments later, space lit up in a series of multicolored explosions. Unable to reverse direction in time, a considerable portion of the HibAdu fleet blew up. In close formation, many ships that were not hit by the mines crashed into the others, and were themselves destroyed.

A chain reaction of demolition surged through the front of the HibAdu armada. Finally, the bulk of the force was able to turn around and go back in the other direction.

Anton saw them regrouping, splitting up into new attack formations. "I'm afraid we only made them mad," he said.

"They know we mean business, though," Nirella said. "It will make them more cautious."

For the next phase of the battle, she ordered the Parais, Borealis, and Corona divisions to protect the exposed perimeters of the Andromeda Division. Then she directed thousands of podships filled with Tulyan caretakers to fan out from the Liberator fleet, for yet another tactic. Upon first hearing about this idea, the Council of Elders had been somewhat resistant, but eventually they had come around to seeing the wisdom of it.

Using their arcane methods, the Tulyan web technicians were changing conditions on the battlefield in ways that the HibAdus and their artificial podships might not detect—tearing up the webbing, or making it look strong when it really wasn't. This was a calculated risk, as the Liberators hoped they could later restore what they had damaged.

In only a few minutes, the Tulyans completed their work and returned to share details of what they had done with the commanders. With this information, technicians were quickly preparing a new map of the battlefield. The potential points of ship-to-ship engagement would go out in great arcs in several directions from the Liberators, while leaving better escape routes to the rear.

General Nirella smiled, displaying a confidence that Anton did not share. "That should slow 'em down and enable us to customize new attacks," she said.

"I hope it works," Anton said, "but I told Noah to be ready in case it doesn't."

CHAPTER SIXTY-EIGHT

Liberators.
We're not just about rescuing Human and Mutati worlds.
We intend to rescue the whole galaxy.
                                    —Master Noah Watanabe

High Ruler Coreq had decided to get his hands dirty. Now he sat in the pilot's chair of his immense flagship, operating the touch-pad controls while the actual pilot sat next to him, giving technical advice. With a laboratory-enhanced brain, Coreq was a fast learner, and operating this lab-pod seemed easy to him. Though he looked to be of an adult age, the laboratory-bred hybrid was barely fifteen years old, having been grown in an Adurian laboratory. That didn't mean he was emotionally or intellectually immature. Far from it. The scientists had done a terrific job on him.

Speeding the flagship from one area of the fleet to another, he satisfied himself that his warships had regrouped into the new attack formations he had specified. Earlier he had done this with arm gestures from the command bridge, which in turn transmitted electronic signals, but he had decided on impulse to handle the flagship controls himself for a while. At just the right moment, his armada would divide and hurtle themselves at the opposing forces from multiple directions, using a variety of methods and a panoply of weapons.

He refused to stay back on the Adurian homeworld, wanted

447

to go out and destroy the enemy himself. He'd been at the vanguard of the coordinated assaults on Human and Mutati planets. Great victories—but as yet incomplete. Two Human-ruled worlds remained stubbornly outside the HibAdu empire, along with a number of upstart independent worlds, the foremost of which was Yaree. Against all odds, Humans and Mutatis were allies now, and were working with the Tulyans, and even a number of other races in lesser roles. Calling themselves "Liberators," they had more than a hundred thousand natural podships that were armed—a formidable fleet, but one that should be no match for his own. Those enemy ships were among the spoils of war that he wanted to save, at least as many as possible.

His triumvirate companions—Premier Enver and Warlord Tarix—did not have his hands-on, adventurous spirit, so they had remained back on the Adurian homeworld, making themselves look busy supervising the bureaucracy. Coreq thought it was a particular fallacy that Tarix called herself a warlord. The extent of her violent acts were confined to police activities on Adurian- and Hibbil-controlled planets. Coreq, on the other hand, was reaching for the stars. That was the stated purpose of the HibAdu Coalition, after all: Conquer all Human and Mutati worlds, and then the rest of the galaxy. Annihilate all enemies.

But getting his hands dirty was one thing. Getting them slapped was quite another.

So far, the Liberators had put up a surprisingly strong resistance. He had not really expected the sabotaged firing mechanisms to still be in place on the Liberator warships, even though the tactic had worked fabulously in the initial surprise attacks against hundreds of enemy planets. As anticipated, the enemy had figured this out afterward, and had replaced the Hibbil computer chips. Those space mines, however, had come as a complete surprise, not showing up on any scanners or signal probes. And he wasn't sure what all those Liberator ships had been doing afterward around the Liberator fleet—thousands of enemy vessels that advanced and fanned out, but for only a few minutes. What had they been doing out there? Trying to lure HibAdu forces forward into another minefield? That was the assessment of his top Adurian commander, Admiral Silisk, and of other officers. Coreq, however, was not so sure. He doubted if they would try a similar tactic two times in a row.

Already his scanning technicians said they could now detect all space mines—they had proven this by spotting several that had not been detonated, after reconfiguring their detection equipment. Leaving the pilot to control the flagship, Coreq went to a forward window, where he could get a good view through a magnaviewer. There, he watched as squadrons of his own ships went out in forays, scouting the battlefield ahead, seeing what the enemy had been up to. Oddly, his scout squadrons began going in erratic flight patterns. Some crashed into each other, and others seemed to disappear in green flashes. He scowled, trying to figure out what was going on.

Opening all emergency channels, Coreq heard the panicked reports of Hibbil and Adurian pilots.

"Podways damaged! Can't see where we are on any of our instruments. Flying blind out here."

"Lost an entire squadron! They just disappeared!"

"Can't stay on course!"

Then a Hibbil came on, sounding more calm over the powerful, secure channel. "As directed, I took my squad around behind the enemy fleet, several parsecs on the other side. Now we're heading back toward them, with their force just now becoming visible on instruments." He grew more excited. "They've spotted us! We only have a few seconds before they attack. A few rough spots on the podways, but typical of what we've seen elsewhere. Infrastructure much better here."

The transmission fizzled out, but Coreq had learned something valuable. His clever foe had left open an escape route at their rear—and probably more than one—bolt holes into space. Quickly, he ordered his fleet to go around. In a matter of seconds, they split space in green flashes. Then, reforming into attack groups, they surged back toward the Liberator force from a different direction.

The redeployment of the immense HibAdu fleet occurred very quickly. Alarmed, Ipsy watched from his hiding place, while his internal programs absorbed battlefield data, and he recalculated the courses of action that he might take. He wanted to inflict the maximum possible harm on the enemy.

Only a short while ago, he had been heartened by the successes of the Liberator fleet. Now the tide of battle seemed to be changing the other way.

Unless the Liberators were setting a trap. He hoped that was the case, but all indications said otherwise.

Watching everything from his paranormal viewing platform, Noah sent comlink and webtalker warnings to Doge Anton and General Nirella.

Responding right away over the comlink, Nirella said, "We see what they're doing. What about our escape contingency?"

Having emerged from the timetrance to await a response, Noah said, "No longer available. I can't visualize any destination beyond this sector. With their huge force the enemy is sweeping space behind us, covering every available podway. The Tulyan researchers said they use a combination of instruments and artificial podship methods to determine where the podways are. Now they have forces stationed on each of them, more than enough to keep us from escaping."

"Can't we knock them out of the way? We can send more than a hundred thousand podships on any one route."

"They have tens of thousands of heavily armed ships stationed on each route. It would be suicide for us to slam into all those warships, with the bombs and other munitions involved."

"But space is vast. There must be other escape routes!"

"From here, the routes are few, and the HibAdus have found all of them."

"Then we've painted ourselves into a corner," Nirella said.

"I'm afraid so."

Dipping back into Timeweb, Noah noticed something more: Dark little spots all over the hulls of the Liberator vessels. Several of the spots flickered, then grew dark again. But Noah had seen what they were: Parviis.

The tiny humanoids seemed to be camouflaging themselves with their projection mechanisms. But why weren't they flying in a swarm and firing telepathic weapons? He answered his own question almost before it passed through his mind.

Attacking en masse had not worked—some problem with their firepower that the Tulyans had noticed. Taking a different tack, the Parviis were going to focus on individual podships in the Liberator fleet, trying to gain entrance and control any way they could. In the alternate realm, Noah saw more and more of the tiny dark spots appear, until space was thick with them around the Aopoddae ships.

When he reemerged, Noah saw his webtalker already engaged in urgent communication with her fellow Tulyans, all of whom had sensed the presence of their mortal enemies.

CHAPTER SIXTY-NINE

Life, in all of its forms, is ultimately about control. This is linked to survival and to the perception that particular life forms cannot live in harmony, and must take all available resources for themselves. But wars and other forms of mass destruction often rise directly from survival perceptions that are not accurate. We do not need to wipe out other races or life forms to survive. In fact, it is in our interest as Humans *not* to do that, and to harmonize with other galactic peoples.

—Master Noah Watanabe, from one of his early essays

Over the communication links, Noah heard the desperation of the Liberator officers and soldiers, and of the Tulyan caretakers. And through his supernatural link to Timeweb, he saw the changing currents of the battle, with the HibAdus gaining an overwhelmingly superior position. They had cleverly cut off all routes of conventional escape for the Liberator fleet, and were now moving in for the kill. Increasingly confident, the enemy armada was gaining speed. All the while, Parviis continued to mass on the hulls of Doge Anton's podships, and were using neurotoxins and other methods to gain entrance. So far Tulyans were using their own methods to keep them at bay, but more and more Parviis kept arriving and joining the others.

Beside him on the central platform of the auditorium, Thinker whirred noisily, and said, "I have searched for all possibilities, but there are no good choices."

Noah didn't respond, He felt like a man on the edge of a precipice, about to tumble off.

His mind raced at frantic speed, and he thought of the armored memory core Thinker had transferred back to him. The heavily encrypted Aopoddae information lay somewhere in Noah's brain, hiding inside the cells and synapses, waiting to be released.

For the Master of the Guardians, it was like knowing something, and not knowing it at the same instant. The information was there at his fingertips, and around him in the cocoon. But he could not utilize it. Previously, he had touched the podship flesh and had caused it to reshape the space station. Several times he had commanded the cocoon to fly through space, and it had cooperated.

Essential information was locked away in the protected core of data that Thinker had found, and Noah needed the key to open it. Why were the Aopoddae making it so difficult?

Thinking back, he recalled that he had used his own arcane powers to heal wounded podship flesh, and had received a tremendous inflow of data from the sentient spacecraft. It was as if they wanted him to have the information—whatever it was—but first they had to make sure he was qualified to receive it, and that he would not use it for the wrong purposes. The Aopoddae had only given him *potential* access to the critical information. He still had to prove he was worthy of it. How could he do that?

A chill ran down his spine, as it occurred to him that the secret of a powerful weapon might be what was inside the armored core of data. Doge Anton had suggested that Noah might be surreptitiously generating a superweapon inside the cocoon. Noah had dismissed it as an idle comment, but what if the idea had an element of merit? What if the amalgamated podships could generate a powerful destructive force?

If it was a weapon inside the armored data core, that would explain why the sentient spacecraft were not sure if he should receive it. Even now, facing their own destruction, they could be hesitating. Had the Aopoddae looked into his soul for his motives, and if so, what had they seen there? His demented twin sister, Francella?

Precious seconds ticked by.

Taking a deep breath, Noah touched a thick section of flesh on the outer wall. It was soft and almost liquid beneath his fingertips. As before, he let go, and the flesh oozed down onto the deck and flowed over the floor. This time, however, instead of flowing across the room, it pooled around him and rose up around his ankles. The alien material was warm and wet against his own skin.

Noah felt like screaming in terror. It had very little to do with fear for his own personal safety. He had survived so much, had been through so many harrowing experiences, that he didn't worry about such things much anymore—except he didn't want his followers to lose their inspiration, their guiding light. And beyond that, Noah didn't want to be lured into a place from which he could not escape, or used by some diabolical outside entity for its own purposes.

So far he felt as if he could go back, that he could reverse the process and step away from the advancing cocoon flesh. But the sentient stuff was probing around the skin inside his shoes and socks and on his ankles, delving into his cellular structure, seeking to flow further upward on his body. If he allowed that to occur, could he still go back? And did he really want to go through this, to achieve an indeterminate *destructive* power?

Noah sensed that he was subconsciously trying to talk himself out of going further. He had always been a person who followed his instincts, so he asked himself some hard questions now: Did he really sense danger if he proceeded? What was his gut telling him?

This time, when he needed it most, his viscera didn't send him any signals at all. He found this troubling, because it suggested that he was losing contact with an important aspect of his own humanity, a means of perception and survival that had always worked well for him in the past.

Noah tried to command the cocoon to open the fortified data core, and to show him what was inside. But nothing happened, other than a flurry of agitation in the ancient, linked minds of the creatures.

He knew the HibAdus could attack at any moment. The immensity and immediacy of this threat loomed over all others. For the moment, the Parviis were secondary, and even the crumbling galaxy. If the enemy armada got through, it would be the end of the Liberator force.

Suddenly he heard a booming voice over the comlink, overriding other conversations. "This is High Ruler Coreq. You have ninety seconds to surrender, or we will annihilate you."

After listening to Coreq's announcement from his hiding place, Ipsy heard a loud buzzing noise, and looked up. The confined space where he'd been hiding was filling with tiny, droning machines, like a swarm of insects.

"Intruder alert," a voice said. It was an eerie, synchronized voice, emitted by speakers on the bodies of the flying biomachines. Ipsy's programs accelerated as he tried to find a way out.

Suddenly there was a loud clatter, and strong hands pulled the little robot out from behind the instrument console. Two Adurian soldiers dragged him to the center of the command bridge, where the High Ruler stood, waiting.

"How did you get in there?" Coreq said. He interlaced the

fingers of his small, furry hands, pulled them apart, and then interlaced them again. A nervous mannerism, it appeared.

"Manufacturing defect," Ipsy said. "The stupid Hibbils left me in there. I only recently came back to awareness, and wondered what I was doing on your ship. Those Hibbils can't do anything right."

"He's lying," the biomachines said, in their eerie synchronization.

"Yes I am," Ipsy said. "And you just narrowed my options down to one."

He saw the look of alarm in Coreq's bulbous, pale yellow eyes. But before the freak could move or issue a command, Ipsy transmitted a chain-reaction detonation program he had set up, electronic signals that surged into the vessel's operating systems.

"Get him!" Coreq screamed. But it was too late.

"Now you're going to die," Ipsy said in a matter-of-fact tone. He felt a wonderful sensation of internal warmth come over him as his circuits heated up, and then set off the loud explosive charges. Still, it was only a limited detonation to start with, killing everyone on the command bridge, while keeping his own artificial consciousness alive in the enclosure he had armored for it.

He heard a piercing scream that filled the flagship and surrounding space. It was Coreq, dying.

Moments later, the flagship blew up in a fireball that took two nearby vessels with it, and damaged twenty other lab-pods, causing them to drop out of formation. In the midst of the Hib-Adu armada, the event was hardly noticed by Liberator observers. To them, it looked like a relatively minor problem with the fleet, so inconsequential that it had no effect on the massive force. The armada kept going forward, past the floating debris.

"Data projection," Thinker said. "The HibAdus would prefer

not to destroy our fleet of natural podships, because our vessels are superior to theirs in numerous ways. But the High Ruler's priority is complete military victory, and there are always some wild podships to be captured in space. His deadline is not a bluff."

Taking a deep, shuddering breath, Noah let go and the warm cellular material ran up his legs and thighs and waist, over the clothing and beneath it, covering him entirely up to his midsection. He felt a flood of data from the podship cocoon, flowing into his brain.

"Master Noah," Thinker said, "are you sure this is wise?"

"I'm beyond going back," Noah said.

Reaching down with his left hand, he immersed it in the thick fluid and felt it congeal around his Human bone structure. He immersed the other hand, and then let the malleable flesh rise over his torso, up to his neck.

Noah felt compression on his chest, making it difficult for him to breathe. He took deep, gasping breaths.

"Master Noah, are you all right?"

Without answering, Noah slid down into the flesh and flowed with it into the outer wall, where he began to swim. Behind him, he heard Thinker's voice, but fading. Time and space seemed to disappear. Noah was in his own universe, swimming across vast distances of starless space.

In moments, he stood again. This time he was inside a new and combined sectoid chamber, glowing with an ancient green luminescence. He could move about freely inside the enclosure (which was at least five times larger than those of podships), and he felt confident that he could leave it if he wanted to do so. He was separate from the cocoon, but part of it at the same time. Just as every creature in the galaxy was linked, so too was he connected to this prehistoric life form that was both primitive and advanced.

He probed inward with his thoughts, seeking the information

he so desperately needed. Then, in a wordless epiphany, he let go. Something this important did not depend on words, or even on an organized collection of data. The armored core that Thinker had been unable to access did not contain multiple bits of data.

It only contained *one*, and now Noah knew what it was, so simple and yet so complex.

Pressing his face against the forward wall of the sectoid chamber, he felt his own facial features enlarge and flow outward, so that he could be seen in bas-relief on the outside of the cocoon. But it was not a "man in the moon" appearance, and not like the reptilian faces that emerged from podship prows when Tulyans piloted them. Instead, Noah's countenance was repeated many times all around the cocoon, as if each podship had assumed his features on its body. Through his own humanoid eyes now, he looked in all directions: to the farthest reaches of the galaxy, to the Parviis trying to gain control of the Liberator fleet, and to the advancing HibAdu armada, which was much closer than before, with glowing weapons ports on the warships, ready to fire.

Noah felt power building around him. Paradoxically, the Aopoddae were a peaceful race, but he realized now that they had access to a weapon beyond the scope of any others, and finally they were allowing him to use it. Higher and higher the energy built up around Noah, until EcoStation became a brilliant green sun in space. Parviis and Tulyans had their telepathic weapons that could wreak great destruction, but this was potentially much, much more.

His eyes glowed the brightest of all, and beams of light shot from them on the sides facing the HibAdu ships, bathing the enemy armada in a wash of green. Then the ships detonated, in tidal waves of destruction that went through the entire fleet in great surges, until it was gone, turned into powder and dust.

As Noah drew back, he felt himself shuddering. He had tapped into a source of galactic energy that might even reach the core of the entire universe. It was raw, primal, and volcanic. It simmered in his consciousness, waiting to explode. He could fire the primal weapon at will. The amassed violence was awesome, simultaneously thrilling and horrifying to him. Again, he thought of the Francella element in his blood, and he wondered if his mind would hold together through all of its expansions and contractions, or if he would go completely mad and start destroying in all directions.

But his doubts lasted only a few nanoseconds. With his brain running at hyper speed, he didn't have any more time to wonder about anything, or to worry. He only had time to respond.

Now he turned the powerful beams of light toward the Liberator fleet, where Parviis continued to scramble over the hulls of the ships, trying to get in. They were no longer veiling their appearances, and could be seen clearly as tiny humanoids. On the hulls of some vessels, Tulyan faces had disappeared, suggesting that the pilots had been overcome and Parviis had taken over. Increasingly he saw the reptilian prows diminish in number, and wherever this occurred, the ships moved away from the others and began to congregate. So far, this amounted to only a small portion of the fleet, perhaps five percent. But he could not allow it to continue.

Through his hyper-alert, organic connection to the cosmos, Noah figured out more possibilities than Thinker could ever imagine. He saw inside every podship in the Liberator fleet, to the individual battles for each craft, and to the mindlink that Tulyans were trying to use for their fellows, but which was much weaker away from the starcloud.

Remembering how he had originally lost the trust of podships because of his part in developing pod-killer guns for the merchant princes, Noah didn't want to destroy any podships.

He had something else in mind.

Focusing the energy beams precisely and governing their power, he detonated them inside the bodies of the attacking Parviis. Tiny green explosions went off inside his consciousness, and he sensed the anguish of his victims, heard their collective screams. And, as moments passed, he saw Tulyan faces reappear on every hull in the fleet. Secure again, the breakaway ships drew back together with the others.

Intentionally, Noah allowed the Eye of the Swarm and a small number of his followers to escape. Noah had always believed that every galactic race, even the supposedly most heinous, had redeeming qualities. The Mutatis had proven that, and he knew and loved one of the Parviis himself. She would be the mother of his child. Their baby would look like a Parvii, but would be a hybrid, not the same as the originals.

I am not about extermination, he thought. Despite all of the changes in which he was immersed, Noah Watanabe remained true to his core values. A deep sensation of fatigue came over him from tapping into the raw primal power, but he fought to overcome it. From somewhere, a reservoir of strength, he summoned more energy.

Then, using his eyes like powerful searchlights to illuminate space, Noah scanned the vast expanse, questing. He sensed something else out there, more dangerous and destructive than HibAdus, Parviis, or even the crumbling galaxy.

Something he might not be able to stop. . . .

CHAPTER SEVENTY

Battles are never static. Even when they seem to be over,
the tide can change.

—General Nirella del Velli

During the surprise Parvii attack, Tesh had fought for control of
the flagship, trying to keep her own people from gaining
entrance to the vessel. It was a battle within a battle, as the
clustering humanoids tried to use neurotoxins to subdue the
podship, and other ancient methods. Even with thousands of
their tiny bodies all over *Webdancer*'s hull, they had faced a formidable task. Just one Parvii—Tesh—inside the sectoid chamber
of the vessel could ward them all off, counteracting the toxins
and keeping the Aopoddae creature under her sole control.

Then the equation had changed.

Woldn himself—the Eye of the Swarm—had joined the
cluster on *Webdancer*. Tesh had sensed him out there, with his
mind merging deeper into the others and dominating them
more than ever. From his proximity and intense focus, powerful
telepathic waves had slammed against Tesh's sectoid chamber,
like psychic battering rams. She'd fought back valiantly, but
moment by moment she had been losing ground as the neurotoxins began to take effect on *Webdancer* and—soon thereafter—on her. Finally, the eager Parviis had streamed through
openings they made in the flesh, like carpenter bees boring into
soft wood.

Woldn and a handful of others had entered the inside of the sectoid chamber with her, pushing her barely conscious form aside so that one of them could take over. Helpless to resist, she'd only been able to watch.

The Eye of the Swarm had kicked her. "Traitor!" he'd said. "We'll show you what happens to traitors. But first, there is a battle to be won."

He had become the new pilot himself, and guided *Webdancer* away to join other breakaway ships.

Suddenly, the sectoid chamber had glowed bright green, an unnatural condition that prevented Woldn from guiding the craft. *Webdancer* began to go in circles and loops, veering off into space.

"Let's get out of here!" Woldn had exclaimed. "You too, Tesh."

With that, he had swooped her up in a telepathic surge and then left the ship, leading her and the others away from it.

"We've lost!" Woldn had said.

Unable to resist, Tesh had flown with the small group of Parviis that left *Webdancer*—a few thousand individuals who were heading away from the battle, bound for an unknown destination. She'd been caught up in their momentum, which suspended her independence. Curiously, Woldn was having difficulty sending telepathic commands to other Parviis in the swarms that had attacked other ships. Some of those Parviis followed Woldn's small cluster, but others did not, and instead scattered into space in complete disarray.

Now as she flew on, Tesh absorbed psychic currents roiling from Woldn's anger and determination to keep fighting back against all obstacles. Seeking to regain the old glories of his race, he would regroup. He would never give up. Everyone in the mini-swarm knew it, and Tesh felt considerable sympathy for them—and even for Woldn. She had never liked turning against her own people, but under the circumstances there had been no other choice. They had been wrong.

Tesh sensed increased anger focused on her—not only from the Parvii leader, but from the others linked to him. If Woldn permitted it, they could kill her. But he had something else in mind for her. What? She could not tell. Gradually, she was able to fall back to the rear of the group where it was a little more comfortable for her. But she could not pull away entirely, and swept forward with her unwanted companions.

Behind her, Tesh sensed something coming fast. Before she could turn to look, it swept her up and absorbed her.

Webdancer!

The vessel had come of its own volition, taking Anton, Nirella, and others with it. Tesh found herself inside the sectoid chamber, and within moments she was piloting the ship back to join the rest of the victorious Liberator fleet.

But the elation did not last long.

The moment *Webdancer* pulled back to join the other podships, Eshaz flew near and asked for an emergency meeting. His request was granted, and the two podships nudged against each other and opened their hatches, so that Eshaz and two other Tulyans could enter.

Through her connection to the podship, Tesh listened as the Tulyans strode heavily through the corridors of *Webdancer* and entered Doge Anton's office. Tesh heard the voices of Anton and Nirella as they greeted them.

"Dire news," Eshaz said. "We must depart for the starcloud immediately!"

"Another enemy," one of the other Tulyans murmured. "Another enemy."

Alarmed, Tesh left the sectoid chamber and hurried down the corridor in her tiny natural form, moving in a blur of speed along the walls. Then, so small that no one noticed her, she slid through an opening beneath the door of Anton's office and entered. It took her only a matter of seconds to get there, and she slipped inside. Then, scurrying up an interior corner like an insect, she became motionless, like the proverbial fly on the wall, eavesdropping.

The biggest Tulyan of the three, Eshaz, shifted uneasily on his feet. "Noah summoned us to the cocoon, and asked us to timesee. He's been sensing a great danger, and wanted us to help him figure out what is happening."

"I've heard of timeseeing," Nirella said. "You're saying it actually works?"

"We don't talk about it much, but yes. It's an ability a few Tulyans have to see aspects of the future," Eshaz said. "We three are among the few capable of this, and I regret to inform you that we have no time to celebrate. A great and terrible thing approaches. We must leave immediately for the starcloud. It is safer there."

"But what is it?" Nirella asked. "We're victorious here. All of our enemies are vanquished."

"All that you know about. We cannot say what is coming, only that it brings darkness with it, and the probable end of all that we know."

"Darkness for all time," the third Tulyan said.

"The end of the galaxy?" Anton said. "The decay can't be stopped?"

"Something more," Eshaz said. "We can't determine what. Only that we must hurry."

"I'm not going to question your judgment," Anton said. "Or Noah's. Nirella, notify the fleet that we are departing for the Tulyan Starcloud. Without delay."

She saluted and got on the comlink to set it up.

The Tulyans hurried away, and Tesh sped back to her sectoid chamber. Only a few minutes later, Noah Watanabe transported his cocoon, *Webdancer*, and half of the Andromeda division of the fleet back to the starcloud via the visualization method he had used previously—a method that he surmised must use the ultimate of galactic shortcuts. It was not quite instantaneous, but was close to it.

Then, in a matter of seconds, he sped back to the battlefield and signaled that he would escort the rest of the fleet—around seventy-five percent of the ships—to the starcloud via other podways, staying with them for the protective firepower he could offer. But, he worried, even that might not be enough.

Feeling great fatigue from tapping into the primal energy source, and with the continuing demands on his energy, Noah hoped he could find the strength to continue. Intermittently, he went through moments when he didn't think he could. Then he would feel bursts of energy that gave him just enough to keep going.

Now his cocoon and thousands of smaller podships split space in flashes of green light, in a frantic rush to escape an enemy that they could not see. For defensive purposes Noah remained at the rear of the pack, and through the Aopoddae linkages he transmitted details to the other podships about the best route for them to take.

As Noah zipped through space behind the others, he pressed his face against the forward wall of the cocoon's sectoid chamber, peering in all directions through his many eyes in the hull, scanning, searching. Podflesh oozed around him in the chamber, a shallow pool of it.

The route he took involved some shortcuts between sectors, and they passed through regions where web conditions were barely adequate. Tulyan repair teams had already worked on some of these podways, and for the areas where breaks still existed, he went around. In a little over two hours, the group emerged from space just outside the Tulyan Starcloud, and made their way into the protective mists.

Just before entering the mindlink field himself, Noah paused briefly and scanned conditions in the galaxy, seeing far across space with his multiple eyes on the hull of the cocoon . . . eyes that enabled him to view the vast filigree of Timeweb and the farthest reaches of space. As he focused to do this, the cocoon glowed brilliant green, casting light far across the galaxy and even illuminating the distant Kandor Sector he had just left.

He detected a disturbing bulge there, in the paranormal fabric of the galaxy. Abruptly, strands of the galactic infrastructure ripped away, creating what looked like an immense timehole, covering the entire galactic sector. Around the galaxy he saw other bulges, and additional huge holes appeared. One of them sucked up Woldn and the remnants of his attack force, then closed again, like a fantastic cosmic mouth. Another took the entire Adurian homeworld to an unknown place . . . and he didn't think it would ever return.

Then, where the Kandor Sector used to be, huge, dark shapes poured out of the hole and scrambled around on the podways, on multiple legs that scampered along the strands of Timeweb. Even with the illumination Noah cast on them, he could not distinguish details of their bodies—only that they were large, amorphous creatures that moved very quickly.

Viscerally, he knew this was the additional danger he had foreseen, but he had no idea what it was.

CHAPTER SEVENTY-ONE

Time spins its own web.
—Ancient Tulyan Saying

Inside the ethereal mists of the starcloud, Noah communicated with the Council of Elders, this time using one of the comlink channels of the Liberators. Then, after making arrangements directly with First Elder Kre'n, he guided his cocoon to the immense inverted dome of the Council Chamber, which floated over Tulé, the largest Tulyan planet. The cocoon and the chamber were of equivalent sizes, but of very different configurations—and Noah's was much more the organic of the two structures. He commanded the amalgamated Aopoddae to link to a docking station on the chamber.

By prior agreement, Noah strode out of the cocoon and made his way into a tunnel linking the structures. There, he boarded a small, automated motocart that had been sent for him, which carried him rapidly into the central meeting chamber.

The entire Council awaited him, sitting at their high, curved bench. Noah would have preferred to remain inside the cocoon, but the Tulyan leaders had insisted otherwise. Worried about still being able to control the primal weapon, Noah had nonetheless acceded to their demand, subject to the availability of the motocart to get him back in the event of an emergency.

Although some of the Elders had seen him in his present podman appearance, the entire Council had not. He exchanged greetings quickly with the Elders, tried not to let their probing, inquisitive stares bother him. He saw Doge Anton, General Nirella, and Subi Danvar standing nearby, and nodded to them.

Again, Noah was weaker away from EcoStation, but this time it was much more serious than the previous occasions when he had left. He felt drained, a condition of deep fatigue that he had begun to notice after using the primal weapon. He had recovered only slightly since then. The weariness had reached deep into his cells and mind, making him feel as if he could sleep for a week, or longer. He didn't dare. He had to go on, had to keep finding the strength to continue.

As he stood before the high bench, Noah focused on the fact that the Elders were looking down at him closely, and some of them were whispering to each other. Troubled, he had a feeling he should get back to the cocoon as soon as possible, for the restorative energy it imparted to him.

"We have formed a military plan with the Liberator fleet commanders," Kre'n said, "and it is necessary for us to merge you into it—with your newfound powers."

"Though we aren't quite sure how to do that," Anton said.

Noah nodded, pursed his lips in thought. He felt exhaustion seeping over him.

"I think we all need a certain amount of autonomy," Kre'n said. "We have our communication channels and our differing capabilities. Here in the starcloud, we Tulyans will maintain our mindlink as a defensive force, while your Liberator ships can be more offensive in nature, still keeping some vessels back to aid us here. As for you, Noah Watanabe, you can serve both purposes."

She paused, and added, "You are in possession of great power and responsibility, Noah. Surely you are the Savior spoken of in our legends, the one who will deliver us from death."

This subject had come up before, and Noah had tried not to

believe it. Now he was no longer so certain, and chose not to comment on it. But no matter what they called him—or what his destiny might be—he was not certain if he had the capability to stop whatever creatures were tearing the galaxy apart with new timeholes, bigger than any he'd ever seen before, or had ever heard of. The decay of the galaxy—at least the rapid acceleration of the process—had not been from any natural, internal laws of decay. An outside force was involved.

Fighting back his fatigue, Noah looked up at Kre'n and said, "I told you what I saw—all the new timeholes, and huge, dark shapes pouring out of the one in the Kandor Sector. Creatures of some kind. You said you know what they are?"

Kre'n nodded her scaly, reptilian head. Then she narrowed her slitted eyes, and said, "What I am going to tell you has never been revealed to non-Tulyans, not by us or by any of our predecessors. It is one of the things we routinely confirm among our people with the truthing touch, constantly verifying that the information has not gotten out. The terrible secret has become ingrained in our race, but now it is appropriate for you and the others present to know what we are all up against."

Noah trembled in anticipation.

"The creatures are Web Spinners," Kre'n said, following a moment's hesitation. "We have Tulyan observers in deep space, and they have confirmed this. The danger is severe."

When Noah looked at the ancient leader with a blank expression, she said solemnly, "In the first days of the universe, the Sublime Creator formed galaxies on top of galaxies, folding them around each other in cosmic embraces. Our beneficial deity lives in the overgalaxy, a wondrous realm of time-and-space consciousness that is on a higher plane than any other."

"Like heaven."

"Somewhat."

"How many galaxies are there?"

"This is not known, and perhaps can never be known by us." She gazed at Noah for a lingering moment, then said, "Long ago, after the explosion of an incomprehensibly large star, galaxies were formed from the flaming embers, creating suns, planets, and other cosmic bodies. From the earliest days, the Sublime Creator wanted to organize the galaxies and keep their differing qualities separate, so he sought builders for the huge project. He was the grand visionary that generated the universe, but for certain detailed tasks he delegated much of the work."

She smiled sadly. "An early form of management, you might say. He already had the galaxies, but to make each of them an entirely separate enclosure he needed a strong fabric for the separations. This he accomplished with work crews involving various life forms that he created. The scale is beyond our comprehension, as are the details. But for us it all boils down to this galaxy, and how it was set up. Our galaxy received special consideration, giving it beauty that is second only to the ethereal realm of the Sublime Creator. This explains the loveliness of our nebulas and star systems, and particularly of Timeweb— our cosmic filigree whose intricacies are unmatched by any other galaxy. This paranormal webbing was generated by specialized creatures on a rather large scale—though on the scale of the universe it might not seem that way."

"And that's where the Web Spinners come in," Noah said.

"Precisely. Like huge spiders, the Web Spinners extruded the strands of our galactic web, after consuming the fibers of deep-shaft, piezoelectric emeralds. So that the races could travel on this glorious infrastructure, the Sublime Creator formed the Aopoddae podships, a race of sentient spacecraft capable of transporting other races across the galaxy in a matter of moments. Our galaxy is indeed a wondrous creation, containing countless life forms that are supposed to work in harmony with one another. There are even infinitesimally small nanocreatures that live inside the webbing. Another race entirely. But that is another story.

"Since it is spun from ingested emerald fibers, Timeweb glows faintly green. The same glow is also found in the sectoid chambers of podships, making it possible for ship pilots to communicate with each other across vast distances via the galactic web that the chambers are in direct contact with. The nehrcom transmission system of the merchant princes also uses these piezoelectric emeralds in a slightly different fashion, aligning the stones so that they bounce signals off the web."

"And my cocoon can glow, like a green sun in space."

"Yes. Truly remarkable."

"And dangerous in the wrong hands," the towering Elder named Dabiggio added. Scowling more than usual, he sat on one side of her at the long bench.

"Fortunately, that is not the case," Kre'n said, glancing at him and speaking in a scolding tone.

"You say the Web Spinners are spiders?" Noah asked.

"No, I said they are *like* spiders, with certain similarities—but significant differences as well. The creatures are immense in size, with remarkably strong exoskeletons that are not subject to the expansion limitations of planet-bound spiders, which would collapse if they were scaled up too much."

"It should not be possible for them to be so large," Noah said, "just as Timeweb should not be possible. Even though I know the vast web exists and that it links the entire galaxy, I am still amazed that something so intricate holds it all together, and that most of the races can't even detect its existence."

"Truly, Timeweb is a grand and marvelous concept," Kre'n said, "but there have been problems. One has been apparent for some time now. The web is infinitely strong but fragile in many ways, and requires a great deal of work to maintain it. Initially, the Sublime Creator assigned Tulyans to perform this work, and gave us dominion over podships to get us around the galaxy. This system fell into disarray when another race grew in numbers and took control of the podships away from us. *Parviis.* The Sublime Creator didn't actually create Parviis directly; they arose from the biotech laboratories of the Adurians, whom he did create himself."

"And even though your race was cast out so ungraciously," Noah said, "you continued to perform whatever maintenance and repair work you could, on a piecemeal basis. A noble undertaking, I must say."

She looked dismal. "The Adurians caused a lot of trouble in ancient days, as they have in recent times. We have always been wary of them, as we have been of their surrogates, the Parviis."

"Tesh Kori told me that Humans are an offshoot of Parviis."

"That is true," Kre'n said, "which serves to explain some of the problems humankind has caused. But that is another matter, and you are not typical of the race."

The comment made Noah think of Tesh (who also was atypical of her race), and of their unborn baby, which would be a hybrid of the Human and Parvii genetic lines.

Just then, Eshaz hurried into the chamber and addressed the Council. "Our deep-space observers report the Web Spinners are on the move," he said. "Heading in this direction. They're leaving a wake of destruction in their path—planetary systems, even the biggest, hottest suns wiped out and scattered into flaming embers. Nothing gets in their way. They just mow it down."

"And their ETA?" Kre'n asked. She looked very concerned, but amazingly steady. Noah detected no panic there, nor on the faces of the other Elders. But in their long experience, this must be the worst of events.

"Eighteen minutes."

Feeling his pulse quicken, Noah said, "I must return to the cocoon."

"We can have you there in less than a minute," Kre'n said. "But know this, valiant Human, before you go into battle: The Sublime Creator found the Web Spinners difficult to control, especially their leader, the Queen. Like the sentient races that are familiar to us, they were granted a form of free will. In their case, they had to be carefully and forcefully monitored while they built the Timeweb infrastructure—a process that took a very long time. When, at long last, they completed the vast construction project, the Sublime Creator confined them to the undergalaxy and sealed them there, so that they could not disturb him or the showcase of his marvelous creation—our own galaxy. Since then, the Queen of the Undergalaxy has ruled her stygian realm, and only that."

"But we have an ancient prophecy," said one of the other Elders, an elegant Tulyan man. "What the Web Spinners create they can also destroy."

"So you've always known this was coming?" Noah asked.

"Our timeseers have long foretold these days," Kre'n said, "and their visions have finally come upon us. Depending upon what happens next—and that we do not know—these are either the End of Days or a New Beginning."

"And a battle plan?" Noah asked.

"Defend and attack. Against such an onrushing enemy, there can be no other plan."

"I guess we'll find out soon enough where I fit into all of this," Noah said.

Kre'n nodded, and said softly, "Our blessings be upon you, Master Noah."

Then everyone hurried to their battle stations.

CHAPTER SEVENTY-TWO

> If they come for us, there will be no place to hide.
> —Ancient Tulyan warning

The moment Noah set foot on the docking platform of the cocoon, he began to feel physically stronger. His skin wasn't even in direct contact with the mottled gray-and-black flesh—only his shoes were—but he still felt an instant infusion of vitality greater than any before, and the fatigue seemed to fade entirely. The cocoon was becoming like a mother's womb, providing nutrients for him in invisible ways.

But he didn't have time to wonder about the nature or cause of the phenomenon. A tidal wave of destruction was on the way.

Thinker greeted him on the platform. "Did the meeting go well, Master Noah?"

"A new threat is on the way." Taking less than a minute, he told the robot what he knew.

As Thinker listened, the lights around his metal faceplate glowed an angry shade of orange. Then he said, "We must fight back hard."

"That is my intent. Now, I'm afraid you're going to have to wait for me again, my friend. I'm going back into the sectoid chamber of this cocoon."

"The weapon room," Thinker said.

"Essentially, yes. I wish it were not that way, but I have no choice." With a grim expression, Noah gave the sentient robot an affectionate pat on the shoulder, feeling this might be the last time the two of them ever saw each other.

Thinker's metal-lidded eyes blinked, as if fighting away tears that were not actually there. At least not physically.

Noah knelt on the platform, and touched his hands against the podship flesh. It became gray liquid around him. He felt the warmth of the alien cellular material, and allowed it to run up his arms.

"I've been given considerable autonomy in the use of the weapon," Noah said, "and I'll be focused on what I have to do." The soft flesh covered his body, all the way up to his shoulders. "I can't use a conventional webtalker to relay information—they say there's too much disturbance around the cocoon—so I need you to remain in direct comlink contact with General Nirella and Doge Anton. Obtain any specific commands they might have and relay them to me."

"What? Oh, you're thinking I can use my organic interface connection on the podflesh, and that will put me in contact with you?"

"Try it now. Quickly."

The familiar tentacle snaked out of Thinker's alloy body, and darted into the gray-and-black flesh on a nearby bulkhead. "Yes," the robot said, "I am now linked to your mind. It will work."

"Good. One more thing. You've always been a de facto officer in the Liberator fleet, though no one has ever given you a rank."

"No matter. I command the robots, but at the pleasure of Humans."

"It *does* matter, my good friend. For your unflagging loyalty and service, you deserve more. Therefore, as Master of the Guardians, I hereby appoint you Vice-General, in charge of all robots. Tell Anton and Nirella I made a battlefield promotion. I'm sure they won't countermand it."

"Thank you, Master Noah. Where shall I meet you after our victory?"

"Anywhere on the cocoon," Noah said, with a stiff smile. "I'll know where you are, because it will be an extension of my own body."

The alien flesh rose up Noah's neck, to his chin.

"We're very small in this galaxy, aren't we?" Thinker said.

It was the last thing Noah heard before he swam into the flesh and became one with it. Again he seemed to cross a vast distance, as if traversing the entire universe. There were no stars, only a darkness that gradually began to glow with a soft green luminescence. Once more, he reached the sectoid chamber and rose to his feet inside, like an alien life form that had just been born and could already stand.

Again he pressed his face against the glowing green flesh of the sectoid chamber, and his multiple countenances emerged on the outside of the cocoon, this time showing the podman features of his evolved face. He disengaged the cocoon from the inverted dome of the Council Chamber, and floated free of it.

Noah felt like he was in a vast sea that stretched across the cosmos. All around him, as if his presence was connected to a vast cosmic circuit, he felt the energy source building, the raw, elemental power of the superweapon. He became a brilliant green sun in space with shining Noah-faces all around it, looking in all directions with the numerous humanoid eyes, casting spotlights of illumination to the farthest reaches of galactic existence. Noah was the cocoon; he was the weapon, and much more. He was a mote, a micro-organism, an embryonic life form, but he extended across time and space. Again he was in direct contact with the primal energy of the universe.

Peering through the green illumination, Noah saw hundreds of the immense, dark creatures scrambling across the podways like huge hunting daggs following a scent, going toward the starcloud along the identical secondary route that Noah had taken. He felt a chill. He still could not make out details of the monsters, only glimpses of multiple legs beneath their bodies, propelling them forward at high speed.

Web Spinners.

As if in response to his thoughts, the massed Aopoddae stirred around him, an agitation of ancient flesh. Trembling to the very depths of his own soul, Noah Watanabe knew that he would have preferred to hold back, that he didn't really want to be any part of a weapon, and especially not one of this frightening scope and power. But he was coming to believe that this horrendous device stood right in the middle of his evolutionary path, blocking his way until he used it. He could not go around the duty, could not avoid the dreadful task that lay before him, no matter how much he might like to. Causing destruction ran counter to every instinct he had. Throughout history, the very worst genocides and ecological disasters had been brought about by warfare. Even the current galactic-wide crisis might have been started by military conflict, and at the very minimum it had been severely exacerbated by it.

Must I use violence to quell violence, he thought, *to begin the process of restoring the galaxy?* And he wondered if his own hesitation, his own doubts, were causing the agitation in the podship flesh in which he was immersed.

He wondered, as well, how the mysterious cocoon weapon functioned, what its workings looked like. It seemed to be an unanswerable question, of enormous proportions. The thing just existed, and in certain circumstances the incredible weapon could spew destruction across the galaxy—like an immense green-flame thrower. He sensed, however, that even that might not be enough against such a threat.

Less than eleven minutes had passed since the Tulyans had estimated the eighteen-minute arrival time, so there should be seven left. But Noah thought it might be more like three now. In the last few moments, the Web Spinners had increased their speed, in anticipation of reaching their goal.

They were hungry. . . .

Clinging to the forward wall of *Webdancer*'s much smaller sectoid chamber, Tesh Kori monitored the flurry of activity in the meeting rooms and corridors of the flagship, and in space around her. Through her connection with the podflesh, she listened to the interior of the vessel, while looking outward through visual sensors in the hull. The Liberator fleet had been divided up and positioned according to General Nirella's orders, prepared to defend the starcloud against the fast-approaching threat.

Web Spinners, they called them. Ancient creatures from the undergalaxy. Demons? That was the only parallel she could draw to Parvii legends, which described the undergalaxy as a stygian realm, inhabited by evil spirits.

She waited for the next command from her superiors. Agonizing seconds ticked by. Through the misty gases of the starcloud, Tesh saw Noah's cocoon moving to a forward position, where General Nirella had ordered him to go. She thought of Noah's child growing in her womb, and wondered if they would ever form a family—the three of them. She desperately hoped so, but nothing about her relationship with Noah was conventional. Besides, war was filled with uncertainties, and too many of the possibilities were not good.

Tesh had lived for more than seven centuries, and in that time had dated men of many star systems and galactic races. But never before had she met anyone even remotely like Noah Watanabe, nor had she ever experienced feelings for any of them that approached those she felt for him.

And, while she could remember details going back all that

time, she had noticed a recent compression of the memories that mattered most to her, the ones she kept calling up and thinking about over and over. The kisses she had shared with Noah, their brief intimacy, the comforting sound of his voice, the caring way he looked at her with his hazel eyes, which he still had even after his flesh changed.

Since meeting him, the original racial difference between them had widened, as Noah had set forth on a path of evolving into something else. She only hoped that he was not evolving into some*one* else.

At the very heart of her feelings, his appearance didn't really matter to her. She cared much more about what was inside, what he was thinking and where he was going with his life. She cared about what sort of a father he would be for their child.

Tears welled up in Tesh's eyes, and ran down her cheeks. She tasted salt.

I must be strong, she thought. The tears stopped, and she steeled herself for battle.

The great weapon that Noah was about to use and the entire scenario seemed so far beyond the range of possibility that he wondered if he was going completely mad, if he had been infected with a terrible disease of the mind. His own twin sister had gone insane and had died hideously. Noah recalled the dermex injection she had stabbed into him, claiming it was her own blood. It had been her last act of hatred toward him before dying. Could Francella's vicious presence be alive inside him at this very moment, and dictating his very perceptions? It remained an unanswered question, just one of many.

I need to control chaos, he thought, trying to bring himself back, knowing that the monsters of the undergalaxy really were coming. *Order must emerge from chaos. In this galaxy, and in my own psyche.*

Abruptly, Noah felt a shift in time and space around him, and he saw fast-forward images through Francella's eyes as she committed vile acts—scheming to murder their father, stealing his assets, hacking at and stabbing Noah. He felt her hatreds, her twisted views, her petty jealousies and self-serving plots. He felt how much she loathed her twin. It was not the first time he had seen through her eyes—or seemed to—and he wondered if this had something to do with the blood she had injected into him, or to the fact that twins were said to have paranormal linkages.

The eyes shifted; the *view* shifted, revealing a horrific threat to the Tulyan Starcloud. . . .

CHAPTER SEVENTY-THREE

> In some circumstances, it is better to perish than
> to survive. If that be the case in our hour of
> crisis, may death come quickly to us all.
> —Transmitted thoughts, from a Tulyan webtalker

Like an earthquake in space, a terrible upheaval consumed the Tulyan Starcloud. Once a haven like none other in the known galaxy, it was anything but that now. Having slipped out of the control of mindlink, comets and meteors streaked wildly through the mists of the starcloud, threatening the planets, the Liberator fleet, and the Council Chamber.

Focusing and refocusing their telepathic waves, the Tulyans succeeded in diverting the incoming missiles one at a time, but more kept coming. A huge meteor—the size of a small moon—barely missed hitting the planet Tulé.

All across the starcloud, Liberator warships fired their weapons at the incoming objects, hitting some and diverting them, but missing others. With the attentions of the defenders on the larger objects, meteorites got through and crashed into dwellings and community structures. Flaming embers hit the floating Council Chamber.

Noah's cocoon was in motion, moving independently of his commands. It was a survival mode in the amalgamated podships that enabled him to focus his attention elsewhere. The cocoon moved through the mists in great graceful patterns, avoiding the celestial storm. It rose heavenward, then circled over the misty veils and three planets of the starcloud, taking evasive action as necessary.

From his paranormal, web-linked observation and listening post Noah hesitated, sensing that he should not fire his great weapon at the incoming objects yet, that he needed to save it for exactly the right moment. But he couldn't just stand by and watch this. At Yaree, he had minimized the power and spread it around to detonate the invading Parviis.

He realized that he was having a gut reaction now, and he had to ask himself if it was relevant, or if it was a useless remnant of his Human form, something that should be discarded. As he watched the cosmic storm all around him, he could hardly stand it anymore. He had to fire the weapon to divert some of those incoming objects.

But still he hesitated.

Through Timeweb, Noah heard one of the Elders—Dabiggio—cry out in dismay, "The demons of the undergalaxy are breaking through!" Other Council members shouted that this couldn't possibly be happening, that the starcloud was supposed to be the strongest place in the entire galaxy, since mindlink had been improved dramatically by a concerted effort of the defenders.

The Council Chamber was hit again, this time by a small comet that skipped off the bulbous underside, tearing loose a jagged piece of the inverted dome. All over the starcloud, thousands of Tulyans were fleeing for the podships and attempting to board them. But in the chaos most vessels were having to take off before they were fully loaded. Above Tulé, four were hit by meteorites and larger objects, destroying them. Noah heard the screams of the dying Aopoddae and their Tulyan passengers.

Unable to wait any longer, he reduced the power of the great weapon, focused it, and fired bursts of primal green light in multiple directions. All over the starcloud and beyond it, comets, meteors, and meteorites exploded and veered away. A small number of them kept coming, but Noah thought the Tulyans should be able to deter the rest of them with mindlink. He drew the power inward, felt it building up around him again.

Now his humanoid eyes looked at the oncoming Web Spinners, amorphous shapes that were closer than ever, only a minute or two away, surging past one star system after another. Why weren't they coming into focus? Kre'n had said they were *like* spiders, and had exoskeletons that scaled up to amazing proportions. Did they look like spiders, then? So far, he'd only gotten glimpses of long legs beneath dark bodies that almost seemed fluid, as their shapes bent one way and another. Perhaps this was yet another form of shapeshifting.

Again Noah felt the visceral sensation telling him not to fire, not yet. He had to wait for precisely the right moment, and really cut loose with everything he had. This time, Noah went with the feeling, and hoped he had not made a mistake by activating the weapon earlier to protect the starcloud. He felt the power continue to build up around him, and it did not seem to him that he had damaged anything. It could keep going up and up.

But in a matter of moments he reached a point where he didn't feel his brain could encompass any more of the tremendous energy. Although his thoughts extended far and could accomplish a great deal, he still had some connection to his past as a Human, and he sensed that there were distinct limitations on what he could do, and that he should not go beyond certain boundaries. But what were those boundaries? His expanded mind would not, or could not, tell him.

Noah felt like a child-god, one who was not able to understand or fully control his powers. But he had no more time to learn, and needed to utilize what he had immediately. It was the most severe form of on-the-job training imaginable, because any mistake he made would have immense consequences.

He felt the momentum of time around him, a tidal wave of events pushing him toward an unavoidable climax. He looked in all directions at once, absorbed information from everywhere simultaneously.

The dark creatures kept coming, and in anticipation of this the Tulyans were evacuating the Council Chamber. Noah recognized the face of Eshaz on the prow of one of the ships that was taking on passengers. That vessel began to move quickly and headed away with others, going in the opposite direction from the approaching Web Spinners. Incoming thoughts from webtalkers told Noah that the Tulyans were setting up a new defensive bastion on their largest planet, Tulé. Due to changes in cosmic conditions, this would be the most powerful place in the starcloud, where they intended to make a last-ditch telepathic stand against the attackers.

Noah saw a weak spot in the galactic infrastructure near the abandoned Council Chamber, a fraying of the green filigree that would soon send the chamber tumbling one direction or another. Nothing like that had ever happened before in this region of space.

Then, to his amazement, the approaching Web Spinners began to disappear before reaching the starcloud, one after the other. From his vantage over the misty Tulyan domain, Noah saw that the creatures were entering a timehole. In seconds, they were gone, and the hole closed in a flash of green.

But near the Council Chamber he saw a bulge in the barely visible fabric of space, and remembered seeing that effect in the Kandor Sector, right before the creatures poured through from the undergalaxy. Now he noticed other bulges appearing around the starcloud, with the biggest of all forming around Tulé, where podships full of evacuees were still arriving. To his dismay, he realized that Eshaz was piloting one of them.

And Noah had no time to do anything about it.

The surface of Tulé cracked open like an eggshell. Something monstrous and black pushed its way through the molten lava and crust of the world, a creature that was much larger than the others. It had long legs, which waved in the sky and struck several podships as they tried to take off, causing them to crash. The planet cracked open further, and Noah saw smaller creatures, scurrying out of fissures. Near the Council Chamber, other creatures emerged and knocked the chamber aside, sending its severely damaged remains drifting through the starcloud.

The earlier Web Spinners had been scouts. Now many more of them were coming out of the undergalaxy, and the mother of them all was a hundred times the size of Noah's cocoon, with a head and body of odd geometric angles, and yellow-ember eyes that burned as bright as suns. Its legs looked and moved like those of a spider, but its body, just breaking through the crust of the planet, was diamond-shaped, as if cut from an immense, precious stone. It was the darkest shade of black he had ever seen, and seemed to absorb light into it and make the illumination disappear, like a black hole in motion.

The monsters clustered on webbing over the ruined world, having scattered Tulé and its atmosphere into space. Liberator warships attacked the creatures, firing ion cannons, nuclear projectiles, and a variety of other space weapons. But nothing did any good, as the creatures ignored the small blasts.

From his high vantage Noah was sickened to see the torn bodies of Humans, Tulyans, and Mutatis floating in space.

The largest Web Spinner, now free, began to climb the web toward Noah's cocoon, but got on a weak strand that broke, causing a momentary delay before it found another.

The *Queen of the Undergalaxy*, he thought.

Other smaller creatures followed her, and resembled her in appearance. Even the smallest of them were as big as Noah's cocoon.

Seeing through his many eyes in the amalgamation around him, Noah's eyes displayed multiple images of the spiders crawling up the web toward him. It was like an array of video screens . . . all showing horror. The creatures were picking up speed.

Noah focused the primal-energy weapon and fired a blinding green blast that was much more powerful than he had used to destroy the HibAdu armada. But this time it only bounced off the geometric, spidery creatures, without seeming to harm them.

Desperately, he increased the energy level by several factors— beyond what he had earlier thought he could stand. He continued firing, but with very little effect on the monsters of the nether realm. The blasts slowed them, but they didn't seem to be harmed at all, and they kept coming. . . .

CHAPTER SEVENTY-FOUR

In this universe, there is always a way to escape from any
situation . . . even from the greatest danger. It is for us,
with the brains and free will that the Sublime Creator gave
us, to find the way.

—Tulyan observation, in emergency council

The Web Spinners scrambled along the strands, heading directly
toward Noah's cocoon, ignoring the warships of the Liberator
fleet that raced alongside them, peppering them with ion and
atomic cannon fire that didn't phase them at all, didn't slow
them down or make them change course. The monsters just
ignored them.

In the midst of the terrible threat, Noah's mind raced, searching for answers and possibilities. He kept firing his own primal
blasts at the creatures, but they kept coming, and he didn't
want to increase the power any more, fearing it would go beyond
anything he could handle. It could destroy the remains of the
starcloud, the Liberator fleet, and everything in this galactic
sector—with the possible exception of the monsters of the undergalaxy. He wasn't sure if anything could stop them.

For the moment, he continued to fire at the creatures, and at
least his shots were slowing them down—though they kept
regrouping and clamoring toward him. Intermittently, for brief
moments, he saw faint lights and shifting colors inside the bodies and heads, as if illuminated from within. Then the colors

and lights would fade to black-blackness with the exception of the yellow-ember eyes, peering out of the darkness of the bodies.

Noah recalled the Battle of Yaree, where he had experienced a brief vision lasting only a few seconds, in which the cocoon blew up and he tumbled out into a glowing green timehole. That had never really happened, and he strongly suspected now—more viscerally than intellectually—that he had seen a fragment of his own future in that vision. But he also felt, with equal certainty, that he could still avoid this fate if he made the right choices. Perhaps that was why his mind revealed the vision to him again, to prevent it from happening.

The Web Spinners had been opening timeholes all over the galaxy, exploiting natural galactic weaknesses and creating new ones, undoubtedly setting them up as entry points and waiting for their best opportunity to attack. But they had seemed to ignore the HibAdus and their conventional weaponry, and were doing the same with the Liberators. They weren't ignoring Noah, though, and his weapon didn't seem to have much effect on them at all. Not yet.

Should he raise the primal power and see what it could do to the creatures, no matter what the potential risk was to everything else? He might have to.

He realized now that the Web Spinners wanted to get to *him,* to the exclusion of everything else in this galaxy. And they had been after him before. Somehow they'd been sensing his presence wherever he was, especially after he formed the cocoon and began discovering what it contained—a raw, cosmic power that the creatures feared. Earlier they had intended to get him at Yaree and in the Kandor Sector, but each time Noah had eluded them. Crossing space from Kandor, he had displayed an ability to traverse vast distances almost instantaneously, which seemed to cause problems for the creatures. And—if that method of travel was not available—for reasons he did not yet understand—he could still travel at great speeds along the podways. He had the means of escape, though he suspected that would only delay the inevitable. They would find him. They were *determined* to find him, like predators that refused to give up the hunt. But for what purpose? Presumably, to attempt to kill him. But what if they couldn't accomplish that? What then? What sort of integrated mind and energy drove them? What form of extraterrestrial hell did they intend for him?

That particular future—if it existed—had not yet been revealed to him.

These alien organisms were smart, and they would undoubtedly attempt to cut off his routes of escape, as the HibAdus had tried to do with the Liberator fleet. Alternately, the creatures seemed to select both undergalactic routes and routes in this galaxy. But Noah was not without his own options. Maybe he could lure them away as far as possible and set off a huge detonation that would finish them off. If conditions permitted, he could go through a timehole into the undergalaxy and do it to them there—thus shifting the focus of the destruction.

Wipe them out in their own nest, he thought. *Kill all of them. Get the Queen.*

If this worked, it would test the limits of his own "immortality," and his ability to return to this realm through a timehole, or through some other means he did not yet know about. But these considerations were not a priority. For the sake of his own galaxy, and for all he held dear, he was more than willing to sacrifice his own life—in whatever form that sacrifice took. It might just save Tesh and their child, and the Liberator fleet could then attack the weakened HibAdu forces and take back the Human and Mutati planets they controlled.

Thinker, are you picking this up? Noah thought.

Yes.

Tell the fleet to disengage, and why. Tell them to remain here, without me.

I'm doing it now, Master.

Noah envisioned a sector far across the galaxy, a region where he had seen numerous timeholes, through the paranormal lens available to him. It was beyond Yaree and the Kandor Sector—so far away, so desolate and off the beaten path that he didn't know of a name for it, or even an astronomical number. Even with all of the sector mapping that had been completed by the various races, there were still places like this, and it was exactly what he wanted. If he had to set off an explosion there, it would be as far as possible from population centers, and it presented the possibility of escape routes to the undergalaxy, where he would go if necessary. One way or another, he would make a statement.

This time, the movement across space was not nearly instantaneous, as it had seemed to be before. But this was intentional. He needed to set up his trap.

Noah felt the podships tremble around him as he transmitted psychic energy to them, yet he urged them to go—he *commanded* it, and they went into motion. There was a tightening inside his skull, and a searing pain as the collective entity accelerated along one podway and then another, heading for the far reaches of the galaxy at tachyon speeds. The discomfort in his skull was enormous—as if the Aopoddae didn't want to cooperate in this—but he did not let up.

Through his cocoon eyes at the rear, Noah saw the curvature of the web, and black forms scrambling along it behind him, trying to keep up. The smaller Web Spinners were in front of the big one now. He summoned the cocoon to greater velocity, but it resisted. Despite this, he was still going at tremendous speed, because he saw suns and solar systems passing by in a blur.

But as he peered through the eyes behind the pod-amalgam, he knew he was not going fast enough to reach his destination. After initially falling back, the predators were gradually gaining on him, with the smaller ones running along parallel strands and the big one looming behind.

The hybrid space station began to vibrate and slow down slightly, and Noah realized that the strand beneath his ship was disintegrating, about to break. Before he could react, the cocoon spun and somersaulted away through space. It had fallen off the galactic track. He struggled for control, and tried to see what was going on, but for several moments he could do neither. One of the smaller pursuers was ahead of the others, and very near him now. Running along a parallel strand, it reached out to swipe at the cocoon with a claw, but narrowly missed.

Noah managed to engage with another podway strand and he accelerated along it, momentarily leaving the creatures behind—until they got on the same podway and began to gain on him again. He urged the cocoon to greater speed, but it resisted.

Desperately, Noah looked for an alternate way to get to the remote sector where he intended to detonate the primal charge and get rid of these alien bastards. He didn't want to visualize the destination and just *go* there, because that could cause the creatures to wonder why he would do that, and might make them suspicious of a trap. It could even cause them to go back and pursue the Liberator fleet as a means of luring *him*. No, he couldn't risk that.

Noah changed course three times to again head in the direction he wanted, but each time he looked back, the pursuers were a little bit closer. Judging the distance he still needed to travel and the limited velocities the cocoon seemed able to attain, he knew he would never make it that far.

Now he had to find the nearest timehole. Noah took a series of looping turns and skimmed a gray-green membrane that didn't seem to belong there, since it was nowhere near the perimeter of the galaxy. Like a wavering, broken piece of wall, it might be a remnant of the long-ago galactic construction project, a huge unused piece that had just drifted away. Or, more likely, it had something to do with the faltering state of the cosmos. He did find podways that were faster on the membrane, but he couldn't locate a timehole. The geometric spiders were much closer now, only a few seconds behind him. The largest one moved up to the center of the pack.

Again the Web Spinners displayed internal lights and colors, but this time only in their heads, where the energy glowed brightly and danced inside the facets, as if in anticipation of the kill. As the monsters neared, Noah was startled to identify facial features on them that were contorted but still resembled those of various galactic races—Humans, Salducians, Adurians, Hibbils, Jimlats, Mutatis, Churians, and even Tulyans.

The faces were chiseled and hard instead of organic . . . features buried within facets.

The Queen looked like an amalgamation of the others, more ferocious and predatory in appearance than any monster of the imagination. She revealed immense pincers on two of her eight feet—claws that could easily rip the space station apart. Looking like an arachnid, a crustacean, and a host of unknown organisms from her demonic realm, she was a nightmare come to life.

A particularly fast spinner streaked ahead of the others, but this one did not have yellow-sun eyes—these burned red. The contorted face resembled that of Pimyt, the Royal Attaché to Lorenzo del Velli. Noah had no time to be amazed, or to wonder. He fired a blast from the cocoon weapon that slowed the creature down, and it fell back with the others.

The Queen of the Undergalaxy moved to the front of the pack. Focusing through the multiple humanoid eyes at the rear of his cocoon, Noah saw that she and her minions were almost on top of him now. While continuing to run ahead of his pursuers, he glowed brighter green, preparing to fire at them.

Suddenly Noah saw bursts of green light ahead of him, like flowers in space, and thousands of podships emerging, one after the other. It was the Liberator fleet led by *Webdancer,* catching up because of the circuitous route he had taken. But he was not happy to see them, and commanded Thinker to transmit and tell them so. Noah was troubled. The Liberators were not only risking their own safety, but it was a foolish gesture, because their destruction would leave much of the known galaxy in the hands of the HibAdus. With no Liberator force to oppose them, Human and Mutati worlds would be forever lost to the conspirators.

Thinker sent the message, but his comlink call had no effect. The fleet surged around Noah, more than one hundred thousand of them heading en masse toward the advancing Web Spinners, firing every weapon they had. Curiously, most of the vessels did not have Tulyan faces on them, suggesting that they were under Aopoddae control.

This new tactic had no effect on the monsters except to irritate them, causing them to veer off course and come back around. The Queen shifted course in the barrage of fire as well, and when she and her demon-companions took new routes toward Noah, the fleet harassed them. Even so, the Web Spinners tried to ignore them, and did not counterattack. They just kept going around and focusing on Noah.

Send another message! Noah said to Thinker, through their organic link. *Tell them I was trying to lure the Web Spinners to a remote region, and preferably into the undergalaxy, where I planned to set off a big explosion. Now I'll have to do it here, but first the fleet needs to be as far away as possible.*

Moments later, Thinker reported back: *Fleet command reports that most of the podships are flying out of their control, not respond-*

ing to the commands of their Tulyan pilots. Only Tesh, Eshaz, and a few hundred other pilots, for reasons that no one understands, report that they can convince their podships to do what they want. But none of them will leave, either—and they're setting up battle formations with the others.

Tell Tesh to go back! Noah said, worrying about her and their unborn child. *Maybe the others will follow.*

A momentary delay. Then: *She won't do it, Master Noah, won't abandon the fleet. Or you.*

Desperately, Noah looked for opportunities to fire at the Web Spinners, but worried about hitting the thick clusters of Liberator ships, and especially *Webdancer*, which Tesh piloted. He still knew where Tesh was—*Webdancer* was the largest ship in the fleet, and beside that, he saw through Timeweb to the sectoid chamber where she clung to a wall inside, piloting the craft. But he could not linger to watch over her, and couldn't justify trying to save her at the expense of the others. Then he was heartened, but only a little, to see his friend Eshaz bring his ship *Agryt* and others in close to *Webdancer*, forming some protection for the flagship. But against such behemoths of space, the effort couldn't amount to much.

Changing course, Noah went around to a flank position, where he was able to fire the primal weapon at several smaller Web Spinners on the perimeter. He used a little higher intensity than before, but far short of the massive detonation he planned. Once more, the creatures were not harmed, but he did manage to knock five of them further away, forcing them to scramble back. If any of those blasts had accidentally hit a Liberator vessel, however, he had no doubt the vessel would not survive. The Aopoddae ships were now following the lead of the flagship, coordinating attacks on the monsters that had only the collective effect of pesky flies.

Reaching the limit of her patience, the Queen finally began

thrashing around with her multiple legs, snaring podships on the sticky surfaces of her skin and smashing the vessels together, killing the Aopoddae and their passengers. So far, *Webdancer* eluded this fate, as did Eshaz's ship *Agryt*, but to his horror Noah saw them heading straight toward her. This time she had her deadly pincers extended toward them.

Noah fired two bright green blasts of energy across the bows of the ships, hitting the Queen's pincers and momentarily deterring their destructive work. *Webdancer* and Eshaz veered away, but soon came back around to continue the fight.

I've got to change this equation, Noah said to Thinker, across their linkage.

Abruptly, he took the cocoon in a sharp turn and headed through a small spiral nebula, passing through it and heading toward a region that was commonly known as the Heart of the Galaxy, the theoretically exact mathematical center of all galactic mass and gravitation. He wished he'd been able to go farther, into uncharted regions. But at least there were no known resident populations in this region.

The Queen of the Undergalaxy was right behind him, picking up speed. Her pincers were extended in anticipation, and she opened her mouth as well, a black, deadly maw in the expanse of space. Wherever she went, color and light vanished—other than her brilliant yellow eyes. She seemed to inhale entire suns and planetary systems, which vanished after she passed near them, though she did not grow perceptibly larger. Oddly—and he began to wonder if it was because of some power the Aopoddae had—she had not been able to do that to them, or to him.

Just then, Noah saw hundreds of Liberator ships on either side of him, keeping up on parallel podways. All except one—*Webdancer*—had Tulyan faces on their prows. *Webdancer* took a lead position on one side of the cocoon, and *Agryt*—piloted by Eshaz—was at the lead on the other side, like flanking guards.

Soon, more and more podships—the much larger group of face-less ones—caught up.

The Queen still managed to get past the fleet, and attacked the underside of the cocoon. She lashed out at the space station with one of her immense chelicerae claws, and barely scratched the hide of the amalgamated podships, but deep enough to cause them to cry out to Noah in pain. Quickly, they began to heal the wound, while Noah veered off and then slowed, taking a position to protect *Webdancer,* and Tesh.

Behind him, he saw five of the smaller Web Spinners do something unexpected. In concert, they flew directly at the Queen's other pincer, and smashed into it. Enraged, she stabbed them with her pincers and tossed the smaller creatures aside. Noah saw a familiar face in one of the dying spinners—a glimmering, distorted countenance that still had the features of Princess Meghina. Then he saw other Human faces inside the facets of the other dying creatures—and recognized them as the Humans who had consumed the Elixir of Life to become immortals. Were they really dying now? Earlier, he had seen Pimyt's face on one of the Web Spinners. What did it all mean? How—and why—had they been recruited into the ranks of the Web Spinners? At least Meghina and four of her companions had not been converted entirely. They had not lost their loyalty to the cause of humanity. Even Meghina, unhappy at being born a Mutati, had proved that she deserved to be considered Human, in the best definition of the race.

The smaller creature with the face of Pimyt swiped at *Web-dancer,* and struck the ship a glancing blow. Noah darted in that direction and slammed hard into the spiderlike demon, knocking it away into space.

On a Thinker-to-comlink relay, Noah had the robot say to Tesh, "Go away! Save yourself and our baby!"

She did not respond, and returned to her course, flying

alongside the cocoon with the other podships. *Webdancer* had scratches on its hull where it had been clawed and scraped, but the injuries didn't seem to be severe.

In a sudden movement, the Queen struck out at Eshaz's ship, and grabbed it in a powerful pincer grip. Then, to his horror, Noah saw the monster bite into the face of Eshaz on the prow of the ship. For a moment, the entire podship changed shape into a larger-than-life version of Eshaz's natural reptilian body, struggling to get away from the spinner. It was to no avail. She ripped through Eshaz and cast him away. He tumbled, alternately changing shape to Aopoddae and Tulyan, then became amorphous and black, with eight legs sprouting out from his lower body. In a matter of moments, the newborn horror raced toward Noah, and Eshaz's face began to glimmer on its faceted face. It had become one of the small Web Spinners.

Noah didn't have time to grieve, or to think about the other podships and pilots who were being converted when the Queen got to them, vessel by vessel. He continued to take evasive maneuvers from the pack of spinners, all the while trying to keep them away from *Webdancer.*

Filled with anger and frustration, Noah felt a trembling in the cocoon flesh. Casting green light from his eyes around the hull of the space station, he gazed out on the thousands of podships in the fleet, many of which kept flying directly at the Queen's pincers in obvious, though suicidal, efforts to deter her. It was working to some extent, as she continued to deal with them while still pursuing Noah. It had the effect of slowing her down, and her companions with her. She seemed to be the only one who could stab the attackers and convert them into spinners. If it kept going like that, however, Noah realized that she would eventually convert the entire podship fleet and command them as well. But she could only convert as many as she could reach—and so far she'd barely made a dent in the Liberator fleet.

Through Timeweb, Noah expanded his mind into the interiors of all the podships. He wasn't really touching them, at least not physically, but the contact was significant, nonetheless. His mind raced, exploring new possibilities as they occurred to him.

In a form of gestalt, Noah realized that he could do much more than he had previously thought possible with the weapon. The cocoon and all of the other podships could accomplish more than the sum of their individual possibilities. He saw a new way to use the tremendous firepower, a way that even the podships themselves might not realize. After all, they had not used it until he appeared.

In the midst of his racing thoughts, Noah caught himself, and felt a chill of realization as information seeped out of the armored Aopoddae memory core in his brain and entered his consciousness. The sentient spacecraft had known the full potential of the weapon all along, but needed him to prove he was worthy of using it. He had to figure it out himself, while they remained in close proximity to him—taking control of most of the fleet away from the pilots.

Even facing their own destruction, the podships were behaving unpredictably, in ways that did not always seem to help their own survival. Their behavior almost seemed . . . religious to him, as if they believed in fate and destiny. But whatever their motives, they concealed them from him. Noah had the feeling that he would never figure out the ancient aliens to any great extent, even if he managed to get through this great challenge with them.

At that realization, Noah felt a shift in space and time around him, and abruptly his face and eyes appeared on the prow of each ship in the Liberator fleet, in addition to his multiple countenances all around the cocoon. Protectively, he was on the prow of *Webdancer*, with Tesh inside.

In the past, when Noah's powers were embryonic and unpredictable, he had, for a time, been able to guide a single podship by remote control, extending his thoughts into its sectoid chamber. Now he found that he could do this for all of the Aopoddae at once—more than one hundred thousand of them—psychically connecting the sectoid chamber of the cocoon with all of the smaller sectoid chambers in the fleet.

Every ship in the fleet glowed faintly green, and Noah felt the pulsing of the flesh of every vessel, the coordinated heartbeat of one collective organism. Noah was that organism, and it was him. The ships all glowed brighter, matching the intensity and hue of the cocoon.

Then Noah fired the incredible primal weapon at the Queen and her minions, not holding anything back. The blasts were white this time—with the ships in the fleet firing at the smaller Web Spinners and the cocoon firing directly at the Queen of the Undergalaxy. He hit her with far more power than all of her slaves received combined. In all, it was exponentially more force than he had used before.

This was enough to disintegrate every one of the smaller Web Spinners in hot bursts of primal whiteness that turned them into dust particles so infinitesimal that they could no longer be seen. They just seemed to vanish. Yet that didn't happen with the Queen. The tremendous force of the biggest blast knocked her into another star system, but she recovered and roared back, her yellow-ember eyes more intense than ever and her body flashing all of the colors in the universe.

Noah hit her again, this time directing blasts at her from the cocoon and from every podship. The tremendous combined force hit her on all sides and broke her into parts, but the parts kept moving, kept trying to regroup. It reminded Noah of himself, the way he repeatedly regenerated his body after his sister hacked it apart. Tesh had worried about what kind of a monster he might be. He hoped he was not one, and had dedicated himself to proving it. But this Queen was something else entirely. Could she ever be stopped?

He continued to fire in rapid succession, focal blasts from all directions that broke the Queen up into smaller and smaller fragments, until only a black cloud of dust remained. The cloud coalesced more tightly and tried to float away, but Noah used the podship fleet to herd it into a timehole—a cosmic opening that made its presence known like a message from the creator of the universe. In went the Queen of the Undergalaxy—every last particle of her stygian dust.

And when she was gone, Noah used the primal power of the cocoon to seal the timehole over, repairing it for all time. Then, gathering energy into the cocoon from the podship fleet, he transmitted simultaneous bursts of raw power into all astronomical sectors, sealing every timehole in the galaxy and repairing every torn fragment of galactic webbing. This took several hours.

Deeply fatigued afterward, he still had the strength to access Timeweb, and through it he watched as Doge Anton sent wave after wave of podships out into the galaxy, on missions to destroy the HibAdus and recapture every Human and Mutati world. Planet after planet fell to the onslaught.

More would follow, but Noah didn't have the strength to monitor the details. He was not needed for those efforts. Already the enemy soldiers were surrendering en masse. Soon the Adurian homeworld and the Hibbil Cluster Worlds would fall as well.

Just before leaving the paranormal realm, Noah saw the commencement of a big victory celebration on Dij, the new Mutati homeworld. Riding in an open car, Hari'Adab was leading a procession down the main boulevard of the capital city. Beside him sat Parais d'Olor in a custom seat that accommodated her avian form. Finally, she was recovering from her injuries. . . .

Noah sighed in contentment. After all the chaos, things were settling down and new balances were being put into place. Safeguards to prevent future galactic wars and rampant decay of the infrastructure.

On a personal level, it pleased him immensely that Tesh and their unborn baby were safe, along with EcoStation. But a great and true friend had been lost, and for him Noah mourned deeply. *Eshaz.*

Vowing to honor his fallen companion one day, Noah gazed out on the fleet of podships, and saw them revert to their normal mottled appearances, with gray, black-streaked hulls. They floated motionless in space, and he understood why.

Lethargically, he swam back through the podflesh and emerged inside one of the classroom modules, where he found Thinker awaiting him.

The orange lights around the robot's faceplate blinked cheerily as he strutted forward, making whirring sounds that were louder than normal. "Congratulations, Master Noah!" he exclaimed.

Moving slowly, feeling fatigued and sore, Noah extricated himself from the cocoon's podflesh and then watched it solidify into the decking and walls, along with all of the interior appointments that had previously been extruded by the amalgamated entity. His own skin remained gray, streaked in veins.

Around him, he felt the power he had harnessed weakening, fading, dissipating. In a matter of moments the glowing green cocoon-sun went out like a used-up light bulb, and became a gray, faceless shape floating in space. Inside, Noah slumped onto the deck, but waved Thinker away when the robot hurried to help.

"You don't look good, Master Noah."

"Nothing a thousand years of sleep can't fix. Just let me rest."

"Shall I send for a doctor?"

Noah almost didn't have the energy to respond. He heard his own voice winding down. "The doctor doesn't exist who can tend to me. Tell everyone I do not wish to be disturbed."

"As you wish, sir."

So drained of energy that he could barely move a muscle, the podman curled up in a fetal ball and plunged into a deep sleep that transported him far, far away.

CHAPTER SEVENTY-FIVE

The best measure of your life is what you give to others, not what you take for yourself.

—Noah Watanabe

As Noah slept on the deck, he dreamed of far-away places and alien races. Across the wide viewing canvas of his mind he saw the entire galaxy in all of its spectacular, colorful beauty, as the Creator had originally designed it. This gave him great pleasure, but the feeling was ephemeral, as he moved from dream to dream, with each of them compressed into only a few ticks of time.

In one of the dreams, he was the first person in an entirely new galactic race of Human-Aopoddae hybrids who had paranormal powers and the ability to inspire others to take care of the galactic environment. His followers wore green-and-brown Guardian uniforms. They looked upon him with awe and reverence, saying he had a certain glow about him and an unparalleled dynamism, that he was a force of nature unto himself. Truly, they insisted, he must be the Savior spoken of in Tulyan legends, the one sent to save Timeweb and hold dominion over it for all eternity thereafter. He tried to deny this, to tell them otherwise, but they wouldn't listen.

In yet another, even more troubling dream, he detected a resumption of trouble in the galaxy, as Web Spinners regenerated themselves and began poking at weak spots from the undergalaxy to make small holes, but not large enough yet for their sinister sovereign to break through. Past events seemed to merge with a possible future that Noah was seeing in the dream, as if all aspects of time had folded together, and the future, the present, and the past were all one. In the past, even when the Queen had been unable to escape she had still found extrasensory ways to recruit from our galaxy, taking Tulyans, Humans, and other races who metamorphosed into Web Spinners. She also incorporated into her Cimmerian legions the ancient race that originally inhabited Canopa in eons past, and was thought to have gone extinct.

It might explain why Eshaz was taken and became a Web Spinner, and why Princess Meghina and her companions were drawn in as well. Perhaps these recruits had powers or abilities that the aggressive Queen found useful. Pimyt was a complete question mark. As far as Noah knew, he did not have Eshaz's paranormal timeseeing abilities, or the immortal blood of Meghina and her companions.

Noah paused, sensing that the Hibbil, too, must have some link to the others that made him attractive to the Queen. But the members of other galactic races had been drawn into her minions as well. More question marks.

And what about me?

Noah's dreaming mind spread out, trying to absorb all possibilities. He saw the reptilian face of First Elder Kre'n superimposed over the heavens, with the faint green filigree of Timeweb visible beyond. "The goal of the Web Spinners," she said, "is to escape the nether realm where they have been imprisoned, so that they can take control of our galaxy and every other galaxy as well. Working at cross-purposes to her, Noah, you sought to maintain and restore Timeweb, in coordination with us. The Web Spinners—with paranormal abilities to perceive events beyond the undergalaxy—could not stand that. After recognizing the threat from you, and your identity as the Savior, the Queen intended to capture you and convert you to her own purposes . . . as her hapless consort. You are immortal, after all, like some of the others that she coveted, but you possess far greater powers—and she thought she could gain control over them through you. She still believes that."

"But I pulverized her into dust," the dream-Noah said.

"All things arise from dust," Kre'n said, in an ancient voice. "You know that. It's why you swept the particles into that timehole."

"Yes."

An additional worry occurred to Noah, and he was about to ask Kre'n about it when he saw a vast timehole open up behind her, encompassing half the galaxy. Out of that hole came the Web Spinners—more than he had ever seen before. So many that they reminded him of a Parvii swarm, but in nightmarish proportions. They swept through the image of Kre'n, scattering her into particles that drifted away. The dark creatures coalesced and grew more compact, and where Kre'n's face had been, another appeared.

Is this real or imagined? he wondered, struggling unsuccessfully to awaken, to free himself of the visions.

The Queen of the Undergalaxy smiled at Noah, but her faceted face was not like before. This time it bore the countenance of Tesh Kori, and in her swollen abdomen grew the child they had conceived.

"You are the God of the Undergalaxy," she said, "and I have guided you to your true purpose."

Noah cried out, but felt his scream absorbed into the noiseless void of the universe. No one heard him, and no one could help him. Not against something like this.

Awakening in a sweat, Noah found that someone had placed a thick blanket over him. He pushed it off, and lay there on the deck dripping with perspiration, trying to shake off memories of the nightmare. It had seemed so real. At least he was still lying in the classroom module where he had gone to sleep. That gave him a sense of continuity, that the visions had not been real, or even Timeweb excursions.

At the sound of voices, he looked and saw Thinker standing in the doorway of the chamber, speaking in low tones to another robot out in the corridor.

Presently, Thinker whirred into the room and said, "You look much better, Master Noah."

Noah rose to his feet, half expecting to still have sore muscles. But he didn't, and he understood why. The cocoon had transmitted Timeweb nutrients into him, and he felt totally energized again.

"How long did I sleep?" he asked.

"Three days. I'll bet you're hungry."

"Not really."

"You've been through a terrible ordeal," Thinker said. "All of us have, but you've had it the worst. By far."

All of the losses deeply saddened Noah, and particularly that of Eshaz, who had given his life so valiantly in the climactic battle. But the outcome of the horrific series of escalating dangers had been favorable. Eshaz would have said it was worth it.

Moments later, Tesh ran into the room. "Darling!" she said. "I'm so proud of you. How are you feeling?"

"Quite rested."

"Good. Despite what you said to Thinker, we took the liberty of having a doctor check your vital signs and administer fluids to you intravenously."

He nodded, but didn't know if that had been necessary. He had other connections.

She gave him a long, lingering kiss. Then, with a broad smile, she reached up to touch the grayish, alien skin on his mouth.

"Is my face a little rough?" he asked.

"A girl can get used to it."

"Just for you, I could revert to my Human appearance . . . at least for kissing."

"No. This is the way you are meant to look, and this is the way I love you now." She placed a hand on her own stomach, which was beginning to show her pregnancy. "I wonder what our little one will look like."

The reality cast aside the bad dreams. Noah remembered what Tesh had told him earlier, that the baby passing through her birth canal would be tiny, the size of a Parvii. "When you say 'little one,' Tesh, you really mean it, don't you?"

"Big things come in small packages," she said.

"You're evidence of that."

"And you, too, Noah. How you accomplished so much, I don't think any of us will ever understand. We all saw portions of it firsthand, and we've seen the reports from Tulyan survey teams and robotic data banks. It's truly astounding."

A voice came from the direction of the corridor. "But the galaxy is not perfect." First Elder Kre'n strode heavily into the chamber, followed by Dabiggio and two other Elders.

"We have reports of weak infrastructure in a number of sectors," Kre'n said. "Nothing major and no new timeholes—at least not yet—but they are matters that need expert attention. We've dispatched caretaking teams."

"I was only able to work with the existing infrastructure material," Noah said. "It seems that the Creator designed it with inherent flaws, thus necessitating regular maintenance." He smiled. "Sounds like job security for you folks."

"You could override us and continue to perform the repairs yourself," Dabiggio said.

"Perhaps, but the energy requirements would be immense

and wasteful, potentially throwing off the natural balances. I hope I haven't already done that, but there were no options. Now I think it is far better to return to the old ways, to the ancient systems that were set up by someone far greater than any of us."

"Humility looks good on you," Dabiggio said. Uncharacteristically, the towering Tulyan smiled.

"Thanks, but it's a suit of clothes everyone should wear," Noah said.

He grinned as several of his other friends entered the chamber—Doge Anton, General Nirella, Subi Danvar, Dux Hannah, and Acey Zelk. It pleased him to see that all of them had survived, and that they had not sustained serious injuries.

"What do we call you now?" Subi asked. The rotund adjutant had a discolored bump on his forehead, but otherwise looked well.

"Just Noah." He put his arm around Tesh. "I'm adjusting my priorities. From now on, I'm the Master Emeritus of the Guardians. You've done such a great job on my behalf, Subi, that I want you to run things from now on."

"As Master Subi?"

"That has a nice sound to it," Noah said.

"Yes, it does," Tesh agreed.

"But I will not live as long as you," Subi said. "One day you will need to resume your previous duties."

"Not if you set up a proper chain of succession." Glancing at Dux and Acey, he said, "We have a couple of good candidates right here."

The young men glowed proudly.

"Good choices." Subi's eyes brightened. "Oh, I see. You want the Guardians to be self-sufficient."

Noah nodded. "I'd like the whole galaxy to be that way, functioning without the need for my intervention. It's idealistic,

I know, but there are other things I have to do."

"What other things?" Subi asked.

"I'm not sure, only that I must free myself from day-to-day duties and prepare for something else. The various galactic races need to set up workable systems to do things on their own . . . always thinking of ecology, always trying to work together instead of at cross-purposes. Life, in all of its forms, must have a common vision."

They spoke for a while longer. Finally, after the others left, Tesh stood alone with Noah and said to him, "I've been thinking about what you said, that there are other things you have to do. Is the Big Guy giving you a promotion? Are you becoming a god yourself?"

With a scowl, Noah said, "I don't think references such as God, the Supreme Being, or the Sublime Creator are necessarily how it really is. They are just convenient reference points for something the galactic races don't understand."

"How about what they call you, the Savior?"

"Mmmm. I told the Tulyans I don't think I'm the messiah foretold in their legends, but I'll admit to you privately I'm not so certain anymore. Don't tell anyone I said this, but maybe it was my destiny to appear when I did and do what I did. For some time now, I have felt myself pulled along on a tidal wave of events. Sometimes I could steer this way or that, as if I had limited free will, but for the most part I've been forced along a certain path. And I don't know where that path leads."

"Somewhere good, for certain," she said, with a gentle smile. "But you frighten me with this kind of talk. You sound like you're planning to leave me."

He smiled sadly, tenderly. "In my line of work, I can't always make plans. But I do follow my instincts." He took her in his arms and held her tightly. "One of my instincts tells me how much I love you . . . and our baby."

"But is that your primary instinct, your main purpose in life? I know I'm asking a typical female question, but I can't help wondering."

"Maybe it is my main purpose. Maybe I can't do anything without you."

She sighed. "The strong woman behind the great man."

"I didn't mean it that way."

"I know you didn't." She looked up and kissed him.

"I mean, we're a strong team, Tesh. You give me strength and vice versa, I hope."

"And our baby? Could he be our real destiny? Might he hold a special purpose, beyond anything you or I could ever accomplish?"

"After what we've been through, anything is possible. But if he . . . or *she* . . . is healthy and contributes to the welfare of the known galaxy, that will be sufficient."

"For me, just being with you is enough, Noah. Our baby is a bonus." She grasped his rough-textured hand and led him toward the doorway. "Now come with me, Darling. We have some catching up to do. Our own set of priorities."

CHAPTER SEVENTY-SIX

Not knowing in advance often makes life more
interesting. There can be a certain magic in the
process of discovery.

—Noah Watanabe

Near the Ring Moons of the Wygeros race, EcoStation floated
in space with its anchor-jets set for the night. Soon, when the
blue Wygerian sun faded from view, everyone aboard the facility
would enjoy spectacular evening views of lucent ring-shadows
as they played colors across the surface of the planet below.

Noah strode through the corridors of the cocoon, past
instructors, research technicians, and eager young students as
they bustled back and forth to classes and laboratories. All wore
green-and-brown uniforms. He smiled at the people, and called
out to some by name, noting with pleasure how many of the
galactic races were represented here. EcoStation had not only
survived—it had come back more gloriously than ever, and was
filled to the brim with learning stations, research laboratories,
and other features of the latest technology, installed in a
magnificent citadel of ancient podflesh.

The contrasts were startling to some, but not to Noah. Each
passenger on the cocoon had boarded it only recently in cosmic
terms, and they were learning how to live in harmony with
ancient things—with the galaxy and all of its varied contents.

EcoStation was just part of the whole picture, but a very important one. It had become the inspiration that he had hoped for, drawing the most brilliant and idealistic minds from the widest sectors, the greatest teachers from every race. Though the cocoon no longer glowed, since Noah had suspended its weapon function, it was still a beacon, in an important and positive sense. From this place, in new ways, Noah was illuminating the entire galaxy with essential knowledge.

Walking into one of the research and development laboratories, he paused to watch Thinker and Dux. They stood at an electronic drafting table designing eco-monitors—flying robotics that could check a planet's air, land, and water. It was just one of the many aspects of Noah's continuing mission to keep the galactic machine running smoothly. EcoStation was full of environmentally sensitive projects such as this one, and Subi Danvar was doing a terrific job of managing and coordinating the operations. This left Noah time to be creative, to come up with new ideas and approaches.

Thinker and Dux were so engrossed in their work that they did not notice Noah standing behind them, watching quietly. Noah smiled to himself, and left. Back in the corridor he picked up his pace, thinking of his own relatively short past, and his much longer future.

The transformed man had experienced a great deal of change around him, the weaving of evolutionary strands. His apparently immortal lifetime and mottled pod skin were only part of it. Not long ago he had been performing ecological repair work on planets that had been damaged by the industrial operations of merchant princes. Afterward his career had taken unexpected turns, and he'd been required to perform work that was related, but exponentially more important.

And all of it had taken place in only a galactic moment.

Considering his potential lifetime, this made Noah wonder

what more he might accomplish. Would his ecological expertise eventually be needed for operations encompassing the entire universe and all of its galaxies? If that proved to be the case, what role could the Tulyans and Aopoddae play in the work?

But as Noah considered these questions, he realized he was thinking through the filter of his own life experiences. Even with all he had seen and accomplished, he knew there was still a lot more than that. The known galaxy was just one of many realms, each with its own unique story.

I am only a punctuation mark in the unfolding epic of the universe, he thought. He rounded a corner and headed down a long corridor.

It seemed incomprehensible to Noah that his destiny lay elsewhere, beyond the vast frame of reference encompassed by Timeweb and the known galaxy. And yet, he sensed that it did. He felt confident that there were fantastic discoveries ahead of him, realms he could hardly begin to imagine. But he wanted to postpone the wildest (and admittedly most intriguing) possibilities for a while, so that he could spend time with Tesh and their baby. After all, Tesh—and probably the child as well—would not have Noah's life span, so it only made sense for him to spend as much time as possible with his family now.

I have free will, and this is what I want, he thought. Then, as if addressing a higher power, he asked, *Haven't I earned the privilege?*

No answer came, not viscerally or any other way. For the moment—other than the ruminations of his mind—he only had the here and now.

Subi Danvar approached. He looked harried, as if he had too much on his mind and had not been sleeping well. He was doing a good job, but still needed to grow into his job as Master of the Guardians, and become accustomed to the responsibilities. "I have that report you requested," he said, as he reached

Noah. He handed over a thick file.

"Good," Noah said, thumbing through the pages. It was an analysis of piezoelectric emerald veins around the galaxy, a subject that he found interesting on several levels. He studied a chart for a moment.

"Look on page sixteen for evidence of ancient mining," Subi said.

Noah thumbed to the page, nodded. "I'll study this before tomorrow's meeting," he said. He tucked the file under his arm. Leaving Subi, he continued down the corridor.

The information that Noah had just perused had to do with his theory of galactic ecology, of the interconnectedness of the galaxy. It was important documentation, more corroborative evidence. Piezoelectric emeralds were the stuff that the ancient builders of Timeweb had used to spin the fantastic webbing of the cosmos. There was much to learn about those minerals, and about the infinitesimally small life forms that lived in their cellular structures.

A captured Adurian lab scientist had referred to them as "Webbies," and said that those inhabiting the galactic infrastructure undoubtedly had something to do with nearly instantaneous Tulyan communication across the galaxy, and with nehrcom transmissions. They might even have something to do with Noah's recovery from a serious injury, when Eshaz connected him to a strand of galactic webbing, and it healed him. In recent days, cooperative Adurian laboratory technicians had found evidence of the tiny, elusive creatures in samples of Noah's blood.

What a fantastic universe this is! Noah thought. He couldn't wait to discover more of its secrets. And he had a long time to unravel them.

Of great importance, Tulyan teams had been journeying to the farthest reaches of the galaxy aboard their restored fleet of podships, performing critical inspection and maintenance tasks. Having seen the terrible reality of the monsters of the undergalaxy, the Tulyans were working with renewed vigor to keep them bottled up. For the rest of eternity, Tulyans expected to perform many of their traditional caretaking duties. But they could not do it all alone. Other races had to contribute as well—different tasks according to their abilities.

Everything had to function like a biological machine, with the parts moving in synchronization. For it all to work, there had to be harmony among all of the ecological niches, on an immense scale. Old prejudices and conflicts would have to be set aside.

Noah sighed, as he thought of the vastness of space, and the diversity of conditions around the galaxy. A great deal of work remained to be done, and he knew the races could never let their guard down again. They must always be vigilant. It was one of the primary lessons that everyone had to learn. Unexpected dangers could always emerge.

He glanced at a chronometer on the wall of the corridor, paused to stare at it. For several moments he was hypnotized by the digital numbers as they advanced in their relentless, cyclical routine. In a few minutes he would sit in as an observer at a class on cluster-world dynamics. It was being conducted by a full-time Mutati professor, a close associate of the Emir Hari'Adab.

Noah grinned. My, how times had changed.

CHAPTER SEVENTY-SEVEN

"I am my parents, grandparents, and ancestors, stretching back to the beginnings of our race and far beyond, to the entropic materials that were stirred up in the dust of stars and went into the first sentient creature. I am the person you see before you, and much more. I am one cosmic life form and I am many. After receiving the nanocreatures of the webbing into my bloodstream, I began to evolve in a new direction. Now the tiny life forms speak to me in their own way, and transport me to my destiny."

—Noah Watanabe, entry in Thinker's data banks

The podship *Webdancer,* having recovered from its battle injuries, was speeding near the Tulyan Starcloud, dodging comets and meteors, and occasionally racing them. The ancient creature was like a frisky pony, with a tiny Parvii woman flying alongside, keeping up easily, matching every maneuver. Though they were not physically connected at the moment, Tesh and her podship were mentally linked through a morphic field, constantly aware of each other's movements. It was one of the methods of communication used by podships to fly in formation, and *Webdancer* had taught it to her in the wordless way of the Aopoddae.

Ever since the epochal battle to save the galaxy, Tesh had been learning things about the arcane cosmic creatures, picking up subtleties of their communication system, and even noting differences within family groupings—what she called "dialects of motion." Without question, these space travelers—defying their appearances—were far more intelligent and advanced than any other galactic race.

Noah claimed not to know much about their wordless methods. And, although her lover seemed far superior in comparison with her, it was his contention that he could never possibly learn everything there was to know, not even about important matters such as the Aopoddae. It was his view— shared with the Tulyan Elders—that the sentient podships comprised a vast and collective storehouse of cosmic knowledge, a repository of treasures and mysteries that went all the way back to the early days of the galaxy.

"They contain the secrets of the universe within their cells," Noah had said to her recently.

Now Tesh became aware of a change in her Aopoddae companion. The podship was slowing down, and had opened a hatch for her to enter. Moments later, she felt a stirring of life within her own body.

Somehow, *Webdancer* had sensed that it was her time.

It was early morning in the Wygerian Star System, with lucent ring shadows still casting soft colors across the surface of the coreworld below. In only a few minutes the sun would rise and chase the shadows away, but Noah hardly thought about that. His senses were on full alert, stretching outward.

A short while ago, he had again immersed himself into the flesh of the cocoon. Now, from far across space, he detected the same thing as *Webdancer*. It was time.

Noah visualized the Tulyan Star System, and in the blink of an eye he was there, bumping up against the much smaller *Webdancer*. He made the docking connection, lifted himself out of the podship flesh, and strode the short distance into Tesh's podship.

As they had discussed earlier concerning this special moment, Tesh lay in the warmth and security of the craft's sectoid chamber. There, at the nucleus of the ancient creature, she would give birth. The old making it possible for the new. She was a minuscule Parvii form on the soft gray deck, with her magnification system off.

Though Noah had influenced matters of immense scale and importance, he now found himself unable to have any effect at all on the tiny woman in front of him, or on the child she carried in her womb. He felt helpless and awkward.

Carefully he knelt over her, feeling like a giant. "I wish I could do something," he said, softly.

Tesh smiled up at him. Her voice was small and distant. "Don't worry! This is the most natural of processes. You're here, and that's more than enough for me."

Noah didn't know if Parvii women ever suffered labor pains the way Human females did—but in Tesh's case it seemed effortless. As he watched, she seemed to *will* the birth, and then it happened. She made hardly a sound, did not grimace in pain. The precious child slid easily through her birth canal and emerged, dripping amniotic fluids.

With deft motions, Tesh severed the umbilical cord and tied off the connection on the child's stomach. Then, producing a blanket as if by magic, she swaddled the baby and extended it up to Noah. "Meet your new son," she said.

Noah placed his right hand beside her, palm up, and she set the baby onto his palm. Tesh was herself only half the length of Noah's forefinger, and the child much smaller than that. Ever so carefully, he used his other hand to slide the child to a safer position. He held the baby delicately, afraid of harming him.

Such a tiny life form, Noah marveled, *and yet so infinitely important.* He saw pinpoint-eyes of indeterminate color in the round face, glittering like a pair of miniature stars.

"With your permission, I would like to name him Saito, in honor of my father," Noah said.

Tesh climbed onto his hand too, and lifted the baby into her arms. She had tidied up her own clothing, and had even brushed her hair quickly. "Then Saito shall be his name."

Walking across Noah's hand, the pretty brunette hopped back down to the deck. Moving a distance away and activating her own enlargement feature, Tesh became full size again, and stood there with the child nearly as small on her hand as he had been on Noah's. "Little Saito cannot be fitted with a magnification system until he is fully grown," she said with a smile, "at the risk of stunting his growth. And for my people that is a very serious concern!"

Noah exchanged loving smiles with her, and for a moment he forgot that he was more than Human, and that this restricted their possibilities for happiness.

The shared bliss did not last long, before Noah sensed *Webdancer* and other podships communicating with one another in their prehistoric, mysterious way. He identified the characteristic sounds of *Diminian* and his companions—the most ancient of the Aopoddae in the cocoon and in the rest of the Liberator fleet.

Tesh's green eyes opened wide in alarm. "Look at your skin!" she said. "Oh, my God, what's happening to you?"

Looking down, Noah saw that the flesh on his hands was breaking up into tiny, dark particles that seemed to bounce off one another on the surface. He touched one hand to the other, and it didn't feel any different.

"It's happening to your face, too!" she said. She stepped backward and clutched the baby protectively to her bosom. Then she reconsidered, and reached out to touch the skin on

Noah's forehead. To his dismay, he felt her fingertips sink into his own flesh and bone. It was painless to him, but he detected the immersion.

Visibly upset, she withdrew.

When Noah touched his own skin, however, it felt no different to him than normal, and he did not sink in.

Now the dark particles on his skin began to move faster and faster, and seemed to dive into the surface, where they continued their agitation in a foggy realm. The skin had taken on a haziness, a cloudlike quality. This time when Noah tried to touch his hands together, they passed through each other and he felt no tactile sensation at all. Pulling the hands apart, they still had their misty definition.

"Are you vanishing?" she asked, her voice panicky. "Darling, what's happening to you?"

"I don't know." Noah felt oddly calm, and that he should accept whatever was occurring instead of trying to fight it. He was only one life form in a universe of countless sentient creatures and possibilities—an infinite number of individuals that were evolving, and were ultimately connected to one another. Inside his body, the Webbies were doing their work.

Tears streamed down Tesh's cheeks. She kept trying to caress Noah's face, but nothing tangible was there. She touched the sleeve of his tunic and it gave way, as if it had nothing behind it. But Noah could still see her clearly, and still saw a misty quality to his own skin—some substance and integrity there.

"For now, it seems to be holding," he said.

"You're continuing to evolve," she said in a voice tinged with panic, "but into what?"

"I don't know where the path of my life is leading. All I know is that I must follow it." He reached out to her, but could no longer feel her skin. He withdrew, disheartened.

"Can you reverse the process, the way you could mentally

command the podflesh to disappear from your skin?"

"That is no longer possible," he said, as information from the Aopoddae surfaced in his mind. "I am beyond going back."

"I'm trying to understand, Darling. I don't want to be selfish, but I love you so much it hurts."

"We share feelings that no one needs to know about," Noah said. "Now that our Saito is born, there is no more need for my physical body. It has been transferred to him. One day, you will tell him of this, and he will fulfill his own destiny."

Filled with sadness, she could only nod.

Noah leaned toward her and kissed her lips. It gave him an emotional sensation, but not a corporal one. Even so, he could clearly remember the tenderness of her kisses, and knew he would never forget them, no matter how long he lived. He recalled an earlier Timeweb experience in which they'd been together paranormally, and she'd later insisted it had been physically real as well. Their baby was evidence of that. Now, it was similar. But entirely different.

As moments passed, Tesh made herself smaller, and held the child in a normal fashion.

Around Noah the sectoid chamber seemed to melt and morph, and in a matter of moments he found that he stood alone inside the larger sectoid chamber of the cocoon. This time there had been no walking, or swimming through the flesh. Somehow, the Aopoddae had done it differently.

Through visual sensors in the flesh, Noah watched Tesh in her reduced form as she hurried through the main corridor of *Webdancer* with their child, making her way forward in the vessel.

In a matter of minutes, hundreds of the oldest podships in the fleet gathered around Noah's cocoon. They began to glow softly in concert with the larger structure, then led it out into deep space. For a while, *Webdancer* kept up with them, flying of her own accord. Then the gray-and-black Liberator flagship separated from the others and fell back. . . .

Tesh stood inside, at a forward viewing window. She saw the glowing podships and the cocoon accelerate along parallel podways that seemed to go upward from her vantage point. Then, in a brilliant burst of green, the fabric of space split open and they went through. For the briefest moment, Tesh got a glimpse of something beyond, a realm of enchanting lights and colors that danced in the ether like immense living creatures. Then the cosmic portal closed, and Noah was gone.

"Goodbye, my love," she whispered. Crying softly, she held the baby close to her.

ABOUT THE AUTHOR

Brian Herbert, the son of Frank Herbert, has won several literary honors, and has been nominated for the highest awards in science fiction. In 2003, he published *Dreamer of Dune,* the Hugo Award–nominated biography of his father. His earlier acclaimed novels include *Timeweb; The Web and the Stars; Sidney's Comet; Sudanna, Sudanna;* and *The Race for God.* Since 1999, he has written nine Dune series novels with Kevin J. Anderson that have been major international best-sellers. Their 2007 novel, *Sandworms of Dune,* reached number four on the *New York Times* hardcover best-seller list. In 2004, Brian published *The Forgotten Heroes,* a powerful tribute to the U.S. Merchant Marine. He has been interviewed by media all over the world.

www.dunenovels.com